Copyright 2022

All rights reserved.

Published by Amazon Digital Services

Cover art: Ismail Ben

ISBN: 9798403544870

Printed in the United States of America

Chapter 1

I arrived at the Lakeside Health Center, an all-inclusive mental health facility built on beautiful French Island, next to La Crosse Wisconsin. It had been at this location for over one hundred years. The state tore down the original building in 1975 and replaced it with a state-of-the-art facility, currently trying to rejoin its predecessor, outdated and in dire need of repair.

Climbing out of the front seat of my six-year-old Black 2012 Tundra, I took in a deep breath as my shoes hit the worn-out, sunbaked, winter-beaten employee parking lot. My Tundra was the only thing of value I was able to salvage from my adopted parents' estate. Shortly after my sixteenth birthday, my father was murdered in a bank robbery gone wrong; my mother succumbed to colon cancer two years later.

It was going to be another hot, steamy mid-July day in Western Wisconsin, but I would be working in air-conditioned comfort, so it wouldn't matter.

My body went into a convulsive stretch, trying to shake off the consequences of last night's alcohol-induced activities. I let out a satisfying good morning grunt as I glanced at the electric blue waters of Lake Onalaska which bordered the property on the west side, several miles from the Mississippi River. The area was called "God's Country" for a reason: lakes, rivers, and forests were surrounded by bluffs and rolling hills, truly eye candy for the soul.

I halfheartedly walked into the building's main entrance, my ears tuning in to the redundant sounds of patients' unintelligible chatter, walkers scraping across worn-out linoleum floors and orderlies barking out orders to patients with limited comprehension skill sets who probably had no idea what year it was. But what always snapped me back to reality was the smell. An intoxicating mixture of year-old cat litter doused with urine and mixed with watered-down bleach, a constant reminder of my job as a Psychiatric Attendant.

Walking through a series of hallways, I greeted several health center employees on my way to the acute psychiatric unit door.

I inserted the plastic security card which dangled from a lanyard around my neck into the scanner and waited for the door to open. I entered the small security hallway and waited for the first door's lock to click back into place. I repeated the same procedure again for the second door and entered the unit, listening as the door clicked into place.

"Ah, the sights, the smells, back into the never-ending psychotic rabbit's hole," I said aloud, pounding my chest twice with my right fist.

Early morning routines created a unit buzz. I turned to the right as several patients walked by and greeted me with the same stale good mornings while some gestured with their hands and others wandered around like zombies in a Walking Dead episode, optimizing their blank stares. I made another right and opened the waist-high swinging nurse's station door.

"Que pasta amigos and amigesses," I happily chanted, trying to stimulate the graveyard shift.

I get the, you just walked in here and let's see you this cheery in a couple of hours look from the staff. Great energy, I thought I accidentally stumbled into a narcoleptic convention.

I stopped at the kitchen at the back of the nurse's station to hang up my backpack, which housed my laptop, golf shirt, shorts, shoes and socks, then headed to one of three worktables behind the main counter.

Russ Hardy sat at one of the tables working on some patients' charts; he was my height, six-feet-two, but unlike me, a skinny laid-back dude who could handle himself in a fight. He was the graveyard psych attendant, fraternity brother and roommate. He was dressed in a cheap green Walmart golf shirt, jeans, and black Nike tennis shoes.

Russ was a total motor head, most content when his head was buried under a hood. He was smart, holding a degree in engineering but here he was, scraping by at minimum wage in a psych unit in bum-fuck western Wisconsin. Russ was also painstakingly paying off a fifty-thousand-dollar college loan while awaiting replies from the hundreds of resumes he'd sent out nationwide. Like all the Lakeview psychiatric attendants, he kept busy protecting the masses from the would-be street people, who'd be taking up valuable real estate, residing in a variety of cardboard boxes and tents strewn across alleys, freeway underpasses and parks.

Poor Russ was probably wondering why he wasn't making one-hundred-thousand dollars a year as an engineer somewhere. Russ saw me walking over to the table and smiled.

"A peaceful night Steve. Can't believe it. Everyone asleep when I walked in and it stayed that way."

"Lucky you, no Marsha to report?" I inquired.

"Nope, I have her chart and it's a short entry. Her two-week stay at Lakeside's been a real nightmare for everyone."

"I've never seen anyone or anything thing like her, and she ends up here, off the beautiful shores of picturesque Lake Onalaska. I'll see you later, Russ. I'm going to look in on George," I said with a frustrated look on my face."

I walked out and past the station gate when Russ grabbed my shoulder from behind.

"Dude, you need to get over being upset at him for checking back in. He's been here a month now. You need to let it go."

"Yeah, I know. It's hard for me, he shouldn't be here this time. Something's going on and he's not talking."

"Let's ask the doctor."

That created a mutual laugh. The Head Clinical Psychiatrist, Doctor Cameron Wage, must have gotten his degree inside a box of Captain Crunch he found while going to school in Grenada. He reminded me of Dr. Irwin Corey, a character my parents showed me on the old Dean Martin Roast reruns, classic, funny comedians without the F-bombs.

"I checked on him twice; he looked peaceful."

"Thanks, Russ. I appreciate the extra effort."

I left the nurse's station through the day room, toward the patient rooms. The day room was a mental merry-go-round, a collection of broken minds, pierced hearts and damaged souls, all peppered with drugs, nicotine, caffeine, alcohol or any combination of the three, awaiting the quick fix to get them back to the place where they could start the same dysfunctional process all over again. The percentage of patients getting out and staying out are and continue to remain painfully low.

I stopped at room 112 and looked at the temporary room placard next to the door, the name "George Sharp" written in bolded letters. I knocked on the side of an already opened door and entered the room. George Sharp sat on the edge of his bed. He was a tall stately looking man in his late 50's and had made millions with a deep-sea petroleum patent. His head, garnished with salt and pepper hair, which seemed to have an allergic reaction anytime a comb or brush approached it. We'd become close over the past three years of his in-and-out mental health center sojourns. There was something that always drew me near him. Like a pet that I needed to care for.

George's irrational, unexplainable psychotic episodes had plagued him for years. He wasn't Schizophrenic, depressed or bi-polar, according to the head shrink, but here he was again, no rational explanation or medical diagnosis for this extended visit. He was fully dressed from the ankles up, no shoes, no socks, typical George.

"Hi Steve, come on in and have a seat. I'll have my secretary carve out a spot on my morning calendar, just for you."

"Thanks for squeezing me in on such short notice," I said in my usual smart-ass demeanor. "So, how's it going this morning? Forget something?"

George looked down at his feet. "No. And after a pleasant evening of eyelid research, I'm still not quite sure, but things are trending toward... copacetic. How are you doing on this fine sunny morning?"

"Doing great, George. Two months since I graduated, and the university still hasn't asked me to return my diploma."

"You make me laugh." George chuckled. "You remind me of someone I used to know... me."

"Really?"

"Except of course for the side-part-pompadour, blonde hair, blue eyes, muscular build, sitting on a six-foot two-inch frame and the Hollywood good looks, we could have been twins."

"At least you haven't lost your sense of humor."

I walked over to the window of the depressing, claustrophobic room with cheap white and blue painted concrete blocks and pulled back the bland faded blue curtain. The plastic brackets holding the curtain were manufactured to break apart under minimal weight, therefore rendering them suicide proof. An aggressive early morning sun crept its way into the room between the thick iron bars outside the window.

"Not what you're used to, is it George?"

I tapped my knuckles against the unbreakable glass window.

"No, but I'm not here on a vacation either, am I?"

"No, you're not, and that's the problem, George. Why haven't you checked out yet? Come on, you and I both know you don't belong here, not this time anyway."

"I've been feeling better the last couple of weeks and I think I'm getting ready to—"

His sentence was drowned out by loud screams coming from the dayroom and an ear-piercing loudspeaker. Several patients ran by Georges' room.

"Code 99, repeat code 99, all patients return to your rooms. Code 99, code 99, all patients return to your rooms."

"Oh shit, Marsha again. Gotta go."

"Careful, Steve. She's extremely dangerous," George warned as he slid off the bed onto his bare feet and watched me run into the tidal wave of uncontrollable psychotic pandemonium.

I raced down the hall and into the day room where I witnessed chaos: running, jumping, screaming, swearing, a chair careening off a day room wall and panic-stricken patients escaping the day room like rats scrambling off a sinking ship. I saw two nurses creating a vapor trail toward the nurse's station.

"What a cluster fuck," I said to myself.

Then I saw her, all five feet, one hundred pounds of her, Marsha Zemlugs. She was a twenty-something-year-old Tasmanian Devil with blossoming scraggly red hair, attired in a stained blue robe, barefoot, hissing, growling, her head rolling side to side, arms and hands swiping at imaginary objects, looking to damage or hurt anything or anyone. She'd be kind of cute if she fixed herself up… a lot. She made eye contact with me, standing alone in the middle of the dayroom. Game on.

I thought of Michael Buffer and announced to the entire day room, "Let's get ready to Rummmmmmmmmmmble!"

As I dashed toward her, she tossed off her robe, revealing a badly-stained beige nightgown. She charged me with whatever contorted, psychotic gait she could conjure up. A normal person would bet their house on me taking her out. What they didn't know was that a couple of days ago

9

she took a two-hundred-pound aide and flipped him over her shoulder and into a wall, right after putting her fist through a double-paned chicken-wire glass drug dispensary window. And to top it off, it took eight aides and enough Xanax to wipe out a rhinoceros to get her under control.

However, today was not a couple of days ago, and now she was loaded on a variety of medications. I'm not sure she even knew what century she was in.

We collided hard and she took the entire brunt of my tackle and went straight down landing hard on the deeply soiled carpet, her head ricocheting off it. Within seconds Russ came up from behind us and jumped on the pile followed by Bill Aliota, another fraternity brother and roommate, who happened to be six-foot-four and two-hundred-and-forty pounds. He was a workout warrior, a former college linebacker, with a violent on-and-off switch. An injury at another school during his junior year ended his playing days before he transferred to La Crosse. A lady's man, with an ivory smile, GQ looks, mafia black slicked-back hair, brown eyes, and equipped with all the silver-tongued one-liners designed to attract women to his lair. He was dressed in a faded gold Greg Norman Shark Polo, black dress pants, and black Air Jordan high top basketball shoes. A real badass I was happy to call friend.

The three of us went after Marsha's legs, arms and waist while making sure none of our body parts were near her mouth. Marsha was a biter, not a zombie-biter, just a biter. I grabbed her waist and tried to pin her to the floor, Bill went after her flailing arms, and Russ attempted to hold onto her legs.

"Bill, you get us a tee time for Saturday morning?" I asked with a bit of a grunt.

Marsha threw a right haymaker that landed on the top of my head.

"Sorry, Steve," Bill said. "Her arms are like an octopus's! Yeah, we're playing the Kappa's in a two-man, two-team best ball, ten bucks a hole."

Russ was getting tossed around like a rag doll as he tried to hold onto Marsha's legs.

"What time?" Russ agonizingly blurted out, sounding like he was on the losing end of a marlin fishing line.

"Eleven at West Salem."

"How apropos," Russ said.

Marsha landed another zinger on my head.

"Goddamn it, Bill!"

"I'm getting kicked in the calf because motor-head can't keep Marsha's legs together!"

There was an awkward pause as we all understood how funny that sounded.

"I didn't just say that?"

"You most certainly did, lover boy," I answered back.

"Bill, you're the jock. Take her legs. Quick, switch with me! I'll grab her arms. Ready? Switch!"

The two made a valiant effort at switching. However, Russ took a jarring knee to the family jewels and let out a low painful howl. Bill rolled over me and on top of her legs.

"I got her sticks boys. How ya' doin' Russ?" Bill sarcastically asked.

Russ snatched up her left arm like a shortstop snagging a line drive. But her right arm caught him square in the grill. You could hear the pop from the employee parking lot.

"I'm doing—" Russ began to say, right before that punch caught most of his face.

"Fuck you, Bill!"

"Dude, that had to hurt! I didn't know you could take a punch like that," I said partially laughing. "And that denutting you just got, tough day at the office bro."

"Eat shit!"

I drove my body up into her chest and managed to block her right arm just as she was about to unload another bone-crunching punch to Russ's face. It sounded like her shoulder popped on the block. Russ wrangled her right arm as Bill gained full control over her legs, looking like he'd wrapped up a tackle, even though her legs were still trying to break free from his grip.

"Who's the fourth man for our match against the Kappa's, Bill?" I said with a wincing grin.

Russ answered in painstakingly quick time. "I was thinking—"

"I can actually hear you thinking. That three-legged eunuch gerbil that commandeers your white mass is slipping and sliding around the marbles in your head; it's a dead giveaway," Bill nastily added with a grin so wide that it weren't for his ears the top of his head would have slid off.

"That's your mothers' fault for riding me like a mechanical bull, constantly jacking my head into the wall, along with every other rodeo clown who ever worked!" Russ shouted back.

I glanced over and finally saw two nurses charging over to us. Marsha, in a final attempt to break free, began violently and rhythmically arching her back, hoping to buck me off and free herself. She was amazingly strong for someone so tiny.

"Oh look, the cocktail waitresses finally showed up with our order!" I exclaimed, trying to keep Marsha pinned down.

"It must be the wrong table. I don't see Bill's Shirley Temple," Russ chimed in, feeling like he just delivered the one-line zinger of the day.

Three uniformed male aids from the second floor dropped to their knees and joined the pile. They randomly grabbed arms and legs. Marsha tried to bite Russ. However, with more freedom to wiggle, I moved my weight towards her head, and used my hand to grab it and turn it away. Then it got really weird. Marsha winked at me and tried to bite her own arm. I slid up her chest and took my knee and jammed it between her neck and arm making sure I applied enough pressure to keep her from injuring herself but not enough to hurt her.

"We got you now!" Bill victoriously shouted.

Russ answered back, "Shoot her up already, my balls are on fire."

One of the nurses dropped down beside us holding back a laugh while rubbing an alcohol swab over Marsha's arm. She injected the needle deep into her arm and pushed down on the plunger. The ingredients in that cocktail must have had a street value of well over a thousand dollars.

Unbeknownst to all of us, our unit supervisor was standing over the entangled pile of humanity for the last minute. Mary Pearson, forty-two, five-feet-six, sandy blonde hair, emerald eyes, a well-preserved face and a body chiseled from countless gym workouts. She wore a bright white blouse, black skirt, and matching black low heels, carrying herself like a southern belle. Throw in a soft down-home Texas accent and you have Mary.

"Y'all just about done?" she said looking down on us.

The drugs immediately kicked in and Marsha became limp. Another aide from the second floor raced over with a gurney. The aides each took a body part and together they placed her on the gurney, strapping down her arms and legs before they rolled her away to the cozy quiet place known as the seclusion room. Hell, she'd been rolled in there so many times in her brief stay at Lakeside they might as well have placed a placard with her name on it.

Bill got up and muttered, "That crazy bitch is tougher than a two-hundred-fifty-pound fullback."

"Yeah, she rearranged my family jewels. I might need permanent disability," Russ added as he tried to stand but instead slumped over and grabbed his knees.

"Maybe mental disability; you had her chart last night and seeing as how your shift isn't over for," Mary looked down at her Lady Rolex, exposing her meticulous burgundy nail polish and silky smooth skin, "another twenty minutes, please write up your revised version on her chart. Thank you, Russ."

"I'm here for the greater good," he proudly expressed as he gingerly walked back to the nurse's station.

"Steve, I need to see you in my office," Mary politely stated as she performed a perfect one-hundred-eighty degree about face and glided to the nurse's station as only she can. I watched her retreat to her office, admiring her perfectly shaped behind.

"You heard her." Bill said as he put his hands on his hips, swaying side to side as he left for the seclusion room.

"Douchebag."

"Bill, did Marsha bang up your hips?"

Bill looked over and saw Mary looking directly at him.

"Ah, just a little kink. You know, football and other strenuous activities."

"Move along Bill. You coming Steve?"

"Yes, ma'am."

Chapter 2

Mary's office was small; a single window overlooked the nurse's station. The room darkening blinds were pulled completely down. Mary sat at her desk, hands perfectly folded as I entered her office.

"Close the door, have a seat."

I sat in one of the three chairs in her office. A mixture of scenic pictures and prophetic sayings covered her walls. The desk was spotless aside from pens and pencils rising out of an old sorority mug and a daily reminder calendar that fought for space. My eyes always wander to one of the sayings on her wall, "Health is merely the slowest possible rate at which one can die."

"You try out some new MMA moves on Marsha?"

"Yeah, cage match, battle of the sexes. She really knows how to make an entrance, and that wardrobe— it'll push ratings through the roof. Make sure you secure the TV rights."

"Okay, enough. That was foolish; she could have really hurt you. I told you what she did a couple of days ago on the second floor."

"I know. I didn't want anyone to get hurt. That's my job description."

"What am I going to do with you? The other day it took eight aides to finally get her down and in seclusion. She's beyond extremely volatile."

"Yeah, I know, but I didn't work that day, lucky me. And on the bright side, it only took six today. Better working conditions brought to you by better drugs."

"With your testosterone overload, you might need assistance."

"Yes, and I appreciate your continued support, the tenacity and dedication you apply to my testosterone problem. Oh, and by the way, you look absolutely amazing this morning."

"Why thank you, Steve, and of course, I'm always glad to help you with your, big problem. Anyway, you're wanted down at the administrator's office. I didn't have time to investigate the matter, so when you're done, y'all come back here and fill me in."

"Yes, ma'am, Captain Testosterone will report back to you immediately.

"You're just too cute. Run along now."

I walked out of Mary's office and over to Russ who sat at one of the tables, updating Marsha's chart.

"So, guess what? Mendez wants to see me."

"Let me guess. Somebody upstairs not happy with your two-point takedown?"

"Who knows?"

"Well, I got Marsha's chart and I'm gonna go out on a limb and write down possession. She doesn't need a shrink; she needs a priest."

"Boys, there is no such thing as possession, y'all know that."

Russ and I were surprised to see Mary standing directly behind us again.

"Oh, and Steve, you're wanted down at the administrator's office, remember?"

"On my way."

I walked out of the nurse's station, scanned myself out of the unit, and started down the hallway. About halfway there, I stopped at the occupational therapy room and peeked inside the glass window. A male patient, buck-naked, was running around the room with a plastic bucket on his head, being chased by the therapist and an aide.

I laughed. "What am I, in a mental institution? Yes, I, am."

I continued the long walk down the short hall, nodding to several patients being escorted by staff members. I stopped at the door marked 'office'. I looked around like a man about to crack an ATM and cautiously entered the room.

Dr. Mendez's secretary, Krista Wagner, dressed neatly like a presidential press secretary, with brown curly hair and large glasses, looked up at me with her always charming smile. Without saying a word, she pointed to a chair, motioning me to sit.

I sat and picked up a four-month-old Psychology Today off the table next to the chair and nervously thumbed through it, looking at the pages without seeing a thing. I tossed the magazine back on the table and noticed all the dysfunctional art on the walls. I glanced down at my shoes, watching my right heel go up and down like a runaway steam piston.

Doctor Mendez's office door swung open as he hastily emerged, blowing by me like the lead car at a NASCAR event. He was nearing sixty and most of his hair had abandoned him, and at five-eight, he wore a somewhat intelligent look and was dressed in a three-piece black pin-stripe business suit, yellow shirt, and a black and yellow paisley tie. He was closely followed by a man in a gray three-piece suit.

Without stopping or looking at me, the doctor said, "Steve, follow us to the conference room," as he grabbed and pushed open the door.

Krista stood like a soldier in a North Korean military parade, pointing to the door I already knew was opened for me to march through. Being the good loyal employee, I popped out of my chair and followed the two men.

Doctor Mendez crossed the hallway in record time, opened the conference room door which just happened to be directly across from his office, and held it open for the guy in the grey suit and me. The suit entered the room first and stood at the head of the conference table next to a dry erase board. I took a couple of steps into the room and wondered which seat had my name on it. Doctor Mendez, to my surprise, closed the door and left. My mind raced.

The man in the suit, average height, greyish thinning hair, looked to be in his late forties, wearing a blue dress shirt and coordinated tie. He sported an annoying, holier than thou look as he directed me to a chair next to him. Always the optimist, I thought of everything I'd done wrong in the last several years. Totally confused and wondering if he was with some government agency, I obliged and sat down. He took out a briefcase he must have previously placed in the room and propped it on the table. He cautiously opened it, pulled out an iPad, and slid it in front of me, leaving a perfect view of the screen.

"I'm Norman Goldhabber of Goldhabber and Goldhabber, a Las Vegas law firm." He handed me one of his cards. "I represent the late Sonny Tringale. The picture on the iPad is Mr. Tringale. Sonny Tringale is your birth father. You do know you were adopted Mr. Mueller, don't you?"

I looked at the picture in amazement, vaguely nodding. It was one of those surreal moments; at twenty four years old you see your real father for the first time. Unless you've experienced it yourself, it's hard to explain.

"I've flown here today to tell you that you are the major beneficiary to the Sonny Tringale estate, lucky you."

Goldhabber continued with his canned courtroom narration. "Upon his passing, Mr. Tringale, Sonny, wanted you to see this video Mr. Mueller."

"Call me Steve."

"Steve."

Goldhabber leaned in, pushed the enter button on the iPad, and a video played.

I couldn't believe what materialized. Home movies from my fifth birthday party splayed across the screen, then cut to still pictures of my adopted parents and me at a county fair. Shots of my father and me working the farm,

18

dozens of personally invasive still shots of my parents and me, including my father's funeral. More pictures and videos, me playing golf, football, baseball. The premeditated invasion of my privacy enraged me to the boiling point. More recent stills appeared, a fraternity party, shots of me walking on campus, last year's psychiatric bus trip and pictures of my college graduation. What sent me over the top, however, were the pictures of me at my mother's funeral. I slammed the iPad shut.

"Where in the hell did you get all this?!"

"I can see you're a bit irritated but—"

"Irritated? That's your educated assessment of what's happening here?!"

"I don't know. I'm not a shrink. Sonny left this as part of his will. And getting back on topic, a private jet will take us to Las Vegas at ten tomorrow morning. That is, if you choose to go. The reading of the will be the following day at one-thirty. That's all I know."

"What do you mean you don't know? You never saw this?"

"Only after I started processing the estate. I watched it. It's what Sonny wanted… you to view this video. The plane leaves at ten, with or without you."

I got up, sending my chair backwards so hard it bounced off the wall. I stomped on the chair with my right foot and paced back and forth, mumbling a variety of obscenities.

"My birth mother in on this spying too?"

"What? No. I have no idea who she was. I heard she died not to long after you were born. Sonny mentioned it once."

"Just great."

Then I did what any normal person would do after finding out his estranged birth father spied on him his entire life, never once thinking about reaching out.

"Well, here's your fucking iPad back!"

I picked up the iPad and threw it against the wall. Goldhabber took several steps backward not knowing what I'd do next. I gave him my best stay out of my fucking way glare and stormed out of the room.

"Nice arm," the lawyer mumbled.

I walked into the hallway and stared at Mendez's office door for a few seconds before I made my way back to the unit. I became oblivious to anyone or anything around me. This is what being insane must feel like. Even when someone killed my father, I managed to keep my emotions under control. But these emotions, right now, were in a universe of their own.

I swiped my card to both doors and went directly into the nurse's station. I looked around and seeing only one nurse in the kitchen, I decided to go back to George's room. George sat on his favorite and only chair in the room, flipping through today's La Crosse Tribune. I walked in and started ambulating back and forth mumbling the word shit nonstop.

"Steve, what's going on? You're going to wear out the concrete floor pacing around like that."

I stopped and looked at George.

"George, you're not going to believe what just happened."

"Slow down, easy Steve. I'm sure you didn't receive a gold star for taking down Marsha?"

"What? No."

"Okay, what happened?" George closed the newspaper and tossed it on the bed. "Did something happen to Marsha?"

I glanced out the window. "I just inherited my birth father's estate in Las Vegas."

I told George my adoption story several years ago by accident, although I've been taught there are no verbal accidents.

"That's incredible Steve. Amazing news. Sit down and tell me about it."

I sat on the edge of George's bed, my anger subsiding somewhat. He sat next to me and put his arm around my shoulder.

"You never met him, so why are you so upset?"

"He's been spying on me and my family ever since I was five. And this slick-willy lawyer who dumped this on me wants me to fly back to Vegas with him tomorrow morning on a private jet. I never envisioned it happening this way.

"Unimportant now. Listen to me, I don't know what he did or why he did what he did, but in the end, your father brought your best interests to the forefront, your security. He left you his estate. Steve, this is the opportunity of a lifetime, your lifetime."

"I know, but why like this? He could have approached me, called, texted, anything. He let all those years go by. I don't get it."

"Steve, my advice? Go to Vegas and find out more about your birth father. And without being morose, find out what happened to him. Or do you already know?"

I got up and walked back over to the window again with its pristine view of metal bars and stared out at the rest of the shitty view.

"Didn't ask. Too pissed off."

"Understandable, but tomorrow morning, you're going to get on that plane and—"

George was interrupted by his sister, Barbara Kennedy, tall, reddish blonde hair, pointy nose, paper- thin lips, a parasite who fed off George. She was a black widow spider, her body sculpted by personal trainers, dressed to kill, always on George's dime. And that caked on make-up looked like a bad nineteen-forties actress. It wouldn't surprise me if she ate her last two husbands. She had power of attorney every time George checked into the psych unit and her outfits kept getting more and more expensive with every incarceration. She was the queen bee bling-bitch.

"George. George Sharp, how are you ever going to get out of this hospital when you continually skip group meetings and. . ." She stopped cold when she saw me standing by the window.

"Hello, Barbra."

"Steven."

"I have a lot of things to do today, George. I'll leave you two alone. Looks like you have your own dilemma to sort out."

"That would be wonderful, Steven."

"Get out of here and get on that plane!" George commanded, looking like a man about to be beheaded by radical Islamists.

"Thanks again, George."

Barbra gave George a seething look "What plane are we talking about?"

I walked back to the nurse's station wondering how in God's name George and Barbra came from the same womb. Mary immediately motioned me over. She presented me with a document. "Here's your leave of absence form."

"But how—"

"Hurry up and sign it. You have a plane to catch tomorrow morning."

"Mendez is okay with this?"

"He had it ready, apparently."

I quickly signed the form and placed it in Mary's hand.

She gave me a big hug and in her sweetest Texas voice said, "Call when you get settled in to let me know how things are progressing. I'm so excited for you."

I saw Bill and Russ at one of the tables and walked over to them. Bill stood. "What's all this I'm hearing about you heading off to Vegas bro?"

Russ walked over to us, "Yeah, WTF dude."

"My birth father's lawyer showed up in the administrator's office and gave me the news: I'm inheriting his estate. The plane leaves tomorrow morning at ten."

Bill was inquisitive. "How come you never mentioned any of this before?"

"You little bitch. What's with the secrets?" Russ fed off Bill's inquiry in a jerked-chain tone.

"I didn't know. I mean, I knew I was adopted, but that's all man. Really. You guys know I'm adopted."

Russ took hold of me by the arm. "Seriously dude, go to the house and start packing."

Bill came over and took my other arm and handed me my backpack. Together they escorted me out of the nurse's station in unconstrained excitement.

"Hey, check it out. You never know. Sounds like this might be your ticket to the good life my brother. Get rolling," Russ said. "I've got your shift covered, on me. Now hit the pavement."

Bill and Russ meandered back to the chaos of the unit while I walked down the hallway toward the seclusion room. Like every room in this unit, the door could be closed but never locked; can't have patients locking themselves in. The seclusion room door was always closed when a patient was in the room. I walked into the room and looked down at Marsha strapped down in four-point seclusion.

"What a waste," I said softly to her.

To my surprise she opened her eyes and answered back.

"Is that what you think?"

I was awe-struck to see she was conscious after all the drugs she'd been dosed with.

"Yeah, pretty much."

She pulled herself up as far as she could, the restraints tightening with every movement. And then she giggled at me.

"There once was a girl who was furious,

Her family rarely took her serious,
With an axe in her hand and blood in her eyes,
She chopped them up cause she was curious.

Ha, ha, ha, ha, ha," she chanted in this psychotic rhythm.

"That's the best you've got?" I smugly answered back.

She stopped cold; her eyes turned icy.

"There's more where that came from."

"You're going to have a lot of time to work on your delivery. Oh, and I almost forgot, I brought you a little something."

She dropped back in the bed and relaxed. "Really."

"I felt bad about dumping you so hard on the floor."

"How thoughtful, what did you bring me, a knife?"

"Better, a chainsaw. It's in my back pocket."

"Seriously, what did you bring?"

I walked up to her and jammed a Tootsie Roll Pop in her mouth.

"See, not everyone hates you."

I turned and walked away. But before I opened the door she mumbled, "Not everyone hates you either, at least not yet."

She pushed up on the restraints and in one motion spit the Pop out of her mouth with such velocity that the paper stick handle stuck into the wall.

"What the fuck!"

"Have fun in Vegas, Steve. Ha, ha, ha, ha, ha, ha, ha. . ."

I backed out of the room, blown away by what she said and what I just witnessed. I slammed the door shut, staring at her through the double-paned glass observation window. She stared back at me, still ha ha-ing me. The epidemy of a crazy, psychotic, possessed individual.

I scanned myself out of the unit and down the hallway toward the parking lot wondering how she knew

24

about Las Vegas. My conclusion: an unstoppable amount of loud mouths at Lakeside.

Chapter 3

I knocked out a couple of must-do errands in town, drove home, to our three story 1924 fraternity house, walked up to the second floor and unlocked my bedroom door.

As I pondered the day's events, I felt myself bordering on an outright mental meltdown. It was too much information to process, even for me.

I surveyed my shit-hole of a room, with the worn out ceiling fan, sporting three cracked plastic buttercup light bulb holders supporting sixty watt bulbs, two of which were burned out, hanging on to a ceiling with spider web cracks in all directions. The worn out faded brown carpet was the star of this room, it only had a few holes in it. The walls had faded blue paint with chips the size of quarters and dozens of plugged white putty holes from previous occupants. My furniture consisted a night stand, with a small halogen light, a scratched up desk with a twenty by sixteen 2017 desk calendar protecting the desktop and the bottom of my laptop. The queen beds box spring looked like it was harboring mice and the mattress was so soft that if I rolled into the middle too fast it would swallow me up like a hotdog in a bun.

The real kicker was my weather-worn shade constantly losing its battle against the afternoon light or any light for that matter. Sleeping in or late or taking a nap was almost impossible. This is what I came home to every day. However, my fraternity brothers always made it feel like home.

But coming home today somehow felt different. Goldhabber's news brought out this pent-up rage while a surging jolt of fatigue drained my strength. My harsh reality, everything I owned pretty much resided within these four walls. I plopped down on my bed. What a pathetic picture, the sum total of my entire life.

But I fought back the morose shroud sucking me into that dark cypress swamp. I owned a 2012 loaded Tundra, free and clear parked outside, the only remnant I was able to salvage from my birth parents bank-ravaged estate, a bike, a little over three grand in the bank and a jet ride to Vegas tomorrow morning. Okay, it was a little messed up, maybe a lot, but I got this.

My eyes stopped on a picture of my mother; tears began to flow, but I shook them off, laid down on the bed, put my arm across my eyes, and drifted off to sleep.

*

A loud bang on my door instinctively made me jump out of bed, swinging my arms wildly. Totally confused, I reached over to my nightstand and picked up my iPhone, squinting down at the time.

"Seven-twenty at night. Shit."

"Hey open up, you sleeping?" Bill said, pounding so hard I thought he was trying to annihilate the paint off my door.

"No, I'm in the closet getting my stuff together."

"Come on down, bullshitter, a couple of the boys popped in. They want to give you a proper send-off."

"I'm going to Vegas, not Afghanistan."

"Come on, get your millionaire ass downstairs!"

"Yeah, I'll be down in five!"

"Hurry up, it's technically a school night!"

"You ass clowns don't even know what the school looks like! You think the library is a shelter for a bubbler." A bubbler was a Wisconsin term for a water fountain. "And a classroom is a group sleep deprivation experiment."

"Just get your debutante butt downstairs!"

I wrapped a few things up for my flight to Vegas and took the short jaunt down the fourteen steps to the bottom of the of the first floor where Russ promptly jumped my shit, almost knocking me over.

"Hey bro, you didn't think we would let you sneak off to Vegas without a farewell brew, did you? A couple of the boys stopped by when they heard."

"When they heard? You mean when you posted it on Facebook and tweeted it."

"Heard, told, who gives a shit, I'm buying."

"Wait a minute, you're buying me a beer from the fridge I stocked with beer yesterday?"

Russ put his arm around me and steered me into the living room. Bill sat on the huge sectional next to a couple of frat brothers who were drinking beer, my beer. They all raised their bottles when they saw me. Russ jumped on the recliner at the other end of the sectional.

"Hey, I thought you were buying, Russ."

"Well, I had a sudden change of heart when you questioned my integrity. Get your own damn beer and I'll have one too."

"Funny. You jokers all want one, while Russ is buying?"

They all nodded their heads and pounded their feet.

"Five beers, coming right up."

I walked out of the living room and around the corner to the kitchen.

"Surprise!"

I almost dropped a load in my pants. Forty or so partygoers, a rambunctious combination of guys and girls, rushed me. They high-fived each other and hugged me. Bill came up behind me and Russ jumped on my back again.

"Come on dude, you didn't think we would let you escape to Vegas without a proper send-off?" Russ quipped.

Bill started the chaos, pumping his fists. "VEGAS! VEGAS! VEGAS!"

Everyone at the party followed the chant and music exploded throughout the house. "Days Go By" some electronic club music by Dirty Vegas rocked the fraternity house.

My fraternity brothers came up to me one-by-one, with hugs, fist bumps, mafia kisses, the whole nine yards. The girls came up and laid hugs and some mouthwatering kisses on me. Nipples were jammed in my ear holes as some of the girls pulled my head into their scantily covered chests. I heard the sound of the keg being tapped and knew the Titanic would be going down again, with me at the helm.

Bill and Russ pulled me out of the kitchen and over to the bar in our living room.

Bill began with, "We mixed up a little sendoff poison for you."

I looked down at the bar. "You dirty bastards."

The music came to screeching halt when Bill picked up a shot glass and a partially full glass of beer, an Irish Car Bomb, and handed it to me. "It's half Jameson whiskey and Baileys Irish cream poured into a one ounce shot glass, then dropped into six ounces of Guinness dry malt and chugged. When you're finished, pound the empty glass upside down on the bar."

The party goers chanted, "DRINK. DRINK. DRINK. DRINK."

"Fuck you very much!" I said.

I raised the glass to all the party-goers, bombed the shot, and calmly poured it down my throat, four seconds flat, slamming the glass upside down on the bar.

Everyone cheered as I nodded and pulled out the sides of my cargo shorts, curtsying.

Bill and Russ led another chant, fist pumping: "STEVE, STEVE, STEVE, ONE MORE TIME!"

Bill poured the Jameson and Bailey's into the shot glass, always heavy on the Jameson, while Russ cracked open another bottle of Guinness and filled my empty beer glass half-way.

I raised my hands and got everyone's attention. "Oh no you don't, boys, the two of you pour yourselves one and join me in a toast!"

Everyone started doing dog cheers-WOOF, WOOF, WOOF-while the shot glasses were being loaded.

I raised my hands for silence and made a toast. "Yonder porcelain God (the toilet) awaits thee!"

We bombed the beers and chugged them to the sound of everyone chanting, "Drink, drink, drink, drink!"

We all slammed our beer glasses down simultaneously, wiped our mouths with our arms, and high-fived each other, much to the appreciation of all the party-goers. The music exploded through the house again as "I'm Shipping Up To Boston" some Celtic punk by Dropkick Murphys, got the party rolling again.

Of course, they added the words Vegas instead of Boston because that's where I was going and nobody in Wisconsin would ever admit to giving a rat's ass about anything that has to do with those lying, cheating, bastards in Boston.

The party raged on for hours, and countless shots and beers left me shit-faced. I grabbed this girl who'd been hanging on me for the last forty-five minutes, rubbing my crotch like she was expecting a Genie to appear. I corralled Bill and Russ with her riding my shoulder.

"Excuse me darling, I have to have a brief momentary conference with my roomies." I put both hands on her shoulders. "I shall return momentarily," I added grabbing my second of two beers from her hand and dragging my tongue across her enticing perfumed neck.

With a beer in each hand, I put my arms around my roommates' necks, spilling alcohol all over them and gently head-locking them, pulling their ears close to my mouth.

"I love you guys, you've been my only family for the last couple of years," I said just loud enough for them to hear.

They answered back, "We love you too, man."

I released them and the three of us banged glasses together and shouted, "TO FAMILY!"

Chapter 4

The digital alarm on my iPhone featuring Toby Keith's, "Get Drunk and Be Somebody" shattered the silence. The sun penetrated through my cheap window shade again, trying to split my already- pounding head in two. I took a couple of swipes at the iPhone, finally managing to pull it into the bed and on top of my chest. After taking multiple swipes at the snooze button, I finally silenced it. My eyes felt like they were bleeding alcohol, my eyelids weighted down by a couple of bowling balls. I courageously managed to open them long enough to catch the time on the phone.

"I can't believe it's seven forty-five." I mumbled, noticing my breath smelled like Jameson. "I hope no one lights a match around me."

I closed my eyes and tried to roll over on my right side. I only managed to turn partway and came to a dead stop. A soft, warm body prevented me from making my roll. Next to me, a naked girl lying on her right side was facing away from me.

"Got a light?" she groggily asked without moving a muscle.

The fog miraculously cleared, the bowling balls disintegrated, and my eyes opened like they were pinned to my forehead.

"You're funny for eight in the morning."

"Thanks for answering my next question," she playfully said.

"It's almost eight?" I replied, trying to recall her name or something about her from last night.

"Morning is such a beautiful time of the day; too bad it comes so bloody early."

She rolled over on her back and went into a full stretch mode, pausing to gaze at my crotch. I couldn't help noticing that her nipples were erect.

"Oh my, someone's glad to see me," she said. "If I had a little more time, I could do another dance on that pole."

"Another?"

She rolled out of bed like a USA Gymnastics Team member. I couldn't help but watch her every move as she tried to scrape together pieces of her clothing, intertwined with mine, strewn across the bedroom floor. Like trying to win a scavenger hunt, she catapulted individual pieces of her ensemble onto the bed, watching me watch her, until all her items were recovered. She rummaged through the pile, casually dressed, putting on a seductive exhibition, making sure my eyes gravitated to her every twitch. You can throw Kellogg's out the window, this is the way to start your day.

"I'm sorry, I don't remember—"

"Julie, just became an active Delta last spring. Nice to see you again too. And what a party."

"I'm glad you enjoyed yourself; we aim to please. That's quite a body you're sporting. Thank your parents for me."

"I'll be sure to mention it the next time I see them. Good luck in Vegas. I hope to see, all of you again."

"Ditto."

She walked out of the room, gently closing the door behind her. I twisted around and sat up on the edge of the bed, looked down at my one-eyed monster staring back at me, and rubbed my eyes until they hurt. I tried to piece last night together but drew a blank. I glanced at my nightstand where a rose rested with a card opened next to it. I leaned over to read the card, almost performing a perfect nose-dive onto the floor. Still a wee bit trashed, I bumbled around and managed to pick up the card.

I hope you had fun last night. I sincerely hope all goes well for you in Las Vegas. Don't forget to call. Mary.

"Are you kidding me. When was she here?" I bellowed out almost gagging.

After taking a long hot shower to drain the pain, I came back to my room and leaned over my desk. I took another look at the card and laid it down. Reaching into my well-organized desk, I retrieved a stack of bills from inside one of the cubby holes. The tombstone of the stack, a college loan statement, thirty-two thousand dollars, the rest, chump-change by comparison. I thumbed through them quickly, did a double take on the student loan bill, pounded the stack in my fist several times on the desk, and flipped the bills back, scattering them.

"Adios mother-fuckers! I'm off to Vegas and I'll deal with you Smurfs later. I'm about to be a rich man."

9:31 AM

I parked my Tundra at the La Crosse Airport on French Island and walked through the terminal. I was escorted to the private jet by an attractive older flight attendant. I could see why she was still flying the friendly skies.

"I'll bet she was one of the charter members of the mile-high club," I uttered quietly to myself.

I entered the plane around nine forty-five, wearing my Oakley sunglasses, a backwards green and gold Packer hat, jeans, a black tee shirt, black sports coat and perfectly worn-out tan leather cowboy boots. My laptop, iPad, headphones and some personal items were tightly packed in my backpack which I carried onboard. My other suitcase went into the cargo bay. The flight attendant seated me across the aisle from that green pile of mucus, Goldhabber.

"My name is Meryl and you'll need to buckle up; we'll be taking off in about ten minutes."

The attendant left and walked back to the cockpit. I leaned over for a better view. Even through hung-over blood-shot eyes some things never change. Plus, I couldn't believe how luxurious this plane was.

"I knew you'd come. Sonny said you would be here. Sonny is. . . was always right."

I turned my head to the sound of that rancid voice that belonged to Goldhabber.

"Good for you. So fill me in on Sonny."

"The plane is about to take off. When were airborne, I'll start to answer some of your questions."

I opened my backpack and took out my Koss headphones, a birthday gift from Mary and plugged them into my sixty-four-gig iPhone six plus, another gift from Mary. I had around six thousand songs broken down into around twenty play lists. I placed the backpack under my seat. I chose, "Mexicoma" by Tim McGraw and hit play. The initial blast almost cracked my ear drums, but I managed to get the volume down to semi-abnormal.

The flight attendant walked back to me. "Please don't use any electrical devices until we are airborne."

Giving her the dumb-fuck look, I responded with, "Come on, really, terrorists have used knives, box cutters, guns and shoe bombs to try and pancake planes, when all along they could have just used cell phones and music to accomplish their agendas. What a bunch of half-wits."

"Very informative. And thank you for those words of inspiration." She lightly responded while rolling her eyes and walking back to her jump seat.

I'd only been on commercial airliners a few times and was amazed how much faster the private jet ascended into the sky.

After the plane reached its cruising altitude, Meryl returned to us with a bottle of Cristal Champagne. I hit the pause button on my iPhone, took off my headset, and looked at the bottle.

Goldhabber leaned over to me. "Ah, the breakfast of champions. Here, have a glass while I tell you a little bit more about Sonny. You do know what this is?" he said, acting like a know-it-all dick.

"I live in Western Wisconsin, not Northern Siberia. And isn't it a little early for a tip of the bubbly?"

"Oh, I see. All of this, per my arrangement with Sonny, is in the will. And I'll segue into the small portion of the will which you'll find useful."

"I thought the will reading was tomorrow?"

"Again, Sonny wanted this portion revealed to you before the public reading."

"Okay, let's hear it."

"Steve, you have inherited a seventy-five percent ownership of Sonny's Yo Leven Limousine Service."

While Meryl poured Goldhabber's glass, she leaned into his glass and pressed her bottom across my arm rest, knowing full well she was distracting me from Goldhabber's grandstanding confabulation.

"The other twenty-five percent belongs to Sonny's longtime friend and partner Dino Lezcano. He's a hard-nosed son-of-a-bitch and a real prick. However, he's fair, a non-stop workaholic, and he's been with Sonny since the inception of the company in the seventies. They were both cab drivers back then, which, by the way, is a whole other story I'm sure you'll hear from Dino or someone else who has first-hand knowledge."

"I'm inheriting a limo company and my birth father used to be a cab driver?"

"Yes, but let me continue. He also left you his house at the Las Vegas Country Club, four vehicles, his personal bank account, jewelry, clothes, although looking at you, none of his things will fit, maybe his shoes, his enemies, ha, just kidding and some stocks. I'll get into the real numbers with you tomorrow at the will reading. Oh yeah, and Tony. Any questions?"

Goldhabber shot down the rest of his champagne and gave me a smug smile. The kind of smile you want to send the heel of your boot through. He motioned to the flight attendant for a refill.

"His enemies? And what the hell is a Tony?"

"Well, it's not the Broadway award and it walks and talks and has more functions than a Pitbull. You'll have to figure the rest out when you get to the Barn and meet him."

"The barn? They have barns in Vegas?"

"No son, it's the nickname for the limo office." Goldhabber rolled his eyes. He pointed to the bottle of Cristal. Meryl wrapped a towel around her arm again and filled Goldhabber's glass. She motioned to me and I waved her off with my hand. As she walked away, I checked out her cute little butt again. And I noticed she wasn't wearing a wedding ring.

I stared out the window trying to absorb all of Goldhabber's data. Still buzzed from last night, I concluded that the four Tylenol I took this morning had already capitulated to the pain ransacking my head, a mission doomed from the start. My eyes and fingers fumbled around with the playlists on my iPhone until they chose something soothing. I put my headphones back on immediately dozed off.

Like having a chair ripped out from beneath me, some kidney-jarring turbulence woke me up demanding my undivided attention. My eyes focused on Meryl who appeared undisturbed by the incident and calmly continued to push a small cart toward us. I glanced at my watch. I had dozed off for ten minutes or so even though it felt like several hours. It occurred to me in that short time span that my four little Tylenol warriors had rallied from the jaws of defeat and conquered the pain pounding between my ears.

She carried a tray loaded with a variety of caviars, crackers, mini sandwiches, cheeses, nuts, and cookies. A lot of food for just two passengers.

Goldhabber plowed through the tray on a mission to capture his favorite delight which turned out to be a sandwich of some kind. She looked at me and I waived her off. He took a large bite and pointed the remainder of the sandwich in the direction of my face, talking as Meryl retreated to the galley in the front of the plane.

"Ironically, Sonny intended to contact you, especially after your mother passed away. I'm not sure what happened; maybe time got away from him. Steve, Sonny was missing for almost a month until a couple of days ago. Metro found his charred remains in a burned-out car in the desert. That's why I'm here and you're headed to Vegas."

I didn't know Sonny or care much for his spying tactics but hearing that he was found dead in a burned-out car was disturbing.

"Metro?"

"The Las Vegas Police department, Metro."

I could tell he was getting bored answering my questions.

"Charred remains, are you telling me someone murdered him?"

"I'm not saying he was, but I'm not ruling out the possibility either. Metro's working on the case and as of now it's open-ended, no leads. You don't come into that kind of power position without making some enemies, big ones. Sonny was very intelligent. It appears as though somebody got him. As I like to say, or it's the most bizarre suicide in the history of Nevada."

The copilot came over to us and stopped between Goldhabber and me, his leg resting against the snack tray.

"Hey Goldhabber," he extended his hand.

Goldhabber took out an envelope from his inside suit jacket pocket and placed it in the copilot's hand. The copilot ripped it out, glanced at me, and took the short walk back to the cockpit.

"The envelope, Goldhabber?"

"A little something for a friend, prearranged of course. Steve, relax, enjoy this down time; it's going to be hectic once you get to Vegas. Ever been to Vegas?"

"You saw the video. Any pictures of me in Vegas?"

38

"I guess not. Anyway, get some rest, chill out. I'm not the bad guy here, just the messenger. And one other item of interest."

"I can't wait."

"Sonny's remains,; he wanted to be cremated. Although I'm sure not that way. The funeral home more or less condensed him. I'm sorry, bad taste, although Sonny would have appreciated the humor. He could be quite the funny man."

"That's great to know, Norman."

I put my headphones on, hit the play button and "The Good The Bad And The Dread" by Dreadzone nearly blowing out my eardrums. I looked out the window and wondered how this might have played out had Sonny been alive. I remembered a crazy incident that happened several months ago. I was riding my bike downtown when some asshole in a Camaro almost sideswiped me into some parked cars. I wasn't hurt, and I assumed it was an accident. There are bad drivers everywhere, but now hearing of the possibility that Sonny was killed, and me as his sole heir, maybe it wasn't a random incident. Or maybe I was overtired and overthinking everything.

I glanced at Goldhabber who must have consumed a bit too much Cristal. The drool running down the side of his mouth made a picture-perfect portrait. I got up, tossed my sports coat on the seat, and went to the back of the plane to use the restroom. Once inside I marveled at how big and nice it was compared to regular passenger plane restrooms. I dropped my ensemble of pants and underwear around my cowboy boots and sat on the pot, not sure what my body wanted to do after last night's festivities. A wrap on the door disrupted my thoughts.

"Goldhabber, I'll be out in five minutes. I just got in here."

Another lighter knock.

"Jesus Fucking Christ! There's only five people on this goddamn flight and everyone needs the crapper at the same time!"

With my pants and underwear puddled around my boots and my shirt dangling over my private parts, I waddled to the door and opened it.

"Hey asshole!"

Meryl slowly pushed me back until I landed back on the pot.

"I'm not used to seeing someone your age flying private. Usually they're old horny rich men, some women too."

"I've aroused your curiosity?"

"I saw the way you looked at me… was I wrong?"

"No. I think you're dangerously hot."

She opened her blouse and unsnapped a front bra clip, revealing a beautiful set of natural thirty-four C's. What especially captured my interest were the thick nipple rings on each breast.

"We don't have too much time, Steve."

"What would you have done had I been in the process of dropping a deuce?"

"That would have been bad timing on my part, but as you can see, lucky me."

She reached under the sink cabinet and pulled out a padded knee square. I was aroused before her skirt hit the floor.

I joined more clubs in that fifteen minutes than I ever thought possible. The mile-high club, the ribbed condom club, the flight attendant club, the on the pot club, the doing a flight attendant from the rear with her head halfway down the toilet club, the finish-off the attendant on the sink club and most erotic bathroom sex ever club. I wondered if a trophy store made those type of trophies.

Meryl hurriedly dressed and exited the restroom first. I turned around to take a leak when my urine suddenly sprayed wildly on the floor, almost landing on my boots. The condom. I'd forgotten to pull the condom off. What a moron. I waited another couple of minutes and wandered back to my seat. I inconspicuously ran my hand across my crotch, making sure I hadn't deposited any urine on my jeans. A quick check of Goldhabber showed him still out, the same drool now crusting over the corner of his mouth.

"Gentlemen, we are making our final approach into Las Vegas. Please fasten your seat belts." Meryl's voice came across the intercom twenty minutes later in a noticeably sexier and gentler tone.

Chapter 5

The plane landed safely at the Signature airport just before noon. The intense desert heat bounced the plane around during our approach, almost causing me to lose whatever was left over in my stomach. Goldhabber exited first with a polite thank you from Meryl, who waited next to the doorway. As I approached her, backpack in hand, she tenderly caressed both of her breasts and gave me a they're going to be sore for a week but I'd do it again in a New-York-second kind of smirk.

I walked off the plane and onto a sizzling tarmac where a limo awaited my arrival. I could feel the heat rising, trying to incinerate me. I assumed it would be agonizingly hot in Las Vegas this time of year. Today was no different. But actually experiencing it for the first time was a real eye opener.

There were two chauffeurs standing next to a limo, both wearing sunglasses and dressed in dark suits.

"These guys look like they're dressed for a Men in Black audition," I smugly dribbled out loud. "It's four hundred degrees out."

The copilot dropped my suitcase in front of the limo, handed Goldhabber his bag, and proceeded to the terminal. Goldhabber walked up to the chauffeurs and cheerfully shook their hands. He executed a perfect about-face toward me, and with his ten-cent smile, summoned me over with his hand.

"Steve Mueller, I'd like you to meet Dino Lezcano, Sonny's partner and now yours. This is Sonny's boy," he announced like I was the cheapest prize at the Chucky Cheese arcade.

Dino was an older-looking Italian, late sixties, under six feet, and looked like he'd been around the block a few hundred times. Dino's handshake, a vice grip, caught me off guard. I had to suck up the pain without wincing and looking like a pussy. I think he drained the remaining alcohol out of my system with that grip.

"Welcome to Las Vegas, Mr. Mueller," they both said in unison.

"Please, ditch the formalities and call me Steve."

"All right, welcome to Las Vegas, Steve," Dino corrected himself.

Goldhabber pointed to the other chauffeur. "This is Kurt Walker, your driver. Kurt, this is Steve."

Kurt Walker had the chauffeur look. He appeared to be in his late forties, tall, handsome, tan, silver black hair, filled out his suit to perfection, in kick-ass shape, sporting several rings on his left hand. However, his most noticeable feature was his smile, professional, trusting, oozing with confidence.

"Steve, a pleasure to finally meet you."

"Thank you."

Goldhabber looked at the three of us, waved goodbye, and slid his suitcase handle up, pulling it towards a waiting Town Car. "I have to get back to the office; I have business I need to catch up on. Steve, call me if you need something. You have my card. Otherwise, I'll see you tomorrow afternoon. Dino, we'll touch base later."

I watched him walk away, suitcase in tow. Standing next to an open back door was a foxy brunette. Tall, thin, wearing a black pant suit and pumps. Never saw a chauffeur look like that before. An ignorant stereotype on my part.

Goldhabber dropped his suitcase at the door and slid in. She closed the door, put the suitcase in the trunk, and walked over to the driver's side. As she opened her door, she shot me an intriguing glance. The door closed and the Town Car drove off the tarmac.

Kurt tossed my bag into the limo's trunk and walked up to me.

"I'll be taking you to our office, commonly known as, The Barn."

43

I climbed into the back of the limo and the first thing my eyes unexpectedly locked onto was an exotic blonde sitting against the far corner of the front back seat. She wore a low cut skintight white dress, matching heels, and brandished an alluring smile toward me.

I instinctively paused at the door, but thanks to Kurt's unceremonious nudge I found myself neatly tucked into the back seat. After the door closed, I watched him through the dark tinted windows, making his way to the driver's side door. I saw the back of Dino's head in the passenger side of the front seat as Kurt entered the limo.

The limo cautiously pulled out of the airport, and the solid divider between the front and back slowly rolled up. The music uncoincidentally came on and I recognized the smooth jazz tune "Inside Myself" by Art Porter as it played in the background.

"Hi Steve, my name is Ruby. I'm here to make sure your first day in Vegas is a memorable one."

Like a third grader, I asked, "Are you a chauffeur too?"

The solid divider clicked shut.

She looked down at my junk and smiled. "I'm whatever you want me to be."

Had I been thinking straight I would have asked Kurt to stop, turn around, and pick up Meryl.

*****

Las Vegas Signature Airport
11:46 AM

A black limo followed by a black Town Car rolled onto the Signature tarmac.

"The plane should be arriving in ten minutes," Kurt told Dino as he pulled the limo alongside an eight-foot chain link fence.

"I still can't believe this shit. Sonny gives this kid seventy-five percent of my… his limo company. He doesn't even know the little prick; his estranged bastard son, my ass."

"Why don't you tell me how you really feel, Dino?"

"Yeah, yeah, I get it, it's over. He's almost here and I can't change this."

"Let's see how this plays out; maybe the two of you can get things back on track."

"What in the hell does a punk college kid from Wisconsin know about anything? He probably just started pissing standing up a couple of years ago. Goddamn it, Kurt, I want to punch something… really hard!"

"Keep this up and you'll have a stroke. Settle down; it's done."

"Is Bridgette parked behind us?"

"Yes, Dino."

"Good, the last thing I want to do is be around that Goldhabber sleazeball any longer than I have to."

"It's all taken care of. Man, it seems like just yesterday since Sonny went missing, and now he's dead. I don't even have words to describe all this. And still no answers as to who killed him either."

"You mean his unfortunate accident, right?"

"Right, and I know Tony won't rest until this is solved. Somebody's going to end up being scorpion chow."

The two silently stared down the tarmac until Kurt saw the plane making its approach.

"Right on time."

After the plane landed, it rolled its way to the area where the limos were staged.

Kurt drove toward the plane, verifying the tail number.

"That's it. Now remember, Dino, play nice. He's just a kid who fell into something and doesn't realize he's in way over his head."

"That's easy for you to say I always thought I was Sonny's closet living everything. This is the curve ball from hell, this bastard kid thing. All the shit I did for him and this is my reward, second fiddle to a snot-nose bastard. And one he didn't even know."

"I'm sorry Dino, I can't imagine how you're feeling right now. But you're a smart guy, you'll figure things out. Ready? Let's go meet the new boss."

Kurt jumped out of the limo before Dino could take a swing at his arm.

"Smart-ass son-of-a-bitch."

"Remember, play nice." Kurt leaned in and closed the door.

Dino joined Kurt in front of the limo and punched him in the arm just as the plane door opened.

*****

The limo drove up the Strip while Ruby playfully unzipped her dress, tossing it at my feet. Talk about eye candy: Ruby, wearing only heels and my first live view of the Las Vegas strip— what a combo. However, the Strip disappeared as soon as she crawled up to me and unbuckled my jeans. This was going to be the third time in less than twenty-four hours with three different women. Was life good or what?

"I'm glad to you like what you see, Steve."

She turned around and straddled me backward, pulling my boots off, playfully falling forward as each boot slipped off my foot. When the second one came off, she rolled over on her back and started making tiny exotic snow angels. She rolled over on her hands and knees and crawled back to my lap where she pulled my jeans and boxers off in one hard tug, falling back on her butt, swinging my jeans over her head like she was about to rope a calf. She tossed them backward over her head and off the front of the back seat. She leaned in, pushing my legs apart, kissed my thighs several times and went down on me. I grabbed her head softly. It's the strangest feeling to look at all those people walking around knowing what you're doing and enjoying the fact they don't have the slightest clue.

*****

"Candice, Mr. Mueller is on board and we're rolling," Kurt radioed in.

"Candice, we're rolling. What, you drop into a seventies Burt Reynolds movie?" Dino asked.

"Dating yourself again, old man."

"And Kurt, keep your eyes on the road. What's so important that you have to keep looking down at your watch every twenty seconds?"

"A little side bet."

"What do you mean, a little side bet?"

"Well, we have a clock going on Ruby and Steve."

"You're timing the kid?"

"Of course we are. We got knuckles to set it up and book it."

"You got Knuckles involved in this? And how many of you sick degenerates are in on this bet?"

"At last count, a dozen or so."

"Oh, you've got to fill me in on this one."

"Well, as soon as Steve pops a nut Ruby's going to knock on the divider. Under seven minutes is two-to-one, seven minutes is one-to-two and over twenty minutes is three-to-one."

"How did you know when to start the clock?"

"Ruby said I should start clocking at Tropicana Avenue."

"Did I ever tell you how warped you are?"

"On many occasions, and this coming from the gentleman on my right who decided to put a hooker in the back seat of a limo to seduce this unsuspecting young lad from Wisconsin." Kurt took his hands off the wheel and placed them on his cheeks, acting shocked and dismayed.

"I'll play along, what did *you* bet?"

"I laid the one-to-two for a nickel ($500.00) and you have to admit this is a classic."

"You really want to know what I think, Kurt?"

"Can't wait to hear it."

"I think I'm paying you too much."

"Come on Ruby Baby."

"Kurt, what happens if you have to slam on the brakes?"

"You're a cold old man Dino, a very cold man."

Twenty-three minutes later, the limo pulled into the barn parking lot.

"Son-of-a-bitch." Kurt lightly pounded the steering wheel.

"Maybe you ought to quit gambling, Kurt. I'm going inside. And I want to know his time; after all, he's going to be my business partner."

Dino walked into the barn door where six drivers waited by the limo. They backed away to let Dino pass.

"You're all warped," Dino added as he passed by.

Kurt got out of the limo and glanced at his watch. Another five minutes passed.

"WTF."

Kurt looked at everyone standing around the door and shrugged his shoulders. Everyone left and walked back into the barn.

"What is this kid, a porn star?" Kurt mumbled to himself.

The back door of the limo finally opened, and Ruby came out shaking her head.

"You'll understand if I don't kiss you goodbye," Kurt said with a shit-eating grin.

She gave Kurt the finger and got into a waiting Town Car.

*****

Kurt stood by the front limo door.

"Welcome to the barn, Steve," he said as he approached me.

"Thanks for the ride and the ah, you know, the other stuff."

"What other stuff?" Kurt innocently answered.

"You know. Ruby."

"You mean Dino's daughter; did something happen between you two?"

"Dino's daughter!"

Kurt looked at me, arms folded, a blank stare across his face. There was an awkward pause, then my brain lights flickered.

"That wasn't Dino's daughter."

"It's not too late to drown yourself in Lake Mead. Come on in and meet the gang."

*****

An Older Office Building in North Las Vegas.
1:05 PM

In a dimly lit suite, Woody Churchfield, a man in his early forties, under six feet, overweight, greasy hair, glasses, overly long fingernails, his right pinky finger painted silver, dressed in a dark blue Armani suit, sat in a high-back leather chair. Being around him was like trying to pick up the clean end of a turd. He was going through files when a text message appeared on his screen. Woody picked up the cell phone.

The meeting at YLL is about to start. I will text you later with more info.

"Amazing what money can buy. This is going to be a very profitable week," he said to himself.

He pushed the intercom button on his desktop phone.

"Maggie, tell Letterman to pick me up out front in an hour. And make sure Eddy Morrow is with him. We have some delicate issues that need his special expertise."

"Of course, Mr. Churchfield. Any particular vehicle you want him to bring?"

"The Bentley Stretch. I want to be noticed today. And Maggie, make sure these files are returned to my safe and locked-up after I leave."

"Of course, Mr. Churchfield, anything else?"

"Not now, but later, I need you to contact the Pope; I have a prayer I need answered."

"I'll let him know there's a possible prayer meeting later today. Anything else?"

"No."

*****

Kurt and I walked into the YLL lobby from the garage entrance. To my left sitting at a receptionist's desk was a rather large woman with red hair. She rose when she saw Kurt and me enter.

"Steve, this is Candice, our main dispatcher, receptionist, and gopher extraordinaire. This company would be lost without her. Candice, this is Steve Mueller, Sonny's boy. He prefers to be called Steve," Kurt said.

Candice shuffled from behind her desk, came up to me and gave me a big bone-crunching hug, probably rearranging most of my vertebrae.

In her thick Irish accent, backing off to hold both of my shoulders, she joyfully expressed, "Mr. Mueller, pardon, Steve, it's so very pleasant to meet you. Aye, yes, I can see the resemblance, not a spitting image mind you, but most definitely related."

At five feet five and probably pushing over two-hundred-and-fifty pounds Candice was built like a brick shithouse. She could probably take a punch too.

"It's nice to meet you too, Candice."

"The conference room is down the hall." She pointed with her right hand. "Everyone's waiting. I'll be right along shortly."

"Thanks." I shuffled down the hallway, flexing my shoulders and slowly twisting my hips, making sure she hadn't broken anything.

*****

Candice dropped back and yanked Kurt by the arm.

In a forceful, quiet voice, Candice ranted, "What the Fuke happened in the back of the limo? She was supposed to polish his knob, not his shoes."

"Hey Candice, I got burned for a nickel. I'll be stopping by Tight Racks later tonight and having a little chat with Ruby."

"My grandmother could have got him off in ten minutes!"

"Your grandmother had a master's degree in gang-banging and could have gotten the whole UNLV football team off in ten minutes."

"You can be such a fukin' asshole, Kurt!"

*****

I did the short walk down the hallway and glanced into the conference room. I could hear boisterous chatter and my name being tossed around like confetti on New Year's Eve. Candice caught up to me and grabbed my arm. She was followed by Kurt and the two of them unexcitedly escorted me into the conference room. I assumed most of the key personnel were here.

"Steve." Dino pointed to a chair. The volume in his voice towered over the noise in the room. "Have a seat right here, next to me. Alright everyone, settle down. We're going to start this meeting," Dino ordered, this time raising his voice an octave.

Like a military tribunal, everyone became quiet and grabbed a seat. You could hear a fly shit a hundred yards away. Back in college, everyone took their sweet-ass time when a professor called for class to commence. Even the wacko-ward meetings never came together this quickly or quietly. I took a seat and looked up at Dino standing on my right.

"Everyone, this is Steve Mueller, Sonny's boy, my new partner and your new boss."

I thought I witnessed Dino coughing up a lung the way he introduced me. I started to stand up but thought otherwise, especially after eyeballing the dissatisfied audience chuckling.

In unison, like a second-grade class, they all responded with, "Hello, Mr. Mueller."

Dino's face wrinkled as he gave the room the fascist dictator stare. The room became still again.

"Steve, these are most of the key people that make YLL run smoothly. I'll start with the introduction of the person on my right: Tony Corleone."

I leaned forward and looked to my right. He must have entered the room after I sat down. My eyes opened so wide I thought they were going to fall out of my head and onto the floor. Tony was massive. He made my frat bother John look like a little schoolgirl. He had to be at least six foot six, well over three hundred pounds, and somewhere in his sixties. His face looked like he had been beaten up by several Navy SEAL training teams, over a decade's worth. Blossoming cauliflower ears kept the sides of his head together while his hands looked like a pair of worn-out nineteen-twenties fielders' mitts. For a second, I thought I had swallowed my tongue. I stood, but Tony pushed Dino back, verbally bull-rushing me.

"So, you're Sonny's kid?"

"Yes sir," I politely answered, not trying to wave red meat in front of the polar bear.

"You goin' to fix this?"

"Excuse me," I said, completely confused. "Fix what?"

Dino moved Tony's hand away from me and interrupted Tony's verbal assault.

"Steve is here as Sonny's heir and his opinions and ideas for taking this company forward into the future will be greatly appreciated, by myself and everyone in this room."

Dino clapped rapidly, looking right at me, followed by everyone else standing up and sarcastically golf clapping. You'd thought I'd just won an Oscar for best suicide in a Vegas nightmare.

Dino stopped clapping and sat down. Everyone else stopped on a dime and followed his lead.

What planet did that jet take me to? I thought.

"Since Sonny's disappearance and now as we know, his death, the company has gotten into a rather tough patch," Dino continued. "Before Sonny's death, we were going to upgrade the company— cars, limos, buses, the office, computer system, advanced GPS, everything." He paused for several seconds. "I'd like to personally thank all of you for sucking it up and toughing it out until Steve's arrival."

I thought I had walked into an Ed Wood Jr. script. I gripped the arms of the chair so tightly my knuckles turned white. I couldn't believe what I just heard. The place was going down like the Titanic and now that I was here, things were going to get better. As if to add insult to injury, everyone joined in on another golf clap.

Dino left the room, followed by Tony. I rose and joined the let's get the fuck out of Dodge parade. Except, I had nowhere to go. I wanted to find Goldhabber and beat the snot out of him. I stopped just outside the door.

Dino and Tony walked into an office next to the conference room. Candice raced by me and returned to her receptionist area. Various people nodded and walked past me. Talk about feeling alone in the world. I saw the men's room and wandered in to relieve myself. I felt a little acid climbing out of my stomach, ready to explode across my tongue and onto the floor. But I wasn't a puker, and the pile of whatever slid back down my esophagus and into my stomach. I grabbed a piece of gum out of my sport coat's inside pocket, tossed the wrapper in a cheap waste basket, and began chomping away. I innocently strolled back out into the hallway and stood there looking stupid.

A tall gentleman approached me.

"Mr. Mueller."

"Call me Steve."

"Alright then, let me begin again. Hello there Steven, my name is Edmond Hollingsworth."

"My mother called me Steven."

"Alright then, let me begin a third time. Hello there Steve, my name is Edmond Hollingsworth."

He was tall, about six foot four, dressed in a light blue suit and coordinated bow tie, and looked like a lost literature professor with a huge overbearing English accent. He grabbed my arm in a friendly way.

"Walk with me, Steve."

"Sure Mr. Hollingsworth." I looked around for someone to throw a bag over my head and drag me to an isolated area for execution.

"You must call me Edmond, Steve. I mean, now that we're on a first name basis," he regurgitated as though we'd been long-established English Fox Hunting chap partners.

"If you say so."

"I'm Sonny's most trusted chauffeur and it would be an honor to assist you in any way possible, making your transition to Vegas a positive and memorable one."

"Ah, thank you Edmond, that would be nice."

What a load of horse manure. This guy was as phony as Hillary and Bill Clinton's marriage. And cologne had a thirty-yard radius and smelled like he bought it at a gas station. I needed a stiff shot about now as he continued forcing me to listen.

"Steve, there are many in this company who will say they are loyal, but over the years Sonny entrusted me with his high-valued clientele."

While in the process of handing me his card, a shorter Spanish-looking man dressed in an expensive gray pinstripe suit walked up to us.

In a light Spanish accent, he said, "Did Edmond invite you into the men's room for a little game of pocket pool?"

"Steve, we'll talk later when the hallway isn't so odoriferous. Excuse me."

He turned to the Spanish guy and loudly said, "Piss off," as he walked toward the lobby.

"What a giant douche bag. My name is Ramone Constantine, chauffeur extraordinaire, and you're the new boss. Welcome to the Barn"

"Thank you."

"No problem. Glad to rescue you."

Ramone stood five foot eight, and couldn't have weighed more than one hundred and sixty pounds. With his gray hair combed back, he was a good-looking older man. I'm sure he did well in Vegas.

"So, is Edmond gay?"

"I doubt it, can't stand him. He's such an ass kisser." We watched Edmond walk toward Candice when he turned around and flipped off Ramone.

"Awe, don't go away mad, just go away!" Ramone yelled down the hallway, catching the attention of everyone within twenty yards. "If you need anything, just let me know. Kurt and I are really tight. And what just happened to that phony British accent when he got mad?"

"Sounds like you two have some issues to work out."

I saw Candice handing Edmond a set of keys as he left the building by way of the garage.

Kurt walked over to us along with the tall brunette from the airport. A black guy followed by an Asian guy approached me as well. I assumed Sonny was into some sort of diversity.

"Getting to know the gang, are we?" Kurt asked. "Edmond might be a little stuffy, but he does make the company money. Isn't that right,

Ramone turned his head away from Kurt and didn't say anything.

"He has a way with the geriatric crowd, especially with his fake British accent. And when you get a chance and you're feeling a little suicidal, ask him about his time spent with the, wait for it," Kurt used his hands to air-finger quote and say, "The Queen."

Everyone within listening distance laughed when they heard the word Queen.

"The Queen?" I inquired.

"Trust me, you don't want hear Edmond's British royalty bullshit tale," Kurt sarcastically blurted out. "Steve, let me introduce you to all these fine people surrounding you. This is Bridgette Saunders, you might have seen her at the airport, the one who drove Goldhabber back to his snake pit."

She stood five foot nine, pretty face, long flowing black hair, perfect make-up. Her black pant suit looked custom-tailored. The blistering white shirt she wore highlighted her Middle Eastern complexion.

"Nice to meet you, Bridgette."

"Welcome to Vegas, Steve. You and Ruby engaged yet?"

"We're still working out the divorce details," I snarkily replied.

"Sorry, couldn't resist."

"Everyone here a smartass?" I said feeling a little embarrassed that everyone knew the goings on in the back seat of the limo.

"I'm not," the Asian guy interjected. He had slicked back dyed blonde hair, late twenties, medium height, must have weighed in the low two hundreds, spoke perfect English, looked like a body builder.

"Steve, this is KiKo Tsundrian, our head mechanic and Asian exotic dancer. He can fix anything; he's a genius, Kurt added."

He extended his hand, "Nice to meet you, Steve."

"Likewise, you must hit the gym pretty hard?"

"No."

He turned away and walked toward the garage door.

"Guy can talk up a blue-streak."

They all gave me a courtesy laugh.

Kurt continued with the final introduction, "Steve this is our affirmative action, Gang Bangin' brother from another mother, Black Panther, Obama lovin', Al Sharpton apologist, Spike Lee film society critic and racist prick extraordinaire, commonly called by his friends as Prez, Mr. Jackson Jefferson Washington. Did I miss anything?"

Everyone was laughing except me. I had no idea how to respond. I was wondering if Kurt skipped out on a Grand Dragon meeting of the KKK to be here.

"Why, thank you Maser' Kurt for that blazing endorsement." Prez high-fived Kurt.

"As always, my pleasure, Mr. Jackson."

"Nice to meet you, Prez."

"Likewise, Steve."

Jackson showed me his knuckles and we fist bumped.

"Alright, alright man," Jackson answered giving Kurt a shoulder bump as though Kurt and he were besties.

"You can learn a lot from Prez," Kurt added.

"So why do they call you Prez?"

Kurt air fingered a hand holding a rope and stuck his tongue out like he just hung himself. "Anyone got a rope?"

Bridgette added, "I'll go get Edmond and we can listen to the Queen story."

"Y'all a bunch of broke back comics. So, Steve, here it is. My father, a degenerate gambler, bet two hundred dollars on a long-shot pony, the day I escaped my mother's embryonic prison, that paid twenty to one. Get it? Jackson, Jefferson, Washington."

"Clever, one of the many positives of being a degenerate gambler," I piled on.

"On a serious note, he also works as a part-time doorman at the Pink Slipper, a gay black night club," Kurt continued while grabbing his crotch.

"Fuck you, it's a strip club, you white dick-sucking, mother-fucker," Prez playfully snapped back.

Everyone was enjoying the name calling. Kurt and Prez evidently had a special friendship.

"Sounds like an interesting job." I felt like a ping-pong ball in a verbal arcade, enjoying every bit of the political correctness process being annihilated.

"It is my brother, it is, and one night I'm gonna take you there as my guest; show you around."

"I'm down with that."

"Be careful," Kurt interjected with a big grin on his face.

"I can't wait. Why is that?" I inquisitively asked waiting for the next insult. Don Rickles would have blown a nut listening to these two.

"Ole Prez here has three baby mommas to support. The man gets the ladies knocked up with a handshake."

"Handshake my ass. I work two jobs, pay my bills on time, and take care of my ladies and kids. None of that slavery welfare bullshit for me." Prez grabbed his heart. "That really hurts man, really hurts," he said as he laughed. "I'll see you all back at The Graveyaad later. Steve, a real pleasure to meet you."

"Yeah, me too, Prez."

"And Kurt, I didn't forget. I'll text you the names of some really great strap-on companies, help you out with your pencil dick problem."

Everyone cracked up including me. Prez and I shook hands and shoulder bumped. Jackson left and walked over to

Candice and got his keys. Candice held them out as he walked by and took them without ever breaking stride on the way to the parking garage.

"You can always feel the love in the air at YLL," Bridgette added.

"Entertaining," I said. "And what's the Graveyaad?"

"It's a bar we all hang out at," Kurt answered.

"I have a whale coming into town tonight, so I need to roll. Nice meeting you, Steve," Ramone said as he too left and walked over to Candice.

"A whale?"

"A client who has no trouble tossing money around, a player. Vegas used to be full of them before the corporations turned this city into Toon-Town. When they call us, we pass off all our little runs to other drivers," Kurt explained.

"Nice piece of Vegas history."

"Steve, I'm going to get a car and take you to Sonny's house. We have a big night ahead of us. I'll meet you in the garage."

Kurt walked toward Candice as Bridgette came over to me.

"Steve, we need to sit down and spend a little time together. There are many things you need to... you'll hear about, stories, rumors," she sympathetically said while handing me her card. "We'll talk soon."

"Okay Bridgette," I responded with a puzzled look on my face.

Bridgette joined Candice. I started to follow her but paused to glance into Dino's office. He just happened to be standing where I was sure he'd absorbed all the friendly employee banter.

"Steve, mind coming into my office for a minute?"

I walked into the office and Tony closed the door, his facial expression reminding me of a Russian guard in a Siberian prison.

Dino sat in his chair and Tony and I took seats in front of his desk.

"Steve, I hope you enjoyed our welcome to Vegas package," Dino said with a childish smirk.

"Right up there, Dino."

"Tomorrow will be the formal reading of the will, and as I'm sure you've already been briefed by Goldhabber, you're the majority owner in the company."

"I know. I can't believe what's happened in the last twenty-four hours."

"Makes two of us," Dino sadly added.

I felt guilty, but I wasn't going to let Dino drag me into his pity-party.

Tony looked at me and in a raised tone said, "I watched and protected Sonny for all these years; then one night, he's gone, no clues, vanished. Then a month later he turns up barbecued in the desert."

"I'm sorry. I heard you two were close."

Tony rose quickly out of his chair and it fell backwards. He leaned into me and pounded his fist on Dino's desk.

"Fuck that! I'm going to find the sons-of-bitches who did this to Sonny and fuck them up." His face burned bright red. "And I'm going to keep on fucking them up until they beg me to kill them, then I'm going to really inflict pain and suffering on them. I swear to God, they will suffer like no one has ever suffered on this earth!"

Tony walked over to a corner of the office and kicked the wall. He found another chair and sat down.

I was visibly shaken by Tony's statement. My father was in special ops. I had never heard anything like this.

"Uh, Kurt's waiting for me outside and I'm obviously a little burned out," I said. "So, I'm going to leave now. We can continue our conversation tomorrow afternoon, if that works for you?"

"Yeah, sure Steve. We'll talk before the will reading. Be here around one."

"See you two tomorrow."

"And one more thing, Steve. Kurt's going to show you around Vegas later tonight. Have fun, take it easy. Kurt has been known to, let's just say, go a little overboard at times."

"I will, and thanks for the heads up."

I slinked out of the office, not daring to look at Tony, and took the short walk down the hallway toward the garage.

*****

Tony leaned in on the edge of his chair. "He sounds like a nice boy. You think the kid will do the right thing?"

Dino shrugged his shoulders. "I planted some seeds; let's see what grows."

*****

On my way out to the garage, I passed Candice sitting at her desk. She hopped up and hurried over to me.

"Steve, Steve."

"Hey Candice."

With a mother's warming smile and a deep look of concern, she gave me another hug, leaned into my ear and whispered, "Take your time, get to really know everyone, especially your new partner, Dino. I'd trust my life with Kurt; he's good people." She leaned back and in a loud voice continued, "Sweetie, go to Sonny's, look around, get some rest. There's a lot going on tonight."

"Like what?"

"Kurt has all the info."

She walked back to her desk and I went out to the garage.

*****

Dino and Tony walked out of the office.

"Keep an eye on him, Tony."

"Why, you think he's in danger already?"

"I can't be sure, but when we put him out on display tonight, he's going to create some Las Vegas-style buzz."

*****

As I walked out to the garage, I saw Kurt standing next to a rear limo door, the engine running.

"Welcome to the YLL family. As you probably noticed, most of us are a tight-knit group."

"Yeah, you can staple the welcome mat to my forehead. Do you mind if I ride in front?"

"Sure, hop in."

We pulled out of the YLL parking lot and cruised down a variety of unfamiliar streets in a strange city.

"Well I'm totally lost, and in more ways than one."

"It's gonna' be alright; you'll do fine. It'll take a little time that's all. Be patient, we have a good crew. Is this your first trip to Sin City? It's quite the place, like nothing you'll ever see anywhere."

"Yeah, great. I'm going to inherit a limo company that's about to roll over and croak. I'm headed to a house

I've never seen, and I feel like everyone in this company thinks I'm a douche bag."

"A big douchebag, Steve." Kurt grinned. "That's a big part of your job, to identify problems and solve them. And you've already identified a key one."

We both looked at each other and laughed.

"What's the story on Dino?"

"That's a loaded question. Care to be more specific?"

"Do you trust Dino?"

"Whoa, swinging for the fences right out of the gate. Wouldn't you have to trust me to get the answer you're looking for?"

"I think I can trust you... can I?"

"Get to know me a little better and then ask me that question."

"The will reading is tomorrow, so I'm not really sure how much time I have to flirt," I said blinking my eyes rapidly.

"Funny. Look, you seem like a nice kid, so yeah, okay, you can trust me to be honest with you."

"So, once again, can I trust Dino?"

"On the surface, I think he's trustworthy."

"On the surface? That's like telling me there's a good chance water's wet."

"We all have skeletons in our closet, present company included. No one's going to volunteer to throw stones at you."

"Sounds to me like you have some regrets."

"Regrets is the wrong word. I like what I do, I think I'm the best at it, and in the end, that's all, at least to me, that matters."

"So, you've overcome your regrets?"

"Jesus Christ, you really do work in a psych ward. I feel like I'm on a moving couch. How old did you say you were?"

64

"Twenty four, and I'm only a psych tech. Imagine what the guys with the big sheepskins can do."

Kurt did a double take and chuckled. "Mind Fuck 101. Love it."

The rest of the ride to Sonny's was quiet, and a few minutes later we pulled up to the guard shack at the Las Vegas Country Club. Kurt flashed his I.D. and within a few seconds the gates swung open. I opened the window, stuck my head out and took in the neighborhood views while letting in a blast of Vegas heat.

"What a beautiful place; this golf course looks immaculate."

"You play?"

"Yeah, you?"

"Yeah. Steve, once you get your feet on the ground, that is if you decide to stay, we should play. What's your handicap?"

"That would depend on whether or not we're playing a skins game."

"And you want to know if I trust Dino?"

He pulled up to Sonny's house and stopped in the circle drive covered by a huge brick canopy that could protect four large vehicles. I exited the limo, staring at Sonny's house for a moment before I walked over to the trunk, which automatically opened.

"It's truly a unique house." I scanned the large single story ranch house."

"It is amazing, especially the inside."

"Strange, there aren't any windows in the front of the house."

"Sonny was into his privacy and had all the front windows removed."

"Sounds more paranoid then private."

Kurt gave me a funny look and pulled out my suitcase while I carried my backpack to the front door. Kurt unlocked the door and I followed him in like a new puppy dog. We both stopped in the entryway.

"This is it. It used to be four thousand square feet of party central. Some heavy hitters have been in this house, the biggest dogs around the world. It once was worth a slick two mil, but with the economy as it is, it's worth probably half that. But the markets are roaring back and soon it might be worth even more.

"My God, this place is huge."

"Sonny, quite the man about Vegas, knew how to throw down and have a good time. There are four master bedrooms and five bathrooms. He had a lot of friends in Vegas and around the world."

"And some enemies too," I added.

"Yeah, those too. Anyway, get some rest because I'll be picking you up at ten. You'll be able to experience a night out and see for yourself how Vegas really works. You know, the people who run this town and the way they run it. Not the stereo-typical bullshit you see on TV."

Kurt tossed me the keys to the house. "It's yours now. The housekeepers have been here, they come twice a week, the way Sonny always had it done, Fridays and Mondays. Catch some winks, lots to do, and I'll see you tonight."

"Thanks, I'll see you at ten. What should I wear?"

"You have a poodle skirt?"

"Funny guy, you sure we're not related?"

"What you're wearing is fine."

"Thanks, and thanks."

"Hey, make yourself at home, it's your place now, inside and out. You want me to show you around before I leave?"

"Thanks, but no. I'll be going solo on this adventure."

"Suit yourself. Later."

Kurt walked out the front door, closing it quietly behind him, a sign of respect for Sonny.

It's hard to explain the emotions I felt once Kurt closed the door and left. It was a beautiful house. I took my boots off and left them on the marble floor entryway. My feet cooled by the marble floors throughout, I wandered the house, fascinated by the high ceilings, art, knickknacks, furniture, and the general layout of the place. When I got to the bedroom, besides the beautiful furnishings, I noticed Sonny had a Samsung Bluetooth system. The remote sat on the nightstand and I turned it on. I programed my iPhone to the Samsung and checked it out with, "Drunker Than Me" by Trent Tomlinson; it was powerful with a great sound.

"Nice, I'm sure I'll be putting this bad boy into action soon."

I opened the master closet and was immediately in awe of its size. It must have been three-hundred square feet, with double clothes bars lining both sides, shelving on the top and a large shoe rack with a full-length mirror in the back. Everything appeared to be left in place before Sonny's death. As I walked around the closet I leaned in and sniffed at his wardrobe. I'd found myself doing that when my father died and again when my mother passed. There was a certain comfort in the odors of loved ones. You knew they passed but their smell brought them back for an instant, returning visions of times spent together as if you'd just experienced them.

I never knew Sonny, but maybe his scent would bring me a little peace of mind or something. I smelled several other suits and caught myself missing my parents, not Sonny, so I decided to quit. Leaving the closet, I shut the door hard. I inspected the night stands, peeking inside the drawers. I found several hundred rounds of ammo, an ammo loader, mace, a knife and sheath with a seven-inch blade, some reading glasses, several dozen hotel card keys, some mystery novels and a bible. Not what I expected, but I didn't know the man.

There were French doors leading to the patio. I opened them to an incredible back yard containing marble statues, a water fountain, and a huge kick-ass pool with a water slide and diving board. This snapped me out of my morose state.

I made my way to the deep end and leaned over; it must have been twelve feet deep. I heard the gentle humming of the pool filtration system and heater buzzing along the side of the house and watched as the creepy crawler worked in a rhythmic pattern along the bottom.

The elevated backyard had a perfectly manicured five-foot hedge surrounding all three sides. I noticed a white nylon flag sticking out of a green, lightly waving in the breeze one house down and directly behind the house. Nice, right up against the golf course. I walked back to the patio admiring the half dozen tables with folded umbrellas sticking up through the centers. The chairs perfectly positioned around the tables had red-and-blue-striped decorative cushions matching the umbrellas.

The bar captured my attention next. What a party I could throw here. Bill and Russ were going to shit themselves when they saw the layout. A built-in grill with every cooking utensil imaginable, shelving for glasses and plates, an outdoor spice rack. Then I saw it, the mother of all sound bars, a custom-built Wet Sounds Stealth-10 with ten-inch speakers and subwoofers strategically placed around the pool area. Sonny the player, truly a hardcore partier with the coin and connections to pull it off.

I reached into a small cabinet next to the sound bar and took out the remote, turning the unit on. I yanked my iPhone out of my back pocket and used my Bluetooth to sync it and scrolled down to one of my iTunes playlists, stopping at the one song I felt was appropriate for this occasion. I jacked the Stealth-10 to level 45. "Rock This

Town" by The Brian Setzer Orchestra ignited the neighborhood with a hard-core pulsating sound. I put my thumbs inside my beltloops and danced around the pool. I didn't give a rat's ass if someone got pissed. My house, my rules, fuck all of you. I flailed and sang to the music for all six minutes and thirty-eight seconds of it.

When the music ended and I calmed down from my mini self-induced euphoric high, I noticed two golf carts next to the hedge with four older women standing on each edge of the golf cart peering into the yard with agitated scowls. I thought my singing went well; it couldn't be the cause of their displeasure.

I politely nodded, and with the confidence of a man holding a Royal Flush and a million-dollar smile, said, "I know, I can only handle two of you at once and as you can see, I'm a little busy, so if each one of you can kindly toss your card, with a picture over the hedge, I'll be more than happy to get back to you as soon as my schedule clears."

I went back into the bedroom and nonchalantly back-pedaled through the French doors, seductively peeking at them until the doors were completely closed.

"This is going to be a riot!" I shouted inside the empty bedroom.

I continued my exploration of the house, admiring how well his house flowed. Sonny had accumulated a lot of things, a huge price tag attached to each item. I wasn't an expert, but nothing looked inexpensive.

Once in the kitchen, I stopped to open the biggest stainless-steel refrigerator I'd ever seen, expecting it to be empty, you know, dead man's fridge, and especially because it'd been a long time since Sonny had been here. I opened it, hoping it didn't smell like swamp ass, but it was fully stocked. The maids were either using this place as a cantina or word got out that I was coming.

I took out an ice-cold Dos Equis and rummaged through a couple of drawers until I found a bottle opener.

The bottle cap bounced off the countertop and onto the floor where it swirled around several times on the white marble floor before coming to rest against the molding.

"I don't always drink beer from a dead man's refrigerator but when I do, I drink Dos Equis. Stay thirsty my friends," I said, enjoying the sound of my own voice and humor.

As I reached down to pick up the bottle cap my index finger felt something unusual. I kneeled on all fours and laid my head flush against the marble floor to look at the molding. Above the molding and just under the cabinet I noticed a white colored button.

Being extremely cautious, I instinctively looked around to see if someone had eyes on me. Of course no one did, so I reached across the floor and pushed the button. I heard a click but didn't see anything. I pushed it again and nothing happened. I looked at the cabinet door and pulled it open. There were additional pots, pans, and lids scattered throughout the cabinet. I pulled each one out carefully, looking for a hidden something.

The elongated short cabinet didn't concede the afternoon sunlight, making a visual inspection difficult. I reached into my back pocket, pulled out my iPhone again, and turned on the flashlight. I hurriedly pulled everything out, lightly examining each item as I tossed them to the floor. After I'd emptied all the contents, I managed to wiggle my head and one arm inside. The sides appeared to be normal as did the bottom. I tried looking up, but there wasn't enough room. I pulled my head out and positioned myself on my back and flashed the light above, taking my hand and feeling along the top. I came across a tiny drawer and tried sticking my hand in it, and accidentally shut it.

"Are you kidding me?"

I searched for the button and hit it again. This time I maneuvered my hand carefully inside and pulled out the compartment's contents, a single key. I kicked several of the pots out of the way, stood, and examined it.

"A key. A key to what?"

I looked around the kitchen and back down at the contents lying on the floor and placed everything back, as close to the way I found it. I laughed at myself for doing it; it was my house after all. Taking a long gulp of my beer, I placed the key in my pocket with the intention of making a copy and returning it to its original hiding place. I continued my tour examining and trying the key in every lock.

Upon entering Sonny's office, I sat down on a high back black leather chair. I looked down at his immaculate glass covered desktop. A large gold Roman numeral clock, with Zeus holding the ends together, took up the back center of his desk.

I swiveled in the chair and looked at the back wall covered with pictures of movie stars, political figures, athletes, and some of his employees. It didn't take a genius to figure out that Sonny's close friends were Dino, Ramone, Bridgette, Tony, and Kurt. I grabbed a picture of Sonny standing next to his pool with some exotic dancer. For the first time since this whole thing went down, I realized he'd had an incredible life before someone took it from him, and that maybe he really was going to share this with me before he died.

I carefully examined his face hoping to recognize any features that might resemble mine. In reality, whether or not there were any physical matches, was inconsequential. I found what I thought were several distinguishing features we possibly shared and bought into my own manufactured creative bullshit.

After thirty minutes of opening closets and looking around corners, I finished my beer and tossed my empty bottle in a garbage can hidden in a utility closet in the kitchen and wandered back to the bedroom. Not that one beer would ever knock me out, but the exhaustion from all the extracurricular activity, starting with last night's fraternity party, Meryl in the jet and culminating with Ruby in the back of the limo, created a sperm bank deficiency and my single tail warriors needed time to regroup. Therefore, time to Z-out.

I closed the impressive bedroom blackening curtains which slid on floor and ceiling mounted black six-inch rails. The curtains completely strangled the outside light. The bedroom became dark enough to be used in a vampire movie. I used the flashlight on my phone to guide myself back to the California King bed and sat down.

I voice commanded my phone to have the alarm ring at eight-thirty, and just for the hell of it I clapped my hands, but of course, the lights didn't turn off. He wasn't that old school. It was worth a shot.

I turned off my phone flashlight and crawled on top of an exotic oriental black-and-gold quilt. A small white remote rested next to the lamp on the nightstand.

"Blockhead, it's for the lights," I said laughing at myself.

Completely exhausted in a jet-black room gave me only one option, to pass-out.

Chapter 6

9:55 PM

After a shower and a quick change of clothes, I was ready for my first night out in Vegas. I sent the boys and Mary a text and told them I would call them sometime tomorrow. Mary sent me a response with several heart emojis. It was almost ten, so I went outside and sat on a relaxing three-person covered swing perfectly positioned next to the front door.

Kurt did not disappoint, showing up right on time. He pulled into the semi-circular driveway in a black six-seat limo and strolled up to the door. He was dressed in black all the way down to his patent-leather shoes. He reminded me of a casino hitman in a Bond movie.

"You get in a decent nap?" he asked.

"I passed out the second I hit the bed."

"Good, because your Vegas education is about to begin. You ready?"

"Like the Patriots for a Super Bowl."

Kurt hit another gear I had not seen and I felt both excited and nervous, my adrenalin levels off the charts.

"Steve, where's your cell?"

"It's in my pocket and turned off. I figured I'd have enough going on tonight and didn't want to be pounded with texts or calls. So, if someone from Vegas needs to get hold of me, I figure on them calling you."

"Good first executive decision," he said with his head bobbing a couple of times in approval.

"One for me."

I sat in the front seat as Kurt put the already-running limo into drive and rolled off the property. The cold air flowed through the front seat, knocking out the hot desert evening air.

"Steve, in Vegas our main business is charters, that's our bread and butter," he said while engaging the traffic in front of us. "People call us, and most of the time Candice or whoever is dispatching will book them a limo or Town Car for whatever event. We try for four-hour minimums, but that doesn't always work. However, during conventions and special events, we have eight or twelve-hour minimums and those are pretty much what we and every other limo company books.

I nodded, absorbing every word.

"A Kelly, that's what we look for when things are slow."

A Kelly?"

"A quick run. There are places including hotels where we can park and with the help of the casino doormen, we can pick up clients, for an hour or the entire night. Sometimes, those turn out to be some of the craziest runs we get. Everyone makes money Steve, the company makes their hourly fee, we make ours plus gratuities and we take care of the doorman or whoever turned us onto the run. And on a personal note, if a client gives me twenty percent of the bill as a tip, he won't ever be riding with me again. I usually get fifty to one hundred percent of the bill as a gratuity, always."

"If the bill is three hundred for four hours, you get one hundred and fifty to three hundred dollars as a tip?"

"Welcome to the limo business, kid."

"You're killing me smalls."

"Any less and the next time that client calls me or the company and requests me, I just make up some bullshit excuse and pawn him off to another driver. I never sell myself short. My personal standards always pay off."

"Does anyone ever call you back?" I said with a sly grin.

"I'm the best there is. I know where to go and I have all the hookups. My time is valuable. And the people who know a good chauffeur always call me back."

"I thought Edmond was the best."

"Edmond is the best if you're looking for sightseeing tours, tea socials, and bingo parlors. You might say he's the geriatric king."

"I think I took the wrong business classes in school."

"I like your sense of humor. You're alright kid, for a whack job from Hooterville."

"That's a psych attendant from La Crosse, Wisconsin."

Kurt pulled into the back parking lot of a place called Tight Racks. We exited the limo.

"These are the headlights and this is the hood," gesturing like a Price Is Right model.

"And are these the tires," I said, throwing it back at him.

He took me into the front seat and showed me where the basic switches were, including the infamous back call switch, the glass slide, solid slide and the kill switch. Next, we got into the back and he showed me how he set up his limo and where the client switches were located. I figured out the cd player and bar.

Kurt hit the lock and alarm switch and we walked toward the Tight Racks front door, protected from the heat and rain by a long red canopy protruding twenty yards into the parking lot.

"This club is owned by one of Sonny's best friends, Max Sharone. "

"Looks like a strip club."

"Wow, what a keen eye. All those exotic pictures on the side of the building tipped you off. No one ever going to pull the wool over your eyes. You really got a topnotch education in Hooterville."

"We have one in La Crosse and I've only been to it once for a bachelor party. I don't need to go to a strip club to get my rocks off."

He stopped walking, put his hand on my shoulder and turned me so he could look me in the eyes. "It's not about need, it's about style."

"Style?"

"Only a knuckle-dragging butthead would come here thinking he's going to out hustle a stripper and get laid."

"Never thought about it that way."

"Look, you should know some things about the owner, Max. He's a former Mossad agent whose father, back in 1938, helped bring Jews to Israel and was one of the original agents when the Mossad formed in 1949. His father died in the 1967 war. Max is still well connected, considered untouchable, even over here. He doesn't confirm or deny it, but I know from a reliable source he has killed on multiple occasions. Max is well respected by all in Vegas. One day when we have some time, I'll tell you all about Max and the Vegas mob. Better yet, if you get close to Max, he might tell you himself."

"That's an amazing story."

We walked into the club and were greeted just inside the door by Kenny Gustapolis, a tall muscle-bound Greek wearing a tux, standing behind a Maître d' podium flashing a chic smile, a gold bracelet dangling from his right wrist and a Tag-Hauer watch on his left.

"I see you brought us a high-rolling young caviler looking to spend an evening surrounded by beautiful and exotic women."

"Kenny, this is Steve Mueller."

"I see, this is Mr. Mueller," he said looking somewhat surprised.

"In the flesh," I said with a beaming smile. Kenny put his house radio to his mouth and informed Max we had arrived. He came from behind the podium, even though a line of patrons had gathered behind us, putting his arm around me and giving me a receptive hug.

"Rochelle will take you both back. Have a good time Mr. Mueller."

A tall redhead, flashing silky long legs and a charming smile, came up to us and led the way to a private VIP room in the back of the club. Kurt already knew the drill, so being courteous, he let her lead.

The music pulsated throughout the club. Girls on several stages were showing off their endowed hardware, natural and surgically enhanced. Most of the tables, full of men, trying to act unconcerned as beautiful women, dressed in as little possible, taunted them with their seductive charms. The dancers were smooth operators, relentlessly working them, trying to get them to use all their cash or credit cards, convincing them to spend their money like they won the lottery. The real unconcerned get real concerned after a few cocktails. I struggled, not fixating on Rochelle's scintillating derriere and legs as she jockeyed between men and cocktail waitresses.

She guided us to a bodyguard who stood by a large mahogany door. Black, six-foot-seven, three hundred plus pounds, cauliflower ears, leathery face, extreme tough-guy look. Either MMA, boxing, or some other facial bludgeoning had taken its toll. He wore an all-black tux with black polished cowboy boots. Rochelle kissed me on the cheek and gave Kurt a hug as she departed.

"Boris, you're looking dapper. Ever get the license plate of that bus?" Kurt asked.

"I'm as close to that as you are to getting the Mohle who did your circumcision," Boris answered without changing facial expressions, opening the door to Max's personal VIP room.

Kurt raised his arms as Boris patted him down. When he finished, he looked at me; I followed Kurt's lead. Max sat at his table.

Kurt led us to a large round corner table in the back of the VIP room. Max Sharone, tall, muscular man in his late sixties, well dressed, diamond rings on his right hand, a Rolex on his left wrist, scary, intense looking. His current lifestyle must have added some extra poundage to his frame and his receding black-gray hair. He rose and hugged and kissed Kurt on each cheek. Ruby was standing next to the table, dressed in a red sequined low-cut cocktail dress with matching heels. She intentionally or unintentionally failed to make eye contact. Maybe pulling my dick out would jog her memory.

"Kurt, my good friend, how are you? And this must be Steve Mueller." He sported a thick Israeli accent.

"Max, I want you to meet Sonny's boy, Steve."

Max gave me a bear hug along with several hardy slaps on the back, garnishing me with a kiss on each cheek.

Max pointed to a chair for Kurt and another one next to him for me.

"Let's all have a glass of Dom. I know you're driving Kurt, but your boss won't mind if you have a drink to honor Sonny, right Steve?

"Sorry, I only drink Christal."

Momentary silence as Ruby paused and Max's grin dissipated. He laughed and Ruby reached for the champagne again.

"I like your sense of humor, definitely related to Sonny."

Ruby reached into a champagne chiller stand and pulled out a bottle of Dom, cork already popped. She took a cloth napkin and grasped the bottle head. She poured Max's, walked around to Kurt, poured his and finally mine. This time she looked at me.

"Thank you, Mr. Sharone," I graciously said.

"Ruby, you already know Kurt."

"Hello Kurt," she said before turning away.   "And Ruby, this is the guest of honor tonight, Steve. Steve this is Ruby," Max said with a huge smile on his face.

"A pleasure to meet you Steve," she answered, acting like this was the first time we met.

Although, looking at her from the chin up instead of her head down, where I previously used it like a basketball player warming up at the free throw line, made her look more cunning.

"Hello, Ruby," I answered back, playing the game.

"And it's Max, Steve, for you it's Max. You are like family. Now we toast to Sonny and to his long-lost son, Steve."

The three of us clinked glasses. "L'chiam!" Max shouted.

Kurt and I joined in. I took a sip and started to pull away the champagne glass from my mouth. I stopped when I noticed Max and Kurt chugged the Dom like a shot. I immediately returned the glass to my mouth and finished it off, some of the bubbles backtracking through my nose. All in all, we quickly disposed of the champagne, which pleased Max.

"Good, good. Ruby, again," Max ordered. "Steve, Sonny and I go way back to the 80's. Whatever I can do to help you settle in, you let me know. And I won't rest until I find out who killed… what happened to Sonny. That you can be sure of." He solemnly finished, leaning toward me.

"I appreciate that, Max."

"And don't let the big-five limo companies give you a hard time. They will because they think they are in control now. But we know better, right Kurt?"

"Right, Max. And I hate to end this little soiree, but we have a lot of places to cover tonight and a short time to do it. We really need to go," Kurt said.

"Steve, you and I will talk soon. There is much to discuss and things you should know."

"Thank you for the champagne, Max. Exceptional.

I turned to Ruby. "Nice meeting you, Ruby."

"Likewise, Mr. Mueller," she said, visually carving me up.

She must have taken some heat for her fallacious execution and overly long results.

Kurt finished off the goodbyes. "Thanks, Ruby. Max, I'll be seeing you soon."

As Kurt and I left the room, I purposely slowed my gait to take in some of the seductive action happening around the club. The women were exotic and I enjoyed being hogtied by eye candy. Kurt raced ahead while I focused on the stage dancers crawling around piles of one-dollar bills. Ruby slapped my ass from behind as she walked past me to the front of the club.

"What a body," I said, drowned out by the pulsating music.

Kurt turned the corner just as a large man with greasy hair, reeking of alcohol, accidentally bumped into me.

"Excuse meee," the drunk slurred out while discretely jamming a piece of paper into my right hand.

He grabbed my shoulder and put his mouth up against my ear, whispering, "Read this when you're alone."

He pushed me away, staggering towards the men's room. I put the piece of paper in my right pocket, wondering what just happened. To my surprise, Kurt came back to investigate my dawdling.

"Making friends?" Kurt inquired, not missing anything.

"Some goofy trashed drunk wandered into me."

"Let's get out of here."

*****

11:39 PM

Goldhabber sat at his office desk, working himself up, enthralled with the women performing a variety of sexual acts on his fifty-five-inch computer screen, when a new email chimed in. Norman quickly rejoined reality, minimized the screen, and anxiously opened the email.

He recognized the email address, dreading yet another highly anticipated shit job for a scumbag client. He created this eco rich, financial septic tank crawling with degenerate human beings years ago. The power, money, drugs, and sexual perks made it all worthwhile, mostly. This email request even crossed his imaginary line of shit-dom.

The pictures downloaded revealed a particularly good-looking couple, a man and a woman. He read the attached note.

"You have got to be fucking kidding me," Goldhabber blurted out, pounding his fists on the table.

He picked up a burner cell he kept taped under his desk and dialed a special number. When he heard the word "Yes" on the other end, Goldhabber replied, "N. G.."

"The necessary people will be informed of the situation," the voice on the other end replied and hung up.

Goldhabber clicked his enter button and brought back the porn screen just as his six-year-old son burst into the unlocked office.

"Daddy, I couldn't sleep; can I play on the computer with you?"

*****

Wednesday
Early Morning

After driving me around the strip for an hour, Kurt parked the limo in a well-lit parking area designated for limos only, somewhere off Industrial Street. I checked my watch, one twenty in the morning.

"I'm taking you to a bar called "The Graveyaad,"" Kurt said with a smile.

"Looks like a watering hole?"

"Hang tight, grasshopper."

A couple of big windows framed a big oak door of the building where the occupants appeared to be having a good time. Loud music played as we approached a door facing out onto Industrial Street.

Kurt opened it and turned back to me. "This is it, The Graveyaad."

We walked in; the door closed behind us.

Kurt continued his oratory. "This place is one of the best late-night hangouts for limo drivers, cab drivers, strippers, pit bosses, dealers, dancers, hookers, pimps, bartenders, bookies, smoke eaters, and an assortment of nondescript characters. If you work in Vegas and you're looking for a good time with locals, you're here. Steve, the action doesn't start until after midnight and doesn't slow down till around eight in the morning."

The Graveyaad had a long bar on the left that curved about twelve feet from the front window, allowing a street view. Another sixty or so feet extended to the bar with well-spaced video poker machines working vigorously with about thirty stools, mostly full. Several huge electric fans working at full speed tried to suck up the vast amount of smoke through their vents. It became apparently clear they weren't adequate enough to battle the tide of clouded smoke enveloping the bar.

Two five spigot taps on either side of the bar were being simultaneously used by two female bartenders as a third female bartender took orders in the middle from two casually dressed cocktail waitresses sporting red low-cut tees and push-up bras. To my right were tables and behind them booths lining the wall. The back right portion of the bar had a precut partially raised dance floor and a Juke box cranking out music just off to the left. Tables were lined up in a half square in front of the dance floor. I wondered if they ever had any live entertainment.

To the left of the stage pushed up against the wall was a covered piano and left of that a small grill window. I could see the stainless-steel blower fan behind the grill signaling fried foods were part of the menu.

The walls were lined with Rodriguez Blue Dogs, historical Vegas photos, and a variety of neon beer lights, representing most of the major beer distributors.

"If you're hungry, Buster is one of the better cooks in Vegas." Kurt walked up to the bar and shouted, "Sherry!"

"Hey baby, is that Steve with you?!" She wore a very warm and friendly smile.

She was tall, pleasant to look at, middle-aged, blonde and auburn streaked hair, wearing a tight low-cut green Graveyaad tee like the red ones, designed to pump up and expose cleavage. She had a southern Louisiana Bayou accent, and I could tell by her low raspy voice, she'd been around bars a long time. She leaned over the bar, anxiously awaiting an intro.

"This is Sherry Labelle, Steve, owner and operator of the infamous Graveyaad. Sherry, this is Steve Mueller, Sonny's boy, fresh out of the Wisconsin backwoods."

"As I live and breathe, there's quite a resemblance… yeah, I can see it." Sherry stared at me like a steaming bowl of crawfish while extending her hand. "I'm sorry for the circumstances that brought you to Vegas. Sonny was special, which makes your money no good tonight."

"Hi Sherry, and thank you, thank you so much, nice to meet you." I took her hand, rolling her wrist gently down, bowing, gently kissing the top of it in an innocent chivalrous gesture. "This is quite the place you have. I really like it. Great setup."

She delicately pulled her hand back, leaning in even more, and in an inquisitive nature asked, "So, you know a little something about bars?" Her smile nimbly widened.

I leaned in close to her, widening my own smile. "Just as an enthusiastic observer and active participant in many drinking establishments. But to be honest, I do consider myself a learned mixologist and, on more occasions than I should probably admit to, a guinea pig of the highest order, with many experimental libations ending in an intoxicating bliss for myself and those around me brave enough to pour those concoctions down their pallets. Of course, some of those concoctions have caused an occasional participant to seek refuge in the nearest pukatorium, or accidentally elsewhere."

"You don't say." Sherry said looking inquisitively at me, trying to hold back a laugh while turning her head towards Kurt.

"So, what will it be?" she asked Kurt.

"Dom."

"Let me guess, you were with Max?"

They both chuckled. Kurt ordered a ginger ale and OJ. Since he was driving, I ordered a tap in the large thirty-two-ounce chilled mug, not wanting to take too much advantage of my open tab.

I sat down in a red bar stool and swiveled around, checking out the bar's uniqueness, all strange to me. Back in La Crosse I couldn't walk into a bar without stumbling into someone I knew. I stopped scoping out the place when I noticed a drop-dead gorgeous brunette sitting alone in a back booth, sipping a glass of white wine, dressed in a seductive pink dress, black stockings, and heels. She looked much older, more like Kurt's generation.

I tapped Kurt on the shoulder.

"Who's the booth babe in the back?"

Before I could finish and without looking back, he calmly said, "Kid, that's why you work and live in Vegas. That's Tatyana Kreshnev, the reason you'll need to make the kind of money an owner of a limo company makes."

I found it hard to take my eyes off Tatyana. Kurt motioned a friend of his to come up to the bar. The guy was tall and wide, thinning greyish black hair, tan, dressed in a gold Greg Norman golf shirt, sports coat, slacks, expensive watch and two men's diamond rings on each hand.

"Red!" Kurt shouted above the noise. "I want you to meet Steve Mueller, Sonny's boy. Steve, meet Red Knuckles Taylor. Once you start making money, ole' Red here will find a plethora of tempting ideas, and many of those schemes will originate from places you've never even imagined. And as always, he'll assist in relieving you of those burdensome financial sums."

"A pleasure to meet you, Steve. Welcome to Vegas. You can call me Knuckles." He looked me up and down like a piece of prime beef dangling on a hook.

"Anytime you want a little action on sports, well, pretty much anything, Knuckles is, "The Man" Kurt said, putting his arm around Red's shoulder.

"Rumor has it they have sportsbooks for betting on almost anything," I answered back like the smartass I am, fresh out of college.

"Sure they do and when you're ready for a little action give Kurt a call. He'll give you my number. Sports books, kid's priceless." Red sarcastically replied.

They huddled together and whispered back and forth.

Kurt turned back towards me and said, "Red and I have a few things to discuss, we'll be over there." Kurt pointed to a table where three other men sat. "Try to stay out of trouble," he playfully advised as he walked away.

I turned back to the bar and looked for Sherry as I finished off my first beer.

*****

Inside the Graveyaad's Women's Room

Woody Churchfield sat on the pot enjoying one of the resident hookers in the handicap stall. The pounding and shaking of metal ground to a halt when the irritating chime of his cell phone messenger went off. He instantaneously stopped and reached into his blazer pocket, carefully examining the screen.

Our boy, sitting at the bar.

Woody shot up, spun the hooker around and pushed her off, leaving her ass partially jammed in the toilet. He backed away, pulled off his condom, and threw it haphazardly between her legs, partially hitting her thigh on the way into the toilet. He adjusted and fixed his pants. He slapped the cash between her legs, with most of it falling on the floor.

"Don't forget to flush," Woody said as he unlocked the stall door and walked out.

She picked up the money and under her breath said, "Asshole."

*****

I found myself alone at the bar, listening to the Stones, "Can't You Hear Me Knocking", on the Jukebox. Bose speakers strategically placed around the bar made the sound quality exceptional, especially with the pumping base. Sherry walked up to me with another female bartender.

86

"Steve, I want you to meet Lisa McGovern. Lisa, this is Sonny's boy, Steve Mueller." She turned around and went back to the waitress station.

Lisa was cute, thin, with, green and pink streaks in her black hair. She filled out her tee shirt nicely with perky little breasts pushed up to the max.

"I hear you're the new guy in town. Sherry said drinks are on the house."

"Nice to meet you, Lisa. Everyone I've met is really nice and interesting. I'll have a Dos Equis. Just tryin' to stay thirsty."

"Cute honey, you don't know the half of it. You look like a quick study. I get off—"

Some rude slimeball wearing a ridiculous cowboy suit like a bad guy in an old 50's Roy Rodgers western, his greasy hair combed back partially hiding a bald spot, the receding hairline and repugnant face reminding me of a Walking Dead extra, planted himself on the barstool to my right and turned toward my ear.

"Lisa, get me a double Wild Turkey Honey, on the rocks."

"Woody, you mind not being so rude when I'm talking with a customer, and it smells like you already had a taste of—"

"Lisa, I don't like repeating myself."

I turned and looked at Woody. "That seat is taken."

"So, you're Sonny's kid?"

"What of it, and how do you know? And by the way, the seat, still taken."

"You don't know who I am, so I'm going to let that, "This seat is taken," ignorant comment slide this time. I'm Woody Huntsman and I run this town."

"That must keep you busy."

"Less mouth, more ears, pay attention. Anybody worth knowing in Vegas knows who I am. Just like I know everything going on in this town, just like I know you're

Sonny's boy, just like I know Kurt's sitting in that seat, just like I know Sonny's limo company isn't worth a shit anymore, and just like I know you're going to sell your piece of it to me."

"The omnipotent Woody Huntsman. Wow, I'm impressed, but then again, I'm impressed with Roseanne Barr's singing voice."

Woody didn't take his eyes off me as Lisa threw down a coaster, slamming Woody's drink on it, slid my beer over to me, and stormed away.

Woody reached across the bar and grabbed a bar nap, pulled a pen out of his jacket pocket, and wrote something down on the napkin. He folded it and pushed it over. I read the note, folded the napkin, and without changing my expression, slid it back over to him.

"What if I don't want so sell my piece. Talk to Dino, maybe he's interested in your offer." I could see the muscles in Woody's face tighten, like the wringing out of a wet beach towel. I glanced over and saw Kurt intently watching the exchange, wondering why he hadn't already come over and back me up.

Woody's face turned red. "You have no idea what you're getting into, boy. Take the money and head back to Turdville. I'll have a contract in your hands by tomorrow afternoon. You can sign it and move on, because if you don't sell it to me, I will bury you along with that sinking limo company. I will make you regret ever getting off that plane. Understand?"

Woody and I were in a cold stare down when Kurt came up behind me, placing his arm around my shoulder, looking directly at Woody.

"What's this shithead doing here? I leave you alone for ten minutes and you become an asshole magnet."

Woody immediately changed expressions and demeanor. "Forgetting your place on the food chain, Kurt?"

"More like a food table, Woody, and as you can see, you're less than a fist's length away."

Kurt looked at me and then straight at Woody before he got up and in his face with the look of a UFC fighter about to step into the Octagon.

"Steve, this guy's a cancer, spreading like an STD in a bareback whorehouse. I wouldn't listen to anything that comes out of his piehole."

Woody finished his drink and slid the glass in front of me.

"The offer stands; make it a done deal by tomorrow, because Steve, many things happen in my world, and they happen suddenly."

He nonchalantly threw a twenty-dollar bill on the bar and walked out, glancing back at me one last time.

I eyeballed Woody until he left the bar. Two other men sitting at a back table trailed after him, each one throwing me a forced toothless smile.

"Who in the hell is that guy supposed to be? It looked like he had a couple of sausage jockey's following him out."

"He owns Imperial Limos and Cab Company, plus a bunch of small casinos and bars. He wants to own Vegas. He comes from a long line of inbred megalomaniacs. He's insane, belongs in an institution. And the tall asshole trailing Woody, he's dangerous. Name is Letterman, handles Woody's dirty laundry. Stay clear of him."

"I've got all the psychiatric hookups for Woody... aren't I fitting in nicely?" I said cheerfully holding up my beer in a toast.

"Well, don't get too full of yourself yet. Casually look at the dance floor; the two guys dressed in suits, sitting in a booth."

89

I followed his instructions and nonchalantly looked around the bar, visually picking up the two men, exactly as Kurt described.

"Congratulations, you've unveiled two more impeccable Las Vegas Limousine owners and they're, without a doubt, here to check you out. The hyenas are swarming tonight."

*****

At a table next to the dance floor, two men were absorbing the Woody, Steve, Kurt exchange.

"Hans, that's the kid who's going to inherit Yo Leven," remarked Barry Schuster.

Barry stood a little over six feet, weighed about one-hundred seventy-five pounds, dark complexion, full head of black hair, wearing a black three-piece business suit, pink shirt, a pink and black tie with shiny black leather shoes.

"He doesn't look like much," Hans Stephanner replied. He was six-five, weighing in at over two hundred and forty pounds, short blonde hair, piercing tombstone blue eyes, his look reminding everyone what a German SS officer would look like today, draped in a dark blue sports coat, a light blue buttoned down shirt, no tie, black dress pants and black boots. "And Woody's still a worthless dickhead. Some things never change."

"I'll get hold of Mr. Johnson and the Sheriff, let them know what's going down. Appears as though we have some unanticipated competition," Barry added.

"And that little shit Goldhabber, we're paying him why? He didn't tell us any of this. I thought this deal was a lock. Let's get out of here."

"You go. I'm going to hang back, Hans."

"Let me guess—Tanya."

"So?"

"I don't understand why you pay for it when there's free pussy oozing out of every corner of this city."

"I like her menu, the variety."

"Do me a small favor; piss Kurt off, do Tanya."

"In time, Hans, in time."

"Your balls aren't big enough."

"You don't think I can handle Kurt?"

"I know you can't. You'd have to get one of your flunkies to ambush him in a deserted parking lot. And that would be extremely messy, draw all of us into a sequence of unwanted attention."

"Weren't you leaving, Hans?"

"Good thing we're in a monetary joint venture, Barry. Otherwise—"

"Only, I'm not defenseless like your pig-eating ancestors."

Hans stepped out of the booth, sarcastically chest saluting Barry. "Be careful what you wish for, Barry," he said and left.

"Prick."

*****

For the next several hours, Kurt and I swapped stories. He introduced me to more and more people as Lisa and Sherry kept my beer glass full, throwing in an occasional shot. The night, now morning went quickly. It was important to watch the people come and go, get a feel for the players.

I turned to Kurt. "Hey, what time is it? I'm getting really buzzed, dude.

"It's almost five."

"Time to take me back to Sonny's. I need to crash. It's going to be light soon, and I don't have my sunglasses."

91

"Dude. You're calling me dude? C'mon, it's early, Lisa still has an hour or so before she gets off."

"What do you mean?"

"Really, you haven't been watching her seduce you with her eyes?"

In unison we both looked over at Lisa handing a waitress a couple of drinks. She looked over at Kurt and me, smiling.

"See," Kurt said, elbowing me hard. "See that, huh, what did I tell ya, *dude.*"

"Maybe, but not tonight. I'm worn out. I couldn't get it up with Viagra, two popsicle sticks, and a roll of duct tape."

"Ruby took that much out of you?"

I briefly discussed my send off and the plane ride in.

"No shit?"

"No shit."

"I knew something had to be off."

"What are you talking about Kurt?"

"You and Ruby, she's a pro, no way you should have lasted that long."

"So… you were in on it too?"

"If only you knew, and for your information, I'm just trying to help you out, my young executive."

I gave him a dumbfounded look as we said our good nights to Lisa and Sherry. Lisa carefully slid me a piece of paper with her phone number. I told her I'd call her. When I turned to leave, I noticed Kurt staring at Tanya, she back at him, even though one of those guys Kurt had me check out earlier sat next to her.

"Hey Kurt, something going on between you two? Why don't you just go over there? I can hang a bit longer."

"How long you going to call it Sonny's house Steve? It's your house now. Let's go," Kurt fired back.

I air fingered a couple of cat claws and followed him out of the Graveyaad.

It took twenty minutes to get to the house. The sun crawled over Sunrise Mountain, the early morning rays emanating a glow, causing my pupils to take refuge under my squinting eyelids. Our only protection—layers of smog.

We stepped out of the limo. Kurt made sure I had the keys.

"I hope you enjoyed yourself tonight. I mean, considering the circumstances."

"I did, with the exception of that dickhead Woody.

"Yeah, a real asswipe."

"Well again, thanks for being there and for introducing me to your friends. You have some interesting ones."

"Yes, I do, and now, so do you. You're beginning to know some of them. Just being Sonny's kid will open doors and friendships for you. It's a whole new world out there for your taking."

"I never knew anyone who had that kind of effect on people."

"He did, in so many ways. I, ah, wasn't sure if I was going to tell you this, but in his last days, something was bothering him. I wasn't privy to all the workings behind the scenes, but something was definitely different."

"In what way?"

"His mannerisms were off, I could tell. You know what I mean?"

"No, but I'm sure you did. Let's pick this up after the will reading."

"Yeah, it's late. We'll talk tomorrow." Kurt corrected himself. "Later today."

I opened the door and walked in, making extra sure I locked the door. I'm not a wimp, but a new house, new city, that Woody guy.

"What a fucking night!" I staggered into the kitchen.

A light came on in the living room, scaring the shit out of me. I jumped into a defensive stance, being drunk, tired and not knowing what the hell was happening; it was Tony.

"What the hell, Tony?"

Tony got out of a chair in the living room and walked toward me.

"If you're here to start some shit, remember I'm a Wisconsin farm boy and I hit like a freight train."

Chuckling, he said, "Really, you gonna take me out with one of your punches? Hey, a mosquito doing an elephant would have more impact than one of your punches. I do this shit for a living."

I walked toward Tony, surprising him.

"Hey, I'm not here to hurt you." He raised his hands. "You're Sonny's boy, just making sure you got home okay. And besides, if I wanted to hurt you, you'd never see it or feel it coming. Unless, of course, I wanted you to."

I dropped my hands and Tony did the unthinkable; he walked up to me and gave me a bone-crunching hug.

"I'm going to find out who did this to us." He patted me on the back several times.

It was one of those moments you don't forget. Tony walked out the front door and just before he closed it, he turned to face me. "The house is secure, lock up behind me."

I went straight to the front door and locked it, tempted to slide a chair under the handle and drag a dresser behind that. Tony had ruined a nice buzz, scaring the remaining alcohol right out of me.

I went to the kitchen and remembered the note the big guy gave me. I grabbed a beer, sat down at the kitchen table, and pulled it out of my pocket and read it out loud.

"I have some important information about Sonny. I'll call you soon."

I put the note back in my pocket.

"Great, just what I need, a cloak and dagger mystery tossed in on top of everything else."

I walked to the master bathroom and got ready for some well-deserved sleep.

*****

A convenience store off the Strip.
5:48 AM

Ramone came out of Benny's all-night convenience store located in a rather rough part of town. There was always a wide variety of beverages at discounted prices, and limos and cab drivers used Benny's whenever possible. Benny had an armed guard at the store; all his employees were trained in open carry and they all carried behind the counter. Several would-be robbers had found out the hard way and were members of the proverbial dirt-nap program.

Benny's was not your typical stop and rob liquor store; the word had gotten out to the undesirable element in Vegas. Go into Benny's, try to rob him and there was a high probability you'd be carried out in a body bag.

Ramone walked out of Benny's store with some Crown Royal for his clients. His charter started at ten PM, and he hoped to wrap this up by six. He went up to the limo's back window and knocked on it. He always locked his clients in for their safety.

"Hey, you two, I've got your Crown."

Ramone, being a professional, waited another thirty seconds before wrapping on the window a second time.

"Hey, pull your pants up, I have your Crown."

Another thirty seconds passed; this time Ramone heavily pounded on the glass with the bottom of his fist. "Hey you two, open up!"

Fed up, Ramone clicked the remote and opened the door. In the back of the limo the man and women were dead, each shot in the head at close range, the backseat covered in blood. He had an instant gag reflex, but didn't puke, bravely battling back the acid trying to race up his esophagus.

"Kiko is going to really be pissed at me when he sees this mess," a stunned Ramone complained to the dead bodies in the back.

Ramone closed the limo door, opened the bottle, and took a swig. He sat on the curb behind the limo, set the bottle down on the street, took his cell out of his tux jacket, and dialed 9-1-1.

"This is Ramone Constantine from YLL Limos. I just came out of a convenience store, Benny's, and found my clients shot to death in the back of my limo."

Chapter 7

My alarm went off at exactly eleven, dragging me out of some sort of crazy kaleidoscope dream. I found the phone, barely managing enough energy to open my eyes and turn it off, yet alone get out of bed and begin my daily bodily functions.

I struggled to sit up, grateful the room-darkening curtains kept the light out. My thoughts immediately took me back to yesterday's events.

"I can't wait to find out what kind of shit-storm is coming my way today.

I forced my feet onto the floor and led my body into an earth-shattering stretch.

"Damn it, son, shake it off."

I punched the flashlight button and lit the way to the bathroom, again forgetting to use the light remote.

I had the meeting at YLL at one, followed by the will reading. I jumped in the shower, got dressed in a clean unwrinkled tee, my only sports coat still smelling like an ashtray. When I finished dressing, I checked my cell phone and saw I had twenty or so missed calls, texts, and emails. I was hungover and it would be too much work to explain everything that happened yesterday. I'd answer them all after the will reading. I went out to the kitchen, and grabbed a coke, glancing at a door which probably led to the garage.

"Let's see what's behind the magic curtain." I rubbed my hands together with a certain degree of excitement.

I opened the door, in awe of the contents parked inside. Goldhabber actually told me the truth, at least about the vehicles.

The five-car garage was loaded with four motor-head goodies. I took a brief pause and realized the missing car must have been the one Sonny died in. But the show must go on, and being a Tundra guy, the first thing that caught my eye was a lifted 2017 custom painted slime green TRD Limited crew cab, with twenty-two inch custom rims and tires, running boards, and a brush guard. I hopped in and instinctively reached down under the left side of the dash to pop the hood lock. I rolled out onto the garage floor and popped it open, going nuts when I saw a supercharger with a cool-air injection system.

"This baby must be pushing six-hundred horses," I excitedly blurted out while fist pumping.

I looked around at the rest of Sonny's toys. A Porsche 911, a Shelby Mustang, and a Caddy SUV. I had to stop and admire Sonny, what an incredible life he had. These toys, the house, the limo company, friends, he had it all, and now he didn't have jack. And as bad as I felt for Sonny, I felt a sense of entitlement that all of his shit was going to be mine. I had to take that Tundra out for a spin. After coming up empty looking for the keys inside the truck, I ran into the kitchen and ripped through drawers.

My cell phone rang and I ran back to the bedroom to answer it, catching it on the last ring.

"Hello, hello," I answered out of breath.

"You tell me, where the fuck have you been? I've called you a dozen times."

"Hey Bill, what's going on? Sorry, I left my phone off last night, you know, figure things out, no distractions from home."

"Shit, I thought something might have happened to you. You okay?"

"Yeah Bill, last night was insane. You wouldn't believe the characters I met and the places we went. This city's off the wall."

"What's going on? Fill me in bro."

"I have the will reading at one-thirty and a meeting with my partner at one. It's crazy."

"Everything's fine?"

"Are you kidding me? No, it's a fucking disaster. The limo place is going belly up and they want me to pony up, get this place running again, or something like that. And this douchebag wants to buy me out. And I became a member of the mile high club, a blow-job in a limo, this house is off the charts and the lawyer I met is a dip-shit and I'm rambling on like I belong in an institution, right?"

"Alright, so let's be clear. A disaster, crazy, a total mess. Perfect, you must feel right at home."

"I can put a strait jacket over this city; they're all out of their minds."

"Hey, take your phone with you and fill me in on everything, alright? No more blackouts. Kapish?"

"Got it and got to run. I'll call you after the will is read. Say hi to Russ."

"I'll tell Russ what you told me. And slow down, watch yourself. I don't have your back there."

"Got it. Later."

*****

Metro Police Interrogation Room.
11:18 AM

Detective sergeant Vicki Spiccuzza, five-foot-six, dark complexion, light make-up, soft brown eyes, could have been a cover girl with her long black hair pulled tightly back in a ponytail, thirty-three years old, dressed in a blue business suit, white blouse, and low heels. She sat in an interview room with Ramone. He had been relentlessly questioned since six-thirty this morning. This was her third time in the box with Ramone.

"Again, you say that the couple charted a limo at ten last night. You took them to several night clubs and casinos and just happened to stop at that dive, Benny's convenience store, at five-thirty in the morning. Sounds like a perfect place to take them out and kill them. But why you, Ramone?"

"This is getting redundant, Vicki; I've been here for five hours and I'm getting tired of repeating myself. You know me. Come on. I'm not capable of something like that. I didn't know these people until last night. I picked them up at the Mirage; check it out."

"I'm sorry, but we have two murdered people in the back of your limo, Ramone. I don't care if you don't like the hours I keep."

"Jesus Christ! What, I shot them and then went into a convenience store, bought a bottle of Jack, sat down on the curb, drank it, and then called you. Are you fucking kidding me?"

"I thought you bought Crown Royal?"

"Christ, it was, now I'm... shit."

"No, Ramone. I just want to make sure there isn't something you missed. I know you didn't shoot them. But honestly, your location, five-thirty in the morning, you could have easily been an accomplice. Why were you there at five-thirty in that shithole of a neighborhood? You're going to tell me that's where you just happened to be? Do I look like a moron to you? Do I?"

"Yes! No! I get cheap booze there. I told you and all your other detectives that. It's cheap, just off the Strip. Lots of drivers go there. Ask the owner."

"We did. Go on, get out of here, and don't plan any out-of-town excursions. We'll be in touch."

Ramone walked out of the interrogation room and to the front desk where the sergeant had Ramone's items bagged up and waiting for him.

Kurt sat in an area patiently waiting for Ramone, glad to see him reappear. They walked out of the station and paused at the Metro entryway.

"Man, they sure drilled your ass for a long time. Thanks for the call Ramone."

"I figured you'd know what to do."

"Yeah, lots of hands on experience dealing with people getting whacked in the back of a limo. Right up my alley."

"You know what I mean. Thanks for waiting here. Everyone really pissed?"

"Well, I've filled in Dino and Tony, with the little info I have. Dino's coming here after the will reading and Tony is doing, you know, Tony stuff."

"I mean really, what's going on? Sonny in the desert, two in the back of my limo. Christ, some dangerous shit going down."

"Yeah, I know. I'm keeping my Glock with me at all times, one in the chamber. I'm done playing." Kurt put his arm around Ramone's shoulder and gave him a bro hug. "Let's go, I'll take you back to the barn so you can get your car and go home. You look like the Matador who lost two out of three."

"Once again, thanks partner."

"You'd have done the same for me. Let's get away from here."

Vicki Spiccuzza stood in the lobby of Metro and watched the exchange between Kurt and Ramone. The desk sergeant joined her.

"Vicki, what the hell is going on at YLL? First Sonny and now this. Someone's trying to physically wipe this company out."

"Or someone's trying to drive the value of YLL into the toilet."

"What about that kid from Wisconsin, Sonny's boy, you gonna have a chat with him?"

"I think that's one bet you want to make; I'm going to have a long chat with him."

Chapter 8

Kurt and Ramone walked into the YLL lobby. Candice ran up to Ramone and pulled him in a motherly bear hug.

"Ramone, you had me so worried. I'm glad to see you're alright."

"Another day in the life of a YLL front line chauffeur."

"What, no hug for me?" Kurt sarcastically asked. "I've been up since…I don't even remember. I'm going into Sonny's. . .Steve's office to catch a couple of z's on the couch. Wake me before the meeting, Candice."

"Oh, sorry Kurt, I didn't realize you had two people fucking shot in your limo too. My bad, I'll make sure I don't goddam forget to hug your tender snowflake ass, honey."

Candice gave Kurt a bone-crushing bear hug. "Feeling better now are we?"

"You just assassinated all my one-tailed warriors. There's got to be a lost wrestling federation somewhere on this planet searching for the likes of you."

Candice gave Kurt a smirk and her middle finger as he walked toward the office. Ramone grabbed his keys off the rack and entered the conference room door. Candice returned to her desk.

*****

I was pissed. I searched the entire house for the keys to the garage goldmine and came up empty. On a positive note, after the will reading, I would have those keys and be tearing up the streets of Las Vegas.

At twelve-forty-five, the doorbell rang. I thought Kurt was a little early, but I was ready. I opened the door, caught off guard when Bridgette stood there, her long black hair streaming down her shoulders, mildly ruffled by a hot Vegas breeze. She wore a repeat of yesterday's all black outfit, heels included.

"Pardon me for staring, but you don't look anything like Kurt," I said.

"What, not good enough?"

"No, of course you are, I mean—"

"Come on Steve, relax. I'm just messing with you. Ready?"

"Seriously, where's Kurt?"

"Let's just say his night didn't end when he dropped you off."

"I knew it, that dirty old dog. He went back to the Graveyaad and picked up that lady at the bar, didn't he?"

"Sherry?"

"That Russian lady."

"Tanya?"

"Yeah, I knew they had something going on."

"Steve, no. Don't even go there. Awfully bad topic, those two."

"So, last night him getting pissed at me when I mentioned her, for real?"

"Like sticking your dick in a woodchipper."

"Ouch, you're going to tell me what that's all about?"

"Absolutely not. If Kurt wants you to know, he'll tell you. It's none of my or your business, so feel free to drop it."

"Sorry, I didn't mean to get your panties all knotted up."

"Forget it. It's been a long night for everyone. Let's go to the will reading."

We walked to the Town Car.

"You want me to get in the front seat or the back?"

She gave me a dirty look. I opened the front door and slid in.

"This a good time to ask you about Sonny?" I inquired.

"Sure... fire away."

"Love your enthusiasm. You said I'd hear some things, probably negative, if I caught your drift. Care to elaborate?"

"That's true."

"Well?"

"A lot of rumors started surfacing about Sonny and me."

"What kind of rumors?" I asked, knowing exactly where this was going."

"Some people thought we were sleeping together."

"Okay, I'll bite. Were you?"

"Sonny and I were close, that's all. I never slept with him."

"Works for me."

"That's it? No other questions?"

"No, I'm not a priest and this isn't a confessional. If you say you didn't sleep with him, then you didn't."

"I thought you'd be a little more concerned."

"Why? I never met him. I really don't care whether you sacked him or not. It's none of my business. Just don't lie to me."

"Fair enough."

"But if he did sleep with you, and of course I believe your version, I could see why."

Bridgette looked at me and the two of us remained silent until arriving at YLL.

*****

Tony sat on a couch inside Dino's office, worried about last night's double homicide inside a YLL limo and the fear it could spread amongst the employees; a couple of them might even resign.

"This shit has to end now." Dino demanded.

"Professional, a total setup, the car, the time, the place, everything," Tony angrily answered back.

"After the reading, get some rest, so you can start fresh tonight. And nothing of this to Steve. We've got enough on our plate without this getting back to him. I've told Kurt and Ramone not to say a damn word."

"Yeah, shit's getting way out of control and I'm tired of us being the target clays. Dino, here comes Steve."

*****

Once inside the barn I could feel an eerie tension amongst everyone in the building. I glanced around the corner and walked into Dino's office. Tony was sitting on the couch. I took a seat in front of Dino.

"I'd say who died in here, but that would be in poor taste," I said, trying to lighten the mood.

"Well, did you and Kurt have some fun last night?" Dino asked.

"Yeah, quite informative. Hey Tony, how did your night turn out?"

"Steve, did you sleep well?" Tony said in an unwittingly cocky way.

"Like someone watched over me, Tony."

"Good, you'll need your "A" game today," Dino said. "We've got a few things to go over before the meeting."

"I figured that much."

"I know that you are now the majority owner of YLL," Dino said with a degree of dismay in his voice. "I'm a minority partner. I thought Sonny would... but he didn't, you're his heir. I just want you to know I'm in this for the long haul, to get this company back on its feet. It's been a solid company for years and it will be again, right Tony?"

Tony eyeballed me.

"Thanks Dino, I really appreciate that. Look, I don't know why any of this happened either. It's—"

Dino cut in. "It's been extremely hard on all of us. Sonny and I go a long way back. It never should have ended like this."

"No, it shouldn't have. Not like that," Tony blurted.

"I'm sorry for your loss. If you think my presence here is the curveball from hell, that's fine, I get it, but I'm not here to tarnish my birth father's reputation or legacy. I didn't come here for a grab and go. This is the opportunity of a lifetime, and I'm going to do whatever it takes to get this place cranking again. And there isn't anyone going to stop me, including that grease trap tender, Woody." I began pacing as my anger hit overload.

"And I want the person or persons responsible for killing Sonny in jail or in the desert. I don't care. Either one works for me." I didn't know what came over me, but when Dino and Tony got up, I thought I was in the deep end of the pool wearing a bowling ball vest.

"That's what I wanted to hear." Dino walked up to me and gave me a hug. Tony nodded.

We all sat down, and I regained my composure.

Looking over at Tony, I asked, "What's your official job title?"

"Tony was a remarkably close confidant to Sonny, handled all of the off the book collecting and security work. He's a holdover from Salvatore Fazzio's original limo company. But that's another story for another day," Dino interjected.

"Ah, thanks Tony."

"You're welcome," Tony said.

"Goldhabber should arrive shortly. Any questions you want me to answer before he gets here?"

"No, my brain has reached its capacity for the moment."

Candice knocked on the door and motioned for us to move to the conference room.

"I sent Goldhabber to the conference room like you asked."

Everyone was present: Kurt, Ramone, Edmond, Bridgette, Kiko, Candice, Max, the three of us and Goldhabber.

"This is the last will and testament of Sonny Antonio Tringale." Goldhabber pulled out the document and began to read. I felt uncomfortable, out of place and alone.

"To any of my relatives, living or dead, that lay claim to any part of my estate other than ones individually named, I leave ten rolls of pennies, to be divided up equally." Goldhabber dropped ten rolls of pennies on the desk and continued reading. "Please take your shares and get out of my conference room."

We all laughed. Of course, no one came forward. Sonny was a witty character for sure.

"Okay, to Kiko, my trusted mechanic, I leave three hundred shares of Apple stock, the 1988 classic black and white Lincoln limousine and the keys to my Austin Martin along with instructions to drive it up to the top of Lee Canyon and cut the brake lines. Park it in a safe place, call YLL and arrange transportation home."

Even dead Sonny could muster a room; more laughing took place.

An awkward Kiko looked around. "Thank you, Sonny."

"To Ramone, I leave my two full length mirrors. I know how much you like to watch yourself walk in and out of a room."

Edmond stood and vigorously clapped.

"And, my antique Rolex, three hundred shares of Apple stock, and my 1986 Cadillac convertible."

Ramone jumped to his feet and clapped back, looking at Edmond. "Yes, yes, God bless you Sonny."

Ramone sat down and Kurt patted him on the back. Ramone flipped off Edmond.

"To Candice, my hot Irish receptionist, I leave four hundred shares of my Apple stock, my mother's gold and diamond charm bracelet, my autographed Elvis guitar, and my pimped out 1992 Cadillac limousine."

Candice placed her head in her hands and began to sob.

"Moving right along to Edmond. Fuck the queen, that old, raunchy, stale bitch." Goldhabber read the will with all the character and exuberance Sonny intended.

Everyone in the room except Edmond, Tony, Max, and me, stood and cheered. With one stern glance, Tony got the room to settle down.

"Sonny, thank you for that zinger from beyond. Alright, let's continue. Quiet please. Ah, to Edmond, I leave my 1975 Aston; it's parked at Lee Canyon and Kiko has the keys."

The whole place simultaneously exploded into laughter, including Tony and Max. I thought people were going to slide out of their chairs. People were laughing so hard they had tears forming in their eyes. Edmond's face turned tomato red.

Goldhabber was fighting back a laugh. "Okay, okay. Again, moving on. And three hundred shares of Apple stock."

Edmond flipped Ramone off.

"To Bridgette! Oh, to be thirty years younger. I leave my mother's wedding ring, the 2001 Mercedes Benz stretch, four hundred shares of my Invidia stock, one hundred shares of my Priceline stock, and a from-the-heart thank you."

I couldn't tell if those were tears of joy, sadness, or anger. Looking around the room, I'm not sure anyone knew how to react to her. But I did have to say, Goldhabber knew how to read a will with the author's intent.

"To Kurt, one of my best friends. I leave my 2013 Shelby Mustang, my horseshoe diamond pinky ring, four hundred shares of my Invidia stock, two hundred shares of my Priceline stock, my platinum plated Glock 17, along with two additional twenty-round clips loaded with hollow points, an eighty-year-old bottle of McPhails to be opened on a special occasion of your choice, and a warm thanks for always being there."

Kurt covered his face with his hands as Ramone returned the shoulder hug and pat on the back.

"To Tony, my trusted friend. You can't keep doing what you do forever, so I'm leaving you with a little something for the road: my 2015 Bentley, my gold money chain, and six hundred shares of my Priceline stock. Be safe old friend."

Tony stared at Goldhabber. By his facial expressions and mannerisms I could tell he felt guilty about Sonny's murder and his inability to solve it. I'm sure he believed this will should have been read under a different set of circumstances.

"To my oldest friend Dino, I leave you five hundred shares of my Priceline stock and twenty-five percent of YLL. Show Steve the ropes and make this company grow."

Dino and I looked at each other. He gave me an awkward nod and I nodded back.

"And the last person to receive something from my last will and testament is Steve Mueller, my son. Steve, you're the son I always wanted but never had the time to connect with. There were so many times I wanted to visit you, but that never happened. Your toughness and intellect will get you where you need to go. You now own seventy-five percent of YLL, my house, the 2017 Toyota Tundra and the 2014 Cadillac SUV, my bank accounts, safe deposit box, and all my personal possessions. However, there is one stipulation. In order to keep your percent of YLL, you must keep it profitable within nine months of this will reading or Dino will have the option to buy you out at fair market value. I know you can make this work."

Goldhabber threw me the two sets of car keys.

Everyone looked my way. I had a lump the size of an ostrich egg in my throat. I got to my feet, thinking the will reading had ended along with everyone else, but it had not.

"Steve, everyone, please sit down. There's more."

Everyone quieted down in anticipation of Goldhabber's next words. His demeanor and expression changed.

"Here it is. Sonny sold all the stocks in his portfolio three weeks before he died. His jewelry is gone, his safe deposit box, empty, he has two mortgages on his house and one on the limo property and both are upside down. All his cars, including his collectibles, have loans against them and are awaiting repo.

"Steve and the rest of you, the bank will be here for those vehicles next week. The only vehicles left are the seventeen limos, nine Town Cars, and a last business statement showing twenty-four-thousand dollars in the bank. The rest is gone, vanished. There is really nothing left except the company. Even the property that it sits on is mortgaged to the max. There's really nothing left."

Everyone started bombarding Goldhabber with questions. The room became loud and chaotic. I sat there watching my future get flushed down the toilet. Kurt kept shouting out the same thing over and over. "What about the scotch?"

Finally, Goldhabber answered him. "What?"

"What about the bottle of McPhails? The scotch—is that gone too?"

"I don't know, I haven't been to the house in a while. I guess maybe it's there. Ask Steve. It's his house, for now."

Goldhabber loaded up his briefcase and tried making his way out the door. Bridgette grabbed him by the arm.

"What do you mean it's all gone?"

"You need me to spell it out for you? It's g-o-n-e, gone. Nothing left."

She stormed out of the room. I walked out and started pacing the hallway.

Dino shot to his feet and slammed his fists on the table.

"Everyone, shut the fuck up! All of you, sit down. Goldhabber, get back here. Kurt, bring Bridgette and Steve back. Now, Goldhabber, before everyone in this room collectively knocks your teeth down your throat, what are our options?"

Kurt grabbed me and we came back into the room.

"I got Steve, but Bridgette left a vapor trail out of the building."

"I can only guess, but the total value of his assets he sold, including the mortgages has a market value of around twenty million, give or take a couple million."

"When did you find this out, and why this phony bullshit will reading? You knew it was a farce."

"Look, it's my job to read the will exactly as written, which I did. The catastrophic results at the end were my duty to you, to let you know."

"Are there any clues to the whereabouts of all his money?"

"Dino, I'm a lawyer, not a detective. My job was to bring Steve to Vegas, read the will, and execute Sonny's last wishes. All of which I did."

"But of course, you and your firm were taken care of?"

"Yes. Sonny had a separate account for our firm, along with executor instructions, which I personally followed to the letter. We were paid in full."

From the look on everyone's faces, the news of the missing fortune took the shape of a massive treasure hunt.

Edmond said, "Who's going to look for these missing funds? If the money is found, will it be converted and distributed equitably according to the will?"

"Are you asking my firm to look for the money?"

Kurt got up and walked towards Goldhabber. "That's up to Edmond. I wouldn't hire your firm to empty shit out of a monkey cage."

Then it began to get interesting. Tony walked up to Goldhabber, slid his briefcase across the floor, picked him up by his belt, and laid his massive forearm across his throat, pinning him against the wall. His feet dangled several inches above the floor.

"I find out you touched, moved, or looked at any of that money and I'll take a cheese grader and slowly shred you into little pieces and mail them back to your wife."

A small wet stain appeared on the front of Goldhabber's pants as Tony released him and pushed him up against the wall again. The room grew silent.

"All right. Everyone relax, calm down. We all need to digest this information," Dino ordered.

Max stood up. "I've seen and heard enough, and I'm leaving."

I grabbed Kurt by the arm. "Max wasn't even in the will. I thought you said they were close. What's that all about?"

"I know. In all the chaos I started wondering the same thing."

Ramone leaned toward us. "Max looks like he's about to kill someone."

"Something strange is going on. Max can smell a setup a mile away. I'll see him tonight, pick his brain," Kurt added.

"Maybe it's Edmond," Ramone said flashing an ivory smile.

"Really Ramone, now?"

"Alright, wishful thinking."

I walked over to the greedy lawyer. "Hey Norman, looks like your Depends need some changing. You knew about this all along and made me sit through this charade."

"I did what Sonny asked. And I did not empty Sonny's accounts; that's on him."

"I'll bet you rifled through the house when you found out the money disappeared."

"Yes, so what? We tried to find it. I'm the executor. That way we could figure out everyone's fair shares in dollars and cents. No crime in that."

"My father… Sonny, keeps on screwing me."

"I did exactly what Sonny asked, so what are you crying about? You still own seventy-five percent of—"

"All I'm getting to do is rearrange the deck chairs on the Titanic, Norman."

"Well happy sailings. I'm out of here; we'll be in touch."

Kurt and Ramone came over as Goldhabber left the room.

"Come on Steve, let's get out of here." Kurt snatched up a Town Car and the three of us drove over to the Graveyaad, Ramone riding shotgun. As I opened the door to the bar, smooth Jazz played on the jukebox. Sherry came over to serve us.

"Hey boys, starting a little early, aren't we? Y'all have lots of Sonny's money to toss around?"

"The will reading was a sick joke." Ramone said.

"You really look worn out Steve, honey. You okay? What's goin' on?"

"No, I'm far from okay. My epicurean lifestyle just blew up in my face while everyone keeps shooting shitballs at me. Nothing is what it seems around here."

"Steve, trust me, it will all straighten itself out. You'll see. Vegas has a way of… recycling its trash."

"See why we come here? Free therapy?" Kurt playfully added.

"Oh, and Steve, I want you to meet my twins."

Sherry walked to the end of the bar where two girls were working. She brought them over and introduced them.

"Steve, on my left Samantha and on my right Charlette. Say hi to Steve. He's Sonny's boy, part owner of YLL."

"Nice to meet you ladies. I'm guessing that because you don't look alike, you're fraternal?"

"Another genius in Vegas." Charlette extended her hand. "Good luck with the limo company."

We shook hands and she walked back to the end of the bar.

"Hi, Steve." Samantha extended her hand too.

"Nice to meet you, Samantha. Quite the healthy grip you're sporting."

"Thank you. And for the record, Charlette's the friendly one."

"How often does she polish her fangs?"

"On even numbered days. I have the odd ones."

"Go figure, leaving my anti-venom serum at home."

"I got this, mom," she added.

Sherry left the bar area and entered the kitchen.

"I'm starving. I'm going back to the kitchen and see what Buster is concocting. You coming, Ramone?" Kurt said nudging him.

"I'll see ya there. I have to empty a kidney or two."

They both left.

"I couldn't help overhearing you all had a rough afternoon."

"Samantha, the word clusterfuck comes to mind. Pardon my French."

With a smile and a light laugh, she said, "So, I guess it's just you and me, Steve. And please, call me Sam."

"Alright, Sam. You always have this effect on people's stomachs and kidneys?"

"Ooh, that smarts. A buttermilk for you?"

"Way too strong for a novice like me."

We both smiled and for the first time today I felt somewhat at ease. I also felt an instant chemistry with her.

We enjoyed the small banter that played out for the next ten minutes. A sympathetic ear proved to be the right medicine after the will reading. She had been in Vegas for five years, coming up from New Orleans, where she majored in business at Tulane. Her twin sister moved to Vegas six years ago, in real estate before joining her mother. The twins shared a condo in Henderson, close to Green Valley Ranch Casino. Of course her condo could have been across the street and I wouldn't have had a clue where it was. This city is twenty times larger than La Crosse. But getting invited there sounded like a good idea and there would be no way on this earth I would not be able to find it. I really liked her. Finally, someone who seems normal in Vegas.

"Steve, what are you having?"

"A Diet Coke would be perfect."

She went to the soda gun and poured me a tall diet over a lot of ice, shoved a straw in the glass, and after tossing a coaster down, slid it over to me. I pulled out the straw, not taking my eyes off her, tossed it on the bar, and took a long drink. Exactly what my parched pallet needed.

"Drinking like a big boy, Steve. No straw."

"Hard core big boy diet drinker, that's me."

"Impressive, this must not be your first time. I can see you've . . . done this before."

I leaned in as close as I could. "Yes, I'm very experienced, Sam."

"I like men with experience."

"Sam, could you come here a minute?" Sherry called out.

"Duty calls. Stick around. I'll be back."

"Hopefully without sunglasses, the leather jacket and the IMI Uzi."

She paused a second, smiled, and walked over to her mother standing at the end of the bar. I looked in the bar mirror and stared at myself.

"Maybe Vegas isn't so bad," I mumbled.

She went back to the other end of the bar and started taking orders. Ramone returned and sat down.

"That had to be the longest kidney extraction on record."

"I saw you working on Sam, didn't want to interrupt you. Is this a great place or what? Those twins are so hot. If only I was two years younger."

"Two years. What are you, smoking crack?"

"Okay, maybe three, tops. Anyway, cheer up. Today is only a minor setback. We'll put our collective genius together and figure this all out. You, me, and Kurt."

"Yep, we'll all figure this out."

"Howdy, boys. I just ordered us some cheeseburgers, no onions. Can't stink up the mouth, our best tool. Nothing worse than a limo driver with bad breath or swamp ass," Kurt cheerfully said as he sat down.

"What about both?"

"Now you're talking cab driver," a cocky Ramone answered back quickly.

"The menu in Greek? What took you so long?" I inquired.

"You looked busy. I didn't want to interrupt you. Besides, Sam's nice. You guys looked like you were having fun."

Somehow, I started to feel better. Kurt and Ramone were becoming friends.

"Soon as we're done eating, I'm going to take you out and show you how to be a great chauffeur, Vegas style," Kurt said.

"Yeah, Steve. Learn the ropes from the second best limo driver in Sin City," Ramone snapped back.

"Ramone, when you pocket thirteen thousand in tips in six days, come see me."

"Luck, you know it."

"Skill my friend, skill."

"You made thirteen thousand dollars in tips in six days?" I said, accidentally letting out a burp.

"More like thirteen thousand four hundred, but who's counting?"

"Well, I do more rock stars, movie stars, and porn stars and—"

"And make less gratuities, my short Mexican compadre. It's about the greenbacks, not the trophies, Ramone.

"Bastardo."

Kurt leaned in and gave Ramone a kiss on the cheek. "You're still my favorite asshole."

We all laughed, the insanity of today starting to fade.

Kurt shouted, "After lunch, we ride!"

We high fived each other.

Chapter 9

After a quick bite, Kurt dropped Ramone off at the Barn, parked the Town Car, and he and I went to his limo and drove to the Tight Racks parking lot. This was going to be the backdrop where my education would continue, completing my chauffeur's internal operation tour and learning how to turn my limo into a personal ATM.

"Steve, whenever you open the door for a client, always open the passenger side door of the limo."

"Let me guess, so they don't step out into oncoming traffic, screw up your tip?"

"Smart ass. From now on it's called a gratuity. Cabbies, waitresses, and bell hops get tips; we get gratuities."

"Gratuities it is."

"Whenever you lend a woman or even a man some assistance, always use your arm, not your hand. Nobody wants to be handled by the hand that's been on the steering wheel or in a thousand other places; it's amateur."

"Never would have thought of that. Smart."

"Get into the back."

In a raised male voice, I said, "Why Kurt, we only just met. I'm not a tramp."

"Get your ass back there. And you totally are."

Kurt followed me in the back and showed me where the switches and controls were, a refresher course from last night.

"Here is where you can score huge points with your clients." Kurt pointed to the sides in the back, "Make sure you always have ice on hand in these. I usually stock one side with beer and the other with water, OJ, Sprite, Coke and Diet Coke. In the bottle holders I keep, Jack, Kettle One, Jameson, and any gin. As you can see, my tumblers have double- wrapped multicolor coordinated beverage napkins. When clients enter my limo, they see this and know they

118

have a chauffeur who knows his shit. How much I stock depends on the size of the limo. Sometimes I need to drop this at the Barn and take out a bigger one. Plus, I keep a cooler in the back with ice, extra beer, water, and other beverages."

"So, size does matter?"

"Sam spike your Coke?"

"Sorry. Do you charge them?"

"When they ask you how much for any of your beverages, you tell them to help themselves and to take care of you on the back end."

"Do they?"

"They certainly do. Nobody wants to appear cheap, except Canadians. They think tipping is what you do to cows. They are a bunch of cheap bastards. However, there are always exceptions; you'll discover who the good ones are."

"Does Candice ever give you any Canadians."

"Not if she wants to live. Look, they are genuinely nice people. It's just a different culture, that's all. Hop out and get in the driver's seat."

The limo was still running as I climbed back into the front seat.

"What, no smart ass comment, Steve?"

"Nope."

"You see the bag on the floor?" He pointed on the passenger's side.

"Yes."

"That's my limo bag."

"I've seen it, but what's in it?"

"It's a survival in the city bag. Lots of things can happen in a night, so I keep some items that might come in handy."

"For instance?"

"I keep the bag stocked with, gum, breath mints, blank signs for airport pick-ups, Band-Aids, a sewing kit, flashlight, batteries of all sizes, cologne, first aid kit, condoms, pens, markers, invoices, a Swiss Army Knife, a corkscrew, bottle opener, sunglasses, reading glasses, a few personal items, the basics."

"You really cover your bases."

"It's Vegas. Anything can happen. A good chauffeur must always be ready for the unexpected."

Kurt pointed out all the controls and their functions. But he stopped at one.

"This is your rear cutoff switch. Only use this if things get out of hand in the back."

"Why would you ever need to do that?"

"Trust me. You'll figure it out."

"And that bulge in your left suitcoat?"

"I'm carrying these days; some clients feel extra safe with a chauffeur that carries."

"Cool. You have a cc permit."

"I do. Buckle up. I'm going to drive you around the city."

Kurt showed me the Strip again. This time I looked at the various hotels and people instead of holding onto the sides of Ruby's ears.

"Kurt, the Strip is so slow, why would you ever drive this?"

"Because you need to see where the casinos are. Occasionally, you'll have to do the strip, play-by-play. Show off your expertise and knowledge of Vegas. It's boring, but part of the job, and those that ask love it."

Kurt pulled into the Mandalay Bay, where we swapped places. Under Kurt's watchful eye and direction, I navigated the strip and its afternoon traffic. At five-thirty, we pulled up to the security gate of my new house with the double mortgage.

"You did a nice job, Steve; I was hoping you would be able to handle this."

"Thanks. Driving a limo can be a real pisser. I had fun and a good teacher."

"Good, because you have your first charter in less than two hours. Clean up and be at the barn by seven. Put on your best clothes."

"Holy shit. Already?"

"What, you've got other plans?"

"No, no. I mean I wasn't expecting to—"

"You have to figure this whole thing out, what you're going to do. Unfortunately, the clock is ticking."

"I get it; shit or get off the pot."

"I couldn't have said it more eloquently if I tried. Good luck, have fun, and I'll see you at the Graveyaad later tonight."

"Thanks again, Kurt."

"Don't thank me yet. Let's see how you like it first."

I watched Kurt drive off as I lingered in the driveway wondering what would happen next. I liked an adventure and hoped this would be a simple and smooth transition, unlike the will reading.

Chapter 10

I took the Tundra out of the garage. I was dressed in a nice pair of black pants, a white shirt, dark tie, and my smoke-induced sports coat. I pumped a double dose of cologne all over it. The twenty-minute drive stimulated my senses, the lit up marquees with their gaudy lights emanating in every direction. There was an overabundance of foot traffic acting like ants battling for the rights to a watermelon and the bumper-to-bumper traffic highlighted by taxi cabs and their bright advertisement displays. I stomped down on the accelerator a couple of times just for fun, enjoying the six hundred horses under my command, arriving at YLL fifteen minutes early.

Candice sat at her desk, manipulating phone calls. She paused to give me a hug.

"Hi, boss. I'm so excited for you, your first run."

"Yeah, me too. I'm kind of nervous though. I don't want to crap the bed."

"Honey, you'll be fine. If you can drive, you can do this. It's a vehicle that's just a wee bit bigger."

She looked at my crotch with two fingers an inch apart and then stretched them.

"You certainly know how to take the edge off. And don't call me boss; it's Steve. That boss thing sounds, well, you know, under the circumstances, strange."

"Got it, Steve. Oh, Dino left you a little gift.

"A gift?"

"Dino didn't want you to get lost, at least not with the limo."

"Cute."

"He had Kiko put in a new GPS in your limo. It should make your first run a snap. Soon, you'll know the streets of Vegas like a pro."

"I used my iPhone, Siri and Waze and studied the streets from Sonny's house to the Barn."

"I like that; you did some homework."

"Six years of college, really paying big dividends; I can talk to my phone and walk at the same time."

"Sounds like you're a candidate for the Harvard Doctorate program."

After our friendly banter we walked out to the parking lot and she led me to the limo I'd be driving.

"It's a 2011 Lincoln. Unfortunately, our newest limo in the fleet. But Kiko does an amazing job of making these things look like new. Here you go." She tossed me the keys. "It only has eighty-seven-thousand miles on it, runs like an even money favorite at the Kentucky derby, and the AC cranks out enough cool air to make Eskimos piss ice cubes."

She opened the door.

"Don't worry, you'll be fine. If you get a little overwhelmed call me, Kurt, or Ramone. We've got your back."

"Okay."

Candice handed me a printout sheet with directions.

"Here is where you are going and whom you are picking up. Mrs. Black, a regular. This run should be a piece of cake, no drama. All your info is on the sheet. Any questions?"

"Right, piece of cake, Mrs. Black.

"Steve, this is your limo. Take it home when you're done for the night. You can leave Sonny's, I mean your Tundra here."

"I think it's seventy-five percent mine, and thanks."

"No problem, you're a good kid. I want this to work out for you. Some new blood around here is not a bad thing."

I slid in the limo, played around with the controls which were almost identical to the ones in Kurt's stretch. I read the directions, punched the address into the GPS, and gently pulled out of the Barn. Putting a scratch on this baby would be catastrophic. The GPS informed me it would take approximately twenty minutes to drive to her home.

Every time I hit a red light, I peered around at the other vehicles stopped beside me, wondering if they thought I had some huge Hollywood star in the back.

I stopped the car at the guard gate of the Desert Cactus Country Club and gave the guard Mrs. Black's name and phone number. After a few seconds he emerged with a direction printout and opened the gate.

Darkness began winning its battle against the sun, which methodically began to tuck itself behind Mount Charleston, revealing a majestic purple and reddish-pink sunset. I drove the mile to her house which consisted of elegant homes with pristine front yards. The gate was open, and I drove up the long circle driveway surrounded by California pepper and eucalyptus trees. I parked under the stucco canopy in front of the door to Mrs. Black's. I looked into the rearview mirror and forced an elongated smile.

I was about to get into the back seat, making sure everything was nice and organized when I realized I hadn't stocked anything in the back.

"Screwed up already, moron," I said with a degree of panic in my voice while grabbing the sides of my head.

I reevaluated my situation and noticed a completely stocked back, looking exactly like the back of Kurt's limo. I saw the note.

"You fucked up already. Your humble and loyal employee, Kurt."

"Thank you, Kurt," I chanted several times, closing the back door and nervously walked up to Mrs. Black's front door.

A beautiful mahogany door with a multicolored circular stained-glass center stood before me. I rung the bell and wondered about the appearance of Mrs. Black. Probably some old rich-bitch customer with a walker, dragging an oxygen tank, tubes sticking out in all directions.

"Showtime," I mumbled to myself.

I looked anxiously down at my feet which were shuffling. Mrs. Black's housekeeper, a short older Latino woman dressed in a full-blown maid ensemble opened the door, catching me off guard.

"You must be the chauffeur," she said in a very monotone voice with a slight accent.

"Uh, yes ma'am."

"Please come in and follow me to the library," she said, closing the door gently behind me.

The size of this place made Sonny's look like a well-furnished outhouse. The marbled entryway, the paintings on the wall, the spiral staircase leading upstairs with a huge chandelier hanging down from the second story. She dramatically opened both doors and extended her arm, directing me into the spacious library.

"Take a seat on the couch. Mrs. Black will be with you shortly."

She stepped out and closed the doors behind her. A large redwood desk, almost nothing on it, squatted next to two bookshelves lined top to bottom with books, and sliding ladders, one on each side, and a seventy-five-inch television on the wall to the right of the entry.

I sat on the long leather couch, noticing a leather chair with a reading lamp attached. She must be a history professor or perhaps an English literature professor?

Mrs. Black entered the library like a dust devil, all five-foot-five of her, red-brown-blonde-streaked short hair, bright pink lipstick, and an overly confident smile. She looked stunning in her white business suit, hiding a pink silk blouse, and three inch white-and-pink stiletto heels. Everything she wore displayed elegance and money. Mary and Mrs. Black could have been sisters. So much for the professor on oxygen; her presence drove the oxygen out of the room. She walked straight toward me.

"So, your Sonny's boy?"

I jumped up off the couch. "Yes, I—"

She stopped, her body an inch from mine, her perfume pleasantly enticing my senses.

She proceeded to grab my crotch. I doubled over from the unexpected squeeze, my arms gently grabbing hers.

"I'll be the judge of that."

I quickly straightened and looked her in the eyes. She appeared to be on a search-and-seizure mission, treading cautiously and not trying to make me cry uncle. I noticed her rigid smile just before she dropped to her knees and unzipped my pants.

This was the fourth time in as many days that I'd had a woman holding my love muscle and looking up at me to communicate. She looked like I just gave her a diamond necklace.

"Oh my, you most definitely *are* Sonny's boy."

She popped up in an athletic sort of way, pushed me on the couch, and removed her white jacket. She gracefully turned partially away while continuing to engage her eyes with mine.

"Don't move. I'll be right back."

As she walked away, she unbuttoned her pink blouse, revealing a bare back, bra-less look, slinging both her blouse and white jacket over her left shoulder. She stopped to dim the library lights and exited through the doors like a high-end runway model, dramatically closing them behind her without ever turning back.

I stared at my pants and underwear dangling around my ankles, my pecker eyeballing me back.

"This is a nice look for me," I said while having a full-of-myself chuckle.

I wasn't sure if sitting alone half naked on a stranger's couch in a personal home library, displayed good

126

company business ethics. Or would she be perturbed when I billed her for my entire time, owning prodigious brass balls, enabling me to gaze directly into her eyes and with unspoken words, demand my well-earned gratuity? All those sugar-plumb thoughts quickly vanished as soon as the library doors reopened.

A very thin man in his thirties came through the door, well dressed. The word gay came to mind.

In a high pitched voice, sporting a girly gait and hand gestures, he excitedly began to speak.

"It looks like we're going to. . . oh my word." He stopped short, I'm sure just as stunned to see me in my partial birthday suit. He visually locked in on my exposed package.

I think I turned fifty shades of red when I saw him ogling me.

"That Mrs. Black, always thinking of me," he said, still fixating on my crotch.

At that point, my self-preservation alarm kicked into panic mode. I shot off the couch, staggering around in a circle on one leg trying to pull up my pants and maintain my balance. I didn't want to crash on my face and have my ass stick up like a San Francisco bicycle rack. And the last thing I wanted to do was indicate a green light where he would conveniently find an object to park there.

"Whoa, I am, uh, you know, um, fuck."

I reached backwards, working and feeling my way out of the library.

"I'm Carson," he gleefully professed.

"Carson, um, this isn't what it looks like."

"Really, what does it look like?"

With Carson playfully approaching me, I reached back anxiously hoping to connect with one of the door handles. However, they weren't supposed to feel big and soft. Carson stopped and I quickly looked behind me only to find my right hand on Mrs. Black's left tit.

"Shit, I—"

"Are you done playing with Carson or do you need some more time?"

"No, no, I can't get you into the back of the limo fast enough," I said as I removed my hand from her breast and shook it like it was numb or on fire.

Acting like nothing out of the ordinary had taken place, she walked out the library doors, wearing a black thigh high skirt which showcased her legs and hips, black five-inch stiletto heels and a white see- through blouse.

Smiling, she said, "If you want, I'll arrange it so you can play with the help later."

Carson smiled at Mrs. Black and winked at me.

I pulled my ensemble back together and moved quickly to the limo, the maid holding open the front door.

I opened the back door and extended my arm for her to use as a means of gracefully entering the limo. She warmly smiled as she pulled her skirt up a couple of inches, grabbed my arm, and seductively swung her left leg into the limo. She sat down and put her second leg up on the floor facing me, exposing her thigh high stockings and her fully shaven private area. She paused long enough to watch my reaction, released my arm, and turned facing the front. She looked away as I gently closed the door and settled into the driver's side.

I glanced down at my private parts and mumbled. "Be careful not to break this on the steering wheel."

I left the AC running on high to keep it nice and cool in the back, another lesson learned earlier today from Kurt. I sat down and readied to pull out of her driveway, but I couldn't help but wonder if Mrs. Black were a regular, had she fucked with everyone at YLL or was I the exception? Or could she be a big tease, relishing in the enjoyment of watching me uncomfortably squirm?

The dividing glass window came down. "Take me to the Forum Shops at Caesars Palace."

"Yes, Mrs. Black."

The window went back up and I quickly called Candice.

"Yo Leven Limousine, may I help you?"

"Candice, Candice, where's the Forum Shops? Never mind. I found it, GPS."

"Steve, park in the north side valet; it's easier to get in and out of and it's less crowded. Good luck, sweetie."

I put the divider down and went to the intercom, hoping she wasn't doing an unusual sex act with some exotic foreign toy. At least not without me as a willing participant or observer; observers are important too.

"I'm sorry I wasn't quite ready to leave when you were Mrs. Black."

What a fucking suck up I had become. The divider started its way back up without her saying a word.

I arrived at the Forum Shops back parking area, feeling better after driving like a perfect little chauffeur. Like a cat, I moved out of my door around to the back of the limo and was about to open the door when I noticed the valet standing at attention, waiting for me to open the door. Smart, make me look good. I see how this works. I opened the door and Mrs. Black extended her arm, again making sure my eyes engaged her wide-open legs revealing everything to me for a second time. The valet got a first-time show.

I knew she was enjoying watching me sweat as my eyes wandered between her legs and back to her face while she never took her eyes off mine. She exited the limo and gave me a big approving smile.

"Come on Steve, let's go inside."

"But I have to—"

"Jerry, park the limo. We'll be inside an hour or so."

"Yes, Mrs. Black."

Apparently, he'd seen this show before.

She handed Jerry a twenty.

129

"Come on Steve, we don't have all night."

We walked into the Forum Shops through the north side valet entrance. A pair of automatic doors opened inward revealing a robust crowd of well-dressed male and female shoppers, with some children sprinkled in. The statue of Neptune caught my eye immediately. Mrs. Black quickly put her arm in mine and casually steered me in the direction she wanted to stroll. I must have been doing a perfect Stevie Wonder imitation rolling my head side to side, soaking up the ambiance as we wandered through the mall. It ended up being a short stroll as we stopped at the entrance to Armani's Men's Clothing store. She lightly pulled me in as a salesman strategically waited for us.

"Mrs. Black, an honor as always."

"Claude darling, how nice to see you again," Mrs. Black flamboyantly conveyed her happiness in seeing him.

Claude took her hand and kissed the back of it.

"Claude, this is Sonny's boy, Steve," she said with a Hollywood smile.

"Mister Steve, what an honor to meet you. Sonny was the best, the absolute best."

Being a smart ass, I turned my hand over so he could kiss it but instead he grabbed my shoulders, hugged me, and kissed me on each cheek.

"Claude, take Steve to the back dressing room and get rid of that awful jacket and those slacks... burn the shoes."

"Yes, Mademoiselle Black. As always, I am your honored servant."

"What the——?"

"Let's go, Monsieur Steve."

Mrs. Black grabbed a chair while Claude draped his arm around me and took me to the dressing room.

Once inside with the door closed, Claude began his routine. "Let me help you get this jacket off."

"Okay, but no burning or destroying any of my things."

He hung my jacket in the dressing room. The large dressing room featured one side of only mirrors, another with eight well-spaced hooks, hangers dangling on each. Against another wall, a large dressing couch, and the last wall displayed three leather chairs and a champagne holder in between them, including a table and a rolling stool.

"The trousers, please."

"Wait a minute, what are you doing with my things?"

"You can leave the shirt and tie on for now."

Claude used two fingers to place my pants on the hook.

"Claude?" A voice in the distance said.

"Let's go. Mademoiselle Black is waiting."

"What do you mean waiting?"

Claude gently grabbed my arm. "Follow me."

Mrs. Black sat on a high back Victorian chair waiting for me when Claude led me into another dressing room. Being led around in my shirt, socks, and underwear by a man was not my idea of a good time.

"Steve," Mrs. Black began, "Sonny and I were close, and over the years he has done many things for me. I'm just returning a kindness. Sonny was the epitome of a well-dressed man and I'm going to make sure his son follows in his footsteps."

"Thank you, but I can't afford—"

"Steve, this is on me. Your money or lack of it is no good. Claude, make the man."

"Yes, Steve, stand tall."

Claude started measuring me in every direction as several assistants came into the room. This moment reminded me of Al Jarreau's song, "Boogie Down," from the movie "Night Shift" when the hookers were trying on all sorts of clothes.

I tried on various suits and combinations, all under the watchful eye of Mrs. Black and under the supervision of Claude. She sipped champagne and enjoyed every moment. With a wave she sent back suits and ordered new ones be brought in. I counted six suits, six or seven shirts, six ties and three pairs of shoes as I wandered back into the dressing room to put my original outfit back on.

I heard a knock on the dressing room door.

"Come on in Claude, nothing's hanging out," I answered as the dressing room door swung open.

"What a shame."

My natural reactions took over and I placed my hands between my legs and took a step back, obviously expecting Claude.

Mrs. Black closed the door, reached behind her back and unzipped her dress, letting it fall around her legs and onto the floor. She looked seductive in her black thigh highs, heels, and nothing else. She took her hand from behind her back and showed me a monster ribbed condom as she stepped out of her dress.

"I can get Claude if you like?"

"I think Claude is going to have to sit this one out. You look stunning."

She kicked her dress to the side and playfully guided me to a leather chair and pushed me in.

I tried to kiss her, but she placed her index finger between our lips and softly shook her head no. She leaned into my neck and dragged her tongue across it while grinding her hips around me. After about ten minutes we both climaxed. She kissed my cheek, grabbed some Kleenex sitting on a table, and wiped herself off as she tossed me the box. I pulled off the condom and looked for an inconspicuous place to toss it, definitely a photo moment. Mrs. Black put her dress on, admiring her body in the mirror, glanced at me, and left the dressing room. I rifled the

132

condom into the waste basket, dressed, and walked up to the Armani front counter.

Mrs. Black leaned over the counter, handing Claude an American Express Centurion card.

"Always a pleasure to have you in our store, Mademoiselle Black."

I walked up to the counter next to my wonderful patron.

"Monsieur Steve, I'll have your suits ready for delivery by tomorrow."

"Claude, you've been exceptional," a proud and pleased Mrs. Black complimented.

"Thank you, Mademoiselle Black."

She pulled out a stack of hundred-dollar bills and counted out five for Claude. "Thank you."

"Steve, pick up those three bags and let's go."

"Thank you so much for—"

"Fucking you?"

"No, no for the—"

"You didn't enjoy fucking me?"

"No, yes, of course, for—"

Her quick-witted teasing ended in, "Come on, Steve." She had a roguish expression on her face.

I started having this prophetic conversation in my head… I guess I just have a propensity for sleeping with older women, not by design; it just started happening and I found myself really enjoying them. Mary wasn't my first, making it less complicated for me to connect with her. Older women seem to sense fear and anxiety in younger men; some are excited by it, most are turned off.

According to Mary, she gravitated toward me because of the way I carried myself, my self-confidence, no-nonsense loyalty and of course the way I looked. The mental foreplay and childish games younger women played were almost nonexistent with older women. They seemed to know what they wanted and weren't afraid to go after it.

We exited the mall and headed back to the north valet entrance. Jerry raced over to Mrs. Black, where she handed him another twenty. He ran into the valet shed and produced the keys. The limo was parked about five feet from where I had left it. I opened the door and Mrs. Black handed me a card. She slipped uneventfully into the back. I went to the front door of the limo and read the card with an address neatly written out.

*****

On the Mirage rooftop a shooter sat patiently waiting for Steve and Mrs. Black to exit the Forum Shops, a sharp eye looking down the scope of a German made .338 Lapua Magnum, range 1400 yards, an easy target from where the sniper bore down.

Steve and Mrs. Black exited the Forum Shops, waiting for the valet to retrieve the keys. The would-be assassin held the rifle steady, lined up the shot, and gently squeezed the trigger. Click. Nothing happened. The assassin placed the weapon gently back in the case after wiping it down, uneventfully exiting the rooftop door.

"Soon, I'm going to enjoy another payday," the shooter boasted.

*****

I pulled up to the Desert Willows Estates, where two security guards and a double wide ten-foot-high entry gate blocked my way. The brick walls surrounding these gates were impressive.

"Pull forward so I can give this to the guard," came the order from the back of the limo over the intercom.

I pulled forward, noticing two armed guards at the entry. One came to the back door. The window slid down. In my driver's side mirror, I saw the guard lean into the back while the other guard, still inside the security shack doorway, kept a watchful eye on me. A couple of words were exchanged, and the guard left the rear of the limo and nodded to the other guard. He disappeared inside for a moment and reappeared with a detailed printout. I rolled my window down, took the printout, and drove between the two ten-foot wrought iron security gates, rolling my window up as I entered the elite community.

I drove upward along the winding resident's roads, barely able to see the multicolored tiled rooftops of the desert mansions and their wrought-iron Spanish balconies. Most were hiding behind impeccably landscaped walls and trees, protecting their wealthy owners.

At a second guard shack another security man nodded at me as the ten-foot gates swung open and allowed us to pass. The residents' homes appeared to get larger the farther uphill I drove.

My GPS signaled I had arrived. The name Adams had been carved into the two brick pillars supporting the opened iron gate. I drove forward and stopped in the circle drive. A variety of limos and Town Cars were parked on the front lawn and around the premises.

Two doormen in red crushed velvet jackets and white gloves rushed to the back door and opened it before I had a chance to exit the limo. I hurried to the back door as fast as I could, but Mrs. Black was already waiting outside the limo. She told me to park and wait as she entered the mansion escorted by one of the men in the red crushed velvet coats. The door closed and she disappeared inside.

"You can find a place on the lawn over there." The other doorman pointed.

"What, no valet?" I playfully asked.

"Not for you. Move it."

After finding an open spot on the grass I noticed a group of drivers standing around in a circle shooting the breeze and smoking cigarettes. I decided to join them, being the socialite I am, mostly to find out a little more information about the gathering inside.

"Interesting place. What's going on?" I asked.

They looked at me like the guy in the elevator who just farted. No one said a word.

"Yo, anybody home?"

That's when one driver glanced at me and flicked his cigarette butt off my chest, the little red glowing ashes trailing the butt to the ground. I checked my clothes, just to make sure they weren't on fire.

The limo guy snapped at me. "Limo boy, stay by your own shit. Nobody here gives a flying fuck what you have to say!"

I took a step toward the butt-tossing driver, but three other drivers intervened on his behalf.

"Come on limo boy, start something," the butt tossing driver dared.

Two of the drivers grabbed me from behind and held me. They caught me off guard. This was supposed to be fun. It wasn't.

"Steve, I'm Eddie Morrow and I work for Woody. We don't like it when some hick struts around here like his shit don't stink."

"You looked in a mirror lately?"

The two guys holding me gripped tighter as Eddie wasted no time, walked up to me, and punched my gut. I tightened my stomach muscles as much as possible, though I still felt it. I doubled over as the two guys from behind let me fall to my knees.

"Anything else you got to say?" Eddie added right before he kicked me in the chest and knocked me onto my back. "Yeah… I didn't think so, bitch."

The three had a good laugh and walked away with a minor ass kicking at my expense. I was fuming mad but also realized this wasn't the time or place to do anything. I had to take the loss, suck this one up. It didn't stop me from becoming irate. However, being a rookie in a strange city obviously set up by these Neanderthals, I brushed myself off and retreated to my limo, my ego dragging behind me.

I jumped in the front seat, pounded the steering wheel, the dash, my adrenaline flowing, angry, and venting. I would not forget Eddie Morrow or his limo thugs.

"Payback's going to be a bitch, Eddie!" I yelled.

I pushed back hard against the steering wheel and folded my arms. I started the engine, letting the ice-cold air chill me out, along with some country music I found searching the Vegas radio stations. My adrenaline retreated, so I relaxed, closed my eyes, accidentally drifting off.

Something on the radio woke me. I looked at my watch—almost two in the morning. I stepped out, stretched, and looked around to see what the dickheads were doing. To my surprise, they had all left. However, more cars had arrived. I paced around the limo several times and sat back inside, looking at the front entryway.

"This is boring, I better put some books on my kindle," I mumbled as I took another casual stroll around the limo.

At about two-thirty I saw Mrs. Black walk out of the Adams' house. I put the limo in drive and drove up to the door. I had been there almost five hours.

The two valets opened the door and let Mrs. Black in. I didn't even have time to open the limo door and get out, so this time I didn't make an effort. The door opened and closed, Mrs. Black seated in back.

"Take me home," she said.

"Yes, Mrs. Black."

In less than fifteen minutes we arrived at her house. After opening her door and standing there for a moment, she put her hand in her purse and pulled out another stack of hundred-dollar bills. She counted out ten and put them in my hand, then kissed me on the cheek.

"Go back to your office, give Candice a hunny."

"A hunny?"

"Yes, a hundred-dollar bill."

"That's one I haven't heard."

She was partway inside when I looked down at my hand, enjoying the Ben Franklin's staring back at me. Indoctrination run, my first one. Wow. The minor run-in faded away; ten dead inventors dancing in your palms can have that kind of effect.

"You need to come inside and finish anything?" she cracked before slowly letting the doors close behind her.

"Carson's probably a really nice guy, but I'll pass," came my answer to an already closed door.

Chapter 11

3:07 AM

I stopped at the Graveyaad first. I figured I could always give Candice her hunny later today.

I walked in, noticed some familiar faces sitting around a table, and grabbed a chair and joined them. No one acknowledged me.

"Come on, really?" I said.

They all looked at me and smirked.

"You got your cherry broke, son." Prez broke the silence and burst out laughing.

"All of you know what happened, don't you?"

"Yeah. Sorry, Steve," Bridgette said in an obviously fake sympathetic voice.

I was the joke of the night, but I had a great time anyway, except for the shitheel drivers who acted like they had a vendetta. My self-gloating came to a screeching halt when Sam came over to the table and gave me a dirty look. She must have heard the offbeat running commentary about my virgin run.

"Anybody need anything?"

"I'll have a tap, Sam."

"So, you're all good?" She walked away.

"Whoa, you pissed her off how?" Prez directed the line of questioning.

"I have absolutely no idea what just happened," I said shrugging my shoulders.

"Looks like someone has feelings for you," Bridgette added.

"What, we just met today and yes she is hot but—"

"You better give your Johnson a little time off, Steve," Prez added.

"Great. Anyway, at least the clothes were a nice touch."

139

"Clothes?" Bridgette asked.

"What are you talking about? Clothes?" Prez asked.

"You know, the suits from Armani's."

"You went to Armani's with Mrs. Black?" Prez asked like he'd taken a direct nut shot.

"Cut it out. Oh wait, I get it. Now I see. I'm going to get crushed with a twenty-thousand-dollar clothing bill. Just another game and I got punked. Real funny."

"You're not kidding? She really took you to Armani's and bought you some suits?"

"Yes. Six suits, six shirts, six ties, and three pairs of shoes. The bill was over twenty thousand."

"Shit man, we had nothing to do with that," Prez said shaking his head.

"Over twenty thousand dollars?" Bridgette asked.

"She said… something Sonny did for her back in the day."

Kurt joined us. "What, somebody die?"

"Get this, Kurt. Mrs. B. laid out over twenty G's at Armani's for our young lad," Prez conveyed.

"I guess our new boss must have spent a little extra time in the dressing room?"

"I spent a *lot* of extra time in that dressing room."

"Well then, to the king," Kurt said standing up and pretending to have a drink in his hand.

Everyone at the table stood and shouted, "To the King!"

"The king?" I answered, totally lost.

"Fuc... king," Prez replied.

"All right, but the King and I still need a beer, and so does Kurt."

I pretended like I had a beer and made the toast with an imaginary mug in my hand just as Sam slammed a beer on the table, spilling some on the table and me. She walked away in silence.

"You really know how to make friends and influence people." Prez smirked.

"Something going on between you two, Steve?" Bridgette asked.

"I think she likes our young Centurion," Kurt proclaimed.

Tanya was walking toward our table.

"Hey Kurt, speaking of Centurions."

Kurt turned to find Tanya standing over him. "Hi Kurt, can I talk to you for a minute?"

"Kinda in the middle of something."

"Go ahead, Kurt. It can wait," I said sticking my head in the guillotine.

Prez added, "Yeah, sure brother, we can wait."

Kurt's was pissed and Prez and I were the reason why. Bridgette shrugged her shoulders, leaving Kurt swinging in the wind.

"Please, it's important. It will only take a minute," she said displaying her Ukrainian accent.

Kurt took Tanya's arm. "Sure."

They walked to the back of the bar.

Bridgette looked around the table. "This night is full of surprises."

"Any volunteers here? Somebody want to tell me what the hell is going on with those two?"

"Steve," Bridgette began, "Like I told you, it's a Kurt thing. If he wants to talk about it, he will. Otherwise, let it go."

"I hoped to gain a little insight into their story. And I'm sure it's a really good one."

"It is," Prez continued where Bridgette left off. "But not from anyone at this table. When the time is right, if ever, he'll talk about it. Besides, aren't you going to take what you can out of this and run back to the drunkest state in America?"

"Don't bet on this kid bailing out. And it's Wisconsin, Prez. We just know how to party."

"All right, the young Centurion is showing signs of life."

"I'm considering everything. I'm not going to get ear holed either. That's all."

"Clever football term. I like it," Bridgette said.

A loud explosion outside the Graveyaad shattered the front windows. Instinctively, everyone ducked and put their hands over their heads. Kurt ran up to our table. I paused for a few seconds, making sure the place wasn't on fire. We were joined by other bar patrons, dazed, confused, and looking to exit via the front door. With all body parts accounted for, I wanted to see what happened.

Once outside, I could make out a cab burning in the loading zone, it appeared to be empty.

"An Imperial cab. Woody's gonna come unglued over this," Kurt said, with Tanya on his arm.

We were joined by Bridgette and Prez.

"What the hell happened?" I asked.

"We," Kurt said pointing to Prez and Bridgette standing next to us, "hate most cab drivers and vice-versa, but no one has ever taken it to this level."

Jerry Foster, a five-eleven two-hundred-fifty-pound beer-bellied cab driver, driving for Imperial Cabs, stood behind us and shouted, "What the fuck! You assholes have taken this too far!"

"Jerry, no one I know would ever do something like this. Feel free to go fuck off!"

"Somebody did, Kurt. There's going to be serious payback. You hear me?"

Jerry grabbed Kurt and tried pushing him down. Kurt knocked his hands away and punched him in the stomach just as Jerry took a swing at his face, barely missing. Several patrons watching the cab burn managed to pulled the two apart.

"Jerry, take your Woody bullshit elsewhere. Nobody here did this."

"You better watch your back, Kurt. This ain't over by a long shot!"

Within minutes several Metro squad cars pulled up near the burning cab. Additional sirens sounded in the distance as an officer ran out of his patrol car.

"All of you get back. This thing might blow again. Whoever owns the vehicles parked next to this flaming cab needs to get them out of here!" the Metro officer shouted.

Two more squad cars pulled up and started diverting traffic. There were people leaving the bar as the first of several fire trucks pulled up and started breaking out hoses and gear.

"Steve, let's go inside. Nothing left to see here, just a smoldering lump of Imperial shit. Besides, all this smoke has made me thirsty," Kurt said.

"There's a cab driver limo driver feud on top of everything else? And I was going to find out about this when?"

"You just did. Let's go inside. I'm buying. Oh, and by the way, yesterday morning at five-thirty, Ramone's two passengers were gunned down, mob style, in the back of his limo. Now you know everything. Feel any better?"

*****

Two blocks away in a dark sedan, Woody and his driver Thomas Letterman, tall, muscular, intimidating, with dead brown eyes, were parked behind two cars with a view of the Graveyaad.

"I can't believe I just torched one of your cabs and I get a bonus. You are a really good boss."

"Let's just say you have some exceptional skills that don't show up on a resume or an HR interview. That's why you're here."

"And this plays out how?"

"It's an extended magic trick. You want people to watch your left hand while the right one performs."

"Maybe this will get Sherry a little more motivated to sell," Letterman surmised. "Might drop the price too."

"Baby steps. Always with baby steps."

"What about Sonny's kid?"

"I'm working on it."

"You gonna need me to help persuade him?"

"Not yet. Things are starting to come together. Let's get out of here. I'll be fielding several calls shortly. My cell is elsewhere, because of course, I'm not here."

"Where to, boss?"

"Take me to the Adams' house. My cell is growing lonely."

*****

Kurt and I walked into the chaos that used to be the Graveyaad. There was not a lot of damage, just a lot of broken glass, flipped over tables, and chairs. Sam sat on a barstool. A white towel covered with some blood rested against her right ear. Sherry and the rest of her staff were cleaning up the remnants of the cab explosion.

I walked over to Sam. "You alright? You need anything?"

"A piece of glass caught the side of my head."

"Let me take a look at it."

"You're also a doctor. Impressive."

I examined her head. Her cut looked like it would need a couple of staples.

"That cut needs medical attention, Sam."

"Really? That bad?"

"Way too pretty of a head not to get it attended to."

"Damn it." Sam glanced at the blood on the white cloth towel.

"If you can tell me where the nearest emergency room is, I'll drive you there."

"A limo ride, some explosions, so this is how you lure a women out on first date? Very elaborate scheme. I'll tell my mom you're taking me to the emergency room."

"You ought to see the second date schematics."

Kurt and Tanya came over to the bar.

"Steve, this is Tanya."

"I would have torched that cab sooner had I known how to get an intro. Very nice to meet you, Tanya."

"Steve, I'm sorry to hear about the circumstances that brought you to Las Vegas."

"Thanks Tanya. Sam and I are about to take a ride to the emergency room." I pointed to her ear. "Nasty cut."

Sherry joined our little group.

"That cut stop bleeding yet, honey?"

"Yeah. Steve has offered to run me over to the ER."

"Thanks, Steve. That would be helpful. Still plenty of damage assessment to do here."

Sherry noticed Knuckles sitting at his table. She turned toward him.

"What, you waiting for a free round?"

"Nope. Waiting to take care of my bill. I always square up."

Sam grabbed my arm. "Let's go out the back way. Less commotion."

"I'll see you later, Kurt. Tanya, nice to meet you."

Sherry joined Sam and me as we walked toward the back door. Buster met us at the kitchen entrance, limping.

"Never fails. Every time I tinker with a new recipe, something always goes wrong."

145

"Maybe a little less nitro in the pot," Sherry suggested.

"There you go, always making fun of me."

"Really Buster, I'm the only person in Vegas that would hire an old crotch rocket like you. Your last job, guarding Abe Lincoln, how'd that work out for you?"

Chapter 12

I took Sam to the ER. Two hours she was patched up and we were parked in front of her condo.

"Limo ride to the ER and home. Only in Vegas."

"YLL. We aim to please."

"Seriously, any idea what you're going to do? I know it's been a little overwhelming since you stepped off the plane."

"Yeah, I do. I want to be an ER doctor."

Samantha double pumped and lightly punched me in the arm.

"Really, what are you going to do?"

"I'm glad you're okay. I'll see you tomorrow night at the bar, that is, if you're going to work. Or are you claiming workman's comp on your mother?"

"I'll be there. I'm from N'awlins, a little blood develops character."

I stuck out my hand as she curtsied, kissed my hand, and walked into her condo foyer. She looked back at me with a warm smile. I waved and sat back in the limo, looked around, and realized I had no idea where the hell I was. I set the coordinates on my new GPS and headed home.

After a twenty-five-minute ride, I pulled into the circular driveway. Even at night, the neighborhood looked amazing. The words 'my house' still hard to comprehend. The events of last night still burning in my head gave me an idea. I went inside, got ready for bed, and called Bill.

After six rings, he answered.

"This better be good."

"Wake up."

"I answered, didn't I?"

"Sorry for the early bird call, but I have an idea."

"Really? It couldn't wait a couple of more hours? I'm exhausted."

"Wake up Russ and put him on speaker. I want you both to hear this."

"Dude, he's got a little hottie in his love castle. He's not going to get up again."

"Funny, Bill. Wake him. I don't care if he's doing Lady Gaga. Bang on his door and wake him up."

"This will be fun."

With the speaker phone on, Bill walked down the hallway and started to pound on Russ's door.

"Hey, get your ass out of bed. It's important! It's Steve! Hey, wake up!"

"Jesus Christ, it's eight fifteen. Hold on," a muffled voice answered through the door.

Russ opened the door slightly.

"I have company bro. Can't this wait a couple of hours?"

"Where'd you find her and how much did it set you back? You usually have porn on and beating your dick like it owes you money."

"Yeah, I like your sister's lesbian gangbang videos."

"Anyway, you're on speaker. Steve has something important to say."

"Steve, can you hear me?"

"Yes."

"Fuck off!"

Russ slammed the door shut.

"He just slammed—"

"Yeah. I heard. Get him back on."

Bill started pounding on the door again.

"Shut the fuck up. I'm trying to sleep!"

"Who was that?"

"Brother Tim."

Bill waking up a bit and becoming more irritable answered, "Climb back into that third world outhouse of a room and knock out your wet dream."

I could hear the door slamming shut.

Bill pounded on Russ's door even harder. "God dammit. Get out here!"

Russ begrudgingly walked out of his room into the hallway and shut the door behind him. The two walked back to Bill's room.

"Somebody strangle an Aardvark in here?" I heard Russ say to Bill.

"Actually no, I just did your mother."

"Russ, can you hear me?" I asked.

"The whole house can hear you."

"Well then, how are you doing?"

"Enjoying the shrinkage you've perpetuated on my dick."

"Make sure the door is shut so no one else can hear this."

I calmly revealed my epiphany to Russ and Bill.

Chapter 13

Steve's House Las Vegas

It was around five-thirty in the afternoon. I had already dragged myself out of bed at three, thrown on my shorts, and shoved some cash and keys into my pockets in case I needed to drive myself to the store. I sat down, flipped the remote, and stopped on the local news, getting my head on straight and psyching myself up for another limo adventure. Of course, I would actually have to show up to work for this adventure to begin.

My doorbell rang. Surprised, I tossed the remote on the couch and curiously walked to see who was there. I opened it. I was ecstatic to see George Sharpe at my front door in Vegas and out of Lakeside. He had the biggest grin I'd ever seen plastered across his face.

He joyfully shouted, "Can anyone get a limo around here!"

"You made it!"

George walked in, dressed to the nines in his business suit and rolling a suitcase behind him. We hugged in the entryway and I slammed the door shut. To my surprise the doorbell rang again. George gave me this strange look and pointed his finger towards the front door. I reluctantly opened it a second time. I must have looked like a guy who just received a prostate exam from a circus clown when I saw who stood there.

"Mary?!"

She looked stunning, dressed in a white and green button down blouse, short black skirt and black Gucci two-inch sandals, with fringed leather hanging down from the top of the straps. Her soft red lipstick matched her fingers and toes.

150

"Well, after Bill and Russ saw George this morning and told him about your idea, George came into my office and immediately asked for his release. And as you well know, I have strict orders to call Barbra should he ever ask."

"You mean you called Satan's concubine?"

George covered his mouth trying to hold back a laugh.

"Yes, I did."

"Go on."

"Well, she really couldn't force him to stay. However, she stipulated I accompany George while on his visit to Vegas, her fly on the wall, with the licensed drug dispensary. And George, in his good-natured state, agreed."

"What a cunt. Sorry, George. I mean, she's Mother Teresa incarnated, or should it be, incarcerated?"

"Unfortunately, she's still my sister, Steve," George said, yawning.

Mary leaned in close to me. "I gave him some extra Xanax after we landed to help him relax. Better show him to his room before he drops to the floor, which by the way is very lovely."

"George, leave the bag. I'll roll it in for you. Let me show you to your room."

I took his arm and we did a double-time escort.

"You have your own bathroom over here." I pointed to the door. "The closet is here and the kitchen is back there. Let me help you with your jacket." I threw it on the bedside bench. "Time for you to do some of that eyelid research you're so famous for."

I helped him take off his shoes, grabbed him by the legs, and rolled him on the bed.

"Thanks, Ss. . ."

He went lights out.

I turned around to give Mary the tour culminating with a stroll into her bedroom. However, Mary had slipped out of her clothes, wearing only her sandals. Her hands were neatly tucked behind her back, her head tilted to one side. She seductively glided directly in front of me.

"Ah, George?"

"As you can see, preoccupied."

I knew exactly what to do. I walked over to the nightstand and picked up the Bluetooth remote for this room. Mary's eroticism was electrified whenever I played the club remix "Kissed By Nature", by Eliane Elias. I synched my iPhone to the Bluetooth, opened my after-midnight playlist, and let the music play.

I walked over to the leather upholstered bench at the foot of the bed. She came up to me and gave me a gentle slow kiss, guiding me backwards until she had me next to the bench. She pulled off my tee and undid my belt, kissing my stomach as she worked my shorts and boxers towards the floor. I grabbed her hair, softly running my fingers through it. She pushed me on the bench, directly on top of George's jacket, removed my clothes, and then like an exotic ballerina worked her way onto my lap, exposing her backside to me.

The dresser mirror sat directly in front of us and watching Mary from all sides drove me wild. Mary pulled me off the bench and onto the carpet.

"You sure about George?"

"A Packer-Cowboy scrimmage on his chest couldn't wake him up."

"Remind me never to piss you off."

It was hot, exotic, impulsive and extremely weird doing Mary in a bedroom where George was sleeping almost in an induced coma. But to be honest, a legion of Roman soldiers couldn't have dragged me out of that room.

The house air made the room cool, but we were both dripping sweat when we walked out of George's room.

"Shouldn't you see if he's breathing?"

"As always, you're just too cute. C'mon, show me my room."

I would have bet everything I owned, Mary would not have been my first conquest in this house.

I showed Mary one of the guest rooms and retreated to my shower, beginning the process of getting ready for work.

Mary met me at the door and laid a long wet one on me. I gave her two hundred dollars, the keys to the SUV, and told her about a nearby store.

"Fill up the fridge, anything you need, and don't forget about George."

She refused my money, pushing my hand toward my pocket but she did grab the SUV keys and said, "See you later, baby. Be safe out there," she added laying another soft kiss on my lips.

What an amazing woman.

*****

Woody's Private Warehouse
6:40 PM

Woody wore his dress cowboy hat, plaid boxers, and black knee-high socks. Two young runaways, one male, seventeen, and a female, sixteen, were sitting together in an Italian leather chair in their underwear.

"Your dinner the best ever?" Woody asked.

"Yes mister Woody," they both less than enthusiastically answered.

"I can't hear you."

"Yes, Mister Woody!"

"I'm so glad to hear that. Are you ready to play a little game?"

The male took the lead. "What game would that be mister Woody?"

"It's the whatever-the-fuck-I-want-to-play game."

Fear began to overwhelm the young runaways and they both nodded.

"It's called the limo game. Ever play it?"

They both shook their heads, not sure what to expect.

"You." Woody pointed to the male. "You're the limo. And blondie and I are your passengers. Sounds like fun, doesn't it?"

They both got out of the chair as the male answered in an unnerved, "Okay."

Woody grabbed the girl and put his arm around her, squeezing her tight.

"Baby, this is like no game you've ever played before. Boy, see that nice bearskin rug over there?"

"Yes sir."

"Go over there and get down on all fours. Remember, you're the limo. Come on sweetie, our limo awaits."

One of Woody's men came running into the room with a neck harness and a small flexible steering wheel attached. The boy on the rug looked up at Woody's man as he put the harness around his neck, letting the steering wheel dangle.

"Don't move. You're parked. If you move, the steering wheel will swing side to side, understand?" Woody's man emphasized.

The boy tightly nodded.

Two more of Woody's men entered the room. They were carrying several folded-up murals of the Vegas Strip. They opened them and placed them in a three-quarter circle along the rug's borders, creating a mini Vegas Strip. The pieces were five feet high. His men took a thirty-foot extension cord, unraveled it, and plugged it in. As they exited the room, one of his men stopped to dim the lights, a shade above total darkness. Woody guided the girl to his desk where he picked up a remote.

"Limo time baby."

He placed his hands on her butt cheeks and guided her into his Vegas Strip recreation, next to the boy on his knees.

Lying beside the rug was a four-foot-long by three-foot-wide tan piece of leather which Woody carefully picked up and placed on the boy's back.

"Nothing but the best for my girl. We're riding in style. Go ahead get in."

She looked at him strangely and carefully sat on the boys back.

"No, no, no, no, you're facing the wrong way. Turn around, I want to see your face."

She got off and back on with her legs just inside the boy's arms. Woody reached over the boy and properly rotated the steering wheel directly under his chin.

"Take this. You're the chauffeur, and you need a steering wheel to turn, moron."

With his left hand on the ground and the wheel in his right the weight of his female passenger almost doubled.

"What an excellent chauffeur we have this evening. Don't you agree baby?"

"The best, Woody."

Woody gently sat on the boys back, a few inches from his hips, displacing most of the weight on his legs. Woody gradually released his weight onto the boys back, his smile growing more sadistic with every pound of pressure he put on. He knew the boy would struggle and every pound of weight would cause him excess pain.

"Hey chauffeur, drive us to the Luxor."

The boy looked at the mock Strip, recognized the Luxor, and tried to crawl towards it.

"You hear that crunching sound?" Woody asked.

"Yes, what is it?"

"That's the plastic I keep under the rug so it doesn't get dirty."

The boy completely exhausted from only crawling seven feet stopped next to the Luxor.

"We're here, Mr. Woody." The boy gasped for air as he put both hands on the rug.

"Sweetie, look at that bright light atop the Luxor."

Woody hit a button on the remote and all the lights on his strip arena lit up, including one that reflected off the top of the room emanating from the Luxor.

"So cool." The girl nervously looking back and forth at all the casino lights flashing in Woody's Vegas arena, the tension making her voice squeak.

"Beautiful, isn't it?" Woody announced, raising his arms like an evangelist about to connect with Jesus himself.

Woody tossed the remote and reached over and took her arms into his and softly kissed her right hand.

"Have you ever made love in a limo… on the strip?"

She knew Woody's kindness would eventually lead to some sort of payback. At sixteen, she had turned hundreds of tricks to stay alive on the streets. The food, drugs, and day-to-day living arrangements all measured in sexual favors, and this moment was no different.

"Why no, I haven't Woody," she innocently lied.

"Get ready for a real treat."

Woody slid up the back of his male chauffeur to get close to his conquest. He reached around her back and unsnapped her bra, revealing cute little perky breasts. She turned her head away. Whatever Woody wanted she would do, part of her daily survival game. The boy remained on all fours, looking down at the rug, not wanting to see what was about to unfold. He had been fed, given temporary shelter and drugs of the highest quality.

She got off the boy's back and slipped her pink underwear off and kicked them to the side. She started to lay on the rug next to where Woody sat on the boy's back.

"What do you think you're doing?!" Woody shot up, dropped his underwear, and grabbed the girl by the hair.

"This is my game; we are going to fuck in the back of the limo!"

The boy started to get up.

"Stay down where you belong, boy!"

He quickly assumed his previous position. Woody dropped the girl on top of the boy, straddled the boy while grabbing the girl's ankles. The boy fought to keep from collapsing onto the rug. Woody, intensely aroused, pulled the girl into him, penetrating her and gyrating wildly on the boy's back.

"Fuck me bitch, fuck me!" He yelled while slapping her several times across the face.

The girl fearful of her life forced an exotic smile and erotically chanted, "Give it to me, baby."

Woody was wild eyed and out of control. He drove himself so hard into her that the boy's arms collapsed sending Woody and the girl over the boy's head and onto the rug. The boy lay quietly still while Woody screamed as he came almost simultaneously with the boy's collapse. The girl's legs were rolled up past her ears, her toes touching the rug. Woody's weight was too much for her to bear; a loud unceremonious crack could be heard as the girl's neck snapped and she lay awkwardly lifeless. The boy tried to move, but Woody pulled a knife from his ankle and rolled over on top of the boy's back.

"You suck as a limo driver. You crashed and killed one of your passengers."

Woody grabbed his hair, pulled his head back to the point of breaking, and slit his throat. Blood gushed everywhere.

"Amazing, unbelievably great!" Woody euphorically howled as he looked over at the carnage he created while triumphantly standing over the dead teenagers. He managed to pull his underwear up.

"Drivers without proper training cause way too many accidents in Vegas, he said while admiring the carnage."

His three men came running back into the room, guns drawn.

Woody looked up at his hidden camera and smiled.

"This will bring a small fortune on the black market. Boys, you know what to do. Use that spot near Nelson. It's been dug, ready for some occupants."

The trio left and went into clean-up mode.

"Silly girl, the plastic is for the floor, not the rug."

Woody picked up the girl's pink undies, took a long sniff, and proceeded to clean the blade of his knife.

*****

Chapter 14

I wandered into the office around seven. Candice sat at her desk assigning runs for the evening. Several drivers were in the lounge drinking coffee, shooting the bull. I wondered what crazy ride I would be handling tonight. I walked up to Candice and gave her the hundred from last night.

"That's from Mrs. Black."

"Uh, thanks."

I left Candice and went straight to Dino's office.

"Hey Dino." I tapped on the door and walked in.

"You had quite a first night, Steve," Dino commented.

"I certainly did. Although, I'm hoping tonight will be a little more on the narcoleptic side. But, I'm ready for whatever."

"Good, we cleaned out some of Sonny's things, boxed them up for you, and put them away. You can go through them at your convenience. Sonny's office is your office. Go in. Check it out."

"Thanks, Dino. And tomorrow at eleven I'd like to have a meeting with all the members of YLL. I have an announcement that will affect everyone."

"An announcement?"

"I'm going to make a few changes around here, make sure Candice gets the word out, so all hands on deck. And without trying to be an overwhelming dick, that includes you and Tony. Thanks, Dino. Oh, and make sure Tony delves into that double murder in the back of Ramone's limo. I want to tidy up any loose ends. It's bad for business. And I want to be in the loop on everything from now on. No more secrets."

You want to talk about priceless looks, this one was Oscar worthy. I walked out of his office and into mine, looked around and went back into Dino's office. He was on the phone and paused when he saw me again, raising his eyebrows.

"Sorry, Dino. One more thing. I'm going to need another desk besides the one that's currently in my office. Thanks."

Dino was bitchslapped stunned when I walked out the second time. I continued on to Candice's desk and gave her the all hands on deck order, just in case Dino had a stroke between now and eleven tomorrow morning.

"Okay, Steve," she barely got out.

"What do you have for me tonight?"

"Golden Nugget, downtown. You can pick them up at the valet on Casino Center Drive. Punch your GPS to find it. It's not until eight-thirty, so you've got time. And I typed up a little Hoover Dam speech, the idiot's guide. No offense. They want to see the dam at night. Just type that into your GPS after you pick them up."

"Thanks, Candice. How long will I be out?"

"Four hours tops."

I left Candice and sat back in my limo.

I called Goldhabber on his cell. "Steve, what a pleasant surprise. What can I do you for you?"

"There's a meeting at eleven tomorrow morning. I need you to bring all of the paperwork associated with Sonny and YLL."

"I'm sorry, but I'll have to pass. I have appointments until after three."

"If you're not at my office by ten forty-five, I'm going to have Tony come to your office and drag you out by your feet. The choice is yours."

"I'll see you tomorrow morning, Steve."

"Ten forty-five. Don't be late."

I arrived at the Nugget at eight-fifteen and waited outside the rear passenger's door. I mentioned to the doorman that I represented YLL and would be picking up the Oswald's.

They came out five minutes early and I introduced myself and my company. They gave me a brief description of themselves and where they wanted to go. Mrs. Oswald was a large attractive woman, blonde hair, fake eyelashes, strikingly long nails, humongous breasts, struggling to remain tucked inside her patterned white and red sun dress, garnished with a diamond necklace around her neck, and designer flip flops intended to show off her French pedicure.

Mr. Oswald was short and thin wearing a summer white and blue patterned dress shirt, exposing his Tag-Hauer watch which he wore on his right wrist. Maybe he was left handed like me. He had on black dress shorts and designer sneakers. Normally attired patrons, I assumed, for a 100-degree summer night in Vegas.

I merged onto the ninety five south at Las Vegas Boulevard and proceeded towards Boulder City and the dam. Light traffic made the time pass quickly. The scenery was new to me also, and I enjoyed it as much as the Oswalds, who were reveling in each other's company in the back seat. The divider remained down and the three of us could easily see each other, their intention perfectly clear: they wanted me to watch them. Out of courtesy I tried not to gaze back at them. However, temptation kept getting the better of me.

We arrived at the Nevada side of the dam. The Oswalds regathered themselves. I read them the well-orchestrated speech for dummies and in return they performed all the grateful courtesy nods, Oh's and ah's. I opened the door for them and they wandered around for about fifteen minutes and then returned. I dutifully waited at the back limo door the entire time.

"Take us across the dam," Mr. Oswald politely asked as the two of them slid back inside as I closed their door.

I drove them across to the Arizona side of the dam and parked. I ran back to the door and opened it. They climbed out, walked around for around ten minutes and then came back to the limo.

"Pretty at night, isn't it?" I asked while standing rigid beside the back limo door.

"It is beautiful," Mrs. Oswald replied.

Mr. Oswald looked bored as I opened the door and let them back in.

"Where to now?"

"Do you know where Nelson, Nevada is? It's fairly close I heard," Mr. Oswald asked.

"I'll just punch it into my GPS and we will be on our way."

"Thank you," Mrs. Oswald quietly replied.

It took me about thirty minutes to make the left off Highway ninety five south onto the one sixty five to Nelson. With the soft blue mood lights on and glancing back through my rearview mirror, I could see the Oswalds were becoming less inhibited as their evening wear disappeared somewhere in the back of the limo. They seemed to be putting on an amateur display for me. I kept waiting, almost praying for the rear divider to go up, but in all likelihood, that wasn't about to happen.

A minute later a braless Mrs. Oswald slid up to the divider. I thought her breasts were going to come through and knock me out of the front seat. She glanced down at her breasts and then back up at me.

She asked in a soft and sexy voice, "Steve, can you find a nice quiet turnoff?"

"I'll look for one," I said, finding it impossible not to look at her breasts through the rearview mirror.

"Thank you."

She gracefully, if there is such a term for this situation, worked her way to the back where her husband secured his arousal watching me eyeball his wife. I was about to poke my eyes out and jump out of the limo when I finally found a nice turnoff for them.

"I found you a spot," I shouted out completely ignoring the intercom.

I parked, leaving the limo running, allowing the continual pumping of cool air into the back. I hurriedly stepped out trying to give the Oswalds their privacy, which apparently was not their intended goal. The driver's side rear window rolled down and Mrs. Oswald managed to slip her head partially out. She must have been on all fours.

The exhibition wasn't over. Mrs. Oswald, contortedly, turned her head toward me under the semi dark neon sky.

"My husband wants you to join us," she said gasping for air while her head violently moved in and out of the window.

"Steve, it, will, be, fun," her husband shouted from behind her.

This can't be the way Vegas functions. There can't be this many crazy people confined to one area. I used my twenty four hours of expertise limo training and came up with a brilliant plan.

I walked up to the window, slightly leaning in, forcing Mrs. Oswald to retreat inside the limo. I responded with what I thought might be the company line.

"As much as I would like to, company policy forbids me from participating in any sexual activity inside or outside the limo. But thank you very much for asking."

"We're friends of Mrs. Black. She said you would agree to join us."

"Friends of Mrs. Black?"

So this is how I'm going to have to reciprocate for the gifts she showered on me. The words dumbfuck and moron flashed through my mind.

"I have an idea. Give me your phone and I will film the two of you. Your own special Vegas home movie… it will be scintillating."

163

I threw a blind dart, because there was no way I'd be dropping my pants and joining those two. After a pause, Mrs. Oswald turned around and sat in the rear seat, the two of them discreetly discussing my proposition.

Mrs. Oswald leaned out and handed me her cell phone.

"Please, come in and join us, Mr. producer."

She scooted over and I joined them in the back. I moved over to a side seat and turned the camera function on to movie, then put the phone on the seat and stared at them. Mister Oswald caught on immediately. He reached into his shorts lying in the back seat, went into his front pocket and pulled out a roll of bills. He started the counting with a one-hundred-dollar bill and looked at me. I looked back at him.

"A real entrepreneur this one. Mrs. B was right about him."

He reeled off three more and I nodded. Four hundred for my movie making skills sounded right. Mr. O's dick remained hard during our transaction, not that I was looking in that area, but it was difficult not to notice. He must have been on Mexican Porn Cialis Thirty's. If it doesn't stay hard for four hours demand a refund.

Anyway, they went at it for about six minutes with the two of them showing off for the camera and making all the expected porn grunts and gyrations. My eyes were almost bleeding from the amateur display.

When it sounded like Mr. O was going to blow his load I shouted, "Come on her tits," inspired by the movie "Boogie Nights".

He took my directions flawlessly and finished all over her. She must have seen her share of porn as she rubbed his passion all over her breasts.

I sent myself a copy for protection reasons, and deleted the email. They started getting dressed.

"Back to the hotel?"

I stepped out of the limo and noticed a vehicle coming up the hill. I guess this place was a very popular place for late night activity. I watched the Jeep until it passed us, not sure or caring whether they saw the limo or not.

*****

"See that limo parked over there?" Woody's man asked the other.

"Yeah, we're further up. They can't see shit from there. Like Woody said, the hole's dug, and there's plenty of room for these two kids."

*****

I dropped the Oswalds back at the Nugget where Mr. Oswald reeled off another six hundred dollars for the use of the limo and my services.

I called in to Candice, asked if anyone else would require my services tonight. Her reply was that it was a slow evening and everything was covered so adios amigo. I drove back to the house enjoying the hell out of the Vegas neon scenery. I decided to skip the Graveyaad, especially after last night's chaos, and prepare for tomorrow's meeting, one I hoped would rock YLL. Besides, I wasn't overly anxious to run into Sam tonight.

The excitement of driving my own limo back to my house had a calming effect on me. I pulled into the driveway and saw my SUV parked in the semi-circular drive.

I unlocked the door, finding the house to be rather still. George was probably out from one of Mary's cocktails and Mary must be sleeping from the flight in and my cocktail.

Walking through the kitchen I saw a note on the table.

Dinner is in the fridge, see you in the morning. XOX, Mary

Nice. I could get used to this lifestyle, for a little while anyway.

I opened the fridge and smiled when I saw Mary had made me her Texas-style Lasagna. I scooped it up, along with a Dos Equis, and tossed the chow in the microwave. When the timer rang, I pulled it out, went into the utensil drawer, found a fork and took my late night dinner out to the pool. The hot air was noticeable, but not uncomfortable. A large casino marquee lit up most of the neighborhood. I picked up the remote for the Bluetooth and turned it on, synching it with my iPhone to a nice chillaxing tune "Night Life" by Ray Price, a 1963 classic my mother used to play.

My mind took off at a million miles an hour. So much had happened in such a short amount of time. However, for some insane reason, I didn't feel out of my element.

My alone time crashed and burned when Mary walked out toward me wearing her Texas Longhorns belly shirt, black see-through panties, and flip-flops.

"How's my lasagna, Steve?"

"My eyes aren't hemorrhaging yet. Spicy Texas lasagna. Got to love it."

I rose and pulled a chair next to mine.

"Have a seat."

Mary sat down and slightly moved it so the chair arms were touching. She put her head on my shoulder.

"There are some things you should know about me."

I finished chewing a mouthful of lasagna and answered her. "Like what?"

"I've been married before."

"Okay, I thought so. Someone as pretty as you had to be scooped up at least once."

"I know this crosses our imaginary boundary lines, but I really missed you."

"I missed you too. It's nice to have you here. While we're crossing boundary lines, do you have any little Mary's running around?"

"God no. That's not where I'm going with this."

"Then what's on your hot Texas mind?"

"When my second husband died, well, he left me a substantial sum of money and a free and clear house, which I sold."

"We never really talked about this. So, there was more than one Mr. Mary?"

"Stop. Yes."

"So, two?"

"More like four."

"Four husbands? Are the other three still alive?"

"Silly." She rubbed her eyes, "Of course they are. At least, I think they are."

"Your first?" I asked while finishing up her lasagna and putting the plate on the table. She had my complete and undivided attention.

"We met in college. We had all the passion and were going to lasso the world, but he never grew out of the partying lifestyle and that lasso became a noose. I pursued a career, he pursued drugs and alcohol. It fell apart quickly."

"How quickly?"

"Eighteen months."

"Sounds like a prison sentence."

"It was."

"Okay then, what's behind door number three?"

"Good, I'll just use numbers and not names."

"Sure."

"Number three, substantially older than me."

"Define substantially older?"

167

"Forty years, give or take."

"And how long did that last?" I asked as I gulped down the rest of my beer.

"About three years; it was nice while he was still active. He wanted a prenuptial agreement. I told him to take a long hard look at me and threatened to end our relationship."

"So, no prenup?"

"Well yes, but he made it worth my while to marry him without much red tape, so to speak."

"A healthy prenup?"

"Exactly."

"He got what he wanted for about three years and you ended up getting what you wanted."

"Pretty much. He's since remarried and living somewhere in Houston."

"Without being too nosy, and since we're having this conversation, how old is he now?"

"I think eighty-nine."

"You little jail baiter."

"I know, right?"

"What about Mr. Mary number four?"

"I met him on an all-inclusive trip to Cancun, Mexico."

"And?"

"Within a year, the flame went out. Turns out he had a thing for college girls and wanted me to be part of some sorority threesomes."

"Perverted, but hot. Did you?"

"Steve, twice. Then I ended our marriage and tossed him out. It put my head in a different space, somewhere I didn't want to be."

"And you've been single for how long?"

"Three years."

"I'm guessing you really don't have to work?"

"I don't, but I do. I, let's just say, I have developed an appetite for the finer things in life, and on my terms. But with you, this, I think I'm falling in love with you."

"Mary." I turned and grabbed her hands, "We've talked before, but never like this . . . I didn't know that. It was the two of us enjoying each other's company. Both of us playing it safe, no strings attached. The way I thought you wanted it."

"Steve, I'm twenty years older than you, well, thirteen to be exact, I'm thirty-seven."

"You told me you were forty-five."

"I know. I thought that would deter you from pursuing me other than for, what we have, a sort of friends-with-benefits relationship."

"Age never crossed my mind. You are hot, sexy, fun. You know. You."

"I guess what we did, I did . . . well, I'm rambling on like a high school senior who got dumped on prom night."

"Hey, you're the hottest forty, thirty- something in America. You're amazing."

"But you're not in love with me?"

"I never really thought about it, Mary. We just always happened. Not a lot of conversation, just a lot of us. Today is the first time we even spent half a day together outside of work."

"I have a confession to make and I'm not proud of it, Steve."

"I thought that's what you were doing?"

"Julie."

"Julie?"

"Monday night, your sendoff."

"Oh, that Julie. What about her?"

"I know her."

"What do you mean, you know her? From where?"

"After the party ended, your room."

"You mean the rose and your card."

"I mean Julie, she, you, me, us, I left before you woke up."

"What are you saying?"

"I've been with her before."

"In a relationship?"

"No."

"How long have you known Julie? And why couldn't I remember anything from Monday night? I thought I had a blackout; it had me freaking out."

"Julie has been, well, I'll just say it, black- mailing me for three years."

"What?"

"Yes, number four's fascination with college girls and me?"

"Shit. Julie was one of the girls?"

"She was also sixteen at the time and lied to my husband."

"Is she extorting money out of him also?"

"I don't know. He vanished after the divorce and I haven't heard a word from him since. It's like he dropped off the face of the earth right after she threatened to have my nursing license revoked and have me arrested for having sex with a minor. That almost destroyed me."

"That little bitch, and I thought she was nice."

"She had me drug you. I mean, I got her the drug. She drugged you."

"Julie made you drug me. Why?"

"I don't know. Maybe so you wouldn't remember what happened. But when someone's blackmailing you and they tell you to do something… you pretty much do it."

"That makes no sense."

"I know."

"That psycho bitch. Is that the real reason you came out here with George, to get away from her?"

"Partly, yes and no. She likes to keep an eye on me, guarantee her payday each month."

"There has to be someone you can call to put an end to this."

"I don't know what to do… I have nowhere to turn; she has me boxed in."

"There has to be some way out."

"If there is, I haven't found it."

Her vulnerability made me want her even more and within minutes our clothes were off and we were working our way into the heated pool. The eroticism with Mary never stopped. She was like an exotic drug.

Chapter 15

1:32 AM

*****

Goldhabber nervously sat in the back parking lot of In-N-Out Burger on South Industrial Road. It used to be the main parking lot but corporate decided to build a new one just to the south and use the old building as a warehouse. Goldhabber fixated on a dumpster diver perfecting his craft as a black Town Car pulled alongside him. Two large men squeezed out.

"I'm going to need your Escalade keys," the man who exited the passenger side ordered. "He's going to follow us, sort of. Can't leave a vehicle here for too long without drawing attention."

The driver glanced over at the dumpster, "Friend of yours?" He thumbed at the homeless guy, contorting in all directions looking for a tasty morsel.

"What do you mean, sort of?"

"Can't have the car exactly follow us, in case your cars being scoped out or bugged. A lot of unsavory malcontents getting involved in this Sonny business. Trust is becoming a main topic of discussion amongst the powers-that-be."

Goldhabber slid into the back and the two cars drove off, making the left on Dean Martin and turning west on Tropicana. Goldhabber's Escalade quickly turned off Tropicana and headed south on Valley View. The drive lasted a little over twenty minutes culminating with a minimal security guard check at Red Rock Country Club Estates.

The car entered a circular drive blocked by an electric gate, which opened as soon as the car entered the driveway.

A large five-car garage with only two vehicles inside opened and the driver found a spot. The garage doors quickly closed.

Two armed men escorted Goldhabber into the kitchen from the garage.

"Norman, glad you could get here and on such short notice," Mr. Johnson happily proclaimed.

Johnson had a medium build, around five-foot-ten, weighing around one-hundred-eighty pounds, dark hair, in his mid-forties, dressed in a black buttoned-down shirt, highlighted by the Rolex on his left wrist, beige Khakis shorts and Nike slides. He looked like money.

"I always try to make my clients happy, Mr. Johnson," Goldhabber answered in a less than enthusiastic tone.

"Boys, stay here. I think Goldhabber doesn't bare any ill will toward any of our guests. Isn't that right Norman?"

"Of course not, Mr. Johnson."

Mr. Johnson put his arm around Goldhabber and escorted him into his elegant office. He opened the door. Goldhabber wasn't expecting the three other men sitting in the room.

"I think you know everyone, Norman."

Norman's lower lip had a miniature stroke when he saw the participants seated in the office.

Sheriff Dean Thomas, tall, thinning hair, sporting the beginning of a beer belly, dressed in a blue blazer, country western shirt, blue jeans and polished brown cowboy boots, Barry Schuster, owner of Silver Express Limos, Hans Stephanner, owner of Comstock Transportation and making it four, the host of tonight's meeting, William Johnson, owner of Desert West Resorts.

"The four of us have some questions for you, Norman."

"Why certainly, fire away." Sweat was starting to form on his brow.

Norman knew these people didn't invite you to their homes for a social visit. To get them all in the same room at the same time meant something serious was about to go down.

"What's Woody up to?" Barry asked.

"You know, trying to do what the four of you are trying to do—buy YLL."

"What does he know about our effort to purchase YLL?" Sheriff Thomas leaned forward in his chair.

"Nothing, nothing at all. He thinks he's the only one with an iron in the fire. Really. He thinks he's close to a deal. But the kid is not as stupid as Woody anticipated."

"Apparently not afraid of him either. Do you know why?" Hans remained reclined in his chair, an expressionless look on his face.

"A big set of cojones on him. But that's only my opinion."

"And how did you arrive at such a conclusion?" Hans asked.

"He got angry with me in Wisconsin and threw my laptop against the wall. And then gave me this pathetic apology."

"He might be your son, Hans," Mr. Johnson quipped.

"When are you going to give him our offer, Norman?" Barry asked.

"Tomorrow morning at the Barn. He's called a meeting for all YLL employees, including Dino and Tony."

"And they're going to show?" Hans asked now extremely interested in Steve's motives.

"He owns seventy five percent of the company, who's going to argue with him?"

Hans stood up and walked over to Goldhabber.

"And you were going to tell us this when?"

Hans put his hand on Goldhabber's throat and started driving him into the wall.

174

"Hans, stop! This won't get us what we want." Sheriff Thomas said as he jumped out of his seat.

Both of Mr. Johnson's men rushed through the door, guns drawn when they heard the commotion. Hans released Goldhabber, pushing him against the wall while simultaneously drawing his Walther PPQ 45. In an instant he got off two rounds, fatal head shots dropping both of Johnson's men. They were dead before they hit the marble tiled floor. Hans reeled, turned the gun on the sheriff, and took a step back rolling the smoking barrel side to side, making sure he had everyone's attention.

"Hans, Hans, it's me. Barry. Stop," Barry begged with both hands up in the air.

Everyone remained motionless. No one wanted to catch the next bullet during Hans's psychotic shooting spree.

"Just got a little spooked. That's all," Hans calmly said as he put his Walther back in its shoulder harness. "Where were we now?"

Sheriff Thomas tried to remain calm as he looked over at Mr. Johnson. "Looks like you're going to need a couple more bodyguards."

Hans smiled and looked over at Goldhabber.

"I'll make a call and get this mess cleaned up," Sheriff Thomas announced. "But not Goldhabber's."

The merriment in the room continued at Goldhabber's expense. He pissed himself.

"Mr. Johnson, I'll send over two of my better ones to replace those target dummies you used. Send me the cleaning bill, Sheriff. I did make a terrible mess of this room."

"Sure, sure, ah, thanks Hans," Mr. Johnson replied.

"We good, Johnson?" the Sheriff asked.

"Ah, yes. Totally good."

"Goldhabber, you have work to do tomorrow, don't you?" Hans said, eyeballing Goldhabber with an even more threatening look.

"Yes, I do Hans, Mr. Stephanner, I me—"

"Norman, Hans is just looking out for all of our interests, aren't you?" Barry added.

"Of course. Look at those two lumps of shit on the floor. I thought they were going to harm you, but look at them now."

Hans took hold of Goldhabber's cheeks with his left hand and guided his head toward the two dead men.

"You see, Goldhabber?"

"I do."

"Good."

Hans released Goldhabber's face and mildly pushed him toward Mr. Johnson. He escorted Goldhabber out of the office and into the garage. Johnson's driver had his hand inside his leather jacket making sure the right people with the right attitude walked into the garage.

"Everything okay, boss?" The driver asked.

"Fine, just a little nonsense in the office. Take him wherever the two of you want to meet up and drop him. And when you get back, make sure to dump Don and Rollo's cars at Buddy's chop shop. They won't be needing their company-funded rides any longer."

"Understood, boss. And does your mouthpiece here need any incentivizing?"

"He's been incentivized, haven't you Mr. Goldhabber?"

"Completely incentivized," he answered nervously, his voice quivering.

"Oh, and put a towel down on the back seat. Goldhabber had a minor accident."

The driver looked between Goldhabber's legs and nodded.

The cars met up at the Denny's on West Tropicana, where Goldhabber exited in record time without looking back at the driver.

"Your keys are in the ignition."

Goldhabber kept walking straight to his Escalade, climbed in, started it up, and squealed out of the parking lot.

"I am so fucked, so fucked!" Goldhabber mumbled as he sobbed and raced down Tropicana towards his home.

His cell phone rang and Goldhabber snapped out of his funk, realized he was speeding, and slowed down. He glanced down at the screen on his Escalade and saw the "No Name" and suspiciously pushed the answer button on his steering wheel.

"Yes."

"You have been a very busy boy, Mr. Goldhabber."

"Who is this? And how did you get my number?"

"Let's just say I'm an interested observer in the goings on at YLL."

"This is who?"

"I didn't say, and as of now, none of your business."

"Fuck off!"

Goldhabber hung up and kept driving.

"More assholes."

The phone rang again, this time with a phone number attached to the call with a two-zero-two area code.

"What!"

"Your meeting with the Four Horseman, as they like to be called, went badly for a couple of Johnson's employees. Right?"

Goldhabber saw a pharmacy on Tropicana and Rainbow and pulled into the empty parking spot, braked and jammed the shifter in park.

"Enough of this shit. Who the hell are you?"

"I'm not the person you want to get ballsy with, understand?"

"It's been a rough night." Goldhabber wiped some of the wetness off around his eyes.

"I'm not your priest or your psychologist… I don't care."

"Then why are you calling me?"

177

Goldhabber stepped out of the Escalade, turned off the handset application to the phone setting, and leaned against the back door.

"You really don't have any idea what you've fallen into, do you?"

"What do you want?"

"I want to save your life. Your son shouldn't have to grow up with a stepdad."

"Stepdad?"

"You're not long on this earth, Norman. Your days are numbered, and I'm afraid I'm the only one who can extend your pathetic existence."

"Who's going to shorten my life?"

"You're already in the mouse trap and the hammer's coming down."

"You have no idea what you're talking about."

"Don't I? Norman, you're a dead man walking. I'm your only way out of this."

"I'm an attorney. I'm not a player."

"You poor dumb son-of-a-bitch. You're carrying water for the hyenas. In a couple of days this is going to come crashing down on you. They've got a hole in the desert reserved, and your name is on it."

The phone went dead. Goldhabber stared down Tropicana Avenue.

"This can't be happening."

Within the last a few hours, two men were murdered in front of him by a psychopath, manipulated by a group of men he could never trust, and he still had to answer to Woody, who is worse than Hans. And out of nowhere some unknown player, perhaps the government dangling a golden parachute, offered him a way out of this disaster. Goldhabber took two steps away from the Escalade and puked.

Woody's burner phone rang.

"Yes."

"Goldhabber is convinced either the CIA, FBI, or some other abbreviated federal organization is monitoring him."

"Good work, Eddy."

"He's in panic mode. Hans's little psychotic episode put our lawyer friend back in our home court."

"That ending was exactly what we needed to get our foot in the door with one of the money men in the Four Horseman alliance."

"I'll continue mind fucking Goldhabber."

"Remember, complete silence."

"You can count on me. Thanks for the bonus, the party limo, and my new job title."

"You're the perfect candidate for operations manager, Eddy."

"Thanks again, Woody."

"We'll talk tomorrow."

The line went dead as Eddy continued walking into the Tropicana hotel lobby. He dialed a room number and a woman answered.

"Hello."

"Tanya, this is Eddy, I'm in the lobby."

"I've got your order waiting in room 455. The girl at the bar with the blue dress and blue and white pumps has your room card. She's expecting you."

"Thanks, Tanya."

"And don't be rude. Leave her a nice tip."

"Sure."

Eddy wondered over to the bar and scanned all the women seated until he found the one Tanya described. He creeped up to her, nudged her arm, and whispered in her ear.

"I'm Eddy and I think you have something I need."

She had red hair and looked sizzling in her blue dress which matched her tinted glasses perfectly.

She swiveled partway in her chair and faced him. She reached into her purse and pulled out a card. She seductively reached into the front pocket of Eddy's pants and placed the card in his pocket leaving her hand there for about five seconds. After watching Eddy squirm, she playfully pulled her hand back.

"Hard for you, wasn't it?"

Eddy liked her playful demeanor and began aggressively pursuing her instead of Tanya's option.

Eddy liked playing the tough guy and put his hand on her inner thigh, methodically working his hand upward.

"You like it a little rough I see," she said casually rolling her tongue across her lower lip.

Eddy lived to be in the moment; he liked and wanted her.

"You have an appointment in room 455, Eddy. Remember?"

He removed his hand from her thigh and moved it to her arm and squeezed it.

"I really like you; I don't care who's in room 455. Why don't *you* join me in room 455?"

The lady in the blue dress reached down and put a vise grip on Eddy's groin. He flinched and bent awkwardly forward.

"Listen Eddy, you've got twenty seconds to get to that elevator. I'm not your girl... understand?" she said compressing her hand even further.

"Uncle. Shit, got it. Let go."

She released her grip and Eddy stepped back.

"Fucking bitch."

He gingerly left the bar area after placing a one-hundred-dollar bill in her hand. He walked toward the elevators.

Charlette watched Eddie disappear in the crowd walking toward the elevator. She loved moonlighting for Tanya, dressing up in elegant outfits, wigs of all lengths and cuts, designer glasses, the disguises protecting her real identity. Besides, she could handle herself with the best of them, men or women.

Being Tanya's front girl paid well and she didn't have to put out on her back. Sherry and Tanya came up with the idea late one morning, a real cash cow for the three of them. Three Vegas female entrepreneurs joining forces in a city with a reputation for pleasing men, for a price.

Chapter 16

Once again, Toby Keith's, "Get Drunk and Be Somebody," woke me up out of a dead sleep. The room darkening blinds made it feel like midnight. I used my iPhone's flashlight to light my way into the bathroom. When I turned the lights on, it felt like my head exploded. I looked at the person in the mirror and came to the realization I was no longer the kid who hopped a jet to Vegas a couple of days ago.

The double-headed shower with dual benches called my name and after a twenty-minute soak I felt ready to take on the day.

I dressed to the smell of bacon and cinnamon rolls, an alluring smell that floated me into the kitchen. Mary was working hard at the stove while George was at the table reading the RJ newspaper, feasting on eggs, bacon, and cinnamon rolls.

"One big happy family having breakfast together," George blurted out when he saw me.

"How are you feeling this morning, George?" I asked looking directly at Mary, wearing a green tee shirt, cutoff blue jean shorts, a skimpy apron and flip-flops.

"I'm doing great, slept like the dead. Mary sure knows how to make a nightcap."

"Without a doubt, George."

"You boys eat up; you have a big day today. Let me pour you both some coffee. It's extra strong. It'll get y'all through your big meetin'."

I enjoyed this much more than I ever thought I would. Playing house with Mary, a hidden fantasy come true. In La Crosse, we had passionate flings but both of us would always retreat within our boundaries. There were never any wake-me-for-breakfast goodnights. In Vegas, it appeared as

182

though the rules were dramatically changing. I might have to make a decision, down the road.

George, under Mary's supervision, made it easy for us to get a small glimpse of what playing house together would be like. But she was sleeping in her room and me in mine. But if Mary said she loved me, would that change all the rules we created? And what about Sam? I really liked her.

After a bathroom pit stop, I started to walk out through the kitchen when I saw Mary leaning up against the kitchen island waiting for me.

"George is in the SUV out front," Mary said.

"Great breakfast, Mary. Our first together."

"Our first Steve, and without being presumptuous, I could get used to this again, I mean with you. I know this was our first night under the same roof, but it was nice waking up knowing you're just a couple of doors down."

"The closest we've been since—"

"Since I took you home from that goofy motel bar on French Island?"

"Yeah, the Ramada."

I kissed her.

"Shit, I've got to go."

Mary smiled at me as George began honking the horn.

"Christ, Mary, how much coffee did he drink?"

10:30 AM

George and I arrived thirty minutes early. The limos and Town Cars in the parking lot were all on the older side but polished and had that new car look in the late morning sunlight. Kiko managed the fleet well.

"Well, George, you ready?"

"For you, I'm ready."

We parked the SUV out back next to my Tundra and the two of us walked in the back entrance. Candice stood next to four additional YLL dispatchers, the graveyard dispatcher, Angela who appeared to be ready to leave, Don, a crusty old Marine, Sara, and Kat the swing dispatcher.

"Candice, I want you to meet your other new boss, George."

"What are you talking about, Steve?"

"George is now part owner of YLL."

"How the hell, what?" The color in her face faded.

"A pleasure to meet you, Candice," George extended his hand towards Candice.

"He bought a twenty-four percent interest."

"Dino's going to shit." She regurgitated with a sly smile while shaking George's hand vigorously.

"That's a healthy handshake, young lady."

"Why thank you… boss."

Candice walked behind her desk and sat down, humorously shaken by the news.

"You alright, Candice?" I asked.

"I'll live. I think."

George and I walked down the hallway to my office.

"George, this is it, my new office and right over there a place for you to take a load off, your desk, today, tomorrow, whenever you come to Vegas."

"I like this, part owner of a limo company, and in Vegas no less. I'm thrilled Steve."

"Jaws, I mean your sister, is going to soil herself when she finds out. You've got to let me be there when you tell her."

"Come on, Steve, she's still my sister. But that barracuda *is* going to crap her drawers when she finds out. Not the trip to Vegas she anticipated."

"Maybe you should sell your house in Onalaska, buy one here. Hey, no state taxes, and besides, your sister would be right in her element with all the bling she harnesses."

"Food for thought, Steve."

184

"George, I still can't believe how fast your lawyers put this together. They had an analysis of the company, the house, and a profitability chart done in five hours."

"Steve, they believe the land this company sits on to be of some value, above and beyond the going real estate estimates. There have been an abundant amount of inquiries done on this property over the last six months. Plus, money makes lawyers wet. You'll find that out once we turn this company into a cash cow."

I'd never really seen George this lucid; he was definitely bringing his "A" game to the table. I enjoyed his command of the situation, his perseverance into the future, and his mental imaging. My gut instincts with George were going to pay big dividends.

Kurt peeked into the office and I invited him in.

"George, this is Kurt Walker, my mentor in the limo business."

"Kurt, meet George Sharp."

They both did a quick scan and shook hands.

"So, Candice tells me I have another new boss?"

"That's correct. We're going to nuclearize this company, take it to new heights, blow the doors off the competition. Hey, no pun intended after the cab incident."

"Funny, Steve. Yeah, you can count me in. This is great to hear after all the garbage that's happened around here in the last several months."

Kurt walked out and I sat down at my desk, noticing a couple of limo contracts for what appeared to be upcoming conventions.

Someone knocked on the door.

"Excuse me. I'm looking for Steve Mueller?"

"And you are?" I asked, staring down at a limo contract.

"Detective Vicki Spicuzza."

I looked up. This sweet calming voice and the word detective didn't add up. But there she stood, all five-foot-five of her, long black hair tied up in a ponytail, wearing a black pinstripe pantsuit, white blouse, packing heat on her right hip and a gold shield on her left.

"I'm Steve Mueller," I awkwardly blurted out, my voice partially cracking like I swallowed a shot of one-fifty-one rum mixed with Louisiana Hot Sauce.

"I'd like to ask you a couple of questions if you don't mind."

If you've ever believed in love at first sight, there comes a moment; the air smells like flowers on a spring day, your bones have little endorphins racing up and down and suddenly you're at peace with the world. Well, Vicki had that effect on me the instant my eyes locked on hers. There have been very few times I've felt awkward in my life; add this moment to the list.

"Sure," came my floundering response.

"Could Mr. Mueller and I have the room to ourselves?"

Like waving a steak at a Pit Bull, she was all business, and my idiotic fantasy disappeared faster than a fart in a hurricane.

George nodded and left the room; she closed the door.

"I have a meeting with all my employees in fifteen minutes, and today of all days, I can't be late."

"I understand, Mr. Mueller," she answered with what I observed to be a miniature double-take glance.

"Please sit down. Call me Steve," I pointed to a chair in front of my desk.

Dino walked in. He appeared to be furious. I assumed selling George twenty-four percent of YLL sent him off a cliff.

"Dino, join us. This question is for both of you. What do you know about the two clients shot in the back of Ramone's limo early yesterday morning?"

"I just learned about it yesterday," I answered.

She strategically paused, trying to read me before she interjected her next thought.

"You don't know who they were?"

"No, just a couple of guys."

"It was a man and a woman."

I stood and looked at Dino.

"The meeting, Steve. We need to start. Everyone is waiting."

"Dino, why didn't you tell me about the shootings in the limo?"

"We thought it best not to concern you with it; you have enough on your plate."

"You don't have any right to determine what you think I need to know or don't. As much as this sucks for you, I'm still the one Sonny gave seventy-five percent of this company to. You think I'm some little piss-ant from Wisconsin incapable of handling adverse information about this train wreck of a limo company? For the record, I'm twenty-four, I've lost both parents, one murdered and another to cancer. I've been on my own the last five years, putting myself through college and working full time. So, the last thing I need is someone pandering to me."

I could feel this strange metamorphosis taking hold. I've always been able to step up my game in big moments, but I never envisioned the correlation between my college education and immediately taking ownership and running a business, especially under these horrific conditions. But I wasn't at all panicked. I should have been with everything crumbling around me, but it somehow felt instinctive and natural. Under all this duress, I somehow knew I was destined to be thrown down this gauntlet. I had this natural ability, a fierce and tenacious voracity to lead.

"I'm sorry, just looking out for you. And in the future, I'll give you both barrels at once," Dino countered.

I'd brought George into an extremely dangerous partnership, and with every passing hour some catastrophe was being perpetrated upon me, trying to derail my hopes of successfully running this company. And to add more fuel to the fire these new developments might be enough to make him back out of our agreement. His sister would inevitably rag on him until his ears were hemorrhaging, and he'd capitulate; I was positively screwed. I did catch the change of expression on Vicki's face, reflecting less of a college grad snot and more of a take-the-bull-by-the-horns person.

Dino, that hard-nosed crusty old redneck, slammed the door on his way out.

"I guess that answered my question," Vicki ceremoniously stated as she walked to the door.

"Wait. I'm sorry. I didn't mean to be such an attack dog," I said.

"Yes, you did. And I think you really set him straight. Impressive for a twenty-four-year-old."

"I'm not trying to be impressive, although I wish I could have made more of an impression on you, in a completely different atmosphere."

"Why Steven, I do believe you're trying to come on to me."

"Pathetic under the circumstances."

"Dream on. Here's my card."

She opened the door and walked out, and so did the air in the room, in a negative way.

I had a meeting to run and I had to come up with a different approach to George's introduction. I raised my right fist, made an explosion sound, and opened my hand. I knew exactly what to say.

Kurt took George to the conference room and all were seated when I walked in. I wasn't sure if anyone had told George about the murder of two passengers. I hoped not and decided I would tell George later, when we were alone, and I could control the environment. I walked to the head of the conference table.

"Thank you all for coming on such short notice."

No one said anything. I noticed the rage in Dino's face and the coolness in Tony's.

Pointing to George I said, "Please stand. George has decided to invest in YLL; he will be a partner in this company."

I waited for the golf-clap applause and rumblings to fade. George did a casual wave and sat down.

"We can't fix everything that went wrong. However, if you plan on staying, we are going to make dramatic changes," I continued.

Edmond Hollingsworth shouted, "What kind of changes?!"

"I'm glad you asked. We're paying off the mortgages, buying new limos, Town Cars, and upgrading the computer system. That includes a state-of-the-art GPS system. We want to know where you are; it will increase security for all drivers."

Everyone clapped. I had their undivided attention. The room was mine to command.

"And for the record, Sonny's house is now *my* house, which means the mortgages are going to be paid down."

More clapping.

"And I will keep all of you informed as these changes unfold."

Everyone stood and clapped, including Dino and Tony.

I raised my hands until the room quieted down. "I'll have an open-door policy, having been in some unique conversations in my past, so feel free to contribute to the growth and success of this company. To all of you, don't ever underestimate me because of my age," I finished by briefly shooting a look at Dino.

More enthusiastic clapping. I felt like I'd just led the La Crosse Eagles in a monster pep rally.

I motioned for Edmond to come over.

"Steve, one hell of a fiery speech. Well done."

189

"Edmond, take care of George today. Take a limo and drive him wherever he wants to go. Can I count on you?"

"I'll clear my schedule immediately. You can depend on me."

Kurt and Ramone came up to me and gave me bro hugs.

"I'm glad you've decided to take this head on, Steve," Kurt said.

"Ditto, Steve," Ramone said.

"Ramone, we're going to have to talk about the shootings in your limo. I need to know what you know."

"I understand. We'll pick a day soon."

"Now, Detective Spicuzza already popped in here today. I'm disappointed you didn't tell me. The way I heard about it—"

"Steve, I'm sorry. You just got here and we all… you know too much to dump on you. Everyone underestimated your commitment."

"Come on, Ramone. Let's go to my office where you can give me the details."

"Kurt picked me up from Metro and knows pretty much everything that went down."

"Kurt, you might as well join us."

The three of us entered my office and Ramone briefed me while Kurt dropped in a couple of small details Ramone skipped or forgot or didn't want me to hear. My guard was now up.

*****

Mary, after cleaning up breakfast and enjoying an episode of "The Price is Right", changed into her two-piece bathing suit, grabbed a towel, Ray-Bans sunglasses, and tanning lotion, and walked out to the pool. The Vegas sun had begun turning up the heat.

She tossed her towel on a nearby table, opened an umbrella, and straddled one of the many chaise lounge chairs, taking in the warm rays. She squeezed a healthy portion of the UV eight coconut butter oil into her hand, rubbed her hands together, and softly polished her skin. She placed the oil on the table, lay back, and closed her eyes.

Mary thought about her soul-baring confessions last night while nervously anticipating a call from Lakeside Administrator Dr. Ernesto Mendez. So far, no call.

After fifteen minutes, Mary sat up in the chaise and thought how risqué it would be to have no tan lines. She unsnapped her top, rubbed some lotion on her breasts and lay down. No one would be looking, but the thought that someone could excited her.

But someone was watching, ten feet behind the chaise, studying her moves and waiting for the right moment.

A small rock splashed into the pool; Mary hastily sat up using her hands to cover her breasts. She looked directly at the pool and peered over the hedge. She returned her focus back to the pool.

The killer took advantage of the opportunity and used a double-handled wooden pistol grip supporting piano wire and looped it firmly around her neck while yanking her back onto the chaise. The killer jammed a knee into her back to gain more leverage. Mary tried to scream, but no sound came out. She reached for the wire, but it was embedded too deeply. She violently kicked to no avail. She agonizingly tried to twist her body, but she found it impossible to maneuver. Ten seconds later, she died.

The killer looked at Mary's lifeless body, unwound the piano wire, using Mary's bikini top to wipe off the small beads of blood, and placed the weapon in a back pocket.

191

"What a waste," the killer mumbled, appreciating her beauty, preparing to strategically place her body in the pool.

The killer rolled her body off the chaise and on to a towel with little effort and gently placed her onto the cool deck, face up. He carefully removed her bikini bottom and placed it on a table next to her towel. After taking several pictures, the killer reached down, glanced over the hedge that showcased one of the clubs perfectly manicured fairways, making sure there were no curious onlookers, cautiously carried her to the deep end, and meticulously slid her lifeless body face down into the pool.

"Bon Voyage."

*****

Ramone explained the incident that cost the lives of two of our clients. It sounded reasonable to believe him; someone must have tailed him and waited for the opportunity to strike.

They both left my office; Kurt closed the door behind him. I put my feet up on the desk and let my mind wander.

I'm sure Detective Spicuzza would be looking into all of the possibilities. What were the odds of her revealing the information she'd gathered? My curiosity intensified. What heinous act did the victims commit warranting their execution, especially in our limo? My inquisitiveness of their motives felt more important than my sympathy for the victims. After all, at least theoretically, they got wacked for something they did to somebody else, right?

On another front, it felt great to see George out and about, back in his element. Edmond, the proper choice, would be able to answer his quirky questions.

I took out my cell and dialed Mary. After seven rings her phone went to voicemail. I left her a message about dinner. I thought she might be in the pool, but my best guess was that she was taking a nap. After all, we were all over each other in the last twenty-four hours and I knew what my body was telling me— it was worn out.

Dino knocked on the door a second time and walked in.

"I left a couple of contracts on your desk. I wanted you to see them, get the general idea how they're structured."

"I started reading them before detective Spicuzza interrupted. You have anything you want to say to me about George?"

"I will have a lot to say to you about George… but not today. We have some loose ends to tie up, especially with those clients being gunned downed in our limo. Tony is digging into their backgrounds to see if they have any organized crime connections. It wasn't a robbery, but maybe a hit put out on those two, because we confirmed it wasn't a jealous rage by an ex-spouse or lover."

"It would be great to get that monkey off our back," I said to Dino.

"I'll keep you up to speed on this and let you know as soon as we hear anything. What did you think of Detective Spicuzza, Steve?"

"A fascinating individual, beautiful too."

"I haven't heard that said about her in a long time."

"It sounds like you know something. Care to elaborate?"

"She's my daughter."

"Vicki Spicuzza?"

"Yes."

"No bullshit?"

"No bullshit."

"Her last name is different from yours."

"Married, her husband was killed in the line of duty."

"Military?"

"No, highway patrol."

"That's horrible."

"Happened three years ago; a tough time for all of us."

"My belated condolences."

"Thank you."

Dino walked out the door and I chose not to pursue a line of questioning regarding her. It might have explained her nonchalant attitude toward me. Maybe she was still grieving or maybe she was all work and no play. Or maybe she just wasn't interested. Lots of maybes.

*****

4:30 PM

George exited the limo chauffeured by Edmond and went up to the front door to unlock it. Edmond grabbed several items out of the limo trunk and followed George into the house.

"Edmond, thank you very much for driving me around, showing me the sights."

"My pleasure, George. Is there anything else I can help you with?"

"Here." George handed him a hundred-dollar bill.

"Thank you very much. I'll see you tomorrow at the office."

George closed the door and walked toward his room.

"Mary, I'm here."

No response.

"She must be enjoying the warm Vegas sun," George mumbled to himself.

George went to his room and placed his newly purchased items from The Fashion Show Mall in his closet. He wandered into the kitchen after taking his meds and poured himself some orange juice. He peered out the kitchen door leading to the patio and saw some of Mary's things sprawled out on a table. He didn't have anything important to say so he finished his drink and went back to his room, took off his shoes and laid down.

*****

I walked over to Dino's office and told him I would be back around eight. I really wanted to do another run, enjoying my new profession. I went up to the front desk and told Candice I'd see her at eight.

"You know you don't have to do any runs Steve, don't you?"

"I want to. How else will I be able to understand the driver's experience? As you know, this is all new to me and rather exciting to boot."

"I'll make sure I find you a run sometime after eight."

"Thanks, Candice."

Rush hour traffic like this was new to me. La Crosse had over fifty thousand people, but Vegas was like La Crosse on amphetamines. I arrived at my house at six. It was quiet. I thought there'd be more activity.

"Hey, anyone home?"

I didn't hear anything and began checking out rooms. Mary's was empty, so I went over to George's. He was out cold and snoring in his bed. Mary must be outside. I stopped in the kitchen and took a Coke out of the refrigerator and proceeded out to the pool.

"Mary."

I walked over to the table and saw her clothes and towel. I took a quick look around and didn't see anything. Another couple of steps toward the bar revealed Mary's backside in the pool. I approached her and then noticed something terribly wrong.

"Mary!"

She was face down, her head resting against the edge of the pool.

"This can't be happening, this can't be! George!"

I kicked my shoes off, threw my sports coat and phone on the deck, and dove in. I came up underneath her and used my left arm to rotate her onto her back, dragging her to the shallow end of the pool.

I took a hard look and noticed the red line and bruising around her neck.

I pulled Mary to the steps and sat down.

"George!"

I sat there, staring at her in disbelief.

"George!" My voice lost power.

A groggy George came through the kitchen door.

"What's going on, Steve?"

He stopped when he saw me holding Mary's lifeless body, on the steps of the pool. He looked into her cold grey eyes.

"My God, Steve. What happened?"

"I found her face down in the pool, George. She's dead. Somebody killed her."

"Somebody killed her," George repeated.

George walked into the pool and the two of us pulled Mary out and covered her with a towel.

The dry Vegas air sucked the moisture off my skin and I became cold. George ran into the house and reappeared with a handful of towels.

"Here. Get out of those wet clothes. Dry off."

196

I put my wet clothes in a pile, taking Vicki's card out of my sports coat pocket, and then went over to my phone lying on the deck.

Chapter 17

I sat on a deck chair, holding her bathing suit in my hands, confused, angry, hurt. I heard the sirens approaching, a knot the size of a Cadillac forming in my stomach. George pulled up a chair and sat next to me.

"I left the front door open for the police. My God Steve, what's happening? Only a handful of people knew we were here. Who would want to hurt Mary? It doesn't make any sense. She was so kind."

"She was. Mary and I. . . we were—"

"Sleeping together, I know."

"You know?"

"I might have a couple of loose screws, but I'm not blind."

"Last night was the first time we ever spent a night together under the same roof. We tried keeping it on the downlow."

"Did you?"

"We thought we checked that box."

"Steve, let's just let the police do their jobs. No sense speculating. They'll find out who did this and why."

"Why? I can tell you why! It's because of this fucking limo company, that's why!"

"Steve, you don't know that for sure."

The kitchen pool door opened and Vicki and several other plain clothes detectives emerged on the pool deck.

George raised his hands and took a couple of steps back, almost falling into the pool.

"Steve, are you okay?"

"No, I'm not. Why would someone want to hurt her? She…"

Vicki pulled up a chair and sat next to me.

"Either of you hurt?"

"Like I said on the phone, I found her floating face down in the pool. I pulled her to the shallow end, saw that mark around her neck, and yelled for George. He helped me get her out of the water. I covered her with a towel." I fought back my anger but several tears made their way down my cheeks.

"Steve, were you in a relationship with her?"

"Why would you ask that?"

"The way you're looking at her."

"She's George's private nurse and my supervisor at Lakeside. We were close."

"Is there somewhere private we can talk inside?"

Several Metro officers came out, and one said, "The house is secure."

"Sonny's office," I replied.

I looked over at Mary's lifeless body under the towel. We walked into the house and went inside the office.

I sat behind the desk as Vicki sat in one of the two white Italian leather chairs facing me.

"Steve, this is the second time today we've been seated like this. What time did you get home?"

I told her my story and she jotted it down.

"And George?"

"With Edmond, one of the limo drivers, all afternoon, asleep when I got home."

"Any reason he would want to kill her?"

"None. He's as dangerous as a newborn puppy. She was the head nurse while he was a patient at Lakeside Health Center."

"A patient, right?"

"Yes, and that has what to do with Mary being murdered?"

"And when you got home, you say you found her in the deep end of the pool floating face down. Correct?"

"Yes."

"Were you and Mary intimate?"

"What if we were?"

Vicki stared at me like I had stolen her wallet and was waiting for me to admit it.

A loud knock preceded Dino and Kurt's entry into the office.

"Steve, we got here as fast as we could. Are you hurt?" Dino asked.

"No, Mary…"

"What's going on, Vicki?" Dino asked in a concerned and louder than normal voice.

"George's nurse, Steve's friend, was found dead in the pool."

"What? What are you talking about? Steve just arrived here three days ago."

"George's nurse and Steve's friend, one and the same."

"Are you saying Steve had something to do with this?"

"No. We're just gathering the facts. But we haven't ruled him out either."

I stood and blasted Vicki for not ruling me out as a suspect.

"I would never hurt Mary. We were close. Yes, we slept together, but for me to do that to Mary? You're way out of line!" I leaned across the desk, shoving my face towards from hers.

Kurt walked around the desk and pulled me back.

Vicki stood. "Don't leave Vegas." She said and walked out of the room, followed by Dino.

"She's just doing her job; nobody here thinks you are capable of this. I don't think she believes it either. She's just seeing what you do when you're riled," Kurt said, trying to be the middleman.

"I'm way beyond riled, Kurt. Who would do this to her?"

"That's what she gets paid for. She's intelligent, a gifted detective. She'll find out who did this."

"Like the two who got gunned down in the limo? How's that working out?"

"That's not fair. She just got the case... and now this."

"Kurt, there better not be a connection to these killings."

"I'm not sure what's going on."

"Call Tony and tell him I want to see him."

"Tony?"

"Yeah, Tony. Time for him to do what he's getting paid to do."

"Steve, you're upset. Chill out before you start ordering people around."

I shot him a dirty look as we walked out of the office. I stormed past Dino who was talking to one of the detectives. Vicki was bombarding George with questions. Picking up my pace, I descended on her. Kurt halted directly behind me.

"Vicki, leave him alone," I said. "He doesn't know anything."

One of the other detectives came up to us and stopped between Vicki and me. She got off the couch.

"Back off, asshole. You guys are done here. Pack up your shit and get the fuck out!" I shouted.

The detective put his index finger on my chest. "We're done when we're done. I'm not on your schedule. Understand?"

I didn't know what came over me, but I knocked his hand off and drove my shoulder into his chest, knocking him backwards and onto the living room floor. Several blues came running over as Kurt grabbed my shoulders. Vicki motioned them away and I shrugged myself out of Kurt's grip.

"You want to spend the next forty-eight hours down in Metro holding for assaulting an officer?" Vicki asked.

201

The blues had tasers drawn and were close to lighting me up.

"Easy Steve. I know you're hurting, but Metro isn't the problem," Kurt warned.

"Steve, we're just covering our bases," Vicki continued. "We need to know everything about everyone. Someone targeted her because it doesn't look like a robbery and I need to find out why: that's the way it works."

"George just got out. He's not violent. I've known him for years, worked with him for years. Please, leave him alone."

"It's okay, Steve," George nervously uttered.

Dino moved next to Kurt as the officer on the ground stood and gave me the I'll-be-seeing-you-again-soon look. The two blues holstered their tasers and left the room.

"Steve, you and George should find a place to stay tonight," Vicki suggested. "We'll be here for hours. You can both gather up some things, after we've gone through them of course, and leave. Just not Vegas... understood?"

"I can get them a comp at the Rio," Kurt cut in.

"Good idea," Dino added. "I'm going back to the office. Let me know when he's checked in."

"Yes." I turned to the pissed off detective. "I'm sorry for knocking you down; she verbally assaulted George and he doesn't do well when he's put under a lot of stress."

I could tell he didn't give a shit as he walked away.

I turned back to Kurt. "Seems like you're coming to my rescue on a regular basis."

"Great customer service," he wisecracked.

"That was a nice move you put on my detective; you have any training?" Vicki asked.

"I caught him off guard, that's all, and yes, I horsed around with my father when I was growing up."

"I'm sorry you lost your father," Vicki responded, sympathetically, "but that was a little more than just horsing around."

"He was military, Special Forces, and he taught me how to defend myself. His death was hard on me, and it devastated my mother."

"How old were you?"

"Fifteen."

George went to his room. Vicki sat on the couch and I joined her, putting my head down, looking at the floor. Kurt stepped out of the room and started dialing his connections.

"It's hard to lose someone close, especially this way."

Kurt awkwardly came back into the living room. "We're being comped by the Rio. Jesse is our host. We need to meet her at Concierge's desk, where she'll take care of you and George." He backed out of the room and left.

"To answer your question, we enjoyed being around each other. Mary was my supervisor for about six months and we always got along. We seemed to be on the same page at work. She was always the consummate professional, until one night it became more."

"I know this is hard, but could you describe more?"

"I worked as a psych attendant the last four years."

"I didn't know you worked there that long; I just heard you worked there."

"I put myself through school, got a bachelor's in business, and did it working forty plus hours a week."

"Driven. Impressive."

"About four months ago, Mary and I accidentally ran into each other at a bar, and one thing led to another."

"You kept this discreet?"

"Neither of us told anyone."

"What about your mother?"

She had me in a vulnerable position and relaxed. I just kept answering her questions.

"Died of cancer five years ago. I was eighteen; been on my own since."

I spilled my guts and she listened as a concerned person, not a detective. At least, it felt that way.

"No other family to lean on?"

"No, just my parents; as you know, I'm adopted."

"You've come a long way in a short time and, Sonny being your birth father opened some doors."

"And closed some even faster. A lot of missing pieces sum it up. Dino told me you lost your husband three years ago. I'm sorry."

After several seconds of silence, she partially opened up.

"Yes, killed by a drug dealer." I could sense her mind drifting off. "Wait, I'm supposed to be asking the questions."

"Sorry, I'm just upset and angry. I want to find the person who did this, make them pay."

"Make them pay or bring them to justice?" Vicki said, trying to gauge my intent.

"Both. She didn't deserve this. And what about the dealer who killed your husband? Is he in jail or on the wrong side of the grass?" I strategically asked trying to see where her head was at.

"Nice try, Steve, but if you really want the data on my late husband's killer's fate… Google it. I don't feel like discussing it."

She got icy with her answer, her face tightening while her eyes squinted as she bore down on me, my que to back off immediately.

"Vicki, we're both hurting from the brutal act of someone else, you more so than me because you were married. But that doesn't make it any less painful."

We settled down in silence briefly to regain our composure. Not a bonding moment but a moment where we realized together that someone had been taken from us in a violent way.

"I cornered him outside a bar in North Las Vegas," Vicki began. "My partner was still inside the bar. I didn't wait for backup. He drew his weapon and I emptied half my Sig 45 into him. It was ruled self-defense, a clean shoot. They cleared me of any wrongdoing. It's all in the RJ archives; I'm sure you were going to look it up anyway."

I told her about Mary and me. Surprisingly, she wasn't judgmental. I felt at ease talking to her. It was like we were taking turns being psychologists. After about ten minutes she put her notes away and told me she would be in touch. I asked her to keep me in the loop, but she gave me a doubtful look and let herself out.

There were CSIs everywhere, inside the house, outside the house, and by the pool combing for any clues into Mary's murder. I went to my room, gathered up some of my clothes as did George, all under the enhanced supervision of one of Metro's finest. He was more than happy to expedite us out of the house and send us on our way to the confines of the Rio Hotel Suites.

*****

The killer walked to a parked car and drove off. Once outside the gated community, the car pulled into a small bar parking lot on Maryland Parkway, and using a burner phone, made a call.

"It's done."

"No witnesses to clean up?"

"No."

"What about George?"

"Asleep in his room; I'm sure Metro will be all over his shit and make him a suspect."

"Good. What else?"

"What do you mean, what else?"

"Steve."

"What about him?"

"Does he know?"

"I listened to the recording. She never got that far."

"She was falling in love again, could have exposed us."

"Let's hope Metro doesn't find the bug I placed out by the pool."

"Do they have any reason to search for one?"

"None at all."

"Good, we'll be in touch."

"And?"

"And your funds have been sent to your offshore account."

"Then until next week, or if I obtain something of interest, sooner. Our business for today is concluded."

"It is."

The line went dead.

The killer took a rag and wiped down the burner phone, placed it on the ground, looked around and then stomped on it several times. Using the same rag, picked it up and tossed it in a nearby garbage can. Sirens roared past the parking lot.

"Time to leave and watch the circus by the pool."

Chapter 18

I valeted the SUV at the Rio and George and I made our way to the Concierge's desk. Jesse gave me a twenty-fifth-floor suite with an adjoining suite. We went into the suite, and proceeded to the master suite. The fourteen-hundred-square-foot suite had three bathrooms, a poker area, living room, bedroom, and a Jacuzzi in the bathroom right next to a window facing the north side of the strip.

"Too bad I can't get my head wrapped around this place. The reason we're here is churning up my insides," I said.

"I know Steve, I feel the same way. Look, you take the big suite, I'll take the smaller adjoining one. I've stayed in dozens of these and this is a first for you. Plus, the views will take your mind off what's happened, at least for a little while."

George left via the adjoining door. I unpacked and wandered around the suite admiring the three-quarter view of the city. Someone knocked at my door, and without thinking I opened it.

Woody and two of his muppets stood there.

"What the hell are you doing here?"

"Boys."

The big guys grabbed my arms and walked me back into the suite. Woody trailed them and closed the door.

"You here to kill me too?"

"Release him. Steve, sit. I heard what happened to this Mary woman and I came over here to tell you I had nothing to do with it. Someone else did this."

"How do you know about Mary and what happened to her?"

"I know everything that happens in Vegas, but I don't know who did this or what you did to motivate someone to the point of propagating such a vicious murder."

The front door opened and Tony walked through, gun drawn featuring a silencer and Tony's you-picked-the-wrong-guy-to-fuck-with look.

Woody's men were surprised by Tony's entrance and couldn't pull their weapons fast enough.

"Go ahead. There are lots of new concrete office pads available in Vegas for pieces of garbage like you."

The men froze.

"I didn't anticipate you joining us this evening," Woody protested.

"Tell your flunkies to pull out their guns carefully and drop them on the floor, now. And if I see your hands move in any direction other than up, I will disembowel you. Understand?"

"Relax Tony, we're all on the same side here," Woody softly pleaded. "No need for anyone to do something heroic."

"Steve, step away from them."

I thought this was going to turn into an O.K. Corral shootout as I backed off to Woody's side.

"Tony, I didn't have anything to do with this. Why would I risk going to jail and kill this Mary? There's no money in it."

"You're a parasite."

"Tony, we all have a purpose. There are leaders like me and followers like you, wrapped up in a nice tidy bow. So Tony, put down the gun. We're all civilized. Let's figure this out together."

"What about the money? Killing Sonny? You gonna tell me no money in that either? You just didn't anticipate Steve showing up."

"There were lots of reasons to eliminate Sonny, there were. He mostly failed to meet the high standards of the other transportation owners in Vegas. He wasn't a member of the good ol' boys club, just an outsider with lavish tastes. He fucked your old boss over, and what did you do? You went to work for him. No sense of loyalty at all. Rather disappointing."

"The only reason you have anything at all, Woody, is because of Salvatore Fazio. He bailed your sorry ass father out of the shithole he dug for himself. And your psycho brother, he's a piece of work. He's exactly where he belongs… High Desert Prison."

"Where he's the shot caller."

"And when he gets out … you'll be kissing his ass."

"Getting rather personal in front of your boss. You might be planting some unhealthy seeds, Tony."

"The only reason I don't plant your hillbilly ass in the desert now is because I know you didn't kill Sonny or Mary. And although I would be doing this city an enormous public service by eliminating a scumbag like you. . . today's not that day."

I was pissed. I was sure Woody would be capable of something like this.

"How do you know, Tony?" I asked.

"Because. . . I can't tell you. Just trust me. It wasn't him."

"I don't really know you, Tony, do I? We just met. How do I know you aren't working with Woody? Playing me?"

One of Woody's men took a leap at Tony, reaching for his gun. Like a professional juggler and ballerina rolled into one, Tony sidestepped him, flipped the gun in his hand, and grabbing the barrel and silencer, cracked Woody's man across the side of his head with the force of a hammer. He dropped unconsciously to the floor. The second of Woody's bodyguards reacted several seconds behind the lead man. Before Tony could pivot and take the second man down, he dove on top of Tony and the two rolled onto the floor with the gun sailing across the room.

Woody tried to take advantage of the situation and reached into his sports coat where I knew he packed. The time to unveil my many years of fight training with my father and in countless gyms arrived. I turned on my right side and gave Woody a roundhouse kick with my left leg. The instep of my left boot caught Woody in the mouth. The impact sent him reeling into the couch with enough force to tip the two-seater backwards, propelling Woody into a full somersault. His head and back slammed hard against the window. A momentary look of panic shot across Woody's face and mine as we figured he would go through the glass and plunge twenty-five stories to his death. The unbreakable glass held.

Woody, dazed, blood dripping from his mouth, was unable to stand. I stepped on the overturned couch, ripped open his sports coat, and removed the Beretta from its shoulder harness. Woody registered a surprised look right before he passed out.

Tony wrestled his way on top of the bodyguard and started whaling on his face, blood splattering on Tony's fists. After the fifth punch, the guy's lights went out, but Tony kept pounding away.

I rushed over with Woody's Beretta still in my left hand. "Tony, you're going to kill him!"

Tony backhanded me and I fell to the floor. I rolled onto my right side and jumped to my feet, instinctively coming into my Zenkutsu Dachi frontal stance, the Beretta still in my left hand.

Tony was the ultimate badass, but at his age, agility was not his strong suit.

"Tony, it's me. It's over. They're all out of commission.

"What the fuck dance step was that? And where'd you get the piece?" Tony asked while keeping a knee on top of the bloody bodyguard.

"A defensive martial arts stance, and it's Woody's. He asked me to hold it for him while he took a nap."

Tony crawled a few feet to retrieve his gun, garnering up whatever reserve strength he retained, then pushed himself onto one knee and stood. His effort left him hunched over, unable to fully stand. He struggled to put a hand on each knee as he gasped for air. He turned his head toward the window, observing Woody's current position.

"You're trained?" With a pause and glance at back at me he added, "He looks happy."

"Yeah to both. Woody and I are besties now. However, his defenestration would have been a nice touch."

"Huh?"

"Defenestration, the act of throwing someone or something out a window."

"You don't say?"

"I do, and I'm finally getting to use one of those words I thought I would never use. My sixty-thousand-dollar education is paying big dividends."

Tony's eyes were locked on Woody, passed out against the glass window.

Chuckling, he said, "You're full of surprises. Trained in martial arts and prodigious words. Didn't see that one coming. Any other secrets I should know about?"

"I can carve the shit out of anyone with a foil or Sabre."

"You fence too?"

"Surprise."

"Anything else?"

"I average over two twenty in bowling, I'm a two handicap in golf, a switch hitter, and I'm referring to baseball, I have a degree in business with a three-point-seven-five GPA and a photographic memory."

"You sound like the next coming. Is there anything you can't do?"

"Yeah, bring people back to life."

"It's alright kid, I'm here. Nobody gonna hurt you while I'm on this earth. Anything else?"

211

"Not today. But please, don't tell anyone about the way I took Woody out. It could cause problems for me. People would think, well, you know, I was an educated bully or something. I want them to respect me for my business talents, not the fact that I can beat the living shit out of them."

Tony arched his back using both hands to push down on his lower back, his breathing almost returning to normal, all of which made me happy. I thought the guy was gonna have a stroke and die in front of me. He watched as the guy he pistol-whipped started coming around. The guy he beat senseless was still out. Tony looked back over to the window where Woody was crawling on all fours struggling to get up.

"Tony, now this is what I'm paying you for. Great job, brother."

"Fuckin' smart ass."

Tony walked into the second bathroom and returned with an ice bucket of cold water. He stood over the knocked-out bodyguard and dumped it on his face, the blood-water mix rushing across the tiled floor. Vegas tap water in July is as cold as most cities' bath water. The water doesn't get cold until December. Still, the watery blast proved enough to bring him partially around as the other bodyguard helped him to his feet. The two badly beaten bodyguards staggered over to Woody and picked him up as the three of them struggled to make their way out of the suite. I ran over to the door and held it open for them.

"You guys mind stopping at the deli on the way out of the elevator and ordering us some roast beef sandwiches?" I joked.

"We'll be seeing you again," the bodyguard mumbled as the three of them left the room.

"Not until your cut man works over those pool ball eyes of yours, cupcake," I sneered back.

Woody eyeballed me and when I looked back into his eyes, it was like looking down into a bottomless pit. He was the textbook definition of psychotic. But with my adrenaline still flowing and being jacked up, I personally didn't give a shit.

"I'm hungry, Tony. How about you?"

"I'm hungry," the voice came from off to my left.

George was standing by to the poker table in the side room next to the adjoining door, holding one of Woody's men's guns, a dumbfounded expression masking his face.

"Shit. I forgot about George. How much did you see?" I inquired.

"More than I ever care to see again. I didn't realize my partner had the capabilities you displayed and would go to those lengths to protect our company."

"George, so many bad things have happened. There's an endless supply of shit heels to go around. Are you sure you're up for this?" I gently took the gun out of his hand.

"Hell no! This isn't at all what I signed on for. But let me tell you this. I didn't achieve my wealth by grabbing my ankles… I'll fight until I'm dead."

"All right. Looks like you brought in a partner with Palle."

"Huh?"

"Balls."

George put his arm around me, Tony joined in and the three of us agreed to take this fight to the next level.

Tony left a few minutes after Woody, probably so they wouldn't run into each other in the parking area. After ordering room service, George and I called it a night.

I had trouble sleeping, too many thoughts racing around my mind. I rolled out of bed and pulled the curtains open, amazed at the amount of colorful wattage the Vegas casinos displayed.

Mary's murder made no sense at all. And her confession . . . I knew in my heart I didn't love her. But I

213

really would miss her. Maybe down the road I would have ended up with her. Too many thoughts kept bouncing around. I crawled back into the sack, staring at the city lights, waiting for the sandman to slam my eyelids shut.

Chapter 19

George woke me up around ten with several knocks on the adjoining bedroom door. It felt good to sleep, but thoughts of Mary's murder along with the fight, YLL, Tony, Woody, Vicki, Sam and everything else had taken a toll on my mental well-being. Throw in the guilt about thinking about two other women not even twenty-four hours after Mary's murder felt even more disturbing.

George had brewed some coffee, so I got the morning jolt I needed to start the day.

"How are you doing this morning, Steve?"

George sipped his coffee and took a seat on the couch where I'd blasted Woody less than twelve hours ago.

"I'm feeling perfectly shitty this morning George. Thanks for asking. And how'd you sleep?"

I joined George on the couch.

"I'm on drugs. I always sleep great."

"Snarky and sarcastic. You are feeling better. Just remember who your friends are. Sharing is an important part of friendship."

"I received a call from my sister this morning."

"And?"

"She's flying out tonight."

"I'll leave a spot open in the garage for her broom."

"Steve."

"Here's a dose of reality, George. She's a conniving bitch who's only concerned with how much of your wealth she can steal every time you end up at Lakeside. As a bonus, she's got the personality of a shark swimming in chum."

"She's family, a bit greedy, but still family, and she's always been there when I needed her."

"Look, I'll try to play nice George, but I'll be watching her," I said, using my two fingers to point to my eyes and back to George's several times.

There was a loud knock on the door followed by a "room service," announcement.

"Stay seated. If something happens, get to your room and lock the door."

We put our coffees on the table.

My heart pounded as I got behind the door and whipped it open, waiting for something bad to happen. And it did; a party broke loose as Bill and Russ barged through the door, a beer in each hand.

"What, your mansion ain't big enough?" they said in two-part harmony.

I slammed the door shut.

They looked at me like I'd disembarked a spacecraft.

"Dude," Russ chimed in.

"WTF bro, the chick at your limo company told us you were here. Why aren't you at your digs, man?"

I walked over to them and hugged them, my eyes tearing up.

"You don't know what happened?"

The cheerfulness drained from their faces.

"What's going on, Steve?" Bill asked.

"It's Mary. They killed her," I said.

"What are you talking about? We just saw her two days ago," Russ said.

I told them the story.

"We have to find out who did this," Bill said.

Another knock on the door startled me.

"Stand over here in case there's some more trouble," I told them.

With additional muscle behind me, I felt more confident in answering the door. This time I yanked it open and blocked the doorway.

"How ya holdin' up, Steve?" Kurt asked as he gently moved me aside and walked into the room.

I peeked down the hallway in both directions to ensure no one else would be charging in before I closed the door.

"You Wisconsinites like to party early or finish late, whatever this little soiree is. Who are your pals?"

"You know us Wisconsinites, outdrinking every state since 1848," Russ added.

I introduced everyone and filled them in on all the details of last night's rumble.

"Woody is like that irritating piece of popcorn that gets stuck in your teeth. No matter how hard you try to get it out, it just burrows in. What do you have lined up for me, Steve? I'm here to help."

"Meet the two newest employees of YLL, who by the way, you're going to train."

"Really? You know we have other drivers for training, right? You were an exception, direct orders from Dino—"

"Well, here's exceptions two and three. Get them started tomorrow morning. We have a limo company to run."

"Boys, did you bring all of my things?"

"We packed your Tundra tight."

"Good. I want to take my things back to the house."

"Dino called me an hour ago. It's okay to return to your house any time after three," Kurt said.

I ordered room service for us. It felt great to have old friends together with a new one. I was feeling comfortable for the first time in a week.

George and I checked out at two-thirty, and the five of us caravanned in the three vehicles, my Tundra, the SUV, and Kurt in his limo.

It was hard to miss the police tape draped across the door as we entered the circular driveway. I walked out of my SUV and ripped off the tape under the watchful eye of several neighbors.

217

"Nice crib, Steve. Even bigger than you described," Russ blurted.

"It's amazing, guys. Let's unload everything and get the two of you settled in."

"Your whole life packed into a Tundra," Kurt sympathetically added.

"Pathetic, right?"

"Nomadic… maybe you're a minimalist."

I bent my left arm and slapped my right hand across my deltoid muscle, holding it there for a couple of seconds as I nodded my head. An Italian gesture for fuck you.

"Tony teach you that?"

We dragged everything in and proceeded to give Russ and Bill the tour, apprehensively showing them the pool area.

"What a waste, Steve," Bill said.

"I'm so sorry too," Russ added. "We all knew you two were involved romantically. Your failed attempt at a secret. But we all agreed how cool the two of you were together."

"A great thing we had . . . now it's gone."

My phone rang and I saw Vicki's name. I excused myself and walked over to the bar by the pool.

"Vicki."

"Steve, how are you holding up?"

"I've been better."

"I'd like to swing by the house."

"My college roommates came in this morning, brought me my things. They're here along with Kurt and George."

"That's fine. I'll be there in fifteen minutes."

"I'll see you then."

I hung up and walked toward the kitchen where they had gathered.

"Kurt, do you mind taking everyone to the barn?"

"Sure, everything alright?"

218

"Yes. Vicki needs to talk with me. And while you're there, can you give Bill and Russ a brief limo demonstration?"

"Sure."

"George, you mind going with them?"

"Of course not, Steve."

Within ten minutes, they were seated in Kurt's limo and took off. I had the house to myself and wandered around the place, absorbing short-lived memories. Maybe Vicki had some leads. I was anxious to hear if any progress had been made on any of the murders.

The doorbell rang.

"Detective." I opened the door and let her in. "Is the kitchen okay?"

"That would be fine."

She looked all business in her light blue blazer, white blouse, blue short heels and skinny jeans. She followed me into the kitchen, and I pulled out a chair for her to sit in.

"Can I get you a beverage? Water, soda, beer, an Irish Car Bomb?"

"The Car Bomb would be nice," she fired back catching me off guard with my head stuck partway into the opened refrigerator.

"What?"

"A water."

"A sense of humor under that suit of armor."

"Suit of armor? Do I really come off that Draconian?"

"Yes and no. I understand you have a job to do."

I took out two bottled waters and sat down next to her.

"I have some questions," she began.

"I'm looking for some answers."

"Do you know a patient named Marsha Zemlugs?"

"Marsha. Who could forget her?" I answered.

219

"Well, here's an interesting connection."

"A connection?"

"The two murdered execution style in the back of Ramone's limo. She was a scientist out at Area 51 and the man was not her husband. He worked at the test site in Mercury, Nevada."

"What were they doing together?"

"That's what everyone wants to know, how those two ended up together on an all-nighter. Their supervisors didn't know of any connections in the past. And here's the kicker: both were happily married."

"I'm sure you checked up on the spouses. They're clear, right?"

"Curiously, both of their partners were out of town the morning of the shooting too."

"Were they seeing each other?"

"Conferences, different cities."

"Rather convenient. How does Marsha fit into all this?"

"Mr. Swanson, the male vic, and his first wife Acacia adopted Marsha. He divorced her seven years later."

"Marsha must have been too much for him to handle."

"The opposite, actually. She was a perfect child. Tired of the wife, he met someone else, moved on. Paid the alimony, child support, no problems. Relinquished all rights to Marsha, including visitation, never saw her again. All according to his ex-wife."

"The records I read say something different."

"And."

"And what?"

"Are you worried about a HIPPA violation?"

"Seriously? Not when he comes to her. Marsha came off the streets," I told Vicki.

"That drives a gaping hole in the ex-wife's statement; she never mentioned any of this."

"We never had an early bio on her either, just the last six years. Vicki, you do know about Marsha's condition, don't you?"

"Only from your facial expressions."

"That obvious?"

"Can I get the rest of the answers from you? I'm just trying to piece this together."

"So much for patient confidentiality."

"It's up to you. I understand you have an obligation to your patients, but I have a gut feeling that these events are interrelated."

"Considering I'm no longer employed with them and my supervisor… I thought you came here… had information on Mary's case." I stared down at the table.

"I'm sorry. Not yet."

"Sure. Back to Marsha."

I introduced Vicki to the classified world of Marsha Zemlugs, relinquishing physical and mental accounts accumulated firsthand by various staff members, aides, psych attendants, psychologists and group therapists. My personal knowledge of the doctor's unwritten short-term treatment directives were all confidential. But these three murders changed the all the rules. These included her off-the-wall physical violence, psychotic episodes, Schizophrenia diagnosis, unexplainable contortions and her obsessive-compulsive behavior, all in the six weeks since she'd been admitted. I highlighted our time together with the last physical encounter, skipping my farewell visit to her room.

"That helped. Thank you. Some bio, very disturbing. And by the way, Marsha escaped Lakeside."

"Escaped?"

"Yes."

"Are you saying she's here? You suggesting she wacked those two in the limo?"

"Highly unlikely, but not ruled out. Would you mind if we go out to the pool?" She motioned to the door.

221

"Sure… something you overlooked?"

"No, I just want to look around again."

We stood outside the pool deck door.

"I'm sorry. I know you had nothing to do with this. I have to be thorough. I can't leave—"

"Any stone unturned. Vicki, I looked into her eyes. "Mary and I were seeing each other, not publicly but, well, we enjoyed each other's company."

"You were sleeping with your supervisor and the two of you didn't want to complicate the work environment."

"Sounds ugly when you put it bluntly."

"Sorry. Just stating facts. No emotion or judgments intended."

"She fell in love with me. I wasn't quite there though, and I felt guilty. Do you know what I mean?"

"Of course. We've all been there. But this conversation ends here. No psychoanalytical sessions."

"I wouldn't dream of it, but oh how fascinating it would be to unmask the draconian warrior."

We stared at each other for a few seconds.

She walked to the west wall and disappeared behind the hard-working AC unit.

After a few minutes she came back. "I have to get back to Metro. Call me if you think of anything."

"I'll show you out."

I watched her leave and went back inside. Marsha's escape and the story Vicki just told me was disturbing. Especially when Marsha's last words to me were about my trip to Las Vegas.

Chapter 20

Everyone slept in except George who caught an early ride to the office and began working on the company reorganization. How nice to have an uneventful day. My best friends were staying with me and there was plenty of booze in the house, enough to drop an army. By two thirty, we all were mulling around the kitchen picking random items out of the refrigerator. We gathered up our harvest and went outside to eat, staring at the drained pool. Next week the pool company would clean and refill it like nothing happened.

Twenty minutes into our feast the doorbell rang. Sonny thought of everything, a portable ringer poolside. We looked at each other, wondering who brought a piece out to the pool? I wasn't expecting anyone, and my friends Russ and Bill certainly weren't. We scrambled to the kitchen. I opened the gun drawer and took out one of two Glock 19s. Bill grabbed the other one while Russ ended up with the smaller Sig Sauer P290.

"How come I got stuck with the little one?"

"Little gun gets the little gun," Bill said.

"Fuck you."

Armed, I cautiously took the lead and walked up to the door, cocking the gun, putting a round in the chamber. Russ and Bill followed suit and took up defensive positions in the living room.

I carefully peeked through the hole, surprised by the person standing at the door.

I looked back at my friends. "Did anyone order a pizza?"

I knew the answer to the question before I asked it.

"Get ready."

I whipped open the door, grabbed the collar of the large man masquerading in the delivery outfit, pulled him through the door along with the pizza he delicately balanced on one hand, and immediately kicked the door closed. I stuffed my gun under his double chin.

"This for me?"

"Whoa, don't shoot. I'm just delivering a message. Jesus, I'm the good guy here."

"Message from whom?"

Russ grabbed the empty pizza box and tossed it like a frisbee, watching it glide across the marble living room floor, coming to rest against an antique reading lamp.

"The note, the note you were handed, the first night at Tight Racks, remember?"

I positioned my free hand on his breast pocket and whirled him around like we were auditioning for Dancing with the Stars.

"You don't look anything like him." I pressed the gun into his neck harder.

"Max told me to give you the note. I work for Max."

"Shoot him, Steve," Russ said.

"You'll ruin the nice Italian marble floor," Bill quipped.

I took the gun away from his chin and waved him into the living room.

"Put the guns down. I think he's on our side," I ordered. "What's your name?"

"I'm Moshe Dayan."

"Like the Israeli general?"

"You know your history."

"Go on."

"My father's cousin, I'm named after him."

"Did you eat for him too?" Bill snipped.

"Yes, I have a love for food."

A better look in the light revealed a handsome, overweight man, around forty, about five-foot-ten and easily pushing two-hundred-seventy pounds. But he didn't look too flabby— plenty of muscle on that frame.

"Love might need to be replaced with obsession," Russ continued.

"Enough with the sarcasm. You obviously came here for a reason. What is it?" I demanded.

"Do you mind if I sit down?"

"Sorry, excuse my lack of hospitality." I pointed to a chair with my left hand. "Take a load off. Would you like something to drink, a cocktail perhaps?"

"A water would do nicely. And since you've apparently decided not to shoot me, would you mind putting those toys away before someone accidently shoots someone?"

"These toys you're referring to, we all know how to play with them," Bill said.

"Still, do you mind putting them away?"

"Be a good sport, Russ, and get Moshe a bottled water."

"Yes sir," he said smiling and flipping me off.

Russ placed the gun in his swim trunk rear pocket and walked to the kitchen, tugging on them, fighting to keep them up from the excess weight of the gun. Bill sat down, twirled his Glock several times around his finger, and slid it under the front of his bathing suit. I put my gun in my lap and sat down. Moshe, void of any weapons, parked it.

"Well, let's hear it."

"Again, I'm here for Max. Your hostility toward me is unnecessary. As you well know, Max and Sonny were close. So much that Sonny let Max in on most of his dealings and vice versa. But one thing you must know, Sonny wasn't in any danger. His enemies were not involved. Sonny had everyone and everything under control."

"Yet, he's dead and I'm here sitting next to you. Care to elaborate?"

225

"I know how this looks, but no one was out to hurt Sonny. That's why we're all in the dark. Sonny's enemies were going to wait until after he died and then throw Dino a bone and take over. Dino is nearing retirement and would have left town in a New York second."

"So, no leads at all?"

"No, but Max still wants to meet with you privately. He has information for your eyes and ears only."

"Steve, I'm not sure I trust this guy. How do you know he's really with Max? Maybe, he's just setting you up," Bill said.

"Steve, take the meeting, you won't be set up or disappointed," Moshe said.

"And you'll guarantee Steve's safety, how?" Bill questioned.

"I'll sit with the two of you." He looked up at Russ, who handed Moshe his bottled water.

"What could possibly go wrong?" I said. "Does Kurt know you work with Max?"

"I'm not sure, to be honest, but he's seen me with Max. Max didn't hide me under the table."

"Now that would have been worth the price of admission," Bill joked.

"Can I arrange the meet?"

"Yeah, let's do it. When?"

"I'll set it up for next Thursday, midnight. Does that work for you?"

"Let me check my schedule, yes. But why so late?"

"You've seen Max's environment. Not much happens during the day; that's when he sleeps."

"Makes sense."

Moshe chugged his water down. As he walked out the front door, I couldn't help but envy Max's unique diversion, the pizza van. A nice way to protect his man's identity.

I closed the door after Moshe pulled out of the driveway and rejoined my friends.

"You gonna go through with this, Steve?" Russ asked.

"Sitting around the house waiting for an epiphany doesn't work for me. I'm going to take the meet and find out what's so hush hush."

"You want us to follow you, in case this is a setup?" Bill asked.

"No, but thanks. No need to get you guys involved in this. Not yet anyway."

So, there's a chance of being on your 'A' list?" Russ quipped.

"Only if you're hit or shot at."

*****

Chapter 21

The Horsemen met at the Triple George Grill for lunch, a block down from the Mob Museum, next to Hogs and Heifers on 3rd street. They sat at their usual table in the back where'd they consume mostly a liquid lunch with trays of oysters on the half shell as they discussed business.

Sherriff Dean Thomas, the silent partner in the Horseman, started the proceedings after everyone ordered drinks.

"I'm not liking where this is heading."

William Johnson added, "This George Sharp buying into YLL is complicating things. Someone strangling that nurse at Sonny's, shinning a bad spotlight all around. Maybe it's time to bail, cut our losses."

"I'm leaning with William on this," added Barry Schuster of Silver Express limos.

"Over my dead body," an extremely irritated Hans Stephanner cut in, leaning into the other three with both of his hands on the table. "There's a fortune at stake and you're going to let a couple of unfortunate incidents get in the way? You forget why we started this project? When Sonny turned up dead, it created a green light sooner than anticipated."

"I know we can make a fortune buying YLL," Sherriff Thomas agreed. "But the body count is cause for concern. If the feds get involved, I'll be out of the loop and unable to direct the investigations."

"Aren't you the Sheriff for a reason? Do your fucking job and find the murderers," Hans responded.

"I'll stick around for another two weeks. Fix this or I'm out," William said reconsidering.

"Two weeks," Barry agreed.

"Sherriff, you better come through or I'll get you sent to Pahrump, changing sheets at the Chicken Ranch Whore House, understand?" Hans warned.

"We're all working overtime on this, Hans," the Sherriff assured. "Take a chill pill."

"Then it's settled. In two weeks, we meet back here, all our problems resolved. We move forward," William victoriously declared.

"Or, if the sheriff's boys and Metro fall on their faces, we bail," Barry said.

They all raised their glasses except for Hans who nodded as the group moved on to other business.

Chapter 22

Monday

A week passed. Everything settled down. YLL began making money, Sam and I saw each other a couple nights, nothing serious, just having fun, and Russ and Bill were enjoying the chauffer's life.

I met with Vicki several times to discuss the progress of her investigations, but all roads ended up on the inconclusive highway and the redundant process would start over again.

Someone claimed Mary's body from the morgue and apparently moved her to Texas, where Mary was cremated by one of her former husbands. I kept what few clothes I had of hers boxed up; no one claimed them. I found a place in the garage and stored her things hoping someone someday might show up. I wanted to meet one of her ex's, especially the last one.

*****

Vicki sat in her office, reviewing witness testimonies, when her partner, Dustin Miles, walked into the office. He'd been on a three-week fishing excursion in the Northwest Territories. He was in his early forties, stood six-four, weighed in at two-hundred-sixty pounds, spent three years playing left guard for the UNLV Runnin' Rebels football team while earning a degree in criminology. He had a propensity for changing gears on a dime as situations dictated. His effervescent personality opened a lot of doors. He'd been with Metro for ten years, the last three as a detective. Big and tall men stores put a beating on him every time he walked in.

"You miss me, V?" Dustin said peering at her from a couple of feet above her desk.

"You've been gone so long I began to wonder if you'd joined the Royal Canadian Mounted Circus."

"Your sports bra bringin' those puppies in a bit too tight?"

"Not as bad as those tighty-whitey nut crackers you strap on each morning. No wonder you don't have any offspring."

She stood and the two hugged.

"Great to have you back. Some crazy off-the-wall-crap's been going down since your three-week hiatus."

"Vacation, Vicki. Play nice with the less fortunate."

"We've caught some real work of art. Two gunned down in a YLL limo, hit style, and the new YLL owner's girlfriend strangled in his pool with piano wire. No witnesses to any of them. But I think we might have caught a break on Mary's murder, the YLL owners girlfriend. We need to swing over to the north side gate shack; I think that's how our killer gained access to the property."

"Nice work V. You want some coffee before we head out?"

"Not here. This machine serves up dredged up Lake Mead mud."

"Choose your store wisely, sarg. I'm buying."

*****

1:30 PM

Woody walked into his office and ordered his receptionist Carol, to call Sherry LaBelle.

"Time for that bitch to sell me her joint," he mumbled to himself.

"Change that. Get me Goldhabber first. He's got some explaining to do."

"Yes, Mr. Huntsman," she dutifully answered.

Woody pulled his desk chair out and plopped down hard, digging his cowboy boots deep into the cheap vinyl mat, scooting his chair directly under his desk. He turned his computer on and pulled up the RJ newspaper web site, scanning to see if there were any new murder stories. He was pleased at the usual drug-related shootings and a murder suicide.

"It's getting unsafe in this city with all these California gang bangers trying to move in on the establishment. This city will be running red for years to come. Almost unfair to our boys in blue trying to solve all these murders," he said laughing out loud.

"I have Goldhabber on the line, sir."

"Thank you, Carol."

"Goldhabber, where in the hell have you been? I've tried to reach you the last couple of days. You know I don't like voicemails."

"Sorry, business and family matters."

"What's this I hear about some George guy that kid brought into YLL?"

"It's true. He's a patient at the psychiatric ward where he worked."

"You're going to sit there and tell me some psycho patient with money coughed up the cash to buy his way into YLL?"

"Yeah, but I'm working on it."

"And just how are you working on it?"

"It just so happens George's sister likes cash more than her brother. I dug up some info on her; she's willing to get the deal voided, for financial compensation of course. I'm drawing up papers as we speak. She's going to sign off on his mental instability, claiming coercion while under the influence of anti-psychotics. I'll use our mutually corrupted judge, the honorable Dr. Sciortino."

Woody broke out in boisterous laugh. "The honorable my ass, that overpriced bag of shit. Does come in handy once in a while."

"That he does, Woody. I'll call you in a couple of days as soon as the greedy little bitch gets here and signs the complaint."

"I might have underestimated just how devious you can be. Keep up the good work," he added at the end of the conversation and hung up.

Woody hit the intercom switch. "Call Sherry."

"Goldhabber thought this up on his own? That stupid backstabbing cockroach. If only he knew who the manifestation residing behind the red curtain really was," Woody chirped out loud.

"Sherry is on line three, Mr. Huntsman."

"Thank you."

"Sherry . . ."

2:15 PM

Goldhabber's burner phone rang. "Yes."

"Did Woody buy your plan?"

"All the way, Mr. Johnson."

"Good. How much time did you buy?"

"At least forty-eight hours, more if you need it."

"Some lawyering you just pulled off; we might need to keep you around awhile."

The line on the other end went dead.

Goldhabber's options were dwindling, hemmed in on three fronts, not including everyone from YLL. At least they weren't going to make him dig his own grave.

3:55 PM

233

While he was printing out some documents from his home office, Goldhabber's cell phone rang again. He recognized the Washington DC area code on the screen. He let the phone ring five times before answering it.

"Yes?"

"How's life treating you, Norman?"

"Oh, it's you."

"Answer your phone like you did, only with more enthusiasm next time, even when a name you *don't* recognize comes up."

"I will."

"Good. Did Woody bite?"

"He thinks I'm a genius."

"We both know that's a pile, don't we?"

"If you say so."

"You aren't being a dick, are you?"

"No."

"One phone call gets your ticket punched to hell, Norman. Any questions?"

"Yeah. When do I get my get my golden parachute?"

"Easy Norman, lots to do yet. And trust me, I'm the only person in this city with your best interests at heart. Isn't that right, Norman?"

"Yes. Do you have a name or something I can call you?"

"Sure."

The line went dead.

Goldhabber's sides were hemorrhaging, being ridden like a cowboy on a mechanical bull with two-inch spurs.

Norman flipped off the phone, turned out the lights, and locked up his office. Once outside, he looked up a number on his phone and dialed it.

"Hello, Norman. What can I help with?"

"I need a pair."

"What age, size, and colors do you prefer?"

"I don't care. Mix and match. You choose. And Tanya, have them bring something to make me relax. It's been a rough day."

"Always here to help. Be at the Trop around eight-thirty. The key will be at the bar. Look for a lady in a pink horseshoe tee and matching baseball cap."

"Yeah, I get the drill. The Trop, eight-thirty, lady in pink. She'll have the room number, key, and something to make you relax. Bye, Norman."

*****

Tanya picked up another burner phone and dialed Charlette.

Charlette rested in her GT Mustang parked outside the Tuscany casino, listening to Satellite Radio. She saw the call and answered it.

"Goldhabber is coming over to the Trop at eight thirty. Pick up the key to room 755 and meet him in the bar."

"That little shit knows me."

"Then tell him you're helping me out or wear some sunglasses, Char."

"No problem. I'll figure it out."

"He'll have four thousand dollars for you."

"That's a lot of cash, Tanya.

"It is."

"You know he's in trouble."

"But he's safe tonight, so let's squeeze his credit cards dry. He'll be too jacked up on Mexican porn Cialis. And the two ball busters he's going to be with will screw him dry. He'll be there a long time. We can charge the shit out of

235

him. If you want to join in, there's an extra thousand in it for you, maybe more."

Charlette thought it over for a few seconds: the four of them, a briefcase full of money, credit cards, hotel comps, and excess party drugs could turn into a financial adventure.

*****

Norman emptied forty one-hundred dollar bills out of his briefcase and put the money in his pocket. Once Norman opened his Mercedes, he reached into his glove box and pulled out a bottle of Mexican porn star Cialis thirties.

"This ought to turn my love muscle into a baseball bat," he loudly said, cheering himself on.

Chapter 23

Wednesday
4:09 PM

The Pope stood on his second-floor bedroom balcony, finishing off a cigarette, enjoying the gentle desert breeze flowing across his patio. He leaned over the black Spanish wrought iron railing surveying his meticulously manicured backyard complete with pool, Jacuzzi, bar, stone grill, and luxury cabana. The balcony circled the entire house, offering him total access to the property at a moment's notice. The unobstructed sunrises and sunsets happened to be a bonus.

His thirty-two-hundred square foot house complete with four oversize garage doors on the northwest side of Pahrump rested on two acres, protected by a seven-foot block wall. The wall encompassed a remote security gate, with strategically placed cameras at the entrance and throughout the property. A short winding thirty-yard asphalt road lined with seven-foot pineapple palms took visitors off the dirt and gravel easement to his front gate. The unique entrance kept curious onlookers away, and the Pope's two German Shepherds casually patrolling the property didn't actually spell the words 'visitors welcome'.

The late midday sun drove the temperature up into the low hundreds, its rays cutting into the bedroom's overhanging balcony shades. As he walked back to the bedroom balcony doors, he stopped next to his beige cushioned wicker patio chairs, pondering the absurdity of his chosen profession—killing selected undesirables for profit.

He finished off his cigarette, plunging its bright, red-tipped end into one of the two antique playboy club ashtrays resting on a hand-designed seven-foot long rustic wooden Spanish door which had been converted into a coffee table.

Business continued to prosper. He'd been receiving an unusual amount of job inquiries over the last two weeks. Several competing criminal and government factions were crawling over each other vying for his unique and special talents, unaware that he'd been triple dipping. The seed money for future contracts made his vault gush with greenbacks and recently purchased jewelry.

The Pope entered the bathroom and opened the double doors to his shower, revealing a tall brunette with a leg up on one of the custom benches, soap running off her back. She smiled when she saw him.

"Coming in, are we?" She faced him.

Within a couple of months, his infatuation with her made it easy for him to ask her to move in and share his desert fortress.

"Let me help you get ready for work, Bridgette."

Chapter 24

Thursday
8:52 PM

*****

A jet landed at Mc Carren International airport and Franco Salvatore exited the plane along with his personal bodyguard. They rode the tram to the baggage claim area, then walked down the escalator where three armed men awaited them.

"Franco, I hope you enjoyed your flight from New York."

"Johnny, the flight sucked. That fucking turbulence. As soon as the plane descended into Vegas, I felt like I was riding a jackhammer. The car loaded?"

"Ready on our end."

They grabbed the carry-ons and walked to the baggage claim area. It wasn't long before they were on their way to zero level at the airport.

"Our driver is with the car. I'll let him know we're getting ready to walk out."

"Ramone, the boss is here. Pull up front."

"On my way."

"Don't you think it's a little over the top using Ramone and YLL to pick you up?"

"Of course it is."

9:41 PM

The Graveyaad rocked again. The taxi explosion, ruled an accident, hadn't caused a drop in patronage or

239

revenue. The enhanced news coverage actually heightened the bars notoriety and business was booming. New faces joined in with the regular clientele and they all appeared to be partying earlier than usual.

"Sam, you meeting Steve tonight?" Sherry called out.

"He's picking me up at two."

Lisa heard the conversation and wasn't pleased. She met Steve first and wanted to show him how sexy and wonderful she could be. Steve, no doubt like his father, was a wham-bam-thank-you- mam kind of guy. But on the bright side, Steve would dump Sam after he got what he wanted. Then she'd have her shot.

No worries. Just have to be a little patient, that's all, she thought to herself while pouring several beers.

"Lisa, shake your ass. We're slammed," Sam shouted.

"Why don't you get taps that pour beer instead of foam?" she shot back.

"I'll call the Bud rep and the two of you can clean beer lines Sunday morning. Good call on your part," Sherry answered.

"Wow, overtime. Now I can afford to get off my mac-n-cheese diet."

"You know where the time clock and the doors are, right?"

Lisa didn't appreciate the way Sherry verbally abused her. But she made bank working here. Leaving anytime soon was out of the question. Lisa gave Sherry a phony smile and kept up the false front.

*****

10:15 PM

Things were moving along at a normal pace. Russ and Bill were still enjoying being chauffeurs, especially the generous gratuities. Fortunately, they didn't have to chauffeur any overly sex-crazed clients. They just did the usual strip club runs, clubbers, and a couple of small conventioneers. I even did a run involving a nice couple celebrating their tenth anniversary. Dinner, a show, and a little clubbing. Simple stuff.

George adjusted to the limo business and taking care of the books while Kurt and Ramone were being Kurt and Ramone. Dino stayed to himself and Tony worked on some leads regarding Sonny. The house had ample space for the four of us. We were working well as a group and the money was pouring in.

The pool man came in the morning and got the pool up and running. I was thankful to be sleeping in and grateful Bill handled the details. The water temperature would be cold and it would take at least twenty-four hours for the water to heat up to eighty-five degrees.

Woody seemed to disappear, along with his BS. I blew off the insane idea of Vicki and I somehow becoming a couple as Sam and I continued to see each other after her night shifts at the Graveyaad. We were having fun exploring the clubs until five in the morning. I hadn't slept with her yet but I knew as soon as I made a move it would happen.

Tonight was my midnight meeting with Max; I was nervous. Bill, Russ and I decided not to involve Moshe in any way and trust him at his word. We were positive his information about the meet was legitimate even though Max didn't return any of my phone calls all week. I would drive a limo to Tight Racks just in case some undesirable was expecting me to show up in my Tundra. After all the insanity having gone down since I arrived in Vegas, the word trust was a big leap of faith.

I slept until four in the afternoon and made lunch. This night owl stuff was beginning to grow on me. I went online and did some tedious computer work. It was almost nine-thirty when my cell phone rang. I looked down at the

241

caller I.D.: unknown. Too late for a telemarketer, so, I answered it.

"This is Steve."

"You might not remember me."

"Alright, enlighten me."

"Marsha."

"Marsha who?"

"You know, La Crosse Marsha."

I pulled the phone away from my ear and did a double take on it.

"Marsha, I remember you... how are you and how exactly did you get my number?" I answered not knowing what to say or why she called me. "You have some very upset people looking for you."

"I'm sorry to bother you, but—"

"Marsha... hello Marsha."

The line went dead.

"You have to be kidding me." I stared at my iPhone. "I wonder what she wanted?" Then I thought about my last chat with her, still wondering how she knew I was going to Las Vegas.

I debated whether I should tell Vicki or keep this to myself. If Vicki ever found out I withheld info from her she would really be pissed. Maybe even prosecute me for withholding information on an active criminal investigation or two.

I took my shower and dressed in one of my new suits. I cranked up the Bluetooth sound bar and played, "Doin My Thing," by King Juju, a crazy song from the slasher movie "Sorority Row". I liked the lyrics and jammed to the tune. I left the song on repeat, trying to keep my attitude in the proper mode.

I finished off my wardrobe with a shoulder holster and Glock nineteen. I wasn't going to get killed with my hands up in the air, begging for my life. I enjoyed a vain moment and admired myself in the mirror.

"Lookin' good, young man," I proudly said.

My nervous energy made me jittery. I thought of several places to go but my train of thought was interrupted when my cell phone rang a second time. I looked at the caller ID, extremely disappointed at the caller's name.

"This is Steve."

"Steve, it's your favorite lawyer, Goldhabber."

"Nobody's beaten you brain dead? Congratulations. I guess Tony hasn't returned from New York yet."

"What?"

"Kidding, Norman. What's up?"

"I have a lead on Sonny's money. You want to meet up? I can tell you what I learned."

"Why can't you tell me on the phone?"

"You'd trust this information across open wires?"

"This sucks. You're right. Where do you want to meet, YLL?"

"Another information sink hole. No. How about at the north end valet at the Forum Shops. You know where that is?"

"I actually do. What time?"

"I'm busy now, but can you be there by eleven?"

"How about eleven-fifteen?"

"That will work, Steve. I'll see you there. And come alone. This is for your ears only."

I guess that was the popular phrase for the evening.

Goldhabber hung up. The one person who I knew was a pathological liar was asking me to show up in a dead-end parking lot at the Forum Shops at eleven-fifteen at night. Gee, nothing to worry about with this scenario.

I looked in the mirror again, wondering if this was my farewell pose. I pulled back my suit jacket, pulled out the Glock, cocked it, put one in the chamber, and replaced it. I walked to my nightstand and grabbed a thirty-round clip for my reload. It made the Glock look like a mini AK-47 when inserted. One in the chamber, fourteen more in the clip, and a thirty-round back-up, I guessed I was as ready as I could be. I got this funny feeling inside my gut. I went back to the nightstand and pulled out another thirty-round clip. Seventy-five rounds. Now I felt dressed.

I took the limo out of the gated community, still in awe of the neighborhood I lived in after all of those years in a frat house. After almost fifteen minutes behind the wheel, I pulled the limo into the parking lot of a joint named Sonny's, on Industrial. It wasn't my father Sonny's place but the name gave me a nice false sense of security.

It was too early for the rendezvous, and I needed to collect my thoughts. It wasn't too late to inform Vicki of my meet with Goldhabber. A simple call and she'd have my back. Serious food for thought, but not going to happen. If this were on the up-and-up, then I would look like a chickenshit for getting her involved.

Awe inspiring having a mental argument with myself; thousands just like me in padded cells having some of these same arguments. I nervously played with the radio, channel surfing and wasting time.

My cell phone alarm went off at eleven. I turned it off, pulled the limo out of the parking lot, and finished the short drive to The Forum Shops.

I entered the driveway just past eleven and looked around for one of the attendants, not sure if anyone worked this late. There wasn't anyone around, but several cars remained in the parking lot. I reached into the right pocket of my suit and made sure the Glock would slide out smoothly. After I pulled forward along the north side of the building, I stepped out, and cautiously scouted the area. An Escalade pulled into the valet area and stopped behind me. I didn't know what Goldhabber drove, but the timing led me to believe it was him. The door opened and sure enough, Goldhabber walked out.

"You alone, Steve?"

"You alone, Norman?"

"Yes. Here. I have a folder. Sonny began working on this shortly before he disappeared."

Goldhabber held onto the folder.

"Are you going to give it to me?"

He gave me this weird obtuse look, like he possessed the last life vest on a sinking ship.

"Norman, the folder," I said, reaching for it with my left hand.

I noticed a Metro squad car pulling into the valet booth behind us. I looked over at the car and turned back at Goldhabber just in time to see his head dislocate from his shoulders, blood and brains splattering onto the hood and windshield of his SUV, and all over me. I did a double take as Goldhabber's lifeless torso careened off his vehicle and collapsed into a contorted pile next to his front tire. He was still clutching the folder to his chest.

I reached down and tore the folder away from his bloodied hands and dove belly first, sliding across the short trunk of the limo, rolling and landing hard partway between the curb and sidewalk. I pulled my Glock out and crawled to the back of the limo, keeping my head down, shoving the folder inside my bloodied suit coat. I hoped the vehicle would provide enough cover for whoever was going to take the next shot at me.

I noticed the officer calmly walking up to the front of Goldhabber's SUV like nothing happened. His weapon was drawn, but his nonchalant movement seemed off.

"Hey! Get down. Someone's shooting at me!" I yelled out to the officer.

"Come out from behind the limo with your hands up. You're under arrest, Steve Mueller," he responded.

How in the hell did he know my name?

"I didn't do this. Are you out of your mind? And there's no fucking way I'm coming out from behind the limo." I peeked around the bumper at the officer approaching me.

"Come out with your hands. . ." He looked down at Goldhabber's body.

It didn't matter. A split second later his head dislodged from his shoulders, just like Goldhabber's, as he bounced off the SUV and collapsed in a heap next to Goldhabber.

"What the fuck is going on?" I said.

I retrieved my cell phone out of my suit jacket and speed dialed the office.

"Good evening, YLL, this is—"

"Candice, I'm being shot at," I said loud enough for her to hear but not loud enough to expose my position behind the limo.

"Who is—"

"It's Steve. Call Metro. I'm in the north valet at The Forum Shops and two people have already been shot."

"Steve, my God! I'm calling. Stay with me!"

Candice was on the other line screaming at Metro. Seconds seemed like hours as I waited for the explosion of another round, or maybe it would be the sound I never heard; a bullet would take my head clean off like Goldhabber and the Metro officer.

I heard a noise behind me. I quickly turned around and pointed my Glock. The valet casually strolled toward the back of the Metro patrol car. I almost pulled the trigger and killed the guy.

Headline: Limo owner kills Forum Shop valet for bad service, I nervously thought, a stupid grin appearing on my face.

I crawled to the front passenger side of the SUV, hoping the shooter didn't pick me off between the vehicles. I scraped holes in my new trousers crawling there and was about to warn him when the valet looked my way and figured it out.

"Shit! Holy shit!" he screamed.

"Someone's shooting at me!"

He created a vapor trail back to the north door valet entrance, leaving me alone with the shooter. It wasn't rocket science putting this scenario together. The shooter didn't care what the valet did. His fire power would be concentrated on me. I watched the valet safely race through the north doors.

I continued to frantically scope out the area, moving my eyes and gun hand simultaneously, waiting for someone to pop up, jump on the limo, anything. The soft lighting near the door provided enough light to see blood trails forming into puddles; a river of red was flowing toward the curb.

Maybe the gunman thought he killed me and took off. With the cop dead, maybe he left the scene. Lucky me, unlucky Goldhabber and the Metro guy. I remained tucked behind the SUV tire, in no hurry to pop my head up. I needed Metro here now. Within seconds I heard an army of sirens, the screeching of tires and the sounds of vehicles flying over speedbumps at the valet entrance.

What was this going to look like to Metro? I'm crouched behind a dead man's car, two corpses bleeding out six feet in front of me, Glock in hand, seventy-five rounds of ammo. "I'm fucked" came to mind.

My version came to me: an invisible marksman somewhere in the night, using a high-powered rifle equipped with a silencer, killing anyone near me. And from what I learned from my father, those had to be some sort of magnum rounds, massive carnage with just a single bullet.

My solution to this: I returned the Glock to the holster, no need holding a weapon at a crime scene where you are the only person sporting a heartbeat.

The first Metro officer arrived on the scene, alone in his car. He parked it alongside my limo. I waved at him from behind Goldhabber's SUV with my hands visible; no need to

247

give him a reason to shoot me. He drew his weapon and came over, stumbling over one of the dead men's legs.

"You alright? You hit?" He ducked behind the SUV.

"Stay down. Someone's shooting at me." The officer took cover next to me. He radioed some codes and asked for backup, swat, and ambulances.

He moved to the front end of the SUV, glanced toward the front wheel and saw the remains of Goldhabber and one of his fallen brothers in blue.

"This was done with a high-powered rifle. Who are you?" he asked.

"Someone trying not to get killed in a mall parking lot," I answered.

Two more squads pulled into the valet area; one pulled up behind the SUV and the other pulled in front of and between my limo and the SUV, shielding the two dead men. Several officers ran out of their vehicles, armed with handguns, eyes surveilling the area. More police cars and SUVs rolled into the parking lot and took up strategic positions.

"What the hell is going on out here?" the officer asked me.

"I was meeting my lawyer when someone blew his head off. Then this Metro officer showed up and the same thing happened to him."

More Metro vehicles pulled into valet, sirens blaring, lights flashing. Officers exited their vehicles, spreading out across the parking lot, taking cover behind parked cars, pillars, and the north end block walls. I could see some of the officers were armed with what appeared to be Remington 700 shotguns.

It was like a Die Hard movie without the Christmas decorations.

The first officer on the scene crawled out between Goldhabber's SUV and the Metro car.

"Cover me," he ordered as he moved quickly towards the two dead men.

I was positive he wasn't referring to me.

The officers took up different angles and surveilled the area for anything that looked like an active shooter, but the only people present were armed Metro officers.

He pulled the fallen officer to the back of the limo and then stopped.

"Hey, this isn't one of our guys. His shield is a knockoff."

He instinctively released the partially headless corpse and backpedaled on his butt behind the cars.

*****

Goldhabber, what a double-crossing sack of shit. I should have done him as a community service, she thought. Bridgette picked up the two spent cartridges from her .338 Lapua Magnum, packed up her gear, and walked towards the Mirage rooftop door.

"I can't wait to get back to Pahrump and reorganize my new house. The pope, never saw this one coming," Bridgette gleefully said as the door closed behind her.

*****

Swat units entered the parking lot. Several members of the unit took their ballistic shields and escorted me inside the north end of the mall. A terrified valet sat on a bench deep into the hallway. Six Metro officers were in the hallway guarding the north entrance and blocking anyone from exiting.

This incident rattled me to my core. I never understood my father's role in special forces. He protected me from its horrors, but if even one day went like tonight, I don't know how he or anyone could have mentally compartmentalized this. My father taught me how to be a man, fair, honest. I never respected him as much as I did in this moment, tonight. I really missed him.

The north doors to the valet entrance swung open from the Forum Shops. Vicki and several detectives came through.

She ran up to me and kneeled.

"Are you all right, Steve? You hurt?"

"I don't think I'll ever be alright after what I just witnessed."

"You know him?" a detective said, accompanying Vicki.

"Steve, this is my partner Detective Dustin Miles."

"You're one lucky kid."

"Define lucky."

"A smartass. Great."

"Excuse us, Miles."

She grabbed my arm and pulled me to the north valet wall.

"What's under your suit jacket?"

"My shoulder holster, Glock included, and a folder Norman was about to deliver to me that I took out of his dead hands."

"Have you lost your mind? Someone could have mistaken you for the shooter and dropped you," she angrily whispered, not trying to draw attention to our conversation. "Just what the hell do you think you were going to do? This isn't some college video game night. People are getting killed around you. You've become a death magnet. Anyone who gets close to you ends up in the morgue. Slip me your weapon, slowly. I'll block the view."

"Don't forget I have two thirty round clips on my harness."

She slightly backed away and held up her hand as I reached into my suit jacket.

"Hold on. Two clips? What were you expecting to happen tonight?"

"Yes to the two clips, no to expecting trouble at the mall tonight. I'm carrying for a midnight meeting with Max at Tight Racks. I'm not going to be some lame ass duck in a shooting gallery."

"What do you think tonight was, Daffy? You think Max is involved in this?"

"I don't think so. I was going to meet him alone and didn't want to go there unarmed in case someone else got any crazy notions of ending me tonight. I wasn't going to die without a fight."

"And how's that working out so far?"

"Great, as you can see."

"Did you fire any shots at the person who killed Goldhabber?

"No."

"This isn't on the way to Max's club. What the hell is going on?"

"I thought you were on my side. Jesus Christ Vicki, I almost got killed. You're acting like I instigated this slaughter."

Our voices were moving up the decibel meter and several officers looked our way.

"You have to use the bathroom?" She double winked at me.

"Ah, sure. My kidneys are about to explode."

She pulled me through the double doors and into the mall. She walked me over to the Neptune statue and pushed me down on a bench.

"I know you're hurting. A lot of really horrific things have happened to you since you arrived. There's something

251

evil going on. I don't want you to end up like Mary or Goldhabber," she said, easing off on her tone.

"Two weeks ago, I was a nobody and everyone liked me. Now, people I know are getting murdered. I don't want this to continue. George, Russ, Bill, I've put their lives in danger. I didn't think it would be like this. It was supposed to be the adventure of a lifetime. I wanted to make this work, for everyone. This is worse than a nightmare because there's no waking up."

"It's a nightmare with a body count."

"At least Russ and Bill know how to protect themselves."

"What is that supposed to mean? They carrying too?"

"Yes, we all have our carry, conceal permits in Wisconsin. We all can shoot too."

Kurt shuffled toward us. His demeanor and facial expression said it all.

"I got here as quickly as I could. Candice called me. You alright, Steve?"

I slowly nodded.

"Kurt, follow us. I'm going to escort you both to the men's room," Vicki said.

Kurt looked at her oddly.

"You're the one calling the shots. Lead the way," came Kurt's response.

Detective Miles observed from a distance the chaotic scene at the statue.

We walked to the men's room door. Vicki held up her left arm and gave us the stop sign. She carefully entered and made sure no one lurked about.

"It's clear," she said as she held the door open.

Once inside, Vicki gave Kurt a command.

"Kurt, you're former military, right?" she quietly asked, knowing restrooms could act as echo chambers.

She placed her right index finger across her lips signaling us to keep it quiet.

"Yes," Kurt whispered.

"Give me your gun harness, Steve. Kurt, I want you to put his gun holster on and smuggle it out of here, discretely. I'll call you when he's finished at Metro. I handed everything to Vicki. Here's his gun and the clips," Vicki said handing Kurt everything.

"Arming civilians. Nice touch. Who do you think did this, Steve? Woody? He must have been really pissed after that ass kicking you gave him," Kurt added.

"You got into a fight with Woody?" Her angry response echoed throughout the men's room. "When were you going to disclose that little nugget?" she said bringing her voice down with a disgusting look on her face.

"Like, never. I didn't think it was important. Tony and I made a point. I assumed Woody understood it's meaning."

"You *and* Tony were involved?" she loudly whispered.

"Oops. Sorry, Steve. I think I'll be leaving now." Kurt put his suit jacket on, concealing the Glock and shoulder harness.

"Two thirty round clips, nice touch," Kurt chimed in. He cautiously exited the men's room.

"Who are you, Steve?" Vicki stared at me with her arms folded.

"Just a guy from Wisconsin with a prodigious target on his back for something I inherited."

"The folder stuffed partway down your pants, that's the one you took off Goldhabber?"

"Yes. He was about to hand it to me before someone decapitated him."

"Do you know what's in it?"

I reached into my pants and pulled it out, unfolded it, and took the papers out.

"They're blank. You've got to be kidding me," I said kicking a stall wall. "This was all a setup to get me to the mall." The empty men's room providing the echo chamber of my frustration. "He said he had some information on Sonny's missing money; that's why we met. Now, someone or some organization has executed him or is the worst shot ever and missed me twice," I said knowing full well whoever was the triggerman was an expert marksman.

"Let's go down to Metro and get you out of here. I'm not sure what's going on, but there's never been anything like this in Las Vegas, even when the mob ran this place."

"I have to let Max know I won't be showing up. I worked on this meeting for over a week."

"You think Max has some answers?"

"Max and Sonny were close. I think he has some ideas that can help solve some of the bizarre happenings of the last couple of weeks. At least I hope so."

"Let's both go pay Max a visit. Why waste an opportunity to gather some intel?"

"Have you ever met Max?"

"Let's just say he knows me and I know him."

"I also have another call to make."

"To whom?"

"Supposed to hit a few clubs later with Sam Labelle."

"It's safe to say you won't be clubbing tonight. Sam, huh?"

*****

Woody was finishing up some contracts when his burner rang.

"Yeah."

"Goldhabber is dead, killed at a meet with that Wisconsin kid."

"They both dead?"

"No. Goldhabber and a cop. It has the signature of one of our mutual friends, the Pope."

"The Pope?"

"You heard me."

"Why would he take a contract to kill Goldhabber?"

"Someone must have dropped a dime on that shyster. What a miserable excuse for a human being. Always had his hands in too many cookie jars. His time to leave Las Vegas."

"Yeah." Woody hung up. He dialed his driver's number.

"Letterman, pick me up in fifteen. Someone took out Goldhabber at the Forum Shops. I'm at the office."

"Sure thing, boss. Goldhabber's dead?"

"Yes, and the widow Goldhabber probably needs some consoling."

"You need me to bring any extras?"

"Not tonight. Let's see how grief-stricken she's going to be. Metro will be on their way soon, so we're just going there to comfort her."

*****

Billy Johnson slammed his fist on his desk.

"What the hell!"

"Hans, that psycho, killing Goldhabber. What the fuck was he thinking? I'm out!" he shouted at his seventy-five-inch flat screen.

His cell phone rang again. He looked at the caller ID and immediately answered.

"Thomas talk to you too?"

"Yeah, and before you jump ship, let me call Hans," Barry Schuster said. "There is no way on earth he took out Goldhabber. Not without a green light from all of us."

"Well, I have two dead bodyguards that would disagree, Barry. That is if they were still alive."

"I got this. Let me call him and get his take or alibi on this, okay?"

"He's your problem, Barry. Deal with it or I'm out. There are other multimillion dollar deals out there."

"Not like this one, Billy, and you know it. Grow a pair."

Chapter 25

Vicki and I arrived at Tight Racks around twelve-thirty AM. I cleaned up the best I could in the Forum Shops men's room, leaving my bloodstained suit coat in her car. My scraped-up suit pants wouldn't be noticed in a dark strip club. Max agreed to meet, even after he heard about all the earlier chaos. I guess I had another question to add to the list. Any idea who was in on the Forum Shops shootings?

Kenny Gustapolis was working the door and greeted us. His look indicated he already knew what had just transpired. A line with would-be patrons formed inside the hallway, partially extending through the club's entryway. We walked directly up to the podium.

"Ever get any nights off?" I asked.

"Sure, but tonight's not one of them. Follow me."

He led us into the club and stopped at the bar.

"Desirée will take you to Max. And what happened to your pants?" he asked already knowing the answer.

He radioed the call to Max.

"Ruby not working tonight?" I inquired.

"Ruby doesn't work here anymore," he answered.

The club was rocking tonight, a packed house with strippers gyrating and hustling throughout. As we were escorted back to Max, I noticed Vicki didn't seem phased by the atmosphere one way or the other. Desirée led us to the same back room I'd met Max in before. Déjà vu all over again. Boris stood watch over the door.

"Evening, Boris."

"Steve, good to see you again. Where's Kurt, chasing down urologists?"

"Boris, this is detective Vicki Spicuzza. Vicki, this is Boris."

"I'll need your weapon, detective."

"This is official police business, Boris."

"No weapon, no entry. Those are the rules."

"I don't care about your rules. Again, police business."

"Again, house rules. No exceptions."

Vicki sized up Boris several times. Even on her best day she couldn't put a dent in him.

"Vicki, it's important, or you can wait out here, I don't care. But I need to see Max."

Vicki begrudgingly removed her piece and handed it to Boris.

"The one around your ankle too."

Vicki lifted up her left pant leg and handed a second gun to Boris.

"They'll be safe with me. You can have them back when you leave."

He patted me down first, then Vicki. When he finished, he opened the back door. Another security guard met us on the other side and escorted us to a secluded table. Max sat in the middle, Moshe on his right.

"You have more security personnel, Max. Expecting trouble?" I asked.

"People weren't dropping like flies the last time we met."

"Fair enough, Max. This is detective—"

"Spicuzza. I know. Nice to finally meet you in person, detective. Our paths have never officially crossed."

"Max Sharone. I've heard a lot of things," Vicki said, mostly holding back any judgements.

"Mostly good, I'm sure, or we'd have met sooner. And how is your father, Dino?"

Vicki took notice of Max's intel.

"He's fine. Thank you for asking."

"Congratulations on being cleared of that incident with your husband's killer. He got exactly what he deserved."

Vicki chose to remain silent.

"So, Steve, how you are holding up? I'm sure better than the guy whose blood is partially splattered across your shirt. The clean spots are where your suit coat was. It appears to be someone else's and not yours by the look of you. A lot of bad things have been happening, especially to those around you. Tonight, well, let's agree you are one lucky young man."

"I'm doing shitty, Max. Nothing can describe what I witnessed tonight. Thanks for asking. No champagne?"

"This is a business meeting, not a social gathering. And the detective is on duty, working several homicidal events that seem to be following you around like flies on a donkey's ass."

"You have an uncanny knack for the obvious."

Max looked that one off.

"I have information that might help you Steve, and you too detective."

He turned to Moshe, this time professionally dressed in a grey suit with a black shirt. After getting up from the table, he stood next to Vicki.

"Moshe, retrieve the file."

"The last person attempting to place a file in my hand got his brains splattered all over a parking lot."

"Some nasty business earlier, but as you can see, they didn't shoot you."

"That's reassuring," Vicki said.

"I'm not apologizing for the strict security rules; it's for everyone's safety."

"You mean your safety," Vicki concluded.

Max and Vicki exchanged icy glances. I didn't see this side of him the last time we met. What a difference a couple of dead bodies could make to reformulate one's second opinion.

"Max, can I see the folder?" I said.

"Moshe, hand it to him."

Moshe pulled a file from under the table, following Max's instructions. He looked more at home, like a well-paid bodyguard, than he did wearing a pizza delivery uniform. He

259

placed the green folder on the table and with his left index finger slid it over. As I reached for the folder, Max slammed his fist on it, briefly startling both Vicki and me.

"If you open this, there are rules you will need to follow," Max commanded. "First off, nobody I knew was out to hurt Sonny. I was close to Sonny and his enemies. Sonny had stage four colon cancer, was going to be dead in less than a year. He just started chemo a week before someone murdered him. And yes, I said murdered. I can't prove it yet, but I will.

"How do you know he was murdered?"

"Sonny wasn't suicidal and he had no reason to be driving out towards Moapa at that time of night. So, yes. I say he was murdered. Inside that folder is a letter from Sonny, his will. He entrusted it to me, only to be opened in the event of his death. I've read it, and you need to read it."

"What about the will reading and Goldhabber?" I asked.

"Sonny wouldn't trust him to deliver a bag of donuts. That will was a decoy to keep Goldhabber from digging. Goldhabber dealt from the bottom of the deck. He extended himself too far, too deep, too fast, with the wrong players, all of whom don't have your best interests at heart."

"Why are you allowing me to hear this, Max?" Vicki asked.

"Because you can be trusted. This document was drawn up several months after Sonny gave Goldhabber the fake will and the video you saw. He used my attorney to draw up the final documents. He didn't tell Dino either out of caution, paranoia, whatever. Before he died, his circle of trust came down to me and me alone. I'm sorry to say this detective, but in the end, Sonny didn't even trust your father."

"But you think I'm trustworthy. You just insulted my father."

"I didn't insult anyone. Sonny made some calculated moves and he believed that one or more of his people at YLL were corrupted. I would have eventually found out, but someone possibly. . . let me rephrase that. . . definitely an outsider, took Sonny out."

"What's really inside of here, Max?" I quietly asked.

"Moshe, stand by the door."

Like a soldier he immediately walked away.

"No one knows this. Dino might have had a clue, but this stays here, and that includes you detective or else you can join Moshe by the door."

"Excuse me, Max. My father is involved in this?"

"Detective, this is not a request, is that clear? What you see here stays here. Swear to me on your father's life that what you see stays here, between the three of us."

Vicki backed down and agreed to Max's terms. Maybe the motivating factor for the string of brutal murders rested inside one green manila folder. Max released his fist.

"Take a careful look, both of you," he said as he slid out of the booth and joined Moshe by the door.

A small light went on above the table making it easy to read the document. Together we combed through the ten-page document, cautiously looking at each other every time we cleared a page and flipped it over to begin the next one.

Vicki gave me an astonished look as we combed through the document at a turtle's pace. I couldn't believe what I read. Vicki had to be thinking the same. No one in their right mind could possibly believe this nonsense. It had to be someone's idea of deranged humor. This looked like a malicious attempt to discredit me and turn YLL into an empty parking lot.

We finished the final page with Max standing at the end of the table, calculating our responses.

"Sonny's not my real father… but he left me everything in his will?"

"He did," Max conveyed. "It's true, Sonny is not your real father. A man named Albert is. Albert Ross Edwards. He went by the nickname, Are. He disappeared twenty-four years ago, right after you were born.

"I don't get it... why leave it all to me?"

"Are is responsible for most of Sonny's good fortune. This was his way of settling a debt of gratitude. Sonny made a promise to take care of you and this is how he fulfilled the promise."

"Yeah, leaving me in debt up to my eyebrows. Nice way to honor a promise."

"Sonny would never do something that heinous. There are pieces missing to this puzzle."

"From what I knew of Sonny... this doesn't seem like something he would intentionally do," Vicki added.

I ignored her statement.

"What do you know about my real father, Max."

"According to Sonny, he was a special, unique individual who served in the United States military in WWII and was awarded the bronze star. He grew up on a ranch outside of Roswell, New Mexico and led a rather mundane life after the war as an engineer. Then everything changed for him after the New Mexico incident that took place in the summer of 1947."

"Seriously, do you expect me to believe he was there. Yet alone involved?" I asked.

"I agree with Steve," Vicki added.

"Look, I was skeptical as well when Sonny brought this to me. I assure you, this is as factual a detailed account of what happened as I have ever laid eyes on. And believe me when I tell you I've seen everything from captured Nazi documents to archived historical documents dating back several thousand years, to sworn testimony on deeds, diaries, certificates and records in a variety of languages, encompassing dozens of countries both friendly and hostile.

So, when I tell you this, whatever you want to call this, is real and verified, it is."

I grabbed my arm as Vicki slid out of the booth and stood next to Max.

"You've inherited more than a limo company, Steve."

"Your telling me my father was at the crash site in Roswell?"

"There are a thousand versions of what really happened in Roswell but Are's account is unlike any of them," Max continued. "Depending on your point of view, he was either in the wrong place at the wrong time or the right place at the right time. The government found him several days after the event, questioned him extensively, and decided to tuck him neatly away, in area 51."

"The Nevada Area 51. Spook city?"

"Yes. And while he was there he quickly morphed our physicists and scientists in almost every applied science. His brain doubled or tripled in functionality. Sonny told me Are was involved in our Stealth technology program, jet fuel mixtures and some projects you'd expect to see in some science fiction series."

"Such as?"

"He spent most of his time working FTL technology."

"That's the power source used by dozens of sci-fi novelists and script writers," Vicki interjected.

"You're a sci-fi girl?" I asked.

"Seen a couple of Star Treks and Wars."

"Impressive," I added. "Faster than light technology is possible, but we're fifty to a hundred years away from achieving anything that would resemble it, maybe longer. Finding a power source with infinite energy to create light speed is impossible with our current resources."

Max looked at me curiously after I tossed out the FTL technology info.

"You're right Steve, with our current technology and resources it would take us fifty thousand years to reach Alpha Centauri," Max said.

"What are you saying Max?" I asked.

"Are you implying the Roswell incidents victims were from the Alpha Centauri planetary system?" Vicki asked. "And Are somehow became intellectually contaminated?"

"Sounds like a story no one would believe," Max concluded.

"Except everyone with a Government UFO program," I threw in for good measure.

"We're getting off point," Max said taking control of the conversation again. Are was kept at Area 51 for almost thirty years."

"They made him into a sled dog." I angrily stated.

"No. They treated him like royalty. They gave him everything he needed or wanted."

"Except freedom," Vicki added.

"Yes. Except freedom. Then he vanished and showed up in Las Vegas in 1978."

"They held him there against his own will for all those years?" I said in my most agitated voice.

"He was a decorated war hero and a patriot. While working at Area 51, Are developed some unique technologies, many of those invaluable to this nation and its allies around the globe. And Steve, until recently, no one knew anything about you. Especially your relationship to Are. He and Sonny went to great lengths to protect you."

"So, what you're telling me is a confirmation of what Sonny wrote in that document. I'm the son of the first person to make contact with an alien?"

"Yes."

"Is the US government after me?"

"Let's just say they're keeping an eye on you, just in case."

"In case of what?"

"In case you display any extraordinary talents."

Suddenly, I wondered about any unusual talents I might possess. Vicki was staring at me oddly along with Max.

"Hey, cut it out, both of you. I'm just a normal guy with a really good memory... there's nothing to see here. Tons of people have good memories."

"Of course they do, Steve." Max smirked.

"Not funny, Max."

"And from what I know of you, you're semi-intelligent too," Vicki snarkily commented.

"Thank you, but I'm not auditioning for "Jeopardy", I said raising my tone a notch.

"Steve, relax. Our government isn't out to confine you."

"Define, 'Our government', Max."

"The United States, Steve. However, I can't say as much for the Chinese and Russians. Afterall, you are the son of the man who made first contact, and somehow they found out about you. And that has piqued their interest."

"And who leaked out this little nugget?"

"Another mystery that will be uncovered... one of these days."

"Our government... hard at work."

"Is everyone after Steve because of Are?" Vicki quietly asked.

"Vicki, I'm sure most of the degenerates trying to acquire YLL have no idea what they've stumbled into."

"What about tonight? Was Steve being shot at or protected?"

"In my opinion, there is no way an assassin could have missed Steve and taken out Goldhabber and the Metro officer by accident."

"Then someone *is* protecting me."

"By all indications of what went down at Caesars, I'd say yes."

"Then I have more than just a random killer on my hands," Vicki surmised.

"Vicki, they're here, governmental agency cleaners, ghosts, hitmen, whatever name you want to attach to them, they're here, and unfortunately, the body count is going to go up exponentially. And no matter how many rocks you look under, you'll never find the ones responsible. And anyone getting in their way, well, you saw what happened tonight. They'll either end up in the morgue, buried somewhere in the desert, or wind up in a fifty-five gallon drum of acid."

"That's a lot of intel for someone out of the loop. You were with the Mossad, Max?" Vicki asked.

"True, HaMossad leModi'in uletafkidim Meyuhadim," he said in Hebrew. "The national intelligence agency of Israel."

It was eerie to hear Max say it in a foreign language and with such conviction. Vicki and Max were in a stare down.

"Sonny made some incredible moves all because of Albert Ross Edwards, my birth father," I began. "That's a lot of BS to swallow, Max. No one is ever going to believe this."

"I disagree. The two dead government employees in the back of Ramone's limo, Mary, the shooting tonight; there are some very concerned parties in direct conflict with each other who completely believe what you just read. And there are those who have no clue what's going on other than the acquisition of YLL. Unfortunately for you, all the players have a different opinion on what to do about you. It appears there are some on your side but more that are not. Your allies may have won tonight, but it's a marathon, not a sprint. Goldhabber and his Metro officer were going to dispose of you for all the wrong reasons, to get their hands on the land your limo company sits on."

"Why would anyone want to kill me over a downtrodden limo company?" I asked.

"The land is worth a small fortune."

"This just keeps on getting better and better," I sarcastically said. "Okay, I'll bite. Why?"

"The NFL has plans to purchase the land directly across the street from your property. It was supposed to remain under wraps until the official announcement. However, when it comes to big money deals, anyone with the knowledge of this could have sold this information."

"How many players are we talking about?" Vicki inquired.

"The obvious, Woody and the Four Horsemen, the not so obvious, all the back stabbers implanted throughout this city in all agencies, too numerous to count."

"They'll be coming at me from all sides."

"They want that property. You can see why your inheritance has drawn the attention of Las Vegas's biggest and most ruthless players."

"I must be missing something, If Sonny expected a huge payday for YLL, then why are his assets missing and why the double mortgage on the house?" I inquired.

"That's why Sonny's death was so tragic in more ways than one. I don't have that answer," Max replied.

"Sonny cashing out his assets is another one of the missing pieces to all of this," Vicki added.

"That makes no sense. He could have held on to it or just sold it and had a huge payday," I said.

"Any bank would have shelled out millions for that development," Max added.

"Yet, here I am, being shot at for the rights to a property that was mortgaged to the hilt, at least until I dragged George into this. And then magically, the NFL secret gets out. Now the vultures are swarming and I'm dinner."

"That sums it up nicely," Max concluded.

"Let me see if I've got this correct. Steve is the target of multiple groups, the Russians, the Chinese, maybe Woody

267

or the Horseman. But another group whose purpose is to protect Steve took out Goldhabber and the Metro cop. And there might be one or more other groups out there whose intentions are unknown?" Vicki surmised.

"In a nutshell way, yes. But there's a bigger piece of the pie that all of the Vegas vultures are unaware of."

"That piece of the puzzle, I understand. It's the part about Are and me that—"

"Makes zero sense, looks fabricated," Max said.

"I'm having trouble buying into this Are story, Max," Vicki said.

"Even I had a hard time buying into it. But Sonny was always a straight shooter and an honorable man, especially around his inner circle. He would rather cut off his arm than lie. If he believed it, and he did, I believed it. That's why I held onto his will and we kept this document sealed."

"You were at the staged will reading, Max. I remember seeing you there," I said.

"Yes."

"And you knew all of it was bogus?"

"Yes. Especially when I heard about the pictures and movies. Sonny never went to Wisconsin, nor did he hire anyone to follow you. His sole purpose was to protect you, not risk exposing you."

"Then where'd he get all that intel?"

"That's what I want to know."

"And the other reason you stormed out wasn't because of the will or the pictures, you knew about those, it was because Sonny liquidated his assets and left you in the dark."

Max paused a few seconds. "Yes."

"Maybe Sonny didn't trust you either," Vicki stated.

"Of course he did. I have the will and the documents!" Max snapped.

"I believe you, Max," I said. "But there are still a lot of holes."

"Too many."

"Getting back to Are, it seems like my protectors were delegated by him with Sonny's help and he wanted me safely tucked away. My adoption had to be off the books, completely illegal."

"It must have been fixed. Your adopted parents must have been specifically chosen. You said your father was in special forces?" Vicki asked.

"Yes."

"And he taught you how to fight and a variety of other skills, correct?"

"Yes."

"Are didn't want you exposed and he kept you out of harm's way. It all makes sense now," an excited Vicki interjected. "He wanted to shield you from the government and anyone else. He didn't want your fate tied to his."

"It's sad. I'll never meet him or Sonny," I somberly added.

"Are trusted Sonny, as did I. Are was a very astute man," Max hammered home.

"I think we've discovered more questions than answers," I sadly added.

"It appears so, today. In the future, who knows," Max said.

Vicki's phone buzzed.

"Do you mind, Max, Steve? It's my Captain."

"I'm sure it's important; answer it," Max said.

Vicki stepped away from the group and took the call. By her body language I could sense she was getting grilled.

"Max, that stuff about Are, you think it's true, don't you?"

"Stranger things have not happened; this is a first for me. Sonny had absolutely no reason to deceive me."

"Is that why he never came to see me?"

"He didn't come right out and declare it, but I'm positive he had Are's and your best interests and safety at heart."

"The photos, movies of me… someone knew about me and shot them."

"I wasn't privy to that," Max said.

Vicki walked back to us.

"The Metro cop, the one killed earlier, was not a cop. It was the Pope."

"The Pope? That son-of-a-bitch!" Max said.

"Metro received an anonymous tip. Nobody tips us off on a partially decapitated body still warm at the murder scene. This is insane."

"One mystery after another," I said.

"You know him, Max?" Vicki asked.

"We've crossed paths."

"He's a gun for hire. We've brought him in several times for questioning on local homicides. But there's never been enough evidence to charge him for anything."

"That dirty snake, Hans. He probably ordered the hit on you and used the pope."

"Who is Hans?" I asked.

"A piece of white trash, that's who," Max said.

"Hans Stephaner?" Vicki asked. "One of The Horsemen. They must know about the stadium plan."

"Apparently so, and with Steve pushing up daisies, only Woody would be in their way, and he can always be manipulated for money," Max added.

"Or eliminated," Vicki said.

"Those murderous cockroaches," Max said. He walked to the wall and back several times.

"You think Hans and the Horsemen wanted to take him out?" Vicki asked.

"I don't know. There's always a blood trail with their kind. It's a gun-for-hire network. Whoever set up the mall shooting was a chess master."

270

"I think whoever interceded on my behalf was the real chess master."

"I stand corrected," Max smugly replied.

"Are's avenging angels, protecting Steve," Vicki said with a smile.

"So, is Are still alive?" I asked.

"I doubt it. He would be close to one hundred years old, Steve," Max said.

Vicki grabbed my arm. "I have to get him to Metro, Max. My detour here isn't appreciated, for any reason. Thanks for your help and the information. Be careful Max; you apparently know too much."

"I still can't believe Sonny would will his entire estate to me and cut your father out."

"Just a minute," Max said.

"I have to bring him in, Max."

"Vicki, sit down. Your trip to Metro is going to have to be delayed a while longer," Max said.

Vicki slid into the booth with a troubled look on her face.

Moshe reached into his jacket where he'd harnessed his weapon and walked toward the three of us.

"What's going on?" Vicki asked.

"Your father wrote a story. It's about the first time Are, Sonny, and your father met. He put it to paper, a rather entertaining account of his first encounter with Are."

"Dino wrote down his first meeting with Are?" Vicki said looking confused at the prospect of her father's involvement.

"It affected him too. After all, his life forever changed on that night. Here is the letter Dino wrote. I'm sure he has a copy lying around somewhere. This took place in 1978, well before I ever met Sonny or your father."

Moshe unzipped a plastic folder and handed it to Max.

"Here it is, the written story of that night in 1978, typed up and given to me by Dino Lezcano."

We sat there mesmerized by the prospect of hearing the story of Are, my father, written by Vicky's father.

Max sat down and began reading.

It is a Sunday afternoon that finished on a Monday morning. The temperature is about 90 degrees. We had just finished our swing shift cab jobs that ran well past midnight.

I pull into the parking lot of the Lucky Steer Casino. It is still under mob ownership but their empire is starting to collapse with one indictment after another taking out the Vegas bosses. The skimming brought in the feds and they were in the process of eradicating mob activity. The good ole boy club of Las Vegas, along with their offspring, the first to set up casinos back in the day, were on the sidelines like Vultures, waiting for the mob to die, ready to devour the fruits of the Mafia Empire and the new barbarians at the gate.

I see Sonny's cab back in a corner of the lot. We agreed to meet there at the end of our shifts. There were no cell phones or pagers back in the day. You made plans and tried to stick to them. I walked up to his cab. Sonny is sitting in the front seat with a guy seated in the back.

"I thought you were done working. Who's the guy in the back?"

Sonny looks over at me with this crazy smile.

"The guy looked lost and confused so I picked him up. An hour later he tells me to pull into the Lucky Steer Casino. We get here and I ask for the twenty-dollar fare and the guy looks at me like I'm Clyde Barrow trying to rob him at gun point.

"Excuse me, I drive, you pay, kapish?" I explained to him in a very nice tone.

He tells me he has no money. I can see this fare sinking to the bottom of Lake Meade. Listen to this. Then he tells me he can pay for his fare in the casino. Of course, I'm not letting him out of my sight. So here we are, waiting for you so I can get paid, in the casino."

"Should we just take him out back and beat the snot out of him, Sonny? Metro won't give a shit. We'll say he's a runner and we settled the score."

"No, let's play this out, see where it goes. I'm already in the hole. He says his name is Are."

"Like the letter "R", or the word Are?"

"I don't know. Does it really matter? Ask him yourself. I'll turn the dome light on."

"Hey, is it spelled A-r-e or just R?"

"A-r-e," Are looks at him and shrugs his shoulders.

"Dude, this guy is dressed like he just escaped from a bad sixties beach party movie. Maybe he ditched the whacko ward or some cool Frankie Avalon costume party. I wonder where he stashed his ukulele. Sonny, what do you think?"

"I think you still get a boner every time you think of Annette Funicello. It's time to go get my cashola."

"Stop, stop. Who's Frankie Avalon and Annette Funicello?" I asked.

"Ever hear of Mickey Mouse?" Max answered.

"Of course I have."

"Well, in the fifties, Annette was one of the first Mouseketeers. Frankie Avalon was a singer and actor. They made a slew of low budget sixties beach movies together, which by the way made a fortune."

"Thanks, Max. Sorry for the interruption."

Max continued.

We lock our cabs and go into the casino. I don't trust anything about this guy. Especially the Hollywood good looks with the bleached blonde hair and sky blue eyes, all sitting on top of a six foot frame. I'm eyeballing him all the way. As we walk into the casino, Are gets this big-ass grin on his face.

"It's a casino. We're in Vegas. It's Disneyland for adults."

Mitzi, a really cute cocktail waitress I have bumped uglies with several times, comes up to us.

273

"Are you talking about Mitzi, my mother?" Vicki angrily asked.

"Yes."

"Go on."

"You boys want a couple of Buds? Who's your amigo? He auditioning for "Beach Blanket Bingo? Hey, whacha havin', Frankie?"

"Thanks Mitzi. Yeah, three Buds. That okay with you, Sherlock? We'll be over… where the hell are we going, Sonny?"

Sonny looks over at Are. "Are, where are we going to get the money you owe me?"

Are starts walking around the casino, his head rolling side to side like a Stevie Wonder audition tape. He's touching machines, stopping to hear the bells. Of course, we're both within arm's length ready to grab him if he makes a mad dash for the exit. He stops at a crap table, must have been the Coolers table, where only two guys are rolling the bones.

"Dino, feel the cool air around this table?"

"Yeah, the house must have made bank earlier tonight. It's a morgue."

"Well, it can't stay cold all night. Let's see if we can heat it up a bit."

"What about our pal?"

"We can keep him between us. You know, until he gives me my money."

"Yeah right."

Sonny reaches into his pocket and pulls out what we called a Polish Bankroll, lots of ones and fives, maybe a twenty or two in the back, for looks. As kids, we both grew up in melting pot neighborhoods where all our friends tossed out insults back and forth. But if an outsider came around and said anything derogatory, he'd get his ass kicked. This was one of our Polish jabs. Just as he's about to reach across the table to get change, Are grabs his arm. He pulls him over to a dollar slot machine. "Try this one."

Sonny looks at him. "Slots are for suckers, tourists. There's no skill here, just luck."

"Trust me. Play this one."

Mitzi comes up to us and hands us our beers. "Slots, since when do you guys play slots?"

I just love the way she looks in that cocktail outfit.

"Our beach buddy compadre wants us to play slots, so slots it is."

"Well, this machine is the Iron Maiden, tighter than a frog's ass. Carly usually puts her Whales on these two machines over here, company secret. And what are you doing playing dollar slots?"

"Frankie Avalon says this is the one to play."

"Well, I've never seen him here before, so I don't know where he's getting his dope."

Sonny puts in a twenty and starts to play five coins at a time. He pulls the lever and gets garbage. Plays five again, nothing. Two more tries. Two more losses.

"Well, that was fun. There's twenty down the shitter. Any more hot tips for me?"

"Don't gamble."

I thought Sonny was going to punch the guy's lights out. He started to get out of his seat, but I held his shoulders down.

"Easy, Sonny. He's just bein' funny."

"Yes, easy Sonny. A joke. A funny. Play again."

"It's real funny when you aren't using your money."

Sonny regained his composure and looked back at Are. "Well?"

"Put in another twenty."

The next twenty went into the machine which led to a series of wins and losses. Then bang, back-to-back four of a kind. Some more losses, a couple of wins, and after forty-five minutes, there's three hundred twenty in the machine.

As Sonny is about to pull the lever, Are tells Sonny, "Time to leave."

He's got his forty back, plus the twenty Are owed him and a two-hundred-forty-five-dollar profit. Yeah, a good time to walk. He

275

pushed the cash out button and the coins rained down into the metal tray making plenty of noise. The machine flashes as the coins stop, leaving Sonny two-hundred-ninety short. The slot attendant comes over and pays Sonny the rest in cash. We all start heading for the cashier's window when Are grabs Sonny by the arm and pulls him toward the Coolers crap table. There is no one there except three dealers shooting the breeze.

"Play here," Are demanded.

"Didn't you just pull me away from this table?"

"That was then, this is now."

Sonny pulls out his new-found dollar and coin supply and changes out two crisp one-hundred-dollar bills.

"What are you, fuckin nuts? You just won over two hundred bucks, and you're going to piss it away on craps?" I asked.

"Apparently so."

"Shit, alright. Give me forty in ones. I can kick my own ass later," I say in my best whinny complaining voice.

There we are, two in the morning on a Monday, about to play craps on a table that's colder than a witch's tit in January, listening to some guy we don't know giving us advice on craps.

The dealers are glad to see some heartbeats at their table again. We are the fresh meat. They walk over to their spots next to the table and one of the dealers slides six dice over to Sonny.

"Okay genius, what do you recommend I do? You do know how to play craps, don't you?"

"Put twenty-five on the pass line and one hundred dollars on the eleven."

"You never put more on an eleven than on the pass line. Are you out of your mind?"

"You called me a genius, right?"

"So, now you're taking me literally?" Sonny added.

"I am a genius. Do it."

I place three dollars on the pass line and three on the eleven. Sonny places twenty-five on the pass line and one hundred on the eleven.

"It's only my money, right genius?"

"It's only your money."

"Any suggestions on which of these dice to pick up?" Sonny says as he turns around and looks at Are.

"Yes. Try two of the red ones."

"They're all red."

"Then you have a one hundred percent chance of picking the right ones. Now you can be a genius too."

"A broke smartass. What next?" Sonny gives Are a smug smile.

"Sonny, you sure you want to play? We can book out of here, drop off the cabs, have some real fun."

"No, I'm riding our genius pony straight to the poor house or to the penthouse, no middle ground."

Mitzi leans in. "You boys need another round?"

"Three shots of Crown and make them doubles. I don't want to see the train that's about to annihilate me," I say with this sinking feeling.

"Right away, baby." She scampers off.

Sonny looks at her ass as she wiggles away toward the service bar.

"Hey, go find your own cocktail waitress to ball. She's mine."

"Sensitive little wop."

"Just grab a pair and let's get this over with. "

Sonny picks two out of the six and the dealer pulls the other four away and drops them in his tray.

"New shooter comin' out. Place your bets," the dealer shouts.

Of course, there's just the three of us. His dealer call is strictly for show, trying to coax some of the other gamblers over to the table for the slaughter.

I look at Sonny, then at Are, and shrug my shoulders. "Give em' hell, Sonny!"

Sonny picks up the dice, rearranges them, squeezes them, then fires them hard off the back. They both careen, one of the dice bouncing twice and showing a six while the other spins against the side wall in a tornado-like spin, slamming into a stack of red five-dollar chips and rolling back into the middle of the table turning up a sweet five.

Sonny and I cheer. The dealer reaches into the stack of black one-hundred-dollar chips and counts out fifteen for Sonny and nine red five-dollar chips for me. The other dealer on our left slides Sonny a twenty-five-dollar chip on the pass line and three white ones to me.

"Pay your first forty-five and your second fifteen hundred," the dealer shouts, trying to lure other gamblers to the table. "Place your bets. Same hot shooter coming out!"

Like flies to shit, people start to walk over to the table, the word hot electrifying the gamblers. I look at Sonny, who's looking at Are.

"Alright, genius. Way to go. We done?"

That's when things get interesting.

"Why not let it ride?" Are quietly says without moving a single muscle in his face.

"Let it ride?" Sonny says sarcastically. "Hey, it's only money. Sixteen hundred on eleven and fifty on the pass line?"

"Your math is impeccable," Are says, cracking a sarcastic facial expression for the first time.

I can hear the sweat coming off Sonny's forehead.

"Sonny, you can't seriously be thinking that?"

The dealers meanwhile call over their pit boss.

"The guy is thinking of playing sixteen hundred on the eleven," the dealer smugly says as his pit boss showed up. "He just rolled one. We got action?"

"Well, what's it going to be, sir? You going to let it ride?" The pit boss intervenes, sensing a major recovery.

Mitzi, with impeccable timing, shows up with three Crown Royals, handing one to each of us. I throw two fives on her tray. She gives me that incredible smile which means I'm getting some as soon as she gets off of work. The three of us lightly bump glasses and down the shots.

Sonny yells, "Let it ride!" and slides the stack of fifteen one-hundred-dollar chips to the dealer. "Put them on eleven."

The dealer shatters Sonny's "let it ride" with, "We have action!"

278

About six people put their money on the pass line and toss anywhere from five to twenty-dollars on the eleven. I take thirty and put it on the tray in front of me. I place twenty on eleven and let the six dollars ride.

The dealer slides the dice back to Sonny, the six and five still showing. Sonny picks up the dice, rearranges them, squeezes them, looks down the table at some miniscule target and fires them hard off the back. Everyone at the table yells "eleven" at the same time the dice crashes against the back of the felt table. The players at the table are leaning slightly backwards, making sure the dice doesn't bounce and accidentally hit one of them. A cardinal sin in the world of craps.

Once again, the dice pound against the back and lurch forward. No suspense this time. A one and a two planted firmly on the bottom of the table revealing a six and a five on the top.

"Yo leven. Winner!" The dealer shouts.

In eight-part harmony everyone at the table yells, "Yes!"

People are high-fiving, jumping, slapping each other silly. Sonny drops to his knees and I dump Mitzi's tray trying to hug and kiss her.

Out of the corner of my eye I notice the pit boss motion to the casino manager. He looks like he just shit himself in a Ferrari. The dealers look at one another, and the pit boss calmly calls out the winnings.

Now the entire casino races over, trying to get one of the eight spots left at the table. There is chub in the water and the sharks are coming in for the kill.

Then everything slows down, and it feels like we are all in a movie; Sonny on his knees pounding the table, people with ear-to-ear grins laughing, me kissing Mitzi with my hands crushing her semi-revealed butt cheeks and Are standing statuesque, no emotion, taking it all in.

"Pay three hundred to your first, twenty-two thousand five hundred to your second," the dealer manages to choke out the words.

I watch the dealer set my three black chips in front of me, plus six dollars for the come line bet. But the most amazing thing I've ever seen is when the dealer stacks four flags, five thousand-dollar chips, and *five blacks, and places them in front of Sonny. And there's also the two green twenty-five-dollar chips for Sonny's pass line bet. Then he rattles off the other amounts to the rest of the players at the table. When the house is paying out this kind of money on each roll, the play comes to a complete halt. The air is electric. Zeus just unleashed a lightning bolt in the Lucky Steer.*

Sonny gets up, his Dago face red as a tomato. I've never seen him that color in the four years we ran together.

"Shit. I mean, holy shit, holy fucking shit Dino. Have you ever—"

"Sonny, never. Not in a million years!"

"I told you I'd have your money in the casino, didn't I?"

"You're a saint Are, you're a saint, a man of his word!" Sonny hugs Are, then stacks the chips and puts them in the chip holder in front of him.

"Is that enough?" Are grins.

"What exactly are you saying, Are?"

"Simple. Is this enough? Is this your pinnacle? Have you scaled your highest mountain?"

"I haven't Are. Why?"

"Then let's give it another go," Are replies with a stoic look on his face.

"I'm sorry. The tables closed. Dealers have to go home. Take your winnings and enjoy the rest of the morning," the casino manager calls out.

And this is where Sonny gets the nickname, Sonny Money.

"Hey, chicken shit, you running a casino or a day care center for tourists?"

"You heard me. Tables closed!"

"I see, you take a hit and gather your toys and run home to mommy! What a fucking pussy!"

Now the casino manager is really getting pissed, and a couple of security goons walk over to the table. The rest of the patrons at the table are complaining and getting boisterous.

"I want to play, and if you don't have the balls to make a decision, find me someone who does!"

Now the security guards are blocking the manger in.

"What, you gonna take me downstairs and knock the shit out of me cause I beat you fair and square? I think everyone here will be a witness, that you're a piss-poor loser and a dipshit!"

By now fifty or so patrons have gathered around the table and everyone starts tossing their two cents into the conversation, igniting the current situation.

I must have lost my mind cause I start chanting, "Sonny, Sonny, Sonny…"

Now everyone is chanting, "Sonny, Sonny…"

The casino goes nuts.

The Red Sea parts when the casino owner walks up to the table. You can hear a fly shit a hundred yards away.

Salvatore Fazio, owner, Kansas City King Pin, transplanted from New York via Kansas City to Las Vegas, a made Cosa Nostra boss, walks over to Sonny.

He calmly asks, "Is there a problem?" He snaps his fingers twice and the casino manager comes over.

"Sonny. His name is Sonny Tringale," a nervous pit boss quietly mentions to Salvatore.

"Sonny. Nice Italian name."

Now a smart guy would have said thank you for a lovely evening, here's a thousand for the dealers, cashed out, and ran out the door, but not Sonny, not tonight.

"Yeah, I won twenty-three thousand and your manager is treating me like I'm an asshole! He won't let me play at this table along with these fine other folks. Is that how you run your casino, Mr. Fazio?"

"You dress like a cabby, come into my casino, and talk this way to me?"

"Uh, I am a cabby."

"Yeah, sure. I've seen you around, with this guy," he points to me. "The one that likes to diddle my cocktail waitresses."

"Look, Dino and I like your establishment. It's a great place. We come here all the time. With all due respect, that's why I'm disappointed that you won't let me play anymore."

281

Sonny just backed a powerful mob boss into a corner in front of sixty or so casino gamblers and employees.

"Sonny had a pair on him," I told Max.
"He was one of a kind. But it gets even better."
"Read on."

Mitzi had raced back to the bar and now brings us six more Crown Royal shots.

"Excuse me, coming through. Here Dino, Sonny, and ah, your guy next to Sonny. What's his name, Dino?"

"Are. It's Are."

"Like the letter?"

"No, like the word."

"Oh, hi, Are. I'm Mitzi."

"Mitzi, are you just about through or is there something else more important going on over there?" Mr. Fazio says in his best irritated voice.

"Sorry, boss."

"Hi Mitzi, it's a pleasure to meet you," Are belatedly acknowledges.

"So, what are you proposing, Sonny?" Mr. Fazio asked.

Are puts his hand on Sonny while Mr. Fazio walks back over to where the dealers are standing. The security guards are surrounding him and the casino manager. Several more security guards come over to the table along with a couple of big Italian guys. Are cups his hand over Sonny's ear and whispers something for about fifteen seconds. And as many times as I have asked Sonny over the course of his life, he never revealed to me, or anyone that I know of what Are said to him. No more than what came out of Sonny's mouth.

"Twenty thousand, one roll, same table odds," Sonny tells Mr. Fazio.

"One roll, twenty thousand, table odds. Is that your adviser standing next to you?" Mr. Fazio asked.

"If an "Adviser" told you to play eleven twice, you would take him out back, crack his skull open to see if he had a brain, am I right Mr. Fazio?"

"You're a funny guy, Sonny. Done. This is just between Sonny and the casino. Tables closed to the rest of you. Is that going to be a problem?"

Nobody says a word.

Loud cheering sparks again, everyone jammed up to the table, four deep all around. Sonny grabs the four flags in his hand and looks at them. That's when things get interesting. Again. Mr. Fazio takes Sonny's dice and hands them to the casino manager. He takes the stick from the dealer and slides over six new dice.

"Go ahead, place your bet... let it ride."

Sonny tosses the four flags to Mr. Fazio who catches them in the air. He moves him back with his hand. Mr. Fazio places them on the eleven.

"Go ahead, pick your dice."

Sonny picks out two dice and rubs them on the table.

"I'll take these."

"Good luck, Sonny," Mr. Fazio says with the worst of intentions as he pulls back the remaining four dice and drops them into the tray.

Sonny looks at Mr. Fazio for a couple of seconds and then says, "Put the chips on snake eyes."

"What do you mean, snake eyes?"

"One roll, twenty thousand, table odds, remember?"

Dead silence in the crowd again.

"Remember?"

Fazio would have reached across the table and choked out Sonny had the two been alone.

"Alright, let's do this."

Sonny takes the dice, lines them up, squeezes them, pounds the table twice, and lets them fly. The dice hit hard against the back. One dice ricochets forward landing with a one showing and the other bounces up and over the table.

"No roll. Doesn't count. Shoot again!" A nervous box man shouts.

There are huge rumblings in the crowd, like a batter missing a grand slam home run just outside the foul pole.

The far dealer takes his stick, scoops up the one die, adds it to the remaining four from the tray and slides them all to Fazio, who slowly slides them to Sonny, waiting for him to pick two.

"Go ahead. Pick two. Any two," Mr. Fazio says.

A patron hands one of the dealers the flying die that flew off the table who hands it to the box man sitting in the middle. Normally he would have examined it and put it in the pile along with the other dice. But not this morning. He puts it in his pocket, not wanting to take the time to examine it.

"Well, go ahead. Pick two," Fazio asks again.

The gambler crowd grows eerily quiet, like a golfer making a putt to win the Masters. There are no machines going off, the chatter has stopped, and people aren't moving.

"Everyone is waiting for you, Sonny."

"I've changed my mind."

"You walking out now, after all this?" Mr. Fazio's expression changed on a dime.

"No."

"Then what?"

"Place the money back on the eleven, Mr. Fazio."

"You can't do that. You already made your bet."

Most of the players watching know that is bullshit and start grumbling and commenting, although not loud enough to catch a look from Mr. Fazio or one of his men.

"Table rules, Mr. Fazio. It's technically a new roll, and I don't have the dice in my hand yet."

Mr. Fazio looks over at the manager who nods and shrugs his shoulders. He moves the four flags to the number eleven.

"Go ahead. Pick two." Mr. Fazio orders.

Salvatore Fazio is not a happy man, the wrong man to piss off. Even I am feeling like my face is going to get rearranged. Mind you, we were tough guys, we could fight. The two of us had been in several *bar fights and beat the shit out of some fare skippers, but these guys are the top of the ass-kicking food chain and in their house.*

Sonny palms the five dice and softly rolls them around on the table in front of him. He looks down, grabs two dice, and pulls them up to the side of his face.

Sonny turns back to Mitzi. "Blow on these for me, will you?"

Mitzi looks over at Mr. Fazio like a rabbit about to be thrashed by a hawk. He begrudgingly nods and she, in some sort of contorted gesture, leans in and blows on them. Then she steps back and puts a vice grip on my hand.

Sonny arranges the dice the way he wants, squeezes them in his fist, pounds the table twice with his shooting hand, and softly tosses them against the back. The dice land on top of each other causing one to roll left and the other to the right with a little extra spin.

Now the people at the table have to push back with their bodies to keep the rows of onlookers from pushing them up against the table. Everyone wants to say they saw it, that they were there, at this table, on this Monday morning. Regardless of the outcome, they are going to be forever part of this ambiance, this moment in time with twenty thousand dollars from one roll of the dice. But the high roller isn't one, he's just a cab driver, average Joe U.S.A., soaking up his fifteen minutes of fame.

"Yo leven. Winner!" The dealer puts as much enthusiasm as he can without Mr. Fazio ordering the breaking of his legs for insubordination.

The left one is a six, the right one a five… three hundred thousand dollars on one roll. This is 1978 and three hundred thousand dollars can buy a lot of things, including happiness.

We both start hugging, Mitzi jumping in and the three of us go around in circles several times. The crowd acts like we won the Super Bowl, screaming, cheering, high fiving everybody everywhere. I must have heard the word God a hundred times.

"Where's Are? Where the hell is Are!" Sonny screams.

Are had quietly left undetected, vanished in the pandemonium, nowhere to be found.

285

"Where in the hell is he, Dino? Mitzi, you see him walk out of here?"

"No Sonny, I didn't. Sorry."

Salvatore Fazio walks over to the three of us. "You've had some incredible luck in my place."

"Yes sir, we have," Sonny says, trying not to swallow his tongue.

"My boys will bring your winnings to you in my office. You do know where my office is located, don't you?"

"Ah... in the basement?" Sonny responds trying to act unafraid.

"Correct. Yes, in the basement, a very lovely suite I only show to my special hotel guests. Or you can just walk out of here and we'll say goodbye and you can have a nice life, something like that."

"You have a unique sense of humor, but sorry Mr. Fazio. I would like all of my money this morning. I earned it fair and square. And you were there to see it."

"And where is your beach boy friend? He lit out before the final action finished. I really wanted to have a word with him."

"I picked him up at the Stardust late last night. I never met him before then. Besides, what does he have to do with any of this? I picked the dice and rolled them, just me."

Mr. Fazio leaves, surrounded by three bodyguards, and vanishes into the crowd. The dealers scoop up my money, empty most of the table chips, and are still short two hundred thousand. The two of us continue our celebration for another ten minutes, being congratulated by casino players and having drinks brought to us by excited players. We are big time alcohol buzzed.

Chapter 26

Friday Early Morning

"That's how Sonny acquired the money to start YLL?" I stated.

"Yes. Sonny told me the story several times, but not like that," Max said. "Vicki, I'm sure you have some questions."

"I do. But not for you."

"Go on Max, finish the story," I said.

Max continued.

Time to start our long walk through the casino toward the large metal door, the entryway to Mr. Fazio's private basement elevator. He has two of his men escorting us there. It isn't like we are going to run away. The walk feels like a trip to the electric chair; my heart rate must have exploded to somewhere around one forty. I can feel my heart trying to climb out of its chest.

We stop at the metal door and a security guard from the shadows walks up to the door and punches in a group of numbers on the electric security pad. There is a loud click as the guard pushes the door open and holds it until we pass into the hallway.

"I thought that door was the elevator?" I say to Sonny.

"Me too."

Once in the hallway, the guards close the door and now it's just the two of us. It's not a long hallway. I expected there to be art or something extravagant placed or painted on the walls but it's just this plain old shiny beige paint.

The hallway turns to the right and the two of us reach a service elevator in the back. There are two additional security guards waiting for us along with Mr. Fazio. We look up and see a white man who looks like an ex-hockey player enforcer, the huge black guy, a heavyweight boxer with sixty losses. I glance at Sonny with the let's-get-the-fuck-out-of-here look.

Sonny shrugs and looks at Mr. Fazio. "I can't wait to see your suite. It's an honor to be invited personally by you."

Like out of a bad horror movie the two security guards smile at each other and laugh.

The black guy leans toward Mr. Fazio. "Shall I call the caterers?"

"Let's hold off. I think there is something here."

Now, I'm not afraid of very many things in life, but those guys scared the crap out of me. And for the first time in my young life, I thought I was going to have a permanent residence somewhere in the Nevada desert.

The elevator doors open and inside is another big nasty-looking white guy, about six-foot-five. However, this guy is dressed in a nice suit and has a certain professionalism about him, and is carrying a small duffel bag in his right hand.

"Tony, is everything ready?"

"Yes boss, just the way you like it," he answers Salvatore.

The five of us join Tony in the elevator, Tony at the switch, the two security guards at our back and Mr. Fazio by the door. We get in, slowly turn, watching the elevator doors close in front of us, one last look at our way out.

"There's music in the elevator. Go figure," I said with a nervous laugh.

We know from living in Las Vegas that there aren't many basements. Caliche rock could destroy a construction job with run over costs and the rain we get causes flooding everywhere. Hell, if you plan on digging a pool you take out Caliche insurance. A casino? Forget about it.

The elevator doors open. Tony is followed by Mr. Fazio. The two security guards nudge us forward until the six of us are standing in his office.

"I don't like being hustled, Sonny," Mr. Fazio says.

"You didn't get hustled, you got beat. It happens."

Tony grabs Sonny by the shirt. "Better watch your tone."

"Sorry."

Tony releases him and backs away.

288

"Really, Sonny? Just got lucky, Mr. Fazio. We always come here. It was just his night," I say.

He motions us to sit in two of the three leather chairs in front of the desk. "I got an idea for you, Sonny. As you know, the feds are coming down hard on me and my fellow casino owners. I have several assets; I think there is a way for you to really come out of this looking good."

"How do you mean, looking good?" Sonny asks.

"I have a limo company and I have to sell it quickly before the feds impound it and it goes away. Are you interested? Or do you want to be a cabby hustling fares all your life?"

"Go ahead. I'm all ears."

Tony says to Sonny, "I can show you what you would look like as all ears."

"Tony, relax. We are discussing a legitimate business proposition," Mr. Fazio interrupts.

"Sorry boss. He's a little cocky shit and maybe needs to learn to respect those higher up on the food chain."

"You're right, but not today. There are more important issues at stake."

"I agree," a smug and confident Sonny says.

"Sonny, I'm going to sell you my limo company for the cut rate price of $300,000."

"How convenient, Mr. Fazio. But I've been around your limos and know their condition and the property they're sitting on. I think it's worth half that."

Mr. Fazio stares him down.

"You're a smart kid, maybe too smart. What do you think, Tony?"

"Way too smart."

This was the point where we were going to make a deal or get our asses handed to us.

"Mr. Fazio, you are a well-respected man, and the fact that you are making this offer to a simple cab driver like me is unbelievable. However, the business climate under that fool Carter in the White

House almost guarantees failure. So, here is an offer I think we can both be happy with."

"Go on. I'm listening."

"I'll give you $150,000 for the limo company and after six months I'll give you a thousand dollars a month for ten years, cash, but no interest."

Mr. Fazio wanders around the desk for a minute or so. There is dead silence in the room, except for the ticking of a grandfather clock in the corner.

"Here is my counteroffer: $170,000 now for everything, eleven hundred a month, cash, for eleven years, starting in six months, no interest. There will be a separate contract for the eleven years. We don't want the feds snooping around, do we?"

Sonny agrees. "We have a deal."

"And one more thing."

I'm afraid to hear the one more thing word.

"Tony, he stays with you as your employee, and my eyes on the business."

"Mr. Fazio," Tony protests.

"It will be good for you. I know I can trust you to take care of my interests in Vegas."

"If you say so, boss."

"Then we have a deal and Tony stays on."

"We do."

If Sonny would have said, no, there would be two more holes in the desert. But with over a hundred thousand in seed money and everything finalized on the contract, we were free and clear and going to say goodbye to being cabbies.

Max put Dino's story down on the table.

"That was written by Dino twenty-four years ago and placed in my trust five years ago, a written account of what transpired that night. Dino thought it might be valuable someday. He does not know I have read this to you tonight. With events rapidly declining around Steve, I wanted you to hear this."

"I never knew my mother and father met at the Silver Steer."

"They did, Vicki, and he loved your mother very much."

"This is a great story Max, but it doesn't explain all the events surrounding me, does it? Did Sonny pay off his debt?" I asked.

"No to your troubles and yes to the debt. But there's more to the story and it's for your eyes only. What you choose to do with the information is up to you. Vicki, do you mind waiting over there with Moshe again?"

With a frustrated look on her face, she walked over to Moshe. As Max began to recount the rest of my story, Vicki pointed to her watch, reminding me of my date with the detectives at Metro.

It took another ten minutes as Max filled me in on as many of the holes he was privy to, but there were enormous blanks and time gaps still unanswered. I got up as did Max and he gave me a big hug.

"It's a burden of monumental proportions that has been placed on your shoulders, and I know Sonny would have explained many more of those gaps to me had he not been killed."

"I don't feel any different." I said reexamining my hands and glancing down at my feet in a joking manner.

"You don't look any different either," Max threw in with a distorted laugh.

"What about Kurt and Ramone? Do they know any this?"

"Only if Sonny told them. But I'm almost positive he didn't."

I met Vicki at the door as Moshe extended his hand to me in friendship which I gladly took. Moshe returned Vicki's weapons and together we left Tight Racks for the short pilgrimage to Metro headquarters.

There was an uneasy silence for the first five minutes while we were driving up Las Vegas Boulevard.

"This investigation is unlike any other case ever. It's offbeat, peculiar, incomparable. You've got to be yanking my chain category. And yet here we are: two people died tonight and my job is still to find out everything I can about this and put the shooter or shooters away, even if he, she, or whoever was protecting you. This isn't personal, Steve."

"Wow, spoiler alert, It seems like *your* job is getting rid of everyone trying to protect me and you're making protecting myself a federal crime."

"That's not fair. I have to follow the law too."

She pulled the car off the main street and into a drug store parking lot.

"I'm on your side, even though I can't believe what I read or heard. I want to help you. I just have to digest all this; this was a lot to take in, and the fact that I'm not going to tell anyone about this Are business makes me an accessory to anything you do."

"How do you think I feel?"

"I can't even begin to think of how—"

"Don't even say it."

She gave me an almost apologetic look and then resumed our drive to Metro.

Chapter 27

1:52 AM

*****

Hans entered Barry Schuster's house through the garage, agitated from the failed events at the mall. He walked up to Barry's bodyguard and shot him in the head, the silencer making a muffled pop sound, dropping him into a sitting position, his head slumped over his left shoulder, his body braced up against the back entryway wall.

Hans proceeded into Barry's private home office.

"Hans. What are you doing here? I'm surprised Michael didn't announce you."

"Michael thought it better to sit this one out."

Barry rose from his desk. "Ah, go ahead, have a seat," Barry said pointing the way with his arm.

Barry sat down again at his large mahogany desk, littered with notes, contracts, personal bills, all shined on by a large blue florescent lamp located on the left side of the desk.

"Barry, what the fuck happened out there tonight?" he asked in an almost eerie and low-key way.

"The quintessential setup, disastrous, someone tipped someone off. The perfect plan, eliminate Steve and Goldhabber together… one trip, one contract two dead. The Ice Man couldn't have set this one up more efficiently."

"Yet, here I am, at your office, two in the morning, to discuss this clusterfuck! The element of surprise, gone! The trail of evidence implicating Woody, gone!"

Hans picked up his chair and smashed it on the office floor shattering it into dozens of pieces.

Barry quietly reached into his drawer and pulled out his Sig Sauer P220.

"Oh, Hans."

He turned around, pausing to look directly into Barry's eyes.

"What the fuck do you think you are doing?"

"You're right you know. I agree with everything you just said."

"Then what the fuck do you think you are doing?" He put an emphasis on his heavy German accent, sounding more like he was doing a reading from a 1940's WWII movie script.

"Hans, my psychopathic friend. You're such an ass-backwards thinking human being. Excuse me, wrong species... sloth."

"What the fuck do you mean?" Hans said, wondering how fast he could unholster his Sig and take out Barry.

"Billy Johnson's security men you permanently aired out, remember? Someone has to go down for this, don't you agree? This entire failed operation has your M.O. written all over it," Barry surmised.

"And who the fuck do you think is going to go down for this? And what the fuck does this have to do with you and me?"

"You're just too stupid to keep around. We decided it's time for you to join your Third-Reich friends in hell."

Barry repeatedly pulled the trigger at Hans point blank range, but nothing happened.

"What the... "

"How the you going to kill someone with a weapon that has no ammunition in it, my greedy little friend?"

Sheriff Dean Thomas walked into Barry's office.

"Dean, shoot him. My gun has no ammo."

"Hans, move up against the wall," the sheriff said, motioning with the barrel of his gun.

"Just what do you think you're doing?" Hans asked.

"Hans, slowly ease that Sig out of your suit coat jacket; this ain't my first rodeo."

Barry walked around his desk.

"The gun wouldn't fire. Hans must have somehow tampered with the gun."

"Hans, set the gun down on the floor and kick it over to me. Eeeeasy like."

Hans followed the sheriff's directive.

Barry tried to make a move for Hans's gun.

"I wouldn't do that, Barry," the sheriff ordered. "Stay where you are."

"We have him Dean, like we planned. I'll shoot him with his own gun, you can make it look like he attacked me, like the gun accidentally went off and killed him. Just look at the smashed chair; his fingerprints are all over it. This is better than perfect, Dean."

Dean cautiously picked up Hans's weapon.

"Barry, please stand next to your good friend, will you?"

"What are you doing, Dean? We won."

"You're such an ignorant putz, Barry." Hans confidently replied. "Your tin star sheriff Dean moved the goalposts in the middle of the game."

"What about Johnson? He in on this too?" a nervous Barry asked.

"I'm afraid Billy Johnson had a bit of bad luck." Dean carefully glanced down at his watch. "In about ten minutes from now."

Hans clapped his hands together. "Well played, sheriff. You and your new partner Woody, you put this together all by yourselves?"

"We decided your two limo companies and Billy's hotel casino would create enough capital to buy YLL without stressing our financial portfolio. With all the chaos surrounding that kid, well, we calculated bumping up the offer might get him to pack up his shit and leave. We went for convenient targets."

"You can't possibly believe any judge or court is going to buy into this horse shit?" Barry said.

295

"Surprise. Done already. Just have to pick the pre-date this happened."

The sheriff unloaded two shots into Barry's heart with Hans's Sig. He staggered backwards landing in a chair in the back of his office, a shocked and dismayed look on his face.

"One down."

"Sheriff, you know the best laid plans don't always work out."

"They do for me. I'm an elected official of Clark County; the people voted—"

A bullet tore apart the back of the sheriff's head, and he bounced off Barry's desk.

Hans head jerked towards the door.

"Anyone else coming through that door?"

"Not tonight, Hans."

"You are one unpredictable man, Franco."

Franco looked down at his watch. "And by the way, sorry to hear about the loss of your friend and ex business partner, Mr. Johnson."

"Accidents happen. What are we going to do about Woody?"

"He's a greedy little prick. His time is coming. Shall we, Hans?" Franco pointed to the door.

Three people were standing in the partially lit hallway.

"What the fuck is this, Franco? You know I'm a better asset alive."

"My father always told me to remain loyal to my partners because it creates a trustworthy atmosphere and makes it easier to do deals. Just ask Sonny. He'll tell you. Oh wait, he can't, he's dead."

"You think I had something to do with that?"

"Not directly, but you chartered a limo a week before Sonny disappeared and specifically asked for Bridgette."

"I remember. I like Bridgette. She's hot."

"She spent an unusual amount of private time with Sonny, and somehow you found out."

"So?"

"Someone else was romantically involved with Sonny and thought she was. Someone who has a personality that gets volatile. Isn't that right, Hans?"

"Get to your point."

"You triggered Sherry Labelle's jealous rage, Hans. You told Sherry Bridgette was the reason Sonny tried to end his relationship with her. And you made up details that would agitate her and cause her to lose control, which she did."

"Now you're just guessing."

"Am I?"

"Of course."

One of the three figures emerged from the shadows.

"Tony?"

"Hans, glad you remember me."

"What are you doing here?"

"Franco, hold my weapon. I don't want this to accidentally go off in his face."

"Tony, I'm on your side. Remember?"

"Hans, of course you are. You're on everyone's side, playing all factions against each other. Almost well played." Tony rubbed his hands together and cracked his knuckles.

Hans backpedaled down the hallway.

"That's far enough, Hans."

Hans turned around startled by the voice behind him.

"Ramone?"

"You've always been so good with names; I wish I was more like you."

"Ramone, still backing the losing team like always."

"Where I'm standing, this team has the lead and the ball, and time is running out."

"You know I'm going to need new partners now that Dean, Barry, and Billy have expired. This is your big opportunity, Ramone, so get on board. Be a winner. Join me. Kill those three."

"Franco, Tony, Jimmy, okay if I shoot all of you and join Hans? He sounds like a real team leader, one I could wholeheartedly trust."

"Tony has some issues with Hans. They need to be addressed," Franco calmly said.

Tony walked toward Hans, taking methodical steps, pulling plastic gloves over his hands, snapping each one tight, creating dull popping sound.

Hans tried to backpedal again.

"If you come any closer Hans, I'm going shoot your calves," a well-positioned Ramone threatened.

He stopped cold.

"Boys, we can work this out," Hans begged with his arms at his sides and his palms facing upward.

Hans dropped to one knee attempting to pull out a Colt Mustang XSP, .380 Caliber ankle gun. The perfect Saturday Night Special, for those times when you've been disarmed from your favorite weapon and a knife simply won't do.

Unfortunately, Tony stepped down hard on Hans's hand as he cleared the holster, crushing his hand between the gun and the floor. His thumb bent backwards and snapped like brittle twig. Hans let out a horrific scream as Tony grabbed Hans by his hair and smashed his head into the hallway wall. Tony kicked the gun toward Franco and without letting go of Hans's hair, violently jerked him into his right knee. The blow landed between his mouth and nose, the impact sending blood splattering on Tony's suit pants, the wall, and the floor. Tony maintained his vice grip on Hans's hair, even as swatches of it came loose in his hands.

Hans tried to punch out Tony's arms hoping to free up his hair from Tony's vice grip. But Tony pounded Hans's head into the wall a second time, collapsing the plaster around his head, making a perfect silhouette impression.

Tony released him and Hans slumped to the floor, semi-conscious on his back. His breathing was shallow and irregular, blood flowing from both sides of his head, mouth, and nose. He clutched his bloody face in his hands.

"You going to finish him here?" Ramone asked.

"No."

Franco walked a few feet back into the hallway. A fourth man came over to him and dumped some painter's plastic on the floor.

"He's going to take one of those infamous short rides in a long car," a happy and smiling Franco added.

Hans, partially conscious, heard the plans for his departure.

"Fuck you, you fat fucking piece of shit!" Hans screamed at Tony as he removed his hands from his face.

Tony reached down and took a large swath of plastic and wrapped it around his head and squeezed.

"How does that feel, you cocksucker!"

Tony grabbed on tight, pulled him to his knees, and continued bouncing Hans's head side to side off the hallway walls. Hans was not a small man, but Tony whipped him around like a coyote taking on a poodle.

"How does this feel, huh?"

Ramone jumped over Tony and Hans and walked over to Franco.

"He's not hitting his head as hard as he can."

"I know. He's toying with Hans, making him dizzy, disorienting him."

"He's a total animal, Franco," Franco's man Jimmy added.

"He is, isn't he? My father was smart leaving Tony to protect our interests. And of course, he's the man you want on your side."

Franco raised up his right hand for a high five which Ramone promptly slapped.

Suddenly Tony dropped to one knee, grabbing his chest. A horrified expression on his face.

"Not now," Tony painfully said as he fell forward across Hans's legs, lying motionless.

"Jesus Christ, Franco!" Ramone shouted as he ran over to Tony and rolled him off of Hans's legs and onto his back.

He placed his ear near Tony's mouth. "He's not breathing, he must have had a heart attack."

Jimmy jumped onto Tony and ripped open his suit jacket, loosened his tie, and began performing CPR.

"Come on. Breathe you old bastard. Breathe!"

Ramone ran into the bathroom and brought out a couple of towels making sure he avoided the pooled blood in Barry's office.

He slid up to Franco and placed the towels under Tony's head.

"We can't call 9-1-1. What are we going to do? We have to get him out of here," a panicked Ramone pleaded.

"No we don't. Leave him. Go back to the office and get Hans's gun. Make sure to put your gloves on tight."

Franco watched Ramone walk up to Hans's gun lying on the office floor. He put his gloves on and picked the gun up with his thumb and index finger. He returned to where Franco stood.

"Franco, we can't just leave him," Ramone pleaded.

"Tony would understand. All of us can't go down for this. His time is over," Franco said while frantically yelling down the hallway. "Where's Hans?"

"Shit. He must have bolted when you went for the gun, Ramone," a nervous Jimmy answered.

"He's a tough bastard. Not to worry. He won't say anything to Metro, but he'll call Woody and tell him everything he thinks he wants him to hear. He needs an ally badly," Franco said.

"Fuck that prick. He's not going anywhere. We'll see him soon enough," an angry Jimmy added.

"Here, the two of you, carefully lift and move Tony in front of the office door. Don't let his feet drag," Franco ordered.

Ramone and Jimmy struggled to follow Franco's instructions. Tony's dead weight made him extremely heavy.

"Take off his gloves and put the gun in Tony's right hand. Get his right index finger on the trigger, Jimmy."

"Okay, boss."

"Now place the gun fully in his hand and fire two shots, one into the left wall, the other into the right."

Jimmy did as asked and the hallway filled up with smoke.

"Now Tony's prints will match along with the GSR," an enlightened Jimmy remarked.

"GSR?" Ramone asked.

"Gunshot residue on his hand," Jimmy answered.

"Oh, I get it now. Smart."

"Hans was badly beaten, Ramone. He's not going to turn anyone in. Hell, he's probably on his way taking up safe refuge at one of his strip clubs or bars. He'll follow his survival instincts. This morning and for the rest of the day, nothing's going to happen. He'll lie low, get some medical attention, off the books of course. Tomorrow will be a different story," Franco said.

"Maybe we'll get lucky and he'll die from his head injuries," Jimmy wisecracked.

"If only life were that simple," Franco added.

"Showing up in a stolen car and wearing ski masks was a touch of genius, Franco," Ramone added.

"Tony had so many talents. His plans were impeccable. This city has cameras everywhere; there's no way to trace this back to us," a confident Franco replied.

"The dead security guard at the gate is not going to say much either," Jimmy playfully added.

"Going to be hard to forget this night," Ramone said.

"So true. Farewell, Tony my friend. You were a faithful and loyal soldier. I'll see you on the other side."

They all looked at the carnage in Barry's office as they passed by.

"We'll leave it to Metro to figure out what happened here. Hans's blood and prints are everywhere. He's going to be hunted."

*****

Chapter 28

2:00 AM

On the way to Metro, I made calls to John, Russ, and George, and they all went to voicemail. I'm sure George took his Ambien and would be out cold; he had an easy explanation. I tried Kurt, but got another voicemail, and the same with Ramone. Candice was still at the office. I let her know where we were going and told her to inform Dino and Tony.

We pulled into the back of Metro headquarters on MLK. Several officers were waiting. Vicki and I were escorted through a back entryway where we avoided the usual contingency of drug addicts, prostitutes, DUI's, gang banger wannabees, and petty criminals.

Once we were inside her cubical, the two officers left. I sat down in a chair in front of her desk, she sat in her chair. A couple of pictures, mementos, awards, items that culminated her successes as a sergeant, daughter, and friend were posted around the office. I sensed an emptiness to the space, the same emptiness that prevailed in my fraternity house bedroom.

"A penny for your thoughts," I softly asked trying to break the uneasy silence.

"You don't want to know what I'm thinking. I don't even know what I'm thinking," she quickly snapped back. "And why aren't you more of a wreck after everything that's happened tonight?"

"Way to come out swinging, detective. You always this charming to your victims or is this a special occasion?"

She got up and walked around the desk.

"I'm sorry, I didn't mean…"

"Don't let my outer shell fool you," I said. "I'm hurting right now and my wheels are going a million miles an

303

hour. I don't know what's going to happen next or to whom. This is surreal."

"There's going to be a host of detectives who are going to grill you, disorient you, try to catch you in a lie.

"Why tell me?"

"I know you're innocent, the victim in all this. If half of the things Max told us are true, this is going to turn out bad. Unfortunately for you."

"And what about the meeting at Max's? You going to add anything?" I said turning my tone up a notch.

"Really? You think I'd do that to you?"

"At this point, I don't know what you're going to do. It would be easy to drop me in the grease, make some headlines."

"You're not the bad guy, Steve, just someone dragged into a series of horrific events that I'm not sure are going to end anytime soon."

There was a momentary pause. I was in the eye of the hurricane as I anxiously awaited to be barbecued by Metro. My mind kept creating a series of scenarios: I would be found guilty of something, end up in jail. I couldn't do jail.

Chapter 29

9:40 AM

The desert heat torched the valley with temperatures that made my sweat sweat. It was determined, by the angle of the shots, that the shooter fired from some place high up. Their unofficial findings, the Mirage rooftop. I was ruled out as the target. The shooter had ample time to splatter me across the parking lot. Somebody up there liked me and protected me from some really bad people.

The only question on my mind was who sent this guy and how did he know what was going down? The sequence of events that seemed to be dogging me with every move left me mentally hanging on by a thread.

Before Metro came to any conclusions, they made sure they got their monies worth and drilled me like a ten-cent whore in a men's prison. Often the questions were twisted and manipulative, looking for a lie or changes in the sequence of events. Throw in the ungodly amounts of caffeine they were pumping in me, hoping I would ramble on like a meth addict. Plus, they were parading me in and out of interrogation rooms.

This was unlike any TV police drama I ever saw, where perps sit and stew in one room all night or in my case all morning. The mental beating I survived last night had toughened me up to the realities of being a constant victim. The only person who didn't interview me was the janitor, and even he looked like he had some questions.

The squad car pulled up to the house just before one o'clock. To say my head was pounding was a gross understatement. I had never felt this exhausted in my entire short life, even with the caffeine buzz. The boys were waiting for me at the door when I arrived and each one gave me a bro-hug and a pat on the back.

"We'll be patrolling this area in four-hour shifts, lieutenant's orders," the patrol car passenger officer stated.

"Thanks."

They drove off and Bill closed the door.

"No holes in you, my brother," Bill proclaimed.

"Maybe another orifice might have improved your persona," Russ added.

"I love you butt jammers too. George at the office?"

"Take a load off first," Bill said.

We went into the living room where I plopped down on the sofa. Bill and Russ stood over me.

"You going to tell him, or should I?" Bill asked.

"What are you two talking about?"

"I got this, Bill. Barbra, our favorite psycho bitch from hell, filed a mental instability charge, drug abuse, and ranted on about his suicidal tendencies at a competency hearing in a Vegas Municipal court early this morning. They dropped him off immediately afterwards to a secure psych unit eval at Valley Hospital. Seventy-two hours' worth."

"What? She can't do that. How in the hell did she pull that one off?"

"Someone pulled some legal strings, got this done post-haste."

"If they don't give him his meds he's going to flip out!" I shouted jumping off the couch.

"What are you going to do next, Steve?" Bill asked, the anger showing like someone dumped a pot of hot coffee in his lap.

"How about using Goldhabber?" Russ suggested.

Bill and I stared at him.

"Too soon, huh?"

"I'm going to call Max, use his guy." I said.

"So, the meeting the two of you had went well considering the circumstances?" Russ asked.

"A meeting I'll never forget, and neither will Vicki. She sort of happened to be there with me in tow because of all the chaos last night."

"She likes you. I knew it," Russ gleefully chimed.

"What? No, dipshit. She was there for me after the shooting and escorted me there hoping to find leads."

"A likely story." Bill smirked.

"You guys belong in strait jackets."

*****

10:00 AM

Hans was lying propped up in the bed of his ex-girlfriend's cousin, Jackie. He offered to quietly pay her mortgage one month at a time including a monthly cash deposit using untraceable slush funds for emergencies. Plus, extra perks to keep Jackie smiling. The great sex kept on the downlow, no dates or being seen in public together.

Jackie patched Hans up and butterflied several of the cuts on his face and completely dowsing him in ice bags. He was in rough shape, he had a concussion for sure, and his eyes were almost swelled shut. He could have used a good cut man, not a sack partner after last night's beating.

Hans didn't know who his allies were anymore. He decided to stay out of sight until tomorrow. Hans already crushed and discarded his cell phone on the way to Jackie's just in case someone tried to ping his whereabouts. He also dumped the previously stolen car he used last night.

"You feeling any better? It's been almost ten hours," Jackie asked.

"Do I look like I'm feeling any better?"

"I guess not."

"And if anyone comes through that door unannounced, take my gun and shoot them."

"What?"

"You heard me. I might pass out, be an easy target. And they'll shoot you too, no witnesses."

"What did you get me into, Hans?"

"Don't give me that innocent victim look. It's unattractive. You knew exactly who and what I was when you took on this little safe house assignment," Hans said holding the side of his jaw.

"Yeah, but I never thought you'd be the one all beat to crap in my bed."

"Welcome to the you-got-paid-do-your-fucking-job movement. Of course this shit happens, never to me, at least not until last night. But it's always been a risk *I* was willing to take. That's why I'm fucking rich and you're living in this—"

"Excuse me. You're the one lying half dead in my bed. Money obviously can't buy everything."

"But unlike some people, I'm not in the morgue either."

Jackie walked over to Hans and rearranged his ice bags.

"What about all your men, where are they? Did they get killed?"

"Actually, they defected. Sold me out to the highest bidder. Loyalty, apparently doesn't mean much anymore."

"What are you going to do, Hans?"

Hans propped himself up and dragged his legs over the bed and onto the floor as a couple of the ice bags crash landed next to his feet. He pointed with his arm.

"Take a bunch of hundreds out of my pocket and go out and buy several burner phones. Take your car. Don't buy them anywhere around here. I don't need any red flags. No calls or conversations with anyone either, especially with the people selling them to you, understand? I don't want anyone nosing their way around your house."

"Do you have any Benjamins without blood on them?"

Chapter 30

*****

Vicki walked into her second-story condo in Green Valley, exhausted from last night's interrogation. Her condo was a four-story complex with half the units built facing inwards with recreational views of the pool, jacuzzi, tennis court and grilling areas. This concept placed those condos in high demand.

Last night's mental kicker, besides the two murders, was how to process and digest the meeting with Max and Steve. She leaned against the wall and tossed her shoes, undressing on the move, throwing off her clothes on the way to the bathroom. Once inside the bathroom she turned on the tub water, making sure the temperature reached hot. She glanced at herself in the mirror. It became obvious to her that she needed to shut it down, ease off. Her mind needed a recharge and a hot bath would be her salvation.

With the tub water running she quickly glided to the kitchen, opened the refrigerator, and pulled out a bottle of her favorite wine, Piesporter Goldtropfchen, a German wine, sweet but not too sweet, with a touch of effervescence. A glass wouldn't be necessary; the bottle would do. She tore off the cap.

While standing next to her kitchen window, she glanced out at her neighbor's balcony and saw Jill Wanlase leaning over the rail in her two-piece black bikini, sensually eyeballing her.

Jill, a tall blonde, pretty, long hair, large in the sense that she worked out often, in amazing shape, displaying a Russian athlete on steroids physique. Vicki chatted with her half-a-dozen times since she moved in four months ago, while sunning poolside, and learned she was a flight attendant and often took friends on exotic excursions. She wondered if Jill dosed to develop a body that solid. She could sense Jill's desire to be with her, something about the way her eyes wandered up and down her body while conversing. Vicki didn't care right now, but she also knew Jill would create a worm hole to get inside her condo; she just needed a green light.

Tired, lonely, exhausted, frustrated, a hot bath running in the other room, with someone interested in her and someone whom she could probably command. Someone who would turn her anxiety and frustration into an erotic fantasy. Anyone, even Jill at this moment, would be a pliable option.

Vicki accelerated her role playing, casually opening the wine bottle, locking her eyes on Jill, whose intrigue accelerated with every move, gripping the balcony ledge, squirming side to side. A front row seat for her erotic performance. Vicki ran the bottle up to her lips tonguing the lip before taking a sip from the bottle, purposefully letting some of the wine spill down her lips, chin, and onto her breasts. She clumsily gestured about the silly mishap, carefully setting the bottle on the counter.

She tossed her head back, letting her hair flail backwards. She ran her fingers across her chin and breasts seductively returning her fingers to her mouth, tasting the new and improved bouquet, using her body as an exotic receptacle. Vicki put on this erotic tease for Jill, her inner psyche debating whether to try something different, take an uncharted, unplanned trip into another sexual world. Would she be capable of taking this to the next level? Could she cross that line between experimentation and wanting? Jill moved past the show portion and motioned to her, a hand gesture indicating she was coming over.

The visual playtime ended. It was time to make a decision. Did she really want to go there? Had tired and lonely won out? Her cell phone rang. Vicki stopped everything and walked away, leaving Jill suspended in a voyeur's fantasy.

"What the hell just got into me," she said out loud as she tracked down her phone and answered it.

"Yeah."

"Detective, this is Sergeant Woods. We've got a quadruple homicide."

"I just got home. Is there no one else to handle this for a couple of hours?"

"I think you're going to want to take an active role."

"Really," she said looking down at her toes and listening to the bath water fill up. "I'm listening."

"Sherriff Dean Thomas, Barry Schuster, his bodyguard, and Tony Corleone, Vicki," he roll-called out.

"Oh my God. Where?"

Vicki knew them all, some more than others, but she knew them.

"Schuster's house was a blood bath. The housekeeper came in this afternoon and found them."

"Text me the address. I'll be right there."

"Dustin's on his way there too."

Vicki ran into the bathroom oblivious to what had transpired in the kitchen, turned off the tub water, reached down and popped open the drain plug, watching her stress relief methodically cyclone downward, staring, momentarily hypnotized by the swirling motion of the retreating water. She pulled a towel off the rack, ran water on it, wiping away the sticky residual wine spilled earlier on her breasts, staring at herself in the mirror. Her nipples became erect from the soft rubbing motion.

"Shit."

She snapped out of it and raced to her bedroom, pulled out a fresh set of clothes and hurriedly got dressed, putting her hair up in a ponytail. She strapped up her weapons and yanked the door open. Jill stood there, a yearning expression on her face and pulling a small carry-on bag.

"I thought you—"

"Sorry, you thought wrong. I have to—"

Jill pulled her in hard and kissed her on the lips. The kiss lasted only a few seconds but it felt endless. Vicki looked at her not knowing what to say.

"Was I wrong?"

Jill walked away, not angry but disappointed. She glanced back at Vicki before she opened the stairway door and gave Vicki a reassuring smile, a smile that indicated she'd be waiting for the next time when Vicki would open her door and be ready to take it to the next level, an open invitation, anytime, anyplace.

She watched her walk to the stair exit and leave. Vicki closed her condo door, walked toward the elevator, confused, tired, knowing she inadvertently created an awkward situation between them.

She had to transfer her mental energy to the task ahead. The murders were going to make national news and create an uneasiness among the citizenry. Regrouping her priorities and finding a gallon of coffee to ingest were first on her agenda. Six murders in less than twenty-four hours, not including the ones without headlines attached.

Mr. Johnson hadn't been found yet; he would take the body count up to seven, an unlucky seven.

While waiting for the elevator and on the ride down, she turned her focus to Steve. He has to know more. What's he hiding? Is he playing me? Is Max involved? Too many questions, no answers, so much to do.

Vicki was talented, paid to do a job where the skills she learned moved her up the ranks to sergeant. She formulated a game plan. Once out of the elevator she hit the car alarm switch, took a quick look in the back seat, reassuring herself that some psycho hadn't snuck back there to slit her throat. She set the Waze app to the location and maneuvered out of the parking garage, still unable to thoroughly clear her head of Steve and the Jill incident.

*****

My cell phone rang, shocking me out of a dead sleep. The faceplate read three-fifty-four PM. The name on the call, Vicki.

"Doesn't she ever sleep?" I grabbed the remote and turning on the bedroom light, dimming it immediately.

"Hey," I sluggishly answered.

"I'm sure I just woke you but there's been some new developments."

"You found the shooter?"

"No. And I'm sorry Steve, Tony... he's gone. He died early this morning."

"What are you talking about?"

"A quadruple homicide last night at the home of Barry Schuster, a limousine company owner. Unfortunately, Tony was there. We're still trying to piece everything together."

"Tony is dead?"

"Yes. I thought you should know before you hear it from someone else."

Vicki told Steve the story being vague as possible, leaving out key factors in the homicides. Besides, she'd just been briefed and didn't know much.

"Does this mean I'm going to be escorted back to Metro?"

"No. I've told my father. He'll let your YLL family know. Dino will be calling you shortly. I told him I'd talk to you first."

"Vicki, tell me you've found something out, anything out?"

314

"What I know is confidential. You know I would tell you if I could."

"Is Woody involved?"

"Again…"

"Great, thanks." I hung up and got out of bed taking my Glock off the nightstand.

Vicki impounded one of my Glocks, but I had three more neatly stashed away.

I checked every room inside the house including the pool area outside, but Russ and Bill were gone. I needed someone to talk to. I made myself a ham and turkey sandwich, opened a Coke, and turned on the local news.

Details of the slayings at Barry Schuster's home were highlighted by the sheriff's death, the lead ins on all the local news outlets. I loved how the media left you hanging on the edge of your chair, then dropped the sketchy details. The commissioner was holding his press conference to stall out the wolf hounds from making too much noise. He rah-rahed up the sheriff about all the wonderful things he'd accomplished. Strange how the sheriff died in the house along with Tony, Barry, and his bodyguard. More questions, no answers.

The one certainty I knew, I was going to miss Tony.

My phone rang and I raced back to the bedroom to answer it.

"Hey kid, how are you holding up?" Kurt asked.

"I was about to call you, ask you the same question."

"Well, I'm feeling like someone kicked me in the nuts with a steel-tipped boot."

"Colorful. You've known Tony for a long time. What have you heard? You're in tight with some of the Metro guys."

"No one is saying anything, Steve. It's like they all ate a box of crackers in the desert with no water. Is Metro watching your house?"

"I haven't looked. I'm assuming so, and after seeing the news, who knows? They might have doubled down, brought in some reinforcements."

"I presume you have another piece?"

"Why Kurt, are you presuming I'm a gun-carrying fanatic with ties to the NRA and three hundred terrorist groups?"

"Seriously, you armed?"

"Seriously, fuck yes. I'm not trusting my life to a couple of donut eaters playing pocket pool somewhere in this gated community while my friends and I are being used as clay pigeons."

"Good. Stay armed. I don't want to see you end up on the daisy program."

"You know something I don't and you're not telling me?"

"You think I'm holding back?"

"Are you?"

"Look, this is far from over and your piece of the pie makes you a target. There are a lot of things in play right now. I want to make sure you're not next."

"You talk to Max lately?"

"No. Why?"

"Just curious."

"Seriously, why did you ask?"

"He's on our side, right?"

"Yes. Why the inquisition?"

"I'm just asking."

"Bullshit, Steve. You know something. What is it?"

"Just protecting *my* piece of the pie, that's all."

"I've got to run; I'll call you later and check in on you."

"Sure, thanks. And you will let me know if you hear anything?"

"As soon as I hear something, you'll be my first or second call."

"That's more like it. Later."

My gut told me Kurt knew more than he let on, but I was sure he had his reasons. I guessed he wasn't ready to let go and confide in me. I walked out the front door and looked around, shocked to find no Metro squad car. They were probably cruising the neighborhood in search of a good place to nap.

*****

5:35 PM

Woody's cell phone rang from an unknown caller as he was about to get in his car with Letterman. He had an idea who might be on the other end. Woody hit the answer button and pulled the phone up to his ear.

"This is Woody."

"Woody, Hans."

"Hans, what do you want?"

"Have you seen the news?"

"I've seen it."

"And?"

"Congratulations on getting out of the Schuster house alive."

"And?"

"You did a nice job of eliminating everyone."

"It wasn't me."

"What are you talking about?"

"I didn't kill anyone."

"They just shot each other?"

"No."

"Well?"

"Fazio's crew."

Woody walked away from the car door.

"Letterman, wait in the car for me."

317

"Yes, boss."

"Fazio. What's he doing in Vegas?"

"Apparently still has eyes and ears here. Vengeful ones."

"Tony?"

"Yeah."

"Anyone else I might know?"

"Ramone."

"Ramone?"

"Yeah. He was there when this all went down. He drove the car to Schuster's house."

"He shoot anyone?"

"No. Just pointed his gun at me while Tony did a dance on my face."

"Really? You call the police?"

"Seriously? But I'm going to have to. My blood's all over the place.

"Where are you? You need help?"

"You mean like the help you were going to give me with your back-stabbing friend, the sheriff?"

"He made me an offer I couldn't refuse. It's not my fault he didn't trust you."

"You could have warned me."

"Hans, I don't even like you. You're a prick."

"Yet here we are talking."

"A valid point. Then why call me?"

"Fazio appears to be reestablishing his family ties in Vegas; that's not healthy for either of us."

"What are you suggesting?"

"I'm willing to let our little disagreement slide."

"In return for?"

"A Woody-Hans alliance."

"Just like that, you're going to let bygones be bygones?"

"If we don't organize now, together, we're both going to end up with toe tags."

"Okay, look, don't call anyone, especially Metro. Let me figure this out. Stay low and stay quiet. We need to weed out the Fazio sympathizers."

"What about Steve?"

"I've got it handled."

"I'll call you in four hours. Is that enough time?"

"It's going to take some major cash, Hans."

"I know and I have it. Alone we're dead. Together, we might be able to pull this off."

"I'll talk to you in four hours."

Woody walked up to his car and climbed into the back seat.

After leaving Steve's, Woody and Letterman drove to the Graveyaad. Woody had some unsettled business to finalize with Sherry.

"You going to get the Graveyaad and YLL in the same week? Isn't that going to leave you a little strapped for cash?" Letterman asked.

"It's going to leave me a lot strapped for cash. That's why I'm going to partner up with Hans. He's got the extra capital I need. And as you might recall, our wonderful sheriff was about to eliminate Hans. Mister Schuster and Mister Johnson are currently residing in the morgue. A brilliant plan until Tony and that Fazio stuck their greaseball New York asses into it."

"Hans all of a sudden trusts you?"

"We have no choice. If only that dumbshit sheriff hadn't tossed my name out before Fazio killed him. Hans is not going to all of a sudden vanish because of a few dead bodies. He's almost as bad a money whore as I am. Almost."

"Like you've always said, he's ruthless, which makes him both useful and dangerous."

"His ass is swinging in the breeze and we're his only ticket out."

Letterman took his eyes off the road and looked at Woody. "That business at Schuster's and the mall, Metro's going to turn this city inside out."

"Hans's blood and DNA are all over the place. The mall is a totally different crime scene. There's another player out there we don't know about. That's why I'll be dictating the terms of our brief partnership, Mister Letterman.

Chapter 31

Saturday

After a quiet Friday night of drinking at my pool I finally managed to pass out around three in the morning. The doorbell rang and startled me out of a dead sleep. I checked my iPhone and it was just past noon.

I put the Glock in my bathrobe pocket, not caring if the handle stuck out. I tapped the peep hole, ducked, and backed away, just in case someone had a shotgun aimed there. Nothing happened. The doorbell rang again. Showtime. I yanked open the door with the Glock pointed straight through it. A loud scream followed. Sam stumbled backwards, almost falling over.

"Are you out of your mind?!"

"Oh shit, Sam. You alright?"

"No, I'm not. I almost swallowed my tongue with you pointing that gun at me. Are you insane?"

"Please, I'm sorry. Come in. With all this craziness…"

Sam walked in and waited for me to close the door. Once inside she threw her arms around me and began attacking me, with kisses.

"You almost got killed last night," she passionately whispered in my ear.

"I know. A horrible ploy to get you here," I answered while gently kissing her neck. "But see? It worked."

"Time to take to me to that bedroom of yours."

"I need to take a shower first. It's been a long night and—"

"Hurry. Lead the way," she said pushing me from behind.

As soon as she figured out the direction I was headed she steered me into the bedroom and slammed the door shut. She ripped off my bathrobe and launched it onto the bed. She kicked off her flipflops and took her jeans and panties off. I yanked off her shirt as we kissed our way into the shower. I paused long enough to turn the knob to my favorite temperature as we spun into the shower. I was living in the history of now.

We spent the next twenty minutes exploring each other, using up every inch of the shower. We finally climaxed with her bending over the seat bench, holding on for dear life.

I collapsed on her back, the steamy water flowing over us. She looked up, straightening her back, easing me off.

"There's an issue of soap. We did come in here to clean you up, didn't we?" she playfully said.

"We did."

I reached over for a bottle of body wash when I noticed something strange out of the corner of my eye. I didn't like what I saw through the partly steamed glass shower doors and scrambled for the gun on the other side. However, in all the heated passion, I forgot to bring it with me.

"Damn."

The partially opened bathroom door swung wide open. Woody and Letterman strolled in.

"Looking for this?" Woody said, proudly waving my gun. "Wow, never saw a dick shrink that fast Steve, although, you appear to have plenty left, impressive. Letterman, toss the kids a couple of towels. We don't want to be rude."

"What are you doing here? And how did you get in?"

Sam turned off the shower, covered up, and moved to a corner of the bathroom, the one farthest from Woody.

I wrapped a towel around my waist and walked up to Woody.

"You stop by for another beating?"

"Hey boy!" Letterman said loudly, making sure he captured my attention. "I wasn't at your first get together at the Rio. If I were, that shit wouldn't have gone down the same way," Letterman boasted.

Before I could answer Woody jumped in.

"All this testosterone aside, I wanted to let you know that I'm your new partner. Letterman, show him."

Letterman held up a legal document with Dino's signature on it and shoved it inches from my face.

"See, all legal. Now, you're going to sell me your remaining interests because, I don't envision us having a long, enjoyable partnership."

"Congratulations, that's the only thing you've ever said that makes any sense."

"With Mr. Sharpe in the looney factory, Dino selling you out and Tony lying on the wrong side of the grass, I don't see much of a future here for you."

"That's it. You think you've won?"

"I know I have. You're finished smartass. I have another legal document sitting on your kitchen table. It's a totally unfair deal, but it's time for you to suck it up and move on."

"I just want to know what you offered Barbra? I mean, what's the going rate for screwing your own brother over this badly?"

"Barbra has a lot of needs and so many problems, an endless supply."

"What's that supposed to mean? What do you have on her?"

"Where to begin. She has a monster black tar heroin habit, drinks excessively, is a spendoholic, has a severe gambling problem and is a kleptomaniac. She's the gift that keeps on giving. She didn't want to lose her meal ticket, to you of all people. Seems he cares more about you than he does her. And poor Barbra Kennedy is not going to let that

323

happen. But she does have a compassionate side; she doesn't want to see her dear brother exterminated."

"What kind of maggot dung were you spawned in?"

"Easy boy. Letterman isn't as friendly as I am and would have no trouble opening up your Wisconsin skull and taking a looksee."

Letterman pointed the gun at my head, a sociopathic grin enveloping his face.

"Like he said."

"Sam, get dressed. Oh, and thanks for unlocking the door," Woody said.

"Great timing, asshole," Sam uttered.

"Sam, you have an unattractive moral flexibility about you. Steve, better to find out now."

"Sam, what's going on? You let Woody in? Why would you do that?"

Sam looked at me with contempt for judging her.

"What, you thought you could betray him and be his what, girlfriend?" Woody cheerfully clarified.

"You're disgusting, Woody. I'm sorry Steve, but there are some extenuating circumstances that I can't get into. I really do have feelings for you. I'm sorry it came to this," she sadly explained as tears began to well up.

Sam hastily exited the bathroom dropping her towel on the floor, refusing to look at anyone.

"See, I'm doing you a solid. Maybe we *can* be partners." Woody said, gloating, "She's almost as cold-hearted a bitch as her mother. Business first. So hot and viciously charming."

"What do you mean, business first? What could you possibly have on her?"

"Now you're getting too personal; the pleasantries will have to stop. Letterman, escort him to the bedroom and make sure he gets dressed. I'll be in the kitchen."

Sam was getting dressed when Woody entered the bedroom. "For the record, you have some nice tits."

"Fuck off, Woody."

She pulled her shirt on and started to walk out of the bedroom.

"Sam!"

She stopped dead in her tracks and turned to face Woody.

"What?"

"I said you have nice tits. Unveil them again. I'm not sure Letterman and I had a chance to relish them."

I couldn't stand watching Woody's power trip, even though Sam had deceived me. But this was way out of line.

Sam reluctantly took her shirt off. Sadly, I could only speculate the overwhelming reasons forcing her to capitulate to the whims of a scumbag like Woody. What did he have on her?

"Come here."

Sam confidently walked up to Woody, stopped in front of him, resting her hands on her hips.

"See Steve, everyone cherishes me."

He started fondling her breasts and bent over and started kissing them, peeking up at me to see my expression.

"Now I'll show you what real power is. Sam, take off the rest of your clothes and lie on the bed."

She gave Woody an icy stare, refusing to let whatever Woody had on her dictate her courage. She defiantly did as ordered.

"Letterman, you think she's hot, don't you?"

"Yes, I do boss. Very."

"Woody, come on. You made your point. Let her go," I pleaded.

"Steve, my perishable partner, watch and catalog. Working for me has always created an abundance of perks for Letterman, isn't that right?"

"Yes boss, all about the perks," Letterman sadistically answered, gradually bearing down on Sam.

"Steve, sit down over here." Woody pointed to a chair in my room. "Take some notes, but don't get turned on. That would be ill-mannered."

"Have some cheap fun, Letterman. Sam is oozing with passion at the mere thought of your rugged touch. Aren't you, Sam?"

"Let's get this over with, Letterman."

"Sassy and direct. I like that in a skank."

Letterman's hands sadistically grabbed her throat as he leaned in and licked her cheek. With a cat-like reaction, he leaned back and slapped her face twice.

"You like it rough this way, don't you?"

"Yes, yes I do," Sam answered, tears starting to form in her eyes.

"Good."

"Come on, Woody, enough is enough. Let her go. Let's go to the kitchen so I can read your proposal."

Woody's attention quickly turned to business.

"Back off Letterman. You can have her another time. Turns out our boy doesn't possess the intestinal fortitude required to be my partner after all. By all indications, he's fragile."

Letterman grabbed Sam by the hair and pulled her off the bed and tossed her on the floor.

"Get dressed, and get out of here."

Sam, visibly shaken, dressed a second time and hurried out of the house.

"See how people just naturally gravitate to my personality?"

"I'm seeing it, Woody. You're a natural, almost spiritual."

Woody tossed the gun back to Letterman. "Make sure he finishes getting dressed, then have him come to the kitchen. YLL is about to be our new acquisition."

"You heard him. Get dressed," Letterman said pointing his gun at me.

"Man, have you found a home."

Woody strolled into the kitchen, opened the refrigerator, and grabbed a beer. He glanced around the room several times before he sat down at the table. What a truly great twenty-four hours it had been. Tony was dead, Dino's percentage in his hands and out of the picture, Steve about to sign over YLL and Goldhabber in the ground. And tomorrow, Hans would ceremoniously turn himself in to Metro, creating a media circus and thus exonerating him from the unending deluge of accusations created by the Schuster murders.

Woody had already formulated Hans's police statement. Hans would use one of his greatest assets, his natural ability as a pathological liar. He'd deflect the truth into dozens of false directions, becoming the victim. The Sheriff's department, Metro, anyone involved, were all just chasing their own tails. Hans would blame Tony and some other unrecognizable attackers for the murders at the Schuster house and proclaim how lucky he was to be alive.

Maybe Hans might be a good partner, at least temporarily. He was ruthless, unafraid to get dirty, charming, and a great liar. But all those traits made him an ill-advisable one too.

The front door swung open and the voices of Russ and Bill calling for me echoed throughout the foyer.

Woody pulled his recently purchased Smith and Wesson .45 from his shoulder harness and laid it on the kitchen table, barrel pointing towards the living room entrance, safety off, finger on the trigger.

"Hey, Steve—"

"Steve's getting dressed," Woody replied.

"What are you doing here?" Russ, visibly disturbed, asked.

"Letterman, Steve almost ready?!" Woody called out, his head partially turned toward the bedroom entrance just off the living room.

Letterman led me through the living room and into the kitchen, escorting me by my arm, his Sig jammed tightly against my back.

"See, all dressed and ready to go."

Bill moved toward Woody, keeping his dual focus on Woody and his Smith and Wesson.

"Why don't you take a hike before I call the police and have your ass tossed in jail?" Bill asked.

"You Wisconsin kids think you're all a bunch of tough guys."

"We aren't that tough, but we do possess all the necessary tools to knock a POS like you around," Bill snarkily said.

"Lettermen, these guys look tough to you?"

"No boss, just loudmouth cheese eaters."

"See Bill, no one here thinks you're bringing a lot of fire power to this conversation."

"Last time I checked, Steve knocked your sorry ass out. Or do you have Alzheimer's and can't remember recent events?"

"He sucker-punched, kicked me when I wasn't looking, isn't that right, Steve?"

"Why don't you ask Letterman to release me and I can give you a repeat performance, demonstrate how I did it the first time, jog your memory. Letterman might find it educational, even learn something," I replied.

"You think one lucky kick makes you a badass?"

"Woody, I can take a bitch-ass, loud-mouth greasy pile of shit like you down all day and all night and not even crack a sweat."

Letterman slapped me on the back of the head. "Don't insult Woody."

The doorbell rang.

"Gee, I wonder who that could be, Woody? Maybe Metro's finest are here to arrest your sorry ass," I said, knowing Metro had eyes on the property.

"Yeah Woody, who's at the door?" Russ added.

"It looks like the boys in blue are here. What are you going to do now?" Bill asked.

"Letterman, escort Steve to the door. Remember cheesehead, I'm pointing a forty-five caliber at your friends' chest. Russ, Bill, sit down at this end of the table," Woody ordered picking up his gun and pointing at the chairs.

Letterman pushed the gun hard up against my spine as we walked to the front door.

"Trying to leave a barrel ring?"

"Shut the fuck up and answer the door."

"Letterman, anyone ever mention that you dress like a homeless wino? Your boss should at least dress you up properly."

That earned me another and even harder smack in the back.

"Just answer the door politely or your pals will be the new decor on your kitchen walls."

"You know, Letterman, I'll bet you're one hell of a fighter. Seriously."

"I am. Woody ever gives me his blessings, I'm going to bust you up, pull your balls out through your ears, and feed them to you."

"I underestimated you, Letterman."

329

"Really."

"Yeah, I didn't think a backwoods limp dick like yourself could string that many words together."

I took two quick steps and opened the door.

"Officers, come on in," I said, relieved.

The officer smiled and pushed me aside.

"What's happening, Letterman? Woody with you?"

"You have got to be fucking kidding me. Really?"

"Life's a bitch when you ain't connected. And what did you just say to me?" A cocksure Letterman boasted.

"Don't take it personally, Letterman, but fuck off," I said.

Letterman took a swing at me, one I anticipated and ducked under, but his lightning-fast roundhouse forward kick, not so much. The kick landed flush against my chest and sent me reeling on my back and onto the living room floor. I rolled up and took a defensive stance, awaiting his next move.

"Letterman!"

Letterman, caught off guard, turned around. Woody stood in the doorway between the living room and kitchen.

"What do you think you are doing?" Woody shouted, waving his .45 in the air.

"He asked for it, so I accommodated him."

"Is that what I pay you to do, accommodate people?"

"No sir, you—"

I took two lightening steps forward and dropped my right shoulder square into Letterman's shoulder, driving all six-foot-five, three-hundred pounds of him headfirst into my recliner, both of them flipping over. The recliner took the brunt of the blow. Letterman ended up smashing his head into the drywall, cracking it. He rose in a flash for a big man, blood running down his forehead. The two cops pulled their tasers and pointed them at me. Woody fired a shot into the ceiling. Everyone flinched, becoming immersed in suspended animation.

"Settle down," Woody commanded. I don't want to kill anyone. Not today. So don't give me a reason to do so. Do I make myself clear?" he commanded as drywall dust floated down from the ceiling like January snowflakes.

Nothing like a discharged firearm indoors to get your undivided attention and your ears pulsating.

Woody stopped next to Letterman.

"Just what in God's name did you think you were doing taking this kid on?"

"He's a dick. I wanted him to know."

Woody pulled a handkerchief out of his pocket and handed it to Letterman.

"You don't see me handing a kerchief to him… now do you? You're the only one leaking right now. Go to the bathroom, fix yourself up."

"Boss."

I flipped him off as he walked by; he ignored me.

"This is not going according to script. Steve, get back into the kitchen," Woody demanded, pointing his gun at me. You two, Metro's finest, wait in the living room and pretend to do your job. I'm paying you enough. And if either of you hear any gun shots, feel free to check in on me."

They both gave Woody a dissatisfied look and did what they were told.

"Russ, Bill, you're still here. Great. Stay seated. I thought for sure you two would have hightailed it out the back when the first shot went off."

"Woody, ah, you only fired one shot," I reminded him.

"Thank you, Steve. See? We can all be courteous and respectful without resorting to violence."

Woody placed the warm .45 Smith and Wesson against my forehead, guiding me backwards to the kitchen table.

"The papers." He reached over and slid them to me. "Sit down and read them. You've got three days to show up at Carson Brown's office and sign them. You *are* going to sell me YLL, understood?"

"I have three days to read them over?"

"Sure, take all the time you need. If they aren't read and understood in the next five minutes, your friends' brains are all over the kitchen wall. Does that work for you?"

"It does."

Letterman reentered the kitchen, a wet handkerchief against the side of his head.

"Letterman, back so soon? I was hoping you'd bleed out," I said with a wink.

Letterman dropped one hand on the table next to my hand and leaned down "Read the documents."

"You should have used some mouthwash while you were in there fixing yourself up. Your breath smells like someone took a dump in your mouth."

"You and I, we are going to have a reckoning. This business won't last much longer. Then I'm going to find you and snap you in two like a week-old breadstick."

I looked over the papers and handed them back to Woody. Letterman took his hands and gestured the snapping of a twig as he smiled at me.

"This isn't some one-horse town in a thirties Western. This supposed deal is bullshit."

"You're getting a check for ten thousand dollars and a five percent share in YLL. I think that's extremely generous of me."

"It's worth five-hundred times that amount."

Woody jammed the gun in Russ's temple and looked at me.

"My lawyer's card is attached to the document. Three days. Any questions, young man? Your friends' lives are in jeopardy if you don't show."

"Three days, your lawyer's office, to sign these papers."

Woody removed the gun from Russ's temple and tapped the table several times.

"Bill, your turn."

Woody used his gun and pressed hard against Bill's temple.

"See how uncomfortable it feels, Bill?"

"Yeah."

"Have any questions?"

"I do," I said, looking directly at Woody. "How much was Dino's check?"

"They would be, unethical," he said laughing.

"I'm sure it's more than ten thousand."

"Dino and I go way back. He's a reasonable man. Besides, he earned his money. He helped in the building of that limo company and unlike you, he'll take his money and discretely leave Vegas."

"I can only hope he chokes on it."

"Aw, sour grapes, but well put. I think you're maturing nicely. Remember our first meeting at the Graveyaad?"

"Does a kid forget his first rectal exam?"

"Like I said then, and I'm saying again now, I get what I want. Sometimes it takes a bit longer, but in the end, I get it."

Letterman slammed his fist next to my hand again, startling me momentarily.

"What he said, bitch boy."

Woody and Letterman left the kitchen followed by the two Metro officers waiting in the foyer. One of the Metro officers unexpectedly did an about face and came back into the kitchen.

"Steve, if you need us, we'll be right outside," he said laughing, placing both thumbs on either side of his utility belt as he left.

333

The door slammed.

I looked at Russ and Bill. "Sorry I dragged you guys into this."

"It's comes with the territory, being your friend," Bill said.

"Yeah, short-lived but adventurous," Russ answered.

"Maybe not so short lived. What I'm about to tell you next is gonna blow your fuckin' minds."

Chapter 32

*****

Sam came through the back door of the Graveyaad, slamming it, then sat on a chair in the small employee breakroom.

Sherry heard the loud noise, turned the corner and peeked inside the room, surprised to see Sam, head in her hands, crying.

"What happened, Sam?"

"I just left Steve's. I don't think it's going to work out between us."

"And you cried so hard your hair got wet?"

"Something like that."

"I call bullshit, Sam. What happened?"

"Leave me alone, Mom."

"No. What did he do?"

"He didn't do anything wrong. It's Woody."

"What about Woody?"

"Mom, just leave it."

"Sam."

"Alright. He knows."

"What do you mean, he knows?"

"He knows about you and Sonny."

Sam got up from the table and walked out the back door. Sherry followed her, grabbed her shoulders, and turned her around.

"What does Woody know, Sam?" Sherry asked, nervously glancing around the back parking lot.

"You and Sonny, Mom. Woody came in here one night, pulled me aside, told me the whole story. One of his stooge cabbies saw everything."

"And just what did he tell you that cabbie witnessed?"

335

"Instead of playing games, why don't you tell me what happened so I can wrap my head around this? He knows, Mom."

Sherry walked back inside the bar, Sam following her.

"You don't get to do this to me, Mom. What happened?"

Sherry stopped and hugged Sam.

"Let's go in the office," she said, tears welling up.

*****

Bill and Russ started pacing the living room floor, blown away after I unfurled my unabridged version of the meeting at Max's.

"Your real father's name is Are? He lived in New Mexico?" a bewildered Russ asked.

"That's what I learned."

"No way," Bill added.

"And possibly still alive?" Russ asked.

"Maybe this explains your love for New Mexican green chilies?" Bill quipped.

Chapter 33

Sunday
1:40 AM

*****

Kurt was in the middle of a club run involving four high rollers from Texas. He stood at the front of his limo in the parking lot of Tight Racks when his phone rang. He looked at the name and reluctantly decided to answer it.

"Tanya, what a pleasant surprise. How are you and your business?"

"Kurt, this is important."

"Of course it is. What?"

"Goldhabber."

"What about him? He's dead."

"I know. But the night before he was killed he was with three of my girls at the hotel."

"That's the earth-shattering event you deemed important enough to call me?"

"One of my girls saw Goldhabber's burner phone; it appeared unimportant at the time."

"Real trustworthy employees you have, sneaking around the personal property of others. Bravo."

"Stop it, Kurt. I'm worried."

"That's a first."

"Seriously, I think you're the only one I can trust with this."

"You think it's that important?"

"Yes."

"Look, I'm with clients. Why don't you give one of your Metro officers a call? Put a feather in one of their caps.

They'll be forever in your debt, you mustering up some reliable intel."

"Kurt, this is serious. Anyone finds out we know who Goldhabber talked to the day before he was murdered, we'll be joining him. Please."

"We've been down this road before, me bailing you out of some hole you've dug for yourself. Sound familiar, Tanya?"

"I promise this is deadly urgent. We might be on a hitlist, Kurt. I'm really fearful for my girls' lives and mine. These people don't care who dies. It's that bad."

"Alright. I'll call Ramone and—"

"No! No, you can't call Ramone. Please don't call or tell Ramone anything."

"What are you talking about?"

"He's working with Fazio."

"Fazio. The New York Fazio? The former YLL owner's son?"

"Yes."

"You're lying."

"I know you two are close but he's working with him. It's about the takeover of Yo Leven."

"You're positive about this?"

"I told you, Goldhabber partied with three of my girls. He was trashed, babbling uncontrollably. Geisha accidentally peeked at his phone, saw text messages from Fazio, Ramone, and the Pope. It scared her."

"Alright, let's for arguments sake say this is all true. Where did Goldhabber get his calls from?"   "Geisha wrote down one of the numbers and looked up the area codes, New York and Washington D.C.."

"New York and D.C.?"

"Yes."

Kurt's phone beeped; his clients were ready to move on.

"I've got to go. I'll call you from my next stop. Stay away from everyone."

"Thank you, Kurt. Please hurry."

The line went dead. Kurt began reliving his past with Tanya. She should have been the one. She was beautiful, intelligent, fun. Sadly, her line of work as a madam was toxic; she made bank but deep down he knew she occasionally slept with some of her high-end clients and he couldn't get past it.

Kurt opened the door and let his clients in. They were hammered, jacked-up on a variety of things. One of them slapped a hundred-dollar bill in Kurt's hand.

"Take us to Hakkasan, Kurt."

"The MGM it is. Great choice. Pour yourself some cocktails for the ride. Plenty of Jack to keep your buzz going."

"We've bought some, "Vegas Blitz" rolled up, ready to smoke. You want a hit, partner?"

"Thanks, but I'll get shitcanned if I do. Besides, I like to see you guys twice a year. Unfortunately, I have to pass."

"A true-blue Chauffeur you are, Kurt. That's why you're the man. But I won't tell if you don't. The offer stands."

"Thanks again, but no."

They were all in, passing around the Jack and firing up one of the joints they purchased earlier in the day. Kurt slid the divider up as he left the Tight Racks parking lot. The divider blocked out ninety percent of the noise and aroma. Kurt couldn't wait. He called Tanya back.

*****

2:00 AM

We grabbed beers and sat around the pool, enjoying the mild cool down summer nights provided in Vegas, the temperature hovering in the mid-eighties. Everyone went about their own business, without a single mention about my story. I pretended to take a nap under the dim pool area lights. I glanced Russ and Bill's way, monitoring any changes in their attitudes. I had just dumped the mother of all stories on them. I'm sure deep down their brains were besieged with a potpourri of science fiction stories.

I became antsy and jumped out of my chair. "You guys done mulling over my story?"

They both stopped what they were doing and gave me this bewildered look.

"Something bothering you, Steve?" Bill asked.

"I get it. Both of you think it's major bullshit, right? Let's be honest. There's no time to pull punches. You think I'm full of it. Go on, say it. Bill? Russ? Come on, God dammit, one of you say it!" My blood pressure was skyrocketing.

"Steve, chillax brother, that story you told us is making you crazy. We get it." Bill set his beer can down and dove into the deep end of the pool.

"Russ?"

"Ditto."

He jumped into the pool. That left me steaming on the edge of the pool staring my good friends down.

"Why don't you join us and cool off!" Bill shouted.

"Steve, you're acting kind of crazy," Russ added while laughing at me.

That's the way they wanted to play it, fine. I moved three steps back and took a running jump at Bill and Russ, tucking my legs under my butt, grabbing them, landing a giant cannonball next to their faces.

The water exploded around them as I landed a perfect ten creating a mini tsunami.

"Jesus Christ, Steve," Russ said as he wiped the water off his face.

"Really, Steve?" Bill pulled himself out of the pool. "You got to get out of this funk, bro." He rubbed the chlorine water out of his eyes.

I treaded water in the deep end, then swam to the opposite side, pulling myself out of the water. I took the long walk up to the table, chugged the rest of my beer, and faced my friends.

"This isn't the time to bail on me, but you both do what you've got to do. I'm calling it a night."

I left the pool area through the kitchen, dripping water everywhere. I walked to the refrigerator and grabbed another beer. I slammed the door shut and almost slipped and fell on my ass.

"Shit!" I grabbed the counter and braced myself.

I went to my bedroom, slamming that door too.

The wall-to-wall chaos afflicting me now fully enveloped my friends. They were getting killed, threatened, and George was physically taken and locked up in mental hospital. Blend that with Sam backstabbing me, Woody on the cusp, ready to steal away my company, and Vicki not trusting me completely, and you have the making of a gigantic knot in my stomach the size of Alaska. I opened the nightstand drawer and threw down a couple more Rolaids. It crossed my mind that I might be turning into a Rolaids junkie.

I walked to the bathroom and got ready to call it a day. I brushed my teeth with the intent of removing all my enamel, did my business, and crawled into bed, spent, drained and rundown. I remotely clicked off the lights and stared at the spot where the ceiling fan would be, listening to the hypnotic sounds of the rotating blades cutting through the cool air above my head.

*****

After dropping off his clients at the MGM, Kurt drove across the street to the Trop, parked the limo in a designated area, and walked into the casino. He heard his phone beep and stopped to look. It was a message from Tonya saying she was sitting at the bar.

It wasn't hard to spot Tanya, looking as beautiful as ever, wearing a tight black low-cut dress, which highlighting her sensual curves and matching stilettos accentuating her alluring ensemble.

As Kurt approached her, the casino seemed to go silent as her troubled soft blue-green eyes watched him.

"Thank you for coming, Kurt," she said, taking his hand in hers.

"So much for staying away from everyone."

"It felt safer here than alone in my room."

Kurt looked at her, wondering how he would ever be able to escape his deep-rooted feelings for her. She was his "Sword Of Damocles", destined to psychologically and emotionally wreck him every time he came close.

"You said it was important; that's why I'm here."

She got up and hugged him placing her arms softly around the back of his neck, ever so slightly moving her fingers.

She moved her lips close to his ear.

"I'm in trouble, Kurt, serious trouble." She pulled her head back and buried her eyes deep into his. "Like I told you earlier, Goldhabber was with three of my girls. Geisha looked at his phone and saw those disturbing texts."

"I remember. This have anything to do with Goldhabber's murder?"

"We can't talk here. Let's go to my room where it's quieter."

"You and me in a hotel room? Bad idea. We know where this goes, and it never ends well for me."

"Kurt, this is different. They're going to kill me. I know it." She put her head on Kurt's shoulder and started to cry. "Please."

Kurt gently moved her hands off his shoulders and took her hand. "What's the room number?"

"Room 844. Here's the key."

The two walked hand in hand across the casino floor to the elevator, pushed the up button, and waited. Kurt protectively surveyed anyone who glanced in their direction.

"I'm sorry I called you, but I have no one else to turn to."

"Funny how that always works out for me, isn't it?"

The elevator came and they rode nonstop to the eighth floor. They exited right and walked to the room and stopped.

"Stand back, Tanya." Kurt used his left arm to shield her.

He pulled out his Glock, shoved the electronic key into the slot, and pushed the door open, leaning backwards in case someone had entered the room and had a little surprise waiting.

The door hit the protective wall cover and slowly began to close. Kurt jammed his right shoe against the back edge of the door and it stopped. The only sounds were Tanya's heavy breathing and a distant TV playing across the hallway.

"Here goes. Stay back."

Kurt raced through the door, flipped the light switch, his gun pointed directly to the center of the room. Tanya came bursting in behind him.

"Stay over here," Kurt ordered Tanya, leaning against the entryway hall.

Kurt checked out the room and bathroom, breathing a sigh of relief when he found the suite empty.

"That got my heart rate going," Kurt said as he closed the room door and turned every lock, bolting the door shut.

He walked into the bedroom with Tanya in tow, stopping at the side of the bed.

"More than this?" Tanya dropped her dress to the floor and stared at Kurt.

"Tanya, I—"

She stepped out of her dress and walked up to Kurt.

"You're right. I can't keep doing this. I'm going to quit. You're right. It's too dangerous, so I'm out." She kissed him.

He leaned back, resisting her kiss. "Tanya, we've been—"

She put her index finger across his lips and stopped him mid-sentence.

"It's over, Kurt. All I want is you."

She kissed him, took off his jacket, and back-pedaled him on top of the bed.

"I love you, Kurt."

Kurt, all in again, rolled her over and took off the rest of his clothes, ready to dive into the volcano. This tainted off-and-on-again pernicious relationship drained his soul, but he couldn't fight it. Deep down, this is what he really wanted.

When they were finished, Tanya rolled on top of Kurt. "I still have some information for you."

"Go ahead. I'm listening."

"Ramone."

"You almost made me forget. Almost."

"He's working with Fazio, trying to take back the limo company."

"You said that, but Ramone? He wouldn't do that."

"He's been given a role in Fazio's organization."

Kurt rolled Tanya off and sat on the edge of the bed. "How do you know this, from Goldhabber's phone?"

"Yes, and there's more."

"I'm listening," a disgusted Kurt said.

"Goldhabber played Fazio, The Four Horseman, and Woody. He was shopping the best deal for himself."

"So, do you know who pulled the trigger?"

"Yes."

"How?"

"Goldhabber was all fucked up on a party cocktail, including coke, Cialis, meth. He turned into a life support system for a penis. One of the girls, Charlette, found his burner phone too and started scanning through it."

"Do I know her?"

"Charlette, Sherry's Charlette."

"No way."

"It's true. She's been handling the cash end in the lobbies for us for a quite a while."

"By us you mean—"

"Sherry and me."

"How did she end up with Goldhabber? Does Sherry know?"

"Charlette's call, not mine. I'm sure she didn't tell Sherry either. She wanted to play, rake in some big cash that night."

"With Goldhabber?"

"She asked, even questioned her about it. She committed and was all in."

"Then who killed Goldhabber?"

"I don't know, but the Pope was supposed to eliminate Steve. Instead, the Pope and Goldhabber ended up getting killed."

Kurt's phone rang.

"Shit, I hope it's not my Texans. They just got to the club."

Kurt looked at his phone and glanced back at Tanya.

"It's Ramone, great timing."

"You better answer."

345

"Kurt took a deep cleansing breath and blew it all out. "Hey, Ramone, what's going on?"

"I'm finished and heading over to Sherry's. When you going to be done with your cowboys?"

Kurt gave Tanya an angry look. "As soon as my Texans get done playing at the club."

"Call me when you're done. I have some interesting news."

"I can't wait. I heard some pretty cool shit myself."

"I'll see you when you're done."

"Later."

Kurt stood up, getting dressed as did Tanya.

"What are you going to do, Kurt?"

"I'm going to act surprised."

*****

Vicki was lying in her bed, exhausted, tossing and turning. She glanced at the clock: 3:13 AM. Her liver was working overtime, trying to discard the massive amounts of caffeine poured into her system, counter flushed with wine, in a desperate attempt to get some sleep. Over the last twenty-four hours she had physically and mentally crashed through the envelope, leaving her disheveled. Her head was fighting off a massive hangover, a mixture of chemicals and exhaustion.

She rose, walked to the kitchen, and poured herself a glass of warm Vegas tap water. She drank it down, turning to the window, eye-balling Jill's condo. She walked over to the kitchen window curtains, setting her glass down in the sink, grabbed one end with each hand and violently yanked them shut.

"No more free shows," she mumbled as she walked into the living room and turned on the TV.

She sat on the couch, rifling through the satellite guide, uninterested in every show that speedily passed her eyes. Vicki's cell phone rang.

"Please. Leave me alone," she said breaking down, tears forming in her eyes.

She clicked off the remote and threw it into the couch and angrily stormed into her bedroom to answer the call. "What now? It's three in the morning!"

Silence on the other end. She pulled the phone away from her ear, looked at the I.D., and turned the speaker phone on.

*****

"Steve?"

"I'm sorry, Vicki."

"No, I'm sorry. You in trouble?"

"No, not physically. Sorry I called this late and woke you up. I just—"

"Steve, it's okay, I couldn't sleep either. It's been a bad day: the killings, balancing the press, no sleep, the coffee. Crap, I'm babbling. What's going on with you?"

"I shouldn't have called; it could have waited."

"I'm up. You're up. Talk to me."

"Well, I told Russ and Bill about Albert."

"Albert?"

"Are."

"And how did they respond?" Vicki asked while lying on her bed.

*****

A black Lincoln pulled down a quiet motionless street and turned into an unlit gravel driveway, a few yards away from a seven-foot custom built cyclone security fence, protecting a long, tall block wall. The camera mounted atop the fence was strategically moving, gathering identifying intel. A loud click and the security gate slid open allowing the Town Car to drive through. The gates closed as the car stopped at the overhanging triple wide car port. Two large dogs barked behind the block wall, protecting the property.

Moshe exited the car first, letting Max out of the driver's side rear door. The bullet proof glass and vehicle armor were ample cover in case the wrong person greeted them.

Moshe walked up to the large solid wooden door, a camera following his every move. He pushed the doorbell, took a step back, and waited.

The large door opened inward revealing a tall brunette armed with a handgun.

"Moshe, how nice. Max, you going to hide behind the car or come in?"

"Warm and fuzzy as ever," Max playfully said.

Max walked to the front door where Bridgette gave him a warm, friendly hug. "Welcome to Casa Brigette. It's no longer called "Rome" the emperor has been replaced by the empress.

"Et tu Brute," Max quoted as he and Moshe entered.

Bridgette closed the door and turned over several locks.

"Not my first time here; I like the new proprietor," Max said.

"Excuse the mess. Just an array of useless men's' clothes to dump and burn."

Bridgette took Max's arm, guiding him behind Moshe.

"From the look of things, it appears as though you've found suitable employers able to acquiesce your special talents."

"I have Max; they also encourage it. An equal opportunity company I might add."

Two dogs came charging into the living room. Bridgette shouted, "Pass auf sie auf!" The two dogs sat and growled, baring their teeth.

"Nice, Bridgette. Freilassen Doughboy. Freilassen Fuksy," Max commanded.

The two dogs both laid down and became quiet.

"Well, well, Max, it appears as though you still know your German commands, and the dogs undoubtedly know you. Been here a couple of times, have you?"

"I could ask you the same question."

"You could."

"I'll go first, Bridgette. The Pope and I have done some business in the past, that is true."

"But not lately?"

"Define lately. I can say with a great deal of confidence that *no* would be a proper and correct response."

"What about you, Bridgette? I assume your current employers were unhappy with the Pope's latest job?"

"They were and they," she opened her arms turned and slowly encircled the entire house, "as you can see, gave me a nice signing bonus."

"Well done. Did you use me as a reference?" Max asked.

"The mere fact that I worked for you and am alive, residing in the same city, is a testament to your approval."

"Well played, dear Bridgette. I see you haven't lost your touch with a Lapua."

"Like you pulled the trigger yourself," a confident Bridgette cheerfully responded.

"I'm beginning to think you've morphed me."

"I'm beginning to think you're right."

Moshe walked over to the bar and poured three glasses of Stolichnaya Elit Vodka. Everyone gathered around the bar and toasted while interlocking arms.

Moshe began the toast. "To the Pope. May that bastard rot in hell."

The three laughed and touched glasses.

"After this cleaning, I'm sure you'll be getting many more contracts. Soon you'll own a house at Mountain Springs Motor Resort, too." Max bowed his head in praise of the rapid rise and marksmanship of Bridgette.

"Why, Father, thank you. Too bad we hardly get to see each other these days."

"That is a shame. And it's wonderful to hear you call me father again. There aren't many opportunities for you to acknowledge our relationship."

"You've done a remarkable job protecting our relationship, Father."

"Bridgette, you know your safety always comes first. Isn't that right, Max?"

"So true, Moshe. And with that toast, we'll be driving back to Vegas. Wouldn't want anyone to see us tonight. One can never be too cautious during these anxious times."

"Eliminating Goldhabber Bridgette was a public service. Too bad we couldn't shout it out and pass the hat," Max said. "That alone would have gotten you your half million-dollar lot at the speedway."

"Great minds think alike," Bridgette cheerfully replied.

"It was risky to come here, but we had to make sure you were not implicated in the hits. Too many killings last night."

"Thanks for having my back. There are a lot of bad apples in this barrel."

They all hugged and Bridgette escorted Max and Moshe out of the front door and back to the Town Car.

"I have a limo client in Vegas tomorrow, so we might end up at your place. They love your club, Father."

"What's not to love, dear? I have a question for you before I leave."

"What is it?"

"Did the Pope accept a contract to kill Steve's friend Mary?"

"No, it was someone else. We discussed it several times. The Pope reached out to several of his connections but also came up empty."

"Then there's someone out there we should be concerned with, Bridgette."

"I know."

The gates opened and as Bridgette watched the car drive away, she momentarily relived her experiences with the Mossad, "The Institute", Israel's protective deep state. Unlike America's counterproductive and corrupt deep state, they made the bad ones disappear.

Bridgette's phone rang. A smile appeared on her face.

"I can't wait to see you again."

"Me too," Bridgette said.

"Be careful. As you well know, the morgue's filling up. They're going to need sandbags to keep the bodies from overflowing into the streets."

"You have such a sexy way with words, Bill. Keep that watchful eye out for Steve."

"You know I will. Maybe we can hook up at your place; I'm dying to see it."

"What, tired of limo sex?"

"That would be like being tired of drinking a bottle of Chateau Lafite, 1787. Tomorrow?"

"Pretty good answer, but a Chateau Margaux 1787 is double the price of your one-hundred-fifty-six thousand dollar Lafite."

"I'll have to see how this goes before I go to, Margaux, Bridgette.

"Really. Be careful what you wish for."

"Oh, I'm wishing."

"I'll call you when I'm in between runs, Bill."

Bridgette hung up, closed the door to her new residence, locked up, and walked up the stairs to her bedroom.

"A Lafite, huh. I'm going to really make him suffer tomorrow," she playfully said as she called the dogs.

*****

Bill left the pool area thinking of Bridgette. He really liked her, but for now their cat and mouse romance would have to continue under the radar.

Steve's poolside outburst was real. The Woody-Letterman fiasco should have never happened. Bill trusted Metro, that was on him. He would never let that happen again. He closed and locked the door to the pool, took a beer out of the refrigerator, and retired to his room. The story Steve revealed earlier put many of the puzzle pieces into perspective. For the first time, the circumstances surrounding Steve made sense.

He closed the door to his room and prepared for bed, thinking of Bridgette. He wanted to be with her now, but patience is what she asked, so he would be playing the long game with her. Another first: he'd found a woman who excited and intrigued him.

*****

It was six in the morning when Kurt returned to the Trop. He went up to Tanya's room and knocked several times.

"Tanya, it's me."

He waited a couple of seconds and then used his plastic key to enter the room. He flipped the light switch on and walked in.

"Tanya."

He searched the room before he sat on the edge of the bed.

"Tanya. What a surprise, gone again," he mumbled.

He glanced around the room looking for any sign of a struggle, but concluded there hadn't been one. Tanya had bailed.

It took twenty minutes for Kurt to drive to the Graveyaad. He easily found a spot. A sparse clientele remained from the Friday night/Saturday morning crowd, scattered around the bar. Kurt saw Ramone sitting alone at a table in the back and joined him.

"What's up, Ramone? Man, you look trashed."

"I'm beyond trashed. I've been doing shots for the last two hours."

"Maybe you ought to start doing coffee shooters, and I didn't see your car. How'd you get here?"

"Candice dropped me off."

"Sounds like you came here to get loaded. Something bothering you?"

"What makes you say that?"

"We gonna play this game, Ramone? What's going on?"

"Nothing. Just need a ride home."

Kurt helped Ramone up and with some help he made it to Kurt's car. The sun just rose over Sunrise Mountain exposing another hot, smog-filled valley morning. Kurt pushed the remote and the car unlocked as Ramone staggered into the front and closed the door.

353

Kurt pulled down a deserted side street and jammed on the brakes, sending Ramone lurching forward. Kurt shoved the limo in park and leaned toward Ramone.

"What the fuck are you doing, Ramone? How could you screw us all over like that?!"

"What are you—"

Kurt pulled out his gun, grabbed Ramone by the collar, shoved the gun under his neck, and shook him several times.

"You goddamn traitor… how could you do this? You helped them kill Tony."

"No. No… that's not how it went down."

"So, you *were* there."

"I saw it all… Tony was whaling on Hans and then he just dropped dead across his legs. We tried to revive him, but he was gone."

Ramone told Kurt the entire story from Fazio's arrival in Vegas to the bloodbath at Barry's.

Chapter 34

I awoke around ten-thirty in the morning, reached out across my pillow and found my phone, recalling my conversation with Vicki.

"What a moron," I babbled to myself while staring at the blacked-out ceiling. "I fell asleep with her on the other end."

"She must think… I have no idea what she's going to think or say the next time I have to talk to her. What an embarrassment, waking her up and then passing out on her," I said continuing to berate myself.

I wandered into the bathroom, flipped on the light, and took a seat in the office with the handle.

"What an idiot."

*****

Vicki's doorbell rang, waking her out of a restless sleep. She sat up, causing her phone to slip off the bed and nose-dive toward the hard tile floor. In one motion and with cat like precision, she caught the phone standing upright on the floor. The annoying doorbell rang a second time.

"Damn, I fell asleep on Steve. Brilliant."

She threw on a robe covering her tee shirt and panties, and with as much energy as she could muster went to the door. She peeked through the peep hole and reluctantly opened the door.

"You look beautiful right out of bed," an excited Jill passionately said as she slid her way into the living room, toting a small bag.

"Jill, what are you doing? It's eleven." She said as she closed the door.

355

Jill wore booty cut-off blue jean shorts, a hot pink Aruba tee shirt, and matching flipflops.

"I brought you a little breakfast, thought you might need it."

"Jill."

"You going to put on some coffee or do you want me to rummage through your kitchen and do it myself?"

"How about neither? Look, Jill—"

"I know, I know, but I really felt some chemistry the other night. Let's have some coffee, bagels, and agree to just be friends."

"Look, I have to get ready—"

"Vicki, it's just coffee and a couple of bagels. Look, show me where the coffee is, and I'll make it. Go on, get ready for work," she added.

"Really Jill, I have a busy day."

"I saw it on the news. How horrible it must have been for you. So much violence in this city. Go ahead get ready. Coffee is the least I can do for you after the day you had yesterday." Jill pointed to Vicki's bedroom. "And where's the coffee?"

Vicki pointed to a cabinet just right of the refrigerator.

"I'll get it started. Get ready. You'll feel better after you have some caffeine flowing through your veins."

Vicki and Jill were acquaintances. Vicki didn't fear her, but the awkwardness of yesterday made this feel uncomfortable. This would be a perfect opportunity to clear the air, let her know she wasn't interested.

Vicki walked to her bedroom and closed the door, trying to get ready in gold medal Olympic fashion. A cup of coffee and then end this.

"It just keeps piling on," Vicki said to the image in the mirror staring back at her while hurriedly putting on a light coat of makeup.

It took a little less than ten minutes for her to get ready and walk out the bedroom door. Her sidearm hung at her hip under a dark blue blazer rubbing against a light blue blouse, skinny jeans, and rubber soled black boots, her hair up in a bun.

Jill sat at her two-seat kitchen table with the bagels on plates, the coffee aroma permeating throughout the condo. She stood up as Vicki approached and walked over to the hot coffee pot and started pouring two cups.

"How do you like yours?"

"Black will be fine. I need a jolt this morning."

"I looked around your kitchen and found the cups. I must have poured a million cups of coffee in my lifetime."

"That's right. You're a flight attendant."

"And you're a detective."

"And I carry a sidearm."

"And I pull a tote bag, and you drive a Tacoma, work shitty hours, and don't get enough rest."

"Well put. And you fly all over the world, set your own hours, and party like the sun's about to implode."

"I'm not keeping score, but I think I crushed you," a grinning Jill proclaimed.

"Point, match, set. You win hands down." Vicki bowed to Julie.

"Okay, okay. Have some coffee and a bagel and join the winner. That must be tough, police work being dominated by men and all."

"There's some crap to deal with. But I've handled it."

Vicki sat down and joined Jill. She lazily slid Vicki her coffee.

"I also found plates and took out some butter for your bagel."

"I might have to charge you rent at this pace."

"You could do a lot worse than me as a roommate," Jill playfully said while buttering her bagel. "There's also some cream cheese in those little pads."

"Look Jill, I know what you're doing."

"Do you?"

Jill stood up and pulled off her tee shirt and tossed it on the floor.

Vicki stood up and put her hands up signaling Jill to stop.

"Jill, I'm—"

"I know, in uncharted waters," she said strategically cutting Vicki off.

Jill kicked off her flipflops toward the refrigerator. Only inches now separated the two women.

"Jill, stop."

Jill grabbed Vicki's arms and pulled them against her breasts, she released them and then grabbed Vicki's head and kissed her softly. Jill released Vicki's hands and reached under her blazer and started fondling her breasts, moving her mouth and tongue across Vicki's cheek, stopping at her ear.

The ear play was erotic and sexy. Jill pulled Vicki's blazer back off her shoulders and slid the arms out, excitedly watching it fall to the floor. Without breaking stride and still working Vicki's ear, she unbuttoned her blouse.

Vicki leaned against the wall, closing her eyes. It had been so long since someone made her feel sexual.

Jill undid Vicki's bra and extended her arms out, slipped it over her hands and tossed it behind her.

"Jill, I—"

Jill grabbed Vicki's waist, bent over and started kissing her breasts while simultaneously and forcefully sliding her hand between Vicki's legs. Vicki fought off the pleasure of Jill's touch, but relented and started to softly moan.

"I want you, Vicki."

Vicki was sex deprived, craving to be taken, but quickly realized this was not who she was or the person she wanted to be taken by. Vicki put her hands on Jill's shoulders and softly pushed back.

"Jill, I can't do this."

Jill started moving her hand even faster between Vicki's legs and using her strength pushed her head deep into Vicki's chest sucking one of her breasts with brute force, causing her to flinch in pain.

Vicki had enough and what seemed innocent and playful turned into a show of female force. Jill started tugging at Vicki's belt.

"Stop!"

Vicki used her police training, slid her right arm under Jill's chin, and violently turned her. Jill was strong, solid, and in incredible shape, but Jill was in the sexual moment not the octagon moment and fell backwards onto the floor.

"I'm sorry Vicki, I got carried away. I'm sorry."

Jill sat on the kitchen floor supporting her weight with the palm of her hands.

Nobody moved or talked for about ten seconds, the two of them breathing hard, staring at each other.

"You know a thousand guys would kill to see you sitting on a floor like that, Jill."

"You going to shoot me?" Jill asked.

"On any other day or night, yeah."

"And a million women would love to see you standing there."

Jill moved her legs knee to knee several times, taunting Vicki.

"Shit, Shit," Vicki said, taking a step toward Jill, then back peddling.

Tears started to form, freely running down her cheeks. She methodically placed the gun and belt on the kitchen table. She took off her boots and dropped her pants to the floor. Jill's eyes froze on her. She slowly took off her panties and threw them at Jill's face.

Jill grabbed them and held on tight almost falling over.

"Is this what you want, Jill?" Vicki said, tears continuing to stream down her cheeks.

Jill got up off the floor and calmly walked over to Vicki and took her hands.

"My God, you're so beautiful. I really want you."

Vicki closed her eyes and leaned into Jill.

"I've never been with a woman before. It's been so long... my husband, they killed him, I—"

Jill took Vicki's hands and slowly kissed her arms, looked up at her, and paused.

"Vicki, I wanted you to want me, not to be some inexperienced woman trying to justify having an affair, some sort of sexual experiment."

Jill gently moved back from Vicki.

"What are you saying, I'm not enough for you?"

"No, of course not. I wanted this to be more than a fling. I can find women anywhere. I really wanted you to want me. Understand?"

Vicki backed up and started picking up her clothes.

"You need to leave."

"Vicki, I'm sorry, I'm looking for more... and I thought maybe you were, you know, ready to really want to be with me, but you're clearly not."

"Get out," Vicki said.

Jill moved in and hugged her.

"Hey, it's okay. You're just lonely."

Jill backed away and started to gather her top and flipflops. They both started dressing. Jill finished first and moved to the door and looked back at Vicki.

"You're so hot. Some man is going to be extremely lucky to have you."

She quietly closed the door behind her.

Vicki stood in her underwear, the rest of her clothes on the kitchen table. She walked to her condo door and leaned against it, continuing to cry.

"What am I going to do?" she quietly sobbed, her head and right hand gently touching the door.

*****

Something appeared to be off when I arrived at the office. Everyone kept staring at me like I was a stone-fingered receiver who couldn't hang on to a pass.

Shelly sat in the dispatcher's chair, twirling her hair and playing on her cell phone. Kiko sat in a chair next to the coffee pot, drinking coffee, playing on his phone. YLL looked like a millennial safe space without the crayons and coloring books.

"How are you this Sunday morning, Steve?" Shelly asked.

"Like I caught an STD on a toilet seat. Thanks for asking."

I glanced into my office without entering. I continued to Dino's office. He had left, cleaned out all his personal items. I grabbed his desk chair and flipped it over.

"Some partner you turned out to be. Adios."

I kicked his desk and walked back to mine. I slammed the door and sat down in my chair almost tipping over from the impact of the landing. Glancing at George's desk, I felt remorseful for dragging him into this unmitigated disaster.

"I never meant to hurt anyone, especially you," I mumbled.

Shelly knocked on my door and walked in.

"Steve, I have Dino on line two."

"Dino?"

"You want me to tell him you're busy or are you going to take the call?"

"Oh, I think I'm going to take this one."

Shelly waited for me to click in on line two.

"Anything else, Shelly?" I said giving her an unpleasant glare.

"Sorry, no. I'll be leaving now."

"Thank you, Shelly."

She about-faced on her back heel and closed the door. I punched line two hard with my right index finger.

"Dino."

"Steve."

"We have some issues to resolve."

"Do we now?"

*****

Chapter 35

Monday
2:25 PM

Woody and Letterman drove to the Graveyaad. Woody had some unsettled business to finalize with Sherry.

"You going to get the Graveyaad and YLL in the same week? Isn't that going to leave you a little strapped for cash?" Letterman asked.

"It's going to leave me a lot strapped for cash. That's why I partnered up with Hans. He had the extra capital I needed. He paid me, now were partners. As you might recall, our wonderful sheriff was about to eliminate Hans. Mister Schuster and Mister Johnson are currently residing in the morgue. A brilliant plan until Tony and that Fazio stuck their greaseball New York asses into it."

"Hans all of a sudden trusted you?"

"He had no choice. If only that ass-backwards sheriff hadn't tossed my name out before Fazio killed him. On the positive side, Hans is not going to all of a sudden vanish because of a few dead bodies. He's almost as bad a money whore as I am. Almost."

"Like you've always said, he's ruthless, which makes him both useful and dangerous."

"His ass is swinging in the breeze and I was his only ticket out."

Letterman took his eyes off the road and looked at Woody. "That business at Schuster's and the mall, Metro's going to turn this city inside out."

"Hans's blood and DNA are all over the place. The mall, however, is a totally different crime scene. There's another dangerous player out there, and we don't know who it is. That's why I'll be dictating the final terms of our brief partnership, Mister Letterman."

Woody and Letterman's cab pulled into an apartment complex across the street from the Graveyaad. Letterman exited first, followed by Woody trailing a few steps behind.

"Jerry, I'll call you when I need a ride. And hang back somewhere nearby.

"Sure thing, boss."

Jerry drove off.

"You see Hans anywhere?" Woody asked.

Letterman looked at his watch. "He said he'd be here."

A black and gold taxi pulled up next to Woody. Hans stepped out, limping, wearing large dark glasses and a UNLV hat as he joined them.

"Nice of you to join us," Woody said.

"Why here?"

"Remember your friend Fazio?"

"What about him?"

"I recently learned Fazio is interested in acquiring the Graveyaad. At three, several of his associates have a meet with Sherry. I thought we could start our partnership off with a little payback, a show of good faith on my part."

"Why does Fazio want to purchase the Graveyaad?"

"Don't know, don't care. I'm not privy to his business decisions. He wants the bar, and I don't want him to acquire it."

"*You're* working on Sherry."

"My business, our business, sending a payback message to Fazio. Nobody's rolling over for him."

"In Sherry's?"

"From the looks of you, I'd be thinking sooner." Letterman added.

"Yeah, I'm in."

"Here's how this plays out," Woody began.

*****

Hans came through the main entrance and scanned the handful of patrons scattered around the bar. He took a seat at a corner table and waited. Fifteen minutes later two men walked in, scanning those inside the bar. They walked up to each one individually, flashed them their guns harnessed inside their suit jackets and asked them to leave. Hans knew what they were doing took the hint and exited before they got to him.

Woody called Eddie.

"I need you to drive over to the Graveyaad; park out back."

"A little early for the Graveyaad, boss," Eddie answered.

"Be here in ten minutes."

"On my way."

Hans walked around the corner and walked up to Letterman and Woody.

"They're inside."

"Good. Wait fifteen minutes and then come in through the back door. You see anyone lurking, call Letterman."

"Got it. And you're going through the front door."

Woody and Letterman stopped at the door and put on surgical gloves before entering. As they strutted in Woody nodded at two men seated at the bar. Sam was tending the bar and washing dirty glasses. The two men nodded back at Woody and left.

"Sam, nice to see you again. I brought along a secret admirer of yours," Woody said, bowing his head, mocking her, making sure she didn't see his hands.

Letterman smiled and winked at her, hiding his hands too. "Somewhere in the back we can go?"

Her face hardened as she answered, "My mother's in her office."

The two walked to the back without breaking stride, Letterman eyeballing Sam most of the way. Sherry stood in her office doorway as the two approached.

"I see you both made it. Never a drunk driver around when you need one."

"Nice to see you too, Sherry," Woody acknowledged.

The three walked into her office. The door closed and they all took seats, Sherry behind her desk and Woody and Letterman in the two chairs facing her.

"My lawyer dropped off the purchase agreement documents. I take it you went through them?"

"I did, but there's one sticking point."

"What's that?"

"The part where it says I'm selling you my bar. I don't think that's going to work for me. Buy someone else's joint. This place is not for sale, especially to you."

"Sherry, you know you're selling it. Why be a bitch? You can sign over the documents now or after this place folds while you're awaiting your trial. All your assets magically frozen. Whatever will poor Samantha and Charlette do?"

"Jail? Whatever are you talking about? Oh wait, you mean that phony bullshit story you fed Sam about me and Sonny you fucking lying asshole!" Sherry's expression changed dramatically.

"Sherry, really? You going to play this little charade? Letterman, show her our little nugget."

Letterman began reaching into his pocket when Sam burst through the office door, a full bottle of Wild Turkey clutched firmly in her raised right hand.

Woody and Letterman rotated in their chairs just in time to see the bottle-wheeling Sam.

"You fucking parasite!" Sam yelled as she swung the bottle down toward Letterman's head.

Letterman raised his left arm in time to partially block Sam's downward stroke while Woody jumped up and bumped into a bookcase. The block forced Sam's hand to open and the bottle glanced off the top of Letterman's head exploding on Sherry's floor, sending glass and whiskey in all directions.

Sherry pulled out a Bowie knife from beneath her desk and lunged at Woody, catching a small piece of his left hip. He grabbed her hair with his right hand, her knife hand in his left, yanking her head. He forced her backwards until she was flush up against the desk. With his strength and adrenaline free flowing, he maneuvered her knife-wielding hand up against her throat. Sherry kicked at his shins. Woody ignored the pain and slit her throat. He became ecstatic watching her blood run down her neck and onto her blouse, turning it red.

"Time to die, Sherry," he softly whispered, eyes wide open, wildly staring in her eyes, watching her life drain.

Letterman seized Sam's throat with his right hand and with his overpowering strength pinned her up against the wall. She tried unlocking his grip with both hands but she was no match. Sam's face turned red as he placed his left hand on top of his right, doubling the pressure. Sam tried to break his grip, continually kicking him. Within twenty seconds her strength emptied into his grip, her arms collapsed, her eyes began to hemorrhage.

"You like it rough, right Sam? Isn't that right?" he said a second time wiggling her against the wall as she collapsed in his hands.

He raised her up several more inches before he let her drop onto the whiskey and glass-drenched floor. He bent over her and snapped her neck.

Buster came through the office door wielding a butcher's knife.

"What have you done?!"

"Self-defense," Woody calmly said.

Letterman clutched Buster's right hand with his left and then delivered a bone-crunching shot to Buster's jaw.

Buster's knees buckled. Woody set Sherry free and discarded her to the floor. He took two steps forward and used his right leather boot in a frontal kick cracking Buster's jaw. The impact almost spun him around, partially dislocating his right shoulder, leaving him barely conscious.

Letterman maintained his grip on Buster's knife-wielding right hand, enjoying the results of Woody's jaw-breaking kick. Buster, being an old crusty Marine, had a surprise package for Letterman. He pulled a knife out of his boot and as he began to pull his left hand back, ready to thrust it deep into Letterman's calf, Hans grabbed his arm.

"Sorry I'm early, but I heard the commotion all the way in the parking lot."

Hans twisted Buster's left hand just as Letterman released Busters right hand. He then side-kicked Buster in the throat, bouncing Buster's head off the door entryway. In an uncontrollable rage, he dragged Buster several feet into the office.

Buster lay unconscious at the mercy of the three of them.

"What happened to Fazio's men?"

"They saw us walk in and ran out," Woody answered.

"This one's yours, as you can, see," Letterman said, pointing to Sam and Sherry's bodies. "Partner."

Hans took his right boot, driving it into Buster's head, cracking his skull. He repeated it twice more before Woody stopped him.

"Inspirational. Now drag him over here next to Sam and close the door."

Hans limped several steps as he dragged Buster in and closed the door.

Woody walked up behind Hans, turned him around and drove Sherry's knife deep into his chest. Letterman shoved Hans backwards, sending him over the top of Sherry's desk.

"If only there was a law banning knives, none of this would have happened."

"You're funny boss, but Sherry cut you good."

"Let's see if we can find something in this room that isn't blood-soaked, use it to stop my bleeding."

Letterman stepped over Sam's dead body, found some freshly washed and stacked white bar towels on one of the shelves. He looked down at Sam's lifeless body.

"It's a shame you didn't let me do her when I had the chance."

"My bad. Now toss me a couple of towels. I don't want to bleed out."

"Convenient that they attacked us. We'll even pass a lie detector test," Letterman said.

"It will never come down to that. Unfortunately, it will also prevent me from acquiring the bar for a while too. It will all go to Charlette," Woody said with disgust. "That psycho bitch and her brat pulled out a short-term win. Charlette will sell it as soon as she can; a lot of bad memories here, worse ones to come if she stays."

"Always plotting for the future, Woody."

Woody pulled out his cell phone from his sports coat inner pocket and dialed Eddie.

"I need you to quietly slip in the back door without being spotted and come into Sherry's office."

"I'll be right there."

Within a minute, Eddie came to the door and Letterman opened it.

"Give that document to Eddie. Eddie, take this and drive back to the office, easy like. No stops, no speeding. Understood?"

"Yes, boss. There's quite a mess in here. That is Buster over there, isn't it?"

"They attacked us, came up on the wrong end."

"Letterman, you pulverized Buster with your boot. Shit. What a fucking mess. And Sam, wow, you really fucked

369

her up. Her neck bone's sticking out of the side of her neck. Jesus, Letterman."

"Sorry to disappoint you. Hans gets all the credit."

Letterman handed the document to Eddie.

"Hans is quite the animal."

"Past tense," Letterman said with a smile.

"Eddie, give it to our wonderful receptionist and tell her to put it in a safe place. She'll know where it goes," Woody ordered.

"You got it. Anything else?"

"Leave."

Eddie snuck out the back undetected.

"Fazio and Hans are going down for this," Woody declared.

"Let's hope Metro pieces it together, follows the bread crumbs we left."

"You see that cabinet door?" Woody asked, pointing to a specific door.

"Yes."

"Open it, rip out the security footage, destroy everything else."

"Got a light?"

*****

7:51 PM

Binge watching an old cop show "The Wire" briefly distracted me, allowing my thoughts to circumvent recent events. My cell phone rang. Vicki. My circumventing came to a screeching halt.

"Vicki, have you any—"

"Steve," she abruptly cut me off. "There's been four more homicides. I didn't want you to hear about it on the news."

"Four more! Not again. Who?"

Vicki paused for a moment.

"Hans, Sherry, Buster, and… Sam."

"Oh no. My God, what happened?" I rose and clicked the satellite off.

"Hans was in a meeting with Sherry when all hell broke loose. They were murdered, the office and half the bar burned down."

I was hurt and angry. She might have betrayed me but this.

"It will take time to put this one together."

"Start with Woody and Letterman."

"They're at the top of our list."

"When did this happen?"

"Around four-thirty. I have to go."

"I understand."

"I'm so sorry. Seems to be my new catch phrase."

"Yeah, sounds about right."

"Make sure you keep everything locked up tight."

"Thanks."

I walked into the kitchen, took out a beer, and sat down. This had to be Woody.

Well into my second beer, I was interrupted by the doorbell. I knew it couldn't be Vicki. I pulled my Glock out of the kitchen drawer, approached the door, and looked through the peep hole, surprised by the person looking back. I opened the door.

"Charlette, I just heard what happened. I'm so sorry. Please come in."

"Thanks, Steve."

I closed the door, making sure I locked and bolted it.

"Charlette, again, I'm sorry to hear about your mother and Sam. I don't even have words to describe how upset I am."

I guided her into the living room and onto the couch, taking a seat next to her.

"Thank you," she started. "I'm sorry for barging in you, but what I have to say can't wait."

"You're not barging in. What's going on?"

"First off, *I'm* sorry."

"What do you mean *you're* sorry? You just lost your mother and twin sister."

She reached into her purse. I reached over and grabbed her hand.

"What are you doing Charlette?"

"You think I came here to shoot you?" she asked.

"Nothing surprises me anymore. Just being careful."

I eased up on my grip and let her finish bringing what turned out to be a key chain, with one key swaying on it.

"A key. What's it turn?"

"This is a key to a private security box at Twenty-Five-Hour Security. I've had it in my possession for a couple of months now."

"Why are you be showing this to me? And again, what are you sorry about?"

"Sonny's death. My mother thought she killed him. Then someone spread a vicious lie saying that she did. These killings are technically her fault, all of this, because of her. You should be back in your college town being a shrink or whatever it is you did. None of this should have happened," she said covering her face.

I couldn't form any words, so I just stared at her.

"Take it," she said handing me the keychain. "I was told not to go there. Just to give you this key in case anything ever happened to my mother."

"Who gave her the key?"

"Sonny gave it to her and she gave it to me with those instructions. That's all I know."

"Does Detective Spicuzza know about any of this?"

"No."

"Maybe she should."

"Go ahead and call her. But I have to leave."

"I know you're grieving, but you should stay, at least until we both talk to her. She needs to hear everything you know about this."

"Plus, I have some information for her that you should hear too."

"What do you know about this?"

I dialed Vicki.

"Steve."

"Charlette's here. You need to come here, now. It's important."

"Are either of you in any danger?"

"No. But you really need to be here."

"I'm fifteen minutes out."

We sat mostly in silence until the doorbell rang. I opened the door, looking at Vicki standing steadfast, but unbeknownst to her, those big, sad, brown eyes told a different story. I could sense her duress, the anguish on her face screamed exhaustion. I'm sure she never thought her job would entail the mass carnage she witnessed since I arrived.

"Come in. Charlette's in the living room. You're going to want to hear what she just told me and what I have to say."

Vicki gave me this not again look, shook her head, came in and sat next to Charlette.

"Charlette, tell Vicki what you just told me."

Charlette filled her in, then I took over the conversation.

"Sam came over here Sunday, elated that I had survived the mall shooting. What I didn't know at the time was that she was setting me up for an unannounced visit from Woody and Letterman."

I finished the story exactly the way it happened; I didn't leave out any details. I could feel Charlette's rage and

Vicki's disappointment. Both were in disbelief and frustrated on a variety of fronts.

"Sam went through all that humiliation for nothing!" an incensed Charlette shouted.

"What do you mean?" Vicki asked.

"My mother was afraid; she thought she accidentally killed Sonny. She was positive he died when he slipped and fell down the back steps."

"What are you talking about, Charlette?"

"Sonny came over to the bar the night he disappeared. He had no idea my mother was waiting to verbally ambush him."

"For what?" I asked.

"My mother and Sonny were in a relationship and sleeping together. Sonny, always the player, promised his player days were over, that he was happy to be with my mother. She fell in love with him, and when she heard he was sleeping with Bridgette, someone more than half his age, well, she freaked out."

"Who told her that?" Vicki asked.

"Earlier in the day, Hans stopped by the bar and discussed it in detail, Bridgette and Sonny's relationship."

"That's what led to an argument between the two?" Vicki said.

"Yes. My mother accused him of sleeping with her, but he laughed it off."

"What happened next?"

"He got upset with her and walked out of her office. He was leaving out the back door when she grabbed him and threw a punch. He ducked, but slipped and fell down the back stairs, landing awkwardly on his neck. She ran down the stairs to help him, but he was unconscious and wasn't breathing. She thought he died and that she was responsible. Buster heard the commotion, came out of the kitchen, ran down the stairs and tried to help. He thought Sonny had died too. He carefully dragged him under the steps. Buster told my mother to wait with Sonny as he ran into the storage closet, pulled out a tarp, came back and covered him."

"She could have called 911 and reported it," Vicki said.

"There's more."

"What happened next?" I asked.

"They went into my mother's office and figured out what they were going to do. They were in there maybe ten minutes before they went back down the stairs. Sonny had disappeared, gone, tarp and all."

"What do you mean disappeared? I thought you said they both checked him out, that he wasn't breathing." Vicki said.

"They did. They were sure he was dead."

I began pacing.

"I know it sounds crazy, but that's what happened. She tried calling Sonny three dozen times, but her calls continually went to voicemail."

"We never found Sonny's phone but we found those calls and subsequent phone calls your mother and hundreds of other persons made. She was a suspect, but we never had enough information or motive to convict her of the crime or anyone else," Vicki added.

"Yet he ended up torched in his car," I stated.

I walked out of the living room and into the kitchen where I pulled a beer out of the refrigerator and continued out the kitchen door to the pool. I yanked out a chair from under an umbrellaed table and sat down. I took a long hard gulp from the bottle and followed it with a mild belch. Manners and social etiquette were at the bottom of my list.

Charlette and Vicki followed me out to the pool area and pulled chairs next to me. Vicki sat back and listened as Charlette and I talked.

"I'm sorry for running out here, Charlette, but this is overwhelming, all of this."

"I know."

"I apologize for being selfish. What you're dealing with is horrific. I can't begin to imagine what you're going through right now and yet you still came here to tell me this."

"You needed to know. I promised my mother if anything ever happened, I'd tell you and give you the key," she said pulling an envelope out of her purse and showing it to me. "Here's the rest. I never thought this would happen."

An address and a security code were printed neatly on the front.

"Go there and open it, like I said, it's a key to a private security vault."

"Sherry gave you and Sam a key in case she was murdered, and you both knew about this?" I asked.

"No. My mother never told Sam, just me."

"I don't get it. Why only you?"

"She was always protective of her."

"From what?"

"From every and anything. My mother hung around and sometimes did business with… let's just say some unscrupulous characters. I was always the hard case while Sam was the glass menagerie. My mother always paid extra attention to her. It's how things worked."

"Did you know Woody was blackmailing Sam? He believed he had the evidence to convict your mother of Sonny's murder. She bought into it one hundred percent."

"What are you talking about? Woody didn't know anything. He wasn't there that night."

"He definitely had something on Sam, because she was terrified; he threatened her with it."

After a brief pause I began to surmise what I thought happened.

"This all makes sense. Woody found out, threatened to go to Metro and drop a dime on your mother unless Sam cooperated."

"But how could he have known?" Charlette asked.

"I don't buy it. Not enough evidence. It has to be something else," Vicki said.

Vicki hit a vein with that one. Charlette turned towards her. "Maybe someone told him about Tanya, my mother, and me working together."

"You mean Tanya's escort business?" I asked.

"Yes. My mother let some of Tanya's girls work out of the bar for a cut. I collected the cash for a lot of those transactions, off premises. Nobody got hurt. Everyone made money, a win-win for all of us. Sam wasn't a part of it."

"Everyone got hurt," Vicki added. "But I'm not buying it. Maybe Woody and Hans worked her together."

"Woody had no way of knowing about Sonny. Only my mother saw it happen and Buster helped. He knew Sherry would never kill Sonny, she loved him."

"This Hans guy got this ball rolling and look what happened," I said.

"Another limo company owner just as psychotic and dangerous as Woody, a perfect pair," Vicki added.

"You guys must breed them here?"

"Sometimes it seems that way," a disgusted Vicki concluded.

"Charlette, did this Hans guy know your mother would go off on Sonny if she suspected he cheated on her?" I asked.

"Let's just say my mother had a Louisiana Bayou temper; Hans knew it."

"Whoa, we're jumping to conclusions. Let's get back to Hans being killed at the bar," Vicki said as she took control of the conversation. "The meeting at her office, any chance Woody and Letterman were there?"

"Woody's always wanted the bar. Woody tried to buy my mother out more than once, at a low-ball price."

"Someone who either worked for her or a regular at the bar sold Hans or Woody the information. They used it against Sam and possibly your mother," Vicki concluded.

377

"But who?" Charlette asked.

"Think, Charlette. It's your place. Who's a frequent flyer at the bar?" Vicki asked.

"Lisa. It must be her. Her ears and eyes are everywhere. Plus, she's always bitching about being underpaid and underappreciated."

"Did your mother ever tell you who was there that night?" Vicki probed.

"No. But I can check the employee hours, receipts and dates. Unless they paid cash. All I know is neither Sam nor I worked that night."

I raised my hand while I thought about the nights and early mornings when I was at the bar. "Hang on a second." Then it came to me. "Knuckles, he's been there every time I've been there. Any chance he'd do something like that?"

"No. Knuckles, is always at our place. My mom... Christ, she let him run his book out of the bar, brought in a ton of slot business. But he wouldn't do that to her, sell her out like that."

"Degenerate gamblers and their bookies will pretty much do anything to make a buck and maybe Woody had something on Knuckles. Maybe they cleared each other's slates." Vicki said, looking directly at Charlette.

"Knuckles and my mother were friends."

"Knuckles is friends with a lot of people, especially with the ones that like to gamble with a degree of anonymity. You know, the ones that like to gamble on credit," Vicki said.

"If you know about his bookmaking, why is he still operating? It's illegal, even in Nevada, right Vicki?" I asked.

"Knuckles has a certain "Cart Blanche" with some very influential people in Metro and the mayor's office. He's considered 'off limits'," Vicki responded.

"That's really screwed up."

378

"I don't have the power to make policy. I have superiors who get paid to set parameters in the department."

"Pardon me if I'm totally unimpressed with your ass-kissing superiors."

"Welcome to Metro policies and procedures."

"Charlette, you knew about this too, didn't you?" I asked.

"Yes. They all made a lot of money feeding off each other. It was a good partnership."

"Let's just ask Sonny, Sam, Buster, Hans, and your mother how that panned out. Nothing but rampant blind-eyed, Vulture Capitalism going on at the Graveyaad," I snapped back.

"Both of you, let's get back on point and figure some of this out. Charlette, you get hold of the payroll records and let me know if Lisa worked that night, and if not, who did. Also, check out the receipts from that night. I'll find Knuckles and have a conversation with him."

"Won't that get your ass in a bind with the penthouse police?" I sarcastically asked.

"Maybe next week I'll be applying for a chauffeur's job at your place."

I opened the envelope.

"Don't worry, Charlette. I won't take anything out of the vault that doesn't pertain to Sonny."

"I know you won't, you haven't been poisoned by this city. You're actually an honest person, Steve. Plus, I'm not sure what's even in there."

"Thanks, but let's not get carried away."

"I have to go. I have a lot of arrangements to make."

Together we all left the pool area. Vicki helped Charlette to the door and let her out, then returned to the living room.

"Steve, we need to talk."

"I thought that's what we were just doing. Let's go into the kitchen."

We each pulled up a chair at the table.

"Before you begin jumping down my throat for not telling you about Sam and Woody, in my defense, it just recently happened."

"I'm sorry the two officers assigned to protect you were on Woody's payroll. There is an overwhelming amount of corruption being exposed ever since the sheriff's murder. His tentacles ran deep in both departments and it's hard to tell who the good guys and bad guys are any more. There are so many amazing police officers in the department. Corruption happens in every large institution. Your home invasion should have never happened. Woody could have killed you... that's on me."

"I'm not blaming you."

"Still—"

"Vicki, they would have, but Woody needs my signature to obtain YLL. Your father sold him his percentage in the company and now he's after mine."

Vicki smiled at me. "He doesn't know, does he?"

"Woody's clueless. He doesn't know I own all of YLL. What a con job by Dino."

"Priceless."

It's nice to see a smile on your face again."

"You too."

After a brief pause, Vicki went to the door. "I need to find a way to get Woody and Letterman permanently locked up, the sooner the better."

"I'd prefer it if they end up like Sonny."

"I know how you feel but I'm still a servant of the law.

"I understand your end, but I can still hope."

"Getting back to your situation... I wish I could assign some officers to watch your house; I'm just not sure who's clean anymore. I'm not going to risk it."

"Not to worry. My roommates and I... we got this."

Chapter 36

Tuesday
8:05 AM

My phone rang, startling me out of a dead sleep. I rolled over and threw my arm out several times like fly fishing for trout in a Montana stream, trying to hook and reel in my cell phone. I got it just before it went to voicemail. I wasn't overly thrilled at the name and picture staring back at me on the screen this early in the morning.

"Kurt, what's got you up at the crack of dawn?"

"It's eight in the morning and we need to talk."

"Okay. How about later this afternoon?"

"How about I'm at your front door and you get your pansy ass up and let me in."

"Jesus, who punched in your nut sack. Give me a minute, I'll be right there. And I'm warning you, I'm not decent."

"Cut the shit and let me in."

A violent outbreak of desert sunlight lurked on the other side of the curtains. I fumbled around using my iPhone's light to get me there. I jerked the bedroom curtains wide open, like the protagonist in a vampire movie, allowing the intense sunlight to illuminate the room. I pretended to be Count Dracula and with my right arm dragged an imaginary cape across my face.

"That's so bright!"

I sluggishly moved out of my bedroom and to the front door, dressed in my black silk gym shorts, open heeled grey and black slippers, and a green and gold Brett Favre tee.

"What's going on, Kurt?" I let him in.

"You've got problems."

"Tell me something I don't know," I said closing the door.

"The original owner's son."

"What about him?"

381

"He's back in Vegas, here to reclaim his father's old company, your company."

"And Woody has threatened me and given me an ultimatum: sign over my portion of YLL or my friends and I will be included in the next round of toe-tags."

"Jesus Christ, Steve, when did this happen?"

"Jesus Christ, Kurt, when did that happen?"

"Okay smartass, I'll go first. I met with Tanya early this morning. She informed me that my trusted friend and yours, Ramone, has been working with Fazio, assisting him in the reacquisition of YLL."

"Our Ramone? Sheee-it."

"Double sheee-it on me. I trusted him, brought him into the fold. But he crossed that imaginary line.

"That back stabbing piece-of-shit."

"However, I caught up with Ramone earlier this morning at the Graveyaad; we had a little chat. Actually, I shoved my Glock under his chin, then he explained *his* side of the story. Now he's back on board with us again, apparently."

"What about tomorrow? He going to flip?"

"He said no, and I kind of believe him. He knows you're for real, not some backwoods stooge. Plus, you probably won't threaten to kill him."

"My father told me this once and I never forgot it: Never threaten anyone. If it reaches that point, you better do what you need to do; negotiations are over."

"Great advice. Negotiating time *is* over. Time for action."

"That's comforting, Kurt, knowing I have Woody, Letterman, this Fazio gangster and his crew all coming after me. Sounds like I'm person of the year material."

Kurt explained his conversation with Tanya earlier in the morning, and by the expression on his face, leaving out what I'm sure were some intricate details, those he believed were better left unsaid.

"Steve, you know you can sell out to Woody. Let him deal with this. There's no shame in that."

"I hate Woody and especially Letterman. I want to permanently fuck them up or watch someone do them. At this point I'll settle for either."

"That's a really bad idea, doing it yourself. A surefire way to end up resting on a refrigerated shelf."

"Rumor has it."

"I want you to meet with Max and me this afternoon at his place. He can help. He has some interesting ideas."

"Thanks for being on my side Kurt. I'm sure Bill and Russ will want to be in on this too. But, I don't want them to get hurt."

"But if I get hurt, it's okay?" Kurt said.

"Just call yourself, bait."

"Spoken like a true entrepreneur. And on that note, I'll set it up and call you with a time."

"Thanks."

Kurt left and I wandered into the kitchen and grabbed an energy bar. I shoved it down my throat and began my trek to the shower when the doorbell rang.

"Is this going to be a regular thing every time I want to take a shower?"

I glanced through the peephole, again surprised to see who stood there.

"Vicki, what brings you here again? Am I under arrest?"

"Can I come in?"

"You have a search warrant?" I playfully asked.

"I do."

I gave her this strange look right before she kicked the door closed and started kissing me. She sensually ambushed me, catching me completely off guard. The two of us stumbled and fell backwards onto the cold tile of the entryway, where she dropped anchor, her hips straddling mine.

383

"Is this how you treat perps?"

"Just extremely dangerous ones, like you."

I grabbed her hair and pulled her savagely into my lips and kissed her with every ounce of pent-up passion I could unleash. After twenty seconds she backed off and took ahold of my shoulders pushing her way up and off me. She seductively hovered above me, breathing hard, intently staring me down.

I fumbled around and stood up in front of her, trying to find the right words to say.

"I'm not interrupting anything, am I?" She glanced down at my aroused hardware and then made eye contact again. "Apparently not."

I took her arms and pulled her into me. "You care to explain what's happening here?"

"You need me to explain this to you?"

She jumped on me, straddling my waist with her legs locked in tightly around my waist while her arms interlocked securely around my neck. I wrapped my arms around her back and kissed her nonstop, only loosening up to pry her arms free of her vice grip to rip off her jacket and shirt on the way to the bedroom. She was sensual, erotic, everything I imagined she would be. And the mind-blowing thing, every ounce of her was into me.

I dropped her on the bed and seductively removed her shoes and threw them on the floor. I carefully unstrapped her ankle holster and tossed it on top of the headboard pillows. While playfully kissing her ankles, I nonchalantly undid her belt buckle, yanked the belt through the straps, and threw it over my shoulder. I continued with the unsnapping her of pants while casually pulling down her zipper.

"You have beautiful eyes," she said pulling my hand in and kissing it.

I was in uncharted territory, my heart pounding, my breathing heavy.

"You're—"

"I've wanted you since the moment we first met," she said cutting off my words. "I've been dying to tell you." She moved in closer and sat up where she easily pulled my tee shirt over my head.

She pivoted around on her stomach and glanced back at me. I leaned back and using both hands pulled her pants and underwear off in one forceful move. I kicked my slippers into the wall and dropped my silk shorts. I lazily climbed into bed while gracefully angel kissing her back. I couldn't help admiring her beautifully sculpted body and every curve along the way to the base of her neck. I pulled her long black hair over her head and gently kissed her shoulders and neck watching her hands playfully dig into the sheets. She suddenly rotated under me, wrapped her arms around my neck and rolled me on my back. She leaned backward, pulled her black sports bra over her head, and dropped it on the floor. Like every other part of her body her breasts were beautiful.

She leaned over, her palms resting next to the sides of my head, displaying her sexy muscled arms. She vivaciously rubbed her breasts across my face; they were soft and natural. I raised my head slightly and began kissing them.

She leaned her head back, eyes closed, tenderly moaning, locking her powerful legs into my hips. She began to slide her pelvic bone back and forth across my waist.

"I want you so bad," she whispered. I only wish…" she stopped her sentence while gently placing her lips to mine and gently kissed me.

I rolled her over and looked deep into her eyes, "I've dreamt of this moment a thousand times. I never imagined in my wildest dreams it would be this incredible."

She pulled me in tighter, her legs cloaked around me. It was passionate, erotic; like two hearts beating as one. My eyes were fixated on hers. We climaxed together and were rhythmically breathing deep sighs of elation. I rolled off her

385

onto my right side allowing the late morning sun to consume her anatomy. She stared at me watching me stare at her.

"It's hard to believe you're here," I said running my left hand lightly through her hair and kissing her cheek.

After a long pause her expression changed.

"Steve, I—"

"What is it?"

She rolled over me and bounced out of bed and began to put her clothes on.

"What are you doing? What's going on?"

"I have to go to work."

I slid out of the bed and took her hands, stopping her from putting her clothes on.

"I'm sorry Steve, this should have never happened, I don't know what—"

"What are you talking about? I've been dreaming of this moment ever since you entered my office like a one-hundred-twenty-pound proton torpedo."

"I know, but you're a suspect, a victim, and what I just did is clearly unethical. I could lose my career over this. This can't happen again."

"This is about your career?"

She pushed my arms away and finished dressing, picking up her blouse and jacket on the way to the front door.

"I know you felt something just now. That wasn't some random hookup we experienced," I said.

"I'm sorry, Steve," she said while putting the rest of her clothes on.

"We can make this work. I'm certainly not going to advertise this."

"I knew this was a bad idea. I should have never come here."

"But you did, and here we are. You going to bail on me?"

"I can protect you more efficiently if I'm not involved. We can't do this again," she said while trying to walk out the front door.

I grabbed her arm and turned her. "You can't do this, Vicki."

She pulled me in and kissed me hard. "I can't do this."

She released me and walked to her car. She started up the engine, locking eyes with me until she backed out of the driveway and drove off. I followed her out the door and stood in my driveway.

My heart sank. I didn't know what hit me. This wasn't supposed to happen. After brazenly eyeballing a female neighbor who picked up on the fact I was standing buck naked in my driveway, I retreated through the door slamming it as I stormed back to the bedroom. I sat on the edge of the bed thinking how I'd never been on an emotional roller coaster like this before.

"What the fuck!" I yelled at the ceiling.

My cell phone rang and I could barely hear it. I must have dropped it in the living room. I raced back and took it off the recliner hoping to see Vicki's name on the screen. Disappointment smothered me when I read the name strewn across the face of my iPhone.

"Hey, Kurt."

"Someone else die since I last saw you? What's wrong? You alright?"

"I'm great. Things have never been better. Why?"

"You sound like shit."

"You planning on getting a psych degree anytime soon?"

"Um, the meeting with Max is set for four this afternoon."

"Thanks. I'll see you there."

"Whoa, hold on, amigo. What's going on? Something's not right."

"I'm exhausted. That answer your question?"

"If you say so, but there's one more thing."

"I can't wait to hear it."

"Woody and Letterman were brought in for a questioning regarding last night's murders, and then released."

"Great news, Kurt."

"Oh, and don't forget to strap up."

"That was two things."

I hung up and walked back to the empty bedroom where I had just been involved in one of the most intense and romantic episodes of my short life. But I felt like someone sucker-punched me. She annihilated me with her analytical, hypothetical, one-sided diatribe and subsequent dramatic exit.

"How did making love to her turn into a funeral pyre? This unending Sonny shit-storm, everybody I meet, everything I touch, everywhere I go keeps eating away at me like leprosy!" I shouted into an empty bedroom.

Chapter 37

After wandering around the house and pool for several restless hours, I managed to shower, dress, secure my Glock and put two thirty round clips in my suit jacket. I left the house headed for the meeting.

Today of all days I needed to have my head in the game, not in some desolate, morose place, beating myself up over Vicki. Her abrupt entrance and departure made the simple task of keeping my eyes peeled to the road nearly impossible; I caught myself drifting across the lane divider lines several times.

I decided to take a different route, while still looking for any signs of unusual activity behind me. I took several side roads as a precaution and somehow managed to drive myself directly in to a cul-de-sac. I stopped the truck, got out, wandered around the vehicle several times before pausing at the hood. I needed to stop hosting this pity party.

"Get your shit wired tight!" I screamed into the late afternoon sky.

I was pissed off, angry, frustrated, words dancing around in my head as I arrived at Tight Racks exactly at three-forty-five. On the brief ride in I managed to extricate my head out of my ass and get back to being me. With all the bad things that had happened ever since I arrived in Vegas, finally it was my time to go on the offensive.

Several limos were parked in the lot along with a handful of cars. I shoved my hand against the truck door and jolted it shut. I scanned the parking lot for any unusual activity, like a cyborg executing a contract. I walked into the club in time to catch the last minute feeble attempts of the day shift morning strippers trying to make bank before their shift ended.

Talk about the bottom of the barrel hour. I've seen women hanging around homeless shelters, toting shopping carts, cuddling bagged liquor and sporting beanies half way pulled down their faces with more sex appeal.

I laughed to myself thinking of how much alcohol I would have to consume to allow one of these "Hotties" to purge my loins with a lap dance. Most of them looked like they were either recovering addicts or sliding back the wrong way into more drug and alcohol abuse, but kudos to them for trying. I once again had my attitude where it needed to be and returned to full dickhead mode.

I strutted my shit to the back room where Boris hovered outside Max's door.

"Boris."

"Steve, been a while."

"It has."

He stuck out his enormous paw. We shook hands and shoulder bumped.

"They're inside waiting for you."

I raised my arms waiting for him to disarm me, but he didn't.

"I'm assuming you brought some protection."

"You mean in case one of your," I air finger quoted 'dancers', busts a move on me?"

A stone-faced Boris replied, "It's important to keep your sense of humor intact, as well as yourself."

"Point well taken."

He opened the door and I walked in.

Seeing Bill at the table caught me off guard. He was seated at a table that included Kurt, Dino, Prez, Kenny, Moshe, and Max.

"Max, this is an unexpected gathering for our private meeting. What's Bill doing here?"

"Sit down, Steve. There are some things we need to discuss."

"I'm all ears, Max." I slid in an empty chair next to the door crossing my arms. "You have my undivided attention," I reassured him looking directly at Kurt.

"Good."

"What's going on? I thought this meeting was arranged for the three of us."

"Not anymore. Everyone here has a stake in this too," Kurt answered.

"Bill, you care to explain?"

"I'm supposed to be here."

"What are you talking about?"

Bill took a deep breath and sighed. "I work for Max. Everyone else, they have their own individual reasons for attending."

"You're now magically employed by Max?"

"Yes. I've worked for him for a long time."

"Oh, this ought to be enlightening. Please, do tell."

"He called me four years ago, asked me to come to Las Vegas for an important assignment. Well, he's the legendary Max Sharone. I couldn't say no."

"You and Max, four years ago? You expect me to buy this week-old bag of donuts? He's old enough to be your grandfather. I don't understand the connection."

"Max and I worked for the same people."

"Max worked for the Mossad in Israel."

"I know."

"Stop beating around the bush and get to the point."

"Max and Sonny were close friends. Max called me, asked me to come to work for him, a special assignment."

"You were working for the Mossad? No way."

"It's true, Steve," Max interjected.

"So school, our fraternity, working together all of these years, our friendship, all manufactured bullshit?"

"Except for our friendship and a few classes I took."

I clapped. "Well played, Bill. You got me. Very convincing, almost Oscaresque. And to the rest of you, congratulations. The patience and deceit you've all displayed waiting for the right moment to unload this charade on me, impeccable."

391

"Steve, you're missing my point. I was sent to watch you, Max thought your life might be in danger. But our friendship, the fun and crazy things we've done together, all of that was real," Bill said, apologetically defending his actions. "We're all here today because of you and Sonny."

"You're twenty-four, Bill. How long could you have possibly known Max?"

"I'm twenty-eight, another lie."

"Twenty-eight? No way. School, work, football?"

"Cooked books."

"And I trusted you."

"You did."

"And by the way, I'm dying to know who you work for, Kurt."

"I work for you."

"No bullshit."

"None. I'm here to help you, remember? Sonny and Tony were my friends too."

"Same here," Prez added.

"Everyone seated here has some unfinished business to settle," Max said.

Boris opened the door and Bridgette walked through. Everyone paused and looked at her.

"Bridgette, what are you doing here?" I asked.

"Don't worry, Steve. I've been to the shooting range a couple of times. I know which end of the gun to point. I'll be fine."

With her right hand, she pulled out a Beretta holstered underneath the left side of her black suit jacket. She began to playfully squint with her left eye closed, holding the gun out in front of her and eyeing me simultaneously, rolling the weapon side to side before placing it back in the shoulder harness.

"See?"

Bill looked like he dropped a ten-million-dollar lottery ticket off the Empire State Building.

"Ah… Bridgette."

"Cat got your tongue, Bill?" a smiling Max asked.

"Big time."

"Dino, she's your responsibility," I said.

"No, Steve, she's my responsibility. You want to tell him, Bridgette, or should I?" Max asked.

"Tell me what?" I asked feeling like the unfunny clown in a bad circus.

"Must be the time, Max," Bridgette weakly replied with a smirk developing on her face."

"It is, dear," Max said with a proud smile.

"Can you two tell me what's going on?" Bill and I asked simultaneously.

"Oh my God, she's Max's daughter," Bill announced to the room.

"What are you talking about?" I said.

"True. I'm Max's daughter, Steve. I've been keeping you safe, a promise I made to Sonny and to my father."

"You work for the Mossad too?"

"Yes."

I quickly did double takes on Bill and Bridgette and realized Bill had no idea the two of them worked for the same agency.

"How are *you* liking Bullshit 101, Bill?"

"Quite the class."

"That it is, buddy. Did you take out Goldhabber and his hitman Bridgette? Are you responsible for saving my life at the Forum Shoppes?"

She didn't say a word, just stood there, looking at the wall.

"Bridgette, how did you know? The timing, the…"

She remained silent, choosing not to make eye contact.

"Who ordered the hit on Steve?" Kurt asked. "Goldhabber didn't have any reason to kill him. Who would have that much power?"

393

Max took over the conversation. "We don't know for sure yet but probably someone sporting a toe tag in the morgue I imagine. There are many people working on it, Us, the Mossad, Homeland, the FBI, the DEA and the CIA have formed a joint task force to deal with all this unusual activity surrounding you Steve and several other national security inconsistencies developing around Las Vegas and parts of the west."

"That doesn't bode well for Steve," Bill said.

There was a knock on the door. Boris let four men enter the room.

"Gentlemen, please come in. We were discussing your agencies' involvement."

They took up positions around the outside of the conference table.

Boris followed them in.

Max stood up. "Boris, take a seat over here next to me."

"Everyone, let me introduce to you all of the western directors of the various task forces assigned to eliminate these current hostile conditions that exist in our beautiful city. Tony Rodriguez of homeland, Carey Newsome of the DEA, James Whitcomb of the FBI and Weston K. Fairview, CIA," Max began.

They all nodded as their names were roll-called.

"We're all working together and we're close to launching a two-part assault on these individuals."

Weston K. Fairview took a step toward the table and began to speak. "With the escalation of violence toward Mr. Mueller, the L.A. drug cartels pushing into your city, and because of the massive amounts of illegal intel pouring out of this area, we've put together this unique task force with a plan to cut off the heads off the snakes in both cities simultaneously."

"We won't be assisting in the L.A. part of this operation but we'll play a major role in the Vegas component," Max indicated to the assembled players.

Carey Newsome said, "Weston is right. Our job is to cut off the Vegas end of the drug supply and illegal intel. Our strike date is right around the corner. We're waiting for the green light to go. Expecting it in the next couple of days.

"Gentlemen, we and our international colleagues have determined Woody and Letterman have crossed our imaginary boundary lines of acceptable behavior. They're considered extremely dangerous to the point where they have been contracted out. Complicating things even further is the return of Fazio Junior and his crew. He's trying to reestablish his father's legacy in Las Vegas, which included any number of crimes. Pick one. Anyway, he's returned to Las Vegas. I'm sure he's somehow involved in the recent killing sprees."

Tony Rodriguez continued the summary. "Max and several of his constituents have been contracted to eliminate these threats. And although all our agencies will all be assisting you in one form or another, our footprint, understandably, won't be on any of this."

"Plausible deniability, how convenient."

"Call it what you want," James Whitcomb of the FBI reaffirmed.

"We're supposed to kill them. Is that what you're saying, Max?" Kurt asked. "You're supposed to be the eraser?"

"Cleaners, Kurt," Boris corrected him.

"You're Mossad too?"

"Yes."

"And what about Kenny? He in your little merry band?"

"No, he's an independent. Works for me because of his many unique talents."

"Did you know about this, Dino?" I asked.

395

"Most of what Max is telling you. Bridgette came as a total surprise."

"What about Metro and the Sheriff's office, they in on any of this?" I asked.

"James, you want to answer that one?" Max asked.

"They're in a restructuring process, completely out of the loop regarding any of our actions or movements. They're still continuing to investigate the murders, but aren't getting anywhere. Fortunately, we have an ace inside the department pulling a variety of inconspicuous strings and keeping us informed of all their activities. Anything that could interfere with our current efforts."

This was an easy one to figure out.

"You've got Vicki involved in this? She could be flushed out and become one of the targets. Are you guys out of your minds? Dino, you approve of this?" I asked.

"She's more than capable of taking this horse to the finish line. She's my daughter, our best chance of sequestering Metro and cleaning out this rat's nest," Dino added. "She volunteered."

"And what about this Fazio guy?" I inquired. "Where is he on the roach list?"

"Not to worry, Steve. We're planning a special little surprise for him. The FBI can be very useful in this one, especially when they're not busy tossing around a political football and taking sides. No offense."

"None taken. We're all in on this one."

"I still don't like Vicki being dragged into this," I objected.

"I worry about her every day. This is what she chose. I couldn't drag her away from this with the Budweiser Clydesdales."

"Your daughter's assistance is most appreciated; we both have skin in the game, Dino," Max proudly stated. "What I'm about to tell everyone in this room stays between us, understood? Some of you already know this."

Max looked each one in the room individually and received an approval nod.

"Sonny is not Steve's real father." Max began and told the entire story to everyone in the room.

Everyone took turns looking back and forth at each other, then their eyes trained in on me.

"Are the CIA, Homeland, FBI or any other federal agencies going to lock me up in Area 51 and throw away the keys?" I said staring at the agency representatives.

"Chill out. You've been watching way too many spy movies, Steve," Bridgette answered. "They've got much larger, remote holes to throw you down."

"You're still here," Weston K. Fairview snarkily replied.

"Comforting to know."

"We're keeping you safe from all of those foreign entities," Bridgette added.

"Bill, before we walk into the O.K. Corral, I have a question for you. Is Max still working for the Israelis?"

"No, he is here to help you because of his friendship with Sonny and the promise he made to protect you. He retired a long time before all this garbage went down."

Max cut in, "Let me bundle this the best way I know how. Steve, several agencies asked me to assist them because I live in Nevada. I contracted Bill to keep an eye out for you in La Crosse, a favor to Sonny and me. You see, Are helped Sonny and Sonny promised to protect you, a quid-pro-quo. We are all here today to clean up a lot of those loose ends surrounding you, Are, and Sonny."

"Well, I've recently acquired additional information concerning Sonny," I began.

"Let's hear it," Max asked.

Everyone listened intently as I told the story revealed to me by Charlette. I left out the part about Vicki and the private vault.

The room went quiet. "All we have to do is figure out how Sonny miraculously vanished from the Graveyaad parking lot and ended up in the desert."

"Quite the story," Dino said.

"Seriously, why am I in danger from foreign entities? I don't have any crazy superpowers. Oh wait, except maybe this!"

I jumped out of my chair, "See? I can fly!"

I saw it on all their faces, this brief expectation.

"Really, you thought I could fly around the room? You people watch way too much Sci-Fi network."

"If you could, that would be extremely cool," Kurt said. "Skipping all that rush hour traffic."

The mood temporarily lightened.

"You gentleman can leave now." Max pointed to the agency representatives. "The rest of what I have to say is between us."

The agency members exited the room.

"Let's get back to Woody," Max continued. "We'll pick up the trail of Sonny's disappearance later."

"Woody knows about Are and me?"

"That half-wit cowboy and those other desert turds had no idea about this," Dino said.

"Tony had inside information, which I'm sure Fazio and others deemed incredibly reliable. Someone bribed someone along the way, either here or down the line. Regardless of how they obtained this information, they now have it."

"And people are getting killed over this." Prez concluded.

"They're a bunch of greedy pricks trying to steal my company."

"That's it, mostly all of it."

"Mostly? What do you mean, mostly?"

"Yes, they've started this war. There's a rogue player who knows about you and your connection to Are. That makes them the most dangerous."

"Sucks to be me."

"That's why the task force formed in Las Vegas. There are a lot of people working on this, Steve. And as a favor to me, they'll eventually find out who murdered Mary too."

"I hear Gitmo is lovely this time of year," Kurt added.

"Ready, father?"

"We are, Bridgette."

"Here's our plan," Prez began. "Remember the Adams' house parking lot incident?"

"Yeah, I remember. Woody's boy Eddie Morrow and some of his ass-clown driver friends jumped me."

"Well, Eddie's been a real busy body of late, hanging around my other place of employment, "The Pink Slipper." Turns out he's into drugs, guns, women, and several Mexican cartel associates. They're using the I-15 as their personal tunnel using limos and party busses to transport their products."

"Woody's footprint is all over this." Bridgette added.

"Yes, for his own bad habits and to set up a distribution center."

"We could really screw up Woody's life," I added.

"That's why I'm here, brother. This muscle show he's been applying, strictly for show. Make no mistake about it, he's coming after your company, and doing it behind the scenes. Everyone else is chasing their tales with this YLL limo company business but not Woody, he's been nailing down drug runs, women trafficking and the purchase illegal firearms, all from the Mexican Cartels. He's been receiving mass shipments of fentanyl, heroin, meth and running a variety of sex for citizenship scams with women from all over the world. He's making bank. But he's got bigger plans;

399

he wants to manufacture the drugs here, distribute them all the way east to Denver and into Canada," Prez added.

"And who do you work for Prez?" I asked.

"Me? I work for gratuities."

"Of course you do."

"How did you uncover this, Prez?" Kurt asked.

Max interrupted. "How Prez knows is unimportant. What is important is securing Eddie and taking out Woody and Letterman. And I have a plan for that. In addition, we're going after what we believe to be another serious problem."

Chapter 38

Two days had passed since our meeting at Tight Racks. My ordered home quarantine began to take a toll on my psyche. Bill and Russ came and went along with several Metro detectives needing additional information on a variety of fronts. Vicki sadly passed off my case to another detective tandem and enlightened me with any current news via text messages .

*****

11:10 PM

Prez stood at the front door of the Pink Slipper Gentleman's Club greeting customers, opening cab doors, and valeting cars. His flashy burgundy doorman's uniform was highlighted by a gold-trimmed collar with matching fringed shoulder braids and double custom gold stripes tailored slightly above his white-gloved hands. A matching gold vest and bowtie partially concealed his bright white shirt. His burgundy pilot's hat featured a glistening leather brim promoting another gold braid surrounding the raised portion of the cap. His burgundy pants had a narrow gold stipe running full length down to the cuffs and hovering above his reflective gold-tipped black patten leather boots. Prez, the effigy of a New York doorman.

Eddie Morrow pulled his limo under the large pink-and-white-striped canopy. He whipped open his door. "Prez, still underpaid and working at that YLL shithole. Working four jobs must really suck." He tossed Prez the keys. "Park it nearby. I'll be back in twenty minutes or so."

"Eddie, the Viagra poster boy. Twenty minutes eh, shit's quadrupling your staying power."

Eddie grabbed his crotch and gave Prez his best suck-my-dick expression as he strutted in.

Thirty minutes earlier he valeted some major Cali Cartel dealer's Black Escalade. He and his crew entered the club like they owned it; maybe they did. Prez knew they would be in one of the exclusive high roller rooms enjoying the perks of unlimited cashflow and showering it on a variety of sexy black, Asian, and Latino women.

Prez pulled out a special sequenced radio and clicked it twice.

"Prez," Bridgette answered seated in a Town Car off West Bonanza.

.   "They're all here."

"Good."

She clicked her hand-held radio and made sure everyone heard Prez's message. Another Town Car pulled alongside her. The cars lined up with the driver's windows parallel to each other, facing in opposite directions. The drivers simultaneously rolled down their windows, letting the dry hot, evening desert air rush in, their mirrors several inches from touching.

"Bridgette, you look incredible."

"Bill, you look—"

"Like a man who's been celibate in a fifty-cent brothel," Bill interrupted.

"Along those lines."

"Shock of the century. Max is your father. I never saw that silver bullet."

"You weren't supposed to."

She released her seat belt and leaned out the window. Bill followed suit and the two kissed.

"Bill, you know I would have told you if I could."

"Bridgette, you taste like a thousand-dollar bottle of champagne. And I'm past that already. Security first. I understand."

They both sat back in their seats.

"You ready, Bill?"

"Usual butterflies. This is what we get paid to do," Bill answered.

*****

I was at home pacing the entire property inside and out, waiting for my cell to ring. The plan was to attack Woody, Letterman, his drug mule Eddie and cartel associates. This would begin shortly. My body was overdosing on coffee while trying to remain ready and on point, my head still wrapped around Vicki's disheartening speech. At eleven-eleven, the phone rang.

I clicked the answer button and took Bill's call.

"What's going on?" I asked.

"Plans in motion. Time to meet at our previously discussed location."

"I'm leaving now."

The line went dead. I pulled out the gun drawer in the kitchen, shoved one Glock behind my back and the other in my shoulder holster. I jammed one extra clip into my holster and the other one into my pocket and went into the garage to get the Tundra.

*****

Eddie walked out of the club with four passengers. Prez pointed to Eddie's limo parked several yards away from the club entrance. Eddie came up to Prez and jammed a five in his hand and took his keys.

"A whole five? Shit. Making bank working for Woody," Prez sarcastically called out.

"Can't have you retiring too soon," he answered back laughing.

"Cheap ass."

His clients filed in and Eddie drove off. Bridgette waited twenty seconds and began her tail. Bill waited another ten seconds and followed Bridgette.

Prez radioed Moshe.

"Moshe, he's headed east on Bonanza, four Mexican Cartel members on board."

"Great job, Prez. Looks like this is it."

"They're all packing."

Moshe went to another frequency. "As they pass by, follow at a safe distance."

Within minutes, Eddie's limo cruised by the MLK intersection, followed by Bridgette and Bill. Moshe turned north on MLK and drove toward the guesstimated meet, somewhere on North Losee. With all their transit numbers and license plates altered, they wouldn't be easily recognizable.

Eddie's limo turned north and entered the I-15-ramp on Washington. Bridgette eased off the accelerator and gave Eddie plenty of time to enter without any chance of being spotted. Bridgette entered the I-15 north and merged behind a semi-truck and in front of a lifted pickup truck. Bill pulled in behind the pickup truck, straining to see Bridgette's car. They were all doing sixty-five and perfectly spaced.

As quickly as they merged, they exited. Eddie put on his turn signal and turned off on the Lake Mead exit. Bridgette pulled off and pumped her brakes to avoid detection. The lifted pickup truck in front of Bill stayed on the I-15 north. Bill exited and almost ran up her rear end.

"Moshe, they're exiting on Lake Mead. I'm watching to see whether it's east or west," she said clicking in Moshe.

"Waiting for your directions."

"West. They're headed west, just like Max predicted."

"I heard; I'll be turning east on Lake Mead in a couple of minutes and meet up."

Moshe radioed another order. "Boris, it's North Las Vegas, it's the Crestline Loop warehouse."

"I know what to do," he said.

Boris sat patiently, parked in the Home Depot lot on West Craig Road. He stepped out of the car and waited less than ten seconds as a second car pulled up next to him and rolled down the window.

"Time to do the bank," he commanded.

Boris handed him a minute brick of C-four, complete with blasting cap. "Drop it in the bushes near the front door. Do it exactly as we planned and get back here."

The car pulled away and drove the two minutes to a nearby savings and loan. The driver pulled a black ski mask over his head and walked to the front door of the bank. It took him less than five seconds to set up the charge and walk away. He ripped off the mask and walked back to his car and returned to the Home Depot.

The car pulled alongside of Boris. "Good job, Lenny."

Boris entered his car as the man took off.

"It's done. Say when, Moshe."

"Everyone listen," Moshe radioed. "They're going to the cable and wire warehouse on Crestline Loop Drive. Woody's been using it as his drug exchange."

Bridgette and Bill drove past Losee, did a U-turn on Lake Meade, and pulled over. Within a couple of minutes, Moshe pulled in behind them along with two unknown cars. They all stepped out for a final review of the assault.

405

*****

I called Max.

"We ready?"

"You in the parking lot Steve?"

"Just arrived."

"I'll be right out."

*****

Boris pulled out of the parking lot and pushed a remote detonator. Within seconds, there was a loud explosion at the bank, lots of noise, dirt, and bushes sent hurling skyward.

"The landscape company owes me a solid."

Boris left and drove toward the north exit of Crestline Loop.

"It's done. The NLV police department will be swarming the bank in minutes. There will be no units anywhere near us when we hit Woody," Boris confirmed to Max, monitoring the operation.

"Good," Max answered.

"Party's on. Go get them."

"And Steve."

"He'll be with me, far away from that mayhem."

"Does he know?"

"No."

Everyone loaded up in their Town Cars except Moshe, who commandeered a chopped 1997 F-250 Ford pickup, double reinforced steel front bumper, high-impact, bulletproof glass and a modified sun roof, large enough to support a fifty caliber and operator.

The cars began a caravan, turning north on Losee. Crestline Loop was a mile up the road.

Chapter 39

Max exited the club through a back door and approached me.

"Walk with me to the east side of the building; we'll be taking my vehicle tonight."

We exited the building. Kenny waited at the driver's side door.

"Ready, boss?"

"We are."

I reached the vehicle, admiring Max's pimped-out ride, military style.

"Holy shit, what in the hell is this thing?"

"My Bentley I use on special occasions. I thought we'd give it a run tonight."

"My ass. This thing could take on an M-1 tank."

"Maybe. Get in back."

"Where does one go to get a custom Bentley like this?"

"You should learn some things about your employees. Try Kiko."

"No way."

"Yes way."

The luxurious custom leather back seats, fully stocked bar surrounded by heavy duty bulletproof glass, and reinforced steel doors made this the ultimate bad-ass ride. Max sat in the passenger seat up front, followed by Kenny who took the wheel.

"This is the heaviest back door I've ever handled."

"Kenny, take us up to the west side."

"The west side?"

"Yes," Max replied.

"You didn't tell me we were heading west. I thought Woody was near the I-15 in Northtown."

"Now you know. That's the beauty of planning operations, the surprised looks you receive when the participants find out their actual roles."

"Steve, buckle up. This thing has wings."

Kenny started it up, jammed the transmission in gear, and gingerly rolled through the parking lot.

"Nice wings, Kenny. Real funny."

Kenny put on a police scanner positioned just below an absent sun visor. I observed a large duffle bag lying on the floor next to me. I reached down and pulled it apart.

"Talk, to, me. There are enough weapons in the back to wipe out this entire city."

"A beautiful thing, isn't it?" Kenny answered.

I could feel the power of the engine underneath me, but inside you could hear a chipmunk pee on cotton.

"Glad you're on my side."

"If we were the bad guys, you'd have met your end long before Goldhabber," Max reassured me.

"Comforting to know. Where are we going?"

I watched Kenny make a hard right on Las Vegas Boulevard, driving north. He must have had it in second gear. I could feel the power of the engine waiting to explode as we gradually sped up.

"Don't worry about our destination. Just make sure your head's glued on tight," Kenny ordered.

He made a left on Charleston, heading west. The windows in the back were not made for sightseeing, more for discretion and protection, but I managed to see most of the sights. We sped up west on the ninety-five. The neon jungle of downtown and the strip began to disappear. Traffic was not a problem this time of night.

After exiting on Sahara and the 215 west, Kenny made a series of turns and pulled up to a security gate, a familiar one. We were driving into the development protecting the Adams' house.

"I thought we were going after Woody, he's here?"

"We have one stop to make first," Kenny answered.

After clearing a second security guard, we stopped in front of the house.

This time, the gates were closed. Kenny rolled down his window and stared into a camera that bore down on him. Seconds later, the gates opened, and Kenny drove toward the house, additional security cameras recording our every move. The place seemed more like a fortress this time around and I was curious as a mouse in a cheese factory to know why we were stopping here.

"The Adams' house, Max?" I asked.

"That's right, I forgot. You've been here before."

"Funny, Max. And I didn't like the way they treated me either."

"Let's hope for a more preferable outcome."

"Where's everyone else? This doesn't look like much of a group effort."

"Not to worry, everyone's doing their part, as we speak."

*****

Eddie parked his limo in front of the loading dock and opened the passenger doors. Four cartel members exited. The leader of the group ordered one of his men to bring in a large black duffle bag. Eddie held open the back door next to a double-wide sixteen-foot dock door.

A dimly lit warehouse made it difficult for Woody's special guests to see.

"Just follow the yellow line," Eddie requested. "The arrows on the yellow line take you straight to Woody's office. I'll be right behind you."

"I think it's better if you lead the way," the leader of the foursome demanded while gently shoving a handgun in Eddies belly.

"I don't see much wire," the tallest of the four conveyed.

"There isn't much of anything that stays here long, including the contents of your case," Eddie replied.

Eddie moved to the front and started walking along the yellow line. "It's only fifty feet to his office. Right over here."

"I don't like change, pendejo," the leader interjected.

"Hey, this ain't our first rodeo together, Pedro."

A well-lit office door opened at the top of a second set of stairs. Woody stood there, arms out.

"Hector, amigos, I'm sorry about the change of venue tonight and the little inconveniences this might have caused. As you well know, unscrupulous individuals continue to go into business for themselves, veering away from the normal transactions which you and I are accustomed to. I thought this warehouse would be a safer environment for our transaction."

"Que la chingada! We need to watch each other's backs," Hector agreed.

"Come upstairs. Mucho dinero awaits you, Hector. The product: you have it, correct?"

"In the duffle bag."

"Good."

"My people are in place, just in case."

Woody's men were strategically placed throughout the warehouse, armed and ready for any intruders.

Hector and the man holding the duffle bag hurried up the stairs. Once inside, Hector's expression changed when he saw Letterman.

"You've met Letterman before?"

"Si, on several occasions."

411

Letterman walked over to Hector. "How unpleasant to see you again."

"Est'as pero si bien pendejo, Letterman."

"Hector, that isn't very nice, calling Letterman a fucking idiot."

"Les just say we no like each other."

"Well, today we're both fighting for the same cause. Let's think of all the money we'll be making today… and in the future. Let's agree to get along."

*****

Bill radioed Bridgette. "Make sure your body armor is secure."

"It is. Thanks for checking. You do the same."

"Max's extra men and their specialty vehicles are pulling up behind me now. That ought to give us some overwhelming firepower."

Boris radioed Moshe. "Our men are here. You ready on your end?"

"I am. Let everyone know we go when you hear the explosion. We're green in five."

"Watch your back, Moshe."

"Do the same."

There was a knock on Moshe's window. He unlocked the door and two men went into the back seat as another sat next to him in front.

Moshe turned around. "Izzy, been awhile.   You ready?"

"When the money's right, I'm ready."

"Still the greedy bastard."

"You know what they say?"

"What, Izzy?"

"Consistency is the true mark of a champion."

412

"Then buckle up, Michael Phelps."

Moshe sped the heavily-armed pickup truck east on Loop drive, made a quick right into the opposite lane, and turned the truck so it faced directly in front of the warehouse door. Izzy reached down into the back seat and pulled out a rocket launcher.

"I see you've brought some of my favorite toys."

"Any snipers on our six?"

"Not anymore."

Five Minutes earlier

Two handpicked snipers, Max Sharone's clutch assassins fired one shot each, killing two of Woody's lookouts standing on a second-floor roof across the street.

*****

Izzy stood up in the sunroof, his rocket launcher pointed at the loading dock double-wide door. He checked his watch, took careful aim, and fired.

Metal, wood, glass, mortar, and plastic debris flew in every direction as a mini fireball appeared at the door, the rocket carved out a hole where the warehouse garage door used to exist. The smoke rose into the desert night, a Nuclear café moment as two cars pulled alongside Moshe, one driven by Boris.

Moshe waited ten seconds as the man sitting next to Izzy handed him a fifty-caliber machine gun. He nodded and went full throttle into the remains of the warehouse door, Izzy spraying the opening nonstop, empty cartridge shells bouncing off the roof and onto the street. Two of Woody's men had been chopped to pieces as they approached the door.

413

"Hang on!" Moshe slammed into the side of a vehicle parked halfway inside the warehouse.

The vehicle he crashed into tipped over, exposing it's underbelly. Boris drove in behind Moshe's truck and pulled alongside him. He jumped out and unloaded his AK-47 throughout the warehouse as did two other men riding with Moshe.

Woody and Hector's crew were caught off guard. Woody and Letterman realized immediately they were on the wrong side of this onslaught. While ducking, they began firing wildly, some of the bullets bounced off the front of Moshe's truck. Izzy continued to pour fifty-caliber bullets randomly into the warehouse, bullets were ricocheting off and taking out chunks of the concrete pillars. A stack of pallets and some fifty-four-inch reels lying on their sides scattered throughout the warehouse were shredded, taking out some of Woody's men who made the mistake of taking up positions behind them. A third vehicle stopped to the right of Moshe's. Four men exited the vehicle and randomly fired their AK-47s up and down the warehouse, taking out every inch of space.

"Jesus Christ, Woody, there's an army out there. These guys aren't thieves, they're military!" Letterman shouted. "It appears as though we've been compromised. Hector, any ideas who's behind this?"

Woody turned to Hector, lying on his back, a large piece of metal sticking out of his forehead.

"Probably wasn't him." Woody added. "Grab our merchandise and let's move to the emergency escape."

Nonstop gunfire mangled Woody's makeshift office, taking out all the glass.

Crawling on all fours, Woody managed to retrieve his duffle bag loaded with cash, escaping out of the office. "Grab Hector's bag!"

Lying on his stomach, Letterman crawled several feet toward Hector, trying to retrieve the bag lodged under

Hector's back. That plan disintegrated faster than the office around him as the gunfire from below took out pieces of the office itself. Letterman abandoned his feeble attempt and crawled out.

Bridgette was parked one building south on the west side of the street. Bill stopped in the alley side of the same building. They met in front of the blown-out entryway, entered and fired their AK-47s randomly at the second-floor balcony. As soon as they emptied a clip, they inserted another and continued firing. Moshe ran under the stairs of Woody's office, holding a Walther PPQ in each hand, scanning for any movement.

One of Hector's men rose behind a leaking fifty-five-gallon drum and pointed a Winchester pump shotgun at Moshe. Boris dropped his spent AK-47, reached behind his back, and fired multiple shots from his Glock 17, killing the man. Moshe nodded to Boris. The return gunfire ceased throughout the warehouse as several of Woody's injured crew held up their arms, waved their weapons in the air, and surrendered. All of Hector's crew lay dead on the warehouse floor.

"Cease fire! Cease fire!" Boris shouted.

It became eerily quiet.

"Where's Woody?" Boris shouted, his voice echoing in the now quiet warehouse.

Bill ran into the smoke-filled warehouse and joined Moshe, working his way up the office steps. Bridgette joined Boris and six other men as they did a visual sweep of the warehouse, dead bodies were everywhere. Two of Woody's men who surrendered and abandoned their weapons were wounded. A badly shot-up woman lying on her back tried her best to surrender but couldn't make it to her feet. Bridgette and several of Max's men kicked away their weapons, searching them for additional ones. A couple of Max's men ushered them together.

"Where's Woody?"

One of the injured men, clutching his shoulder, said, "The last place any of us saw him was at the top of the stairs. That was before the door exploded."

"Anyone see Woody or Letterman?" Bridgette called out.

"No! We're all looking for them." Multiple voices responded.

"Anyone see Eddie?"

"Not yet!" another voice answered.

"Fan out and find them!" Bridgette yelled.

Bill and Moshe crashed into Woody's office and found one dead body lying on what appeared to be a duffle bag.

Bill looked down at the body and smiled. "Hector."

Moshe knelt and yanked the case out from under his body. "Jackpot."

Moshe pulled it open. "Well over a million dollars' worth of product."

A loud shot rang out from the second floor. Everyone turned to the sound of the gunfire and wheeled their weapons upward, firing randomly. Bridgette looked to her left through the dust and smoke and saw one of their own down. She raced toward Boris, slid to one knee, and rolled him over, checking for a pulse on his neck. He was gone.

"Boris is down! They killed Boris. We still have an active shooter on the second floor. Find that son-of-a-bitch!"

Six men ran toward the gunfire with their weapons pointing upwards. Anything that twitched would be eliminated.

Bill left Moshe when he heard the shot and ran out of Woody's office, scanning the warehouse floor. He was relieved to see Bridgette standing unhurt.

"Bill, they killed Boris." Bridgette solemnly lamented.

Bill leaned on the railing, looking down at Boris, taking the loss personal. Three men put Boris in the back seat of his car as Bill returned to help Moshe.

Two of Woody's men came racing through an emergency side entrance door on the south side of the warehouse and made a break for one of the buildings across the alley. Unfortunately for the two men, Max had several men covering that door. They were gunned down in seconds.

Moshe went down a hallway with several attached offices; their shattered windows overlooked the warehouse floor.

"Woody could be hiding in any one of these," he said to Bill who reappeared after checking out the gunshot. "What happened?" Moshe whispered.

"I'm sorry, Moshe. They killed Boris. The shot came from this floor. Whoever did it is still up here."

Bill watched Moshe's expression turn from sadness to anger as he moved to the first office door and wildly kicked it in, knocking the door off its bullet-riddled hinges.

"Come out you chicken shit!" Moshe screamed.

He fired two rounds into a makeshift closet and ripped open the door, pointing his Walther's inside. It was empty. They heard a sound coming from down the hallway and together they moved to the office entry way. Moshe peeked his head in and out for a split second drawing several shots that took off a piece of the door molding, sending chipped wood in several directions.

"Too close," Moshe said.

"Woody, you're a dead man!" Bill shouted.

Bridgette and several other of Max's men heard the additional shots coming from the second floor and were looking for another way up. There was a loud booming sound as dozens of empty pallets crashed on the warehouse floor, taking everyone by surprise. A loud continuous war-like scream echoed throughout the warehouse as a man jumped on what appeared to be a zip line attached from the rear of the second floor to a place somewhere on the first floor.

"Die you mother fuckers!" He shouted as he slid down the zip line firing two AK-47's spraying the entire floor. Several men were hit multiple times and died instantly. Bridgette rolled to her right behind a pillar and fired in the area of the shooter. Everyone took cover. No one was safe as the bullets ricocheted off the vehicles, pillars, and concrete floor. The buzz from the zipline ended as the person attached to the line ran out of ammo. Every person in the warehouse returned his gunfire, destroying everything around his landing area, including the shooter.

"Cease fire!" Bridgette yelled.

The gunfire stopped and a man could be seen hanging upside down still attached to the wire, bleeding profusely from a variety of wounds sustained after landing on the end of the dock. The man's hands were duct taped to the guns. Bridgette walked cautiously over to the bullet-riddled body, pointing her Glock at the assailant's head. She stood over the body, blood still trickling down his face.

"Who's insane enough to do something like this?" she said to the agents standing near the body.

"Doesn't make any sense," one of the agents added.

Bill ran to an opening on the second floor. "Is everyone alright?"

"I'm not sure. I saw several of our men go down," Bridgette answered.

Moshe came up behind Bill. "You're going to want to see this."

The two walked back to another office which housed a hidden panel. Behind the panel was a custom dumb waiter, big enough to hold two adults.

"That son of a bitch escaped down this thing," Moshe said.

"I'll bring this back up, take it down, and see where it ends up."

"You sure you want to do this, Bill? Eddie and Letterman might be with him."

"And miss out on getting Woody? Not on your life. See if anyone spotted him or anyone else exiting."

Bill hit a green button and waited as the dumb waiter lumbered its way to the second floor. When it stopped, he climbed in.

"Could be an ambush. I would have disabled it," Moshe warned.

"Me too."

"I'm going back the way we came, see if I can find the exit point."

Bill saw the hand-held remote control and pushed the green button. After a slight jerk, he began the descent to the bottom in this miniature coffin. He leaned back and pointed his gun toward an opening he knew would appear, a thousand malevolent scenarios dancing through his mind.

He had enough room to maneuver his body partially to one side where he trained his weapon. If Woody or any of his men were waiting, he would at least get off a round or two. Bill began to breathe faster as his confined ride came to a rough stop. He dove out and rolled on the floor, coming up in a shooter's position. The surrounding darkness put a damper on his pursuit. Woody came through here, knowing absence of light would be his ally. Bill reached into his belt and pulled out a flashlight and turned it on, hoping Woody didn't have a gun trained on his location.

The light reflected off metal stairs at the end of the tunnel. Bill noticed several hanging single light fixtures, smashed, the shattered glass lying on the ground looking like diamonds in a mine. Woody covered his bases; he knew whoever would chase him down this tunnel would need light to continue.

Bill approached the stairs, the broken glass he stepped on sounding like elephants marching on boxes of Wheaties. He reached the end and carefully pointed his gun and light upwards. This had booby trap written all over it; a wooden trap door twenty feet above him blocked the way out. When he opened it, would Woody be waiting on the other side ready to kill him? Bill felt his heart pounding, an adrenaline rush like no other, a life-or-death situation. With time running out, he charged up the ladder and jammed his shoulder into the trap door.

*****

Moshe pulled out his radio. "Woody, Eddie, maybe Letterman, they're not accounted for. Anyone see them?"

"Two men tried to escape out the south door exit, but they won't be going anywhere. We'll check them out," one of Max's men covering the south door radioed back.

After a few seconds he answered, "Not them, just a couple of mooks."

"Check the adjacent buildings. You've got under a minute; North Las Vegas police and Metro are on their way."

"Got it."

Sirens could be heard in the distance. Time for everyone to bail.

"How many prisoners are there?" Bridgette asked.

"Three, all wounded," one of Max's men answered.

"We don't take prisoners; dead men don't make bail." Bridgette announced.

"I'll handle this," one of Max's men replied

Several men found their fallen team members, picked them up along with their weapons, loaded them inside several waiting cars, and drove out of the warehouse.

One of Woody's wounded men waved his hands wildly and began shouting, "I won't say anything, let me go, I'll leave the—"

His sentence ended when a bullet lodged between his eyes. He dropped awkwardly on the warehouse floor. The other man tried running toward the south exit door; he took two in the back and crashed into small stack of bullet-riddled pallets. The agent walked up to him and put another one in the back of his head. The badly-injured girl lying on the floor smiled and gave her assassin the thumbs up.

"I would have done you too."

"Tough break," he said, right before he put one in her head.

"When they autopsy this disaster, they're going to know we executed some of his people," Bridgette said.

"We're gonna' barbeque this place," another of Max's men added.

Moshe returned to his vehicle, backed out of the warehouse, and faced the warehouse door on Crestline Loop, still holding a Walther in each hand, surveying the area.

"What happened to Woody?" one of the men in the car asked.

"He used a custom dumb waiter to escape. It runs beneath the building and comes out in a small store next to the alley. I'm sure he had a vehicle waiting."

"And Eddie?"

"Disappeared, probably the same way."

"Where's Bill?" Moshe asked the driver.

"I saw him run between the buildings. A minute or so later. He got into his car and drove north on Lossee."

Everyone left in the warehouse ran out to their cars.

Izzy once again stood up in the back seat of Moshe's truck. One car remained inside the warehouse still lying on the passenger side door, its underbelly exposed and facing the street.

421

"All clear. Let there be light," Moshe ordered.

Izzy took aim with his rocket launcher and fired a missile toward the gas tank of the overturned car, it's gas flowing throughout from numerous bullet holes. A loud explosion ensued and could be heard blocks away as the missile's impact sent burning fragments of metal and gasoline throughout the interior of the warehouse, mixing with the wood fragments, turning it into a fiery inferno.

"That's for Boris. No survivors, no witnesses, no fingerprints."

Three fast-moving vehicles screamed off Crestline Loop and drove south on Lossee. Two other vehicles drove cautiously north on Losee.

"You behind me, Bridgette?" Moshe asked.

The line stayed quiet. "Bridgette, you okay?"

Another long pause mixed with ruffled sounds.

"Yes, yes, sorry. I dropped the radio between my legs."

"Don't scare me like that. You know Woody's missing."

"I know."

"Where's Bill?"

"He was seen driving north on Lossee."

"I'll call him."

Two North Las Vegas squad cars with lights flashing sped past Bridgette, heading south on Lossee. She turned right on Cheyenne and then made another right and turned south on the I-15. She could see the smoke billowing out of the warehouse they just destroyed as she drove past it. Several cars pulled off to the side, lookie-looing the carnage created by the blazing yellow fire and black smoke.

Bridgette dialed Bill, nervously waiting for him to answer. The call went to voicemail. She continued to dial his number, producing the same results. She broke protocol and dialed Max.

He answered. "Yes dear."

"Bill's not answering my calls."

"He was doing well when your charter ended?"

"Yes."

"Thank you."

*****

Eddie sat in the back seat of Bill's Town car, pointing a gun at Bill's head. Woody, dirty, tired, but excited to be alive, sat next to him. He leaned into the front seat.

"Nice of you to come charging through that trap door, Bill," Woody said.

"And giving us a ride too," Eddie added.

"Take a left on Carey Avenue; that's the light right here."

Bill followed the instructions.

"Now make a right at the first light, Commerce street."

It took less than a minute until Bill made the right.

"Drive north until you see a stop sign and turn right."

"Where are we going?"

"Just drive. Follow my expertise directions."

"You're the ones with the guns."

"We are, aren't we?" Eddie added.

Bill made the right. Woody gave him his final destination.

"Make a left into the North Las Vegas golf course parking lot."

"The golf course? I figured you for more of a pocket pool player."

Bill turned into a dimly lit parking lot. He noticed several of the lights were knocked out.

423

"Pull into that spot next to the fence. Slowly turn off the ignition and hand the keys to Eddie."

A Cadillac pulled in a couple of spots to their left. The driver exited the Cadillac and walked up to Bill's window, tapping it several times with the front end of a silencer attached to a gun.

"Shithead, roll down the window," Eddie commanded.

Bill obeyed as Letterman stood there waiting to greet him, covered in dirt, with several tears in his sports coat, pointing the gun at his face.

"Looks like you had a rough night Letterman."

"Shut up."

"Interesting you showed up tonight, fully armed, part of a well-organized, high-jacking crew run by Max Sharone. Care to explain?" Woody asked.

"You're a drug dealer and a murderer. Nobody likes you."

"I warned you what would happen to you if you stuck your nose into my business," Woody reminded Bill.

"What were you doing with Max's men, chasing us down... something you've been hiding," Letterman pointed out.

Woody and Eddie climbed out of the back and both came over to Bill's rolled down window.

"You've got some splainin' to do," Eddie added.

"You have leaks, Woody. I joined Max to help Steve get rid of you."

"No shit," Letterman snapped back.

"And the biggest leaker is right here," Bill answered pointing to Eddie.

"He's full of shit, Woody."

"What are you saying?" Woody asked.

Bill, in one swift movement, grabbed the door handle, kicked open the door while leaning over on his right side, and pulled out a gun he'd stashed under his seat. The

424

door hit Letterman's hand and the gun went off, the bullet blowing a small hole in the driver's side passenger window. Woody reached under his jacket and removed his gun, backpedaling sideways toward the rear of Bill's car, and fired randomly into the front seat area. Eddie ducked and stumbled backwards, firing at the front windshield, staying close to Woody. Bill fired several shots through his open window which landed in the door panel of Letterman's Cadillac. Bill's lightning reaction forced Letterman to duck behind the rear wheel well. Eddie dove onto the asphalt and continued firing.

Bill was hit in the shoulder and leg and several more times in his vest. He could barely breathe as he dragged himself out of the car and limped north toward the golf course fence. He rolled down a small hill and up against another fence. He managed to drag himself over, landing near some netted golf course practice mats.

Woody and Letterman retreated to Letterman's car firing numerous more rounds at the course's small club house.

"We need to get out of here," Woody ordered.

Eddie stood several yards in front Letterman when Letterman shouted, "Take Bill's car."

"What?"

Letterman pointed his gun at Eddie, who stopped dead in his tracks and cautiously wandered backwards toward Bill's car. After a brief glance at the car, he realized a variety of fluids were leaking onto the asphalt surface, making it undrivable. Letterman and Woody jumped into the Cadillac and drove off, leaving Eddie to fend for himself. He bent down, leaned up against the car, and made a phone call.

When the person on the other end answered, he asked, "How close are you?"

"Close enough. I have you at some golf course off Brooks Avenue."

"God bless Modern technology."

425

"Run over to the south end of the parking lot and calmly walk westward to Brookspark Drive. I'll be waiting for you there. Hold on a second."

"Letterman and Woody just sped past."

"You were right about them."

"Get your sweet ass over here, baby."

"Love you too."

*****

With Letterman behind the wheel and Woody in the passenger's seat, they turned south on north fifth street and drove back toward Carey.

*****

Bill crawled to the clubhouse and stopped when he landed against the north end of the building. He took aim at Eddie running out of the parking lot, but his shaky hand made him drop his arm into his lap. A group of scared teenagers lingered around the back of the clubhouse, ducking behind chained-up golf cart bag carriers.

Bill watched his blood ooze out of his wounds. He took his left hand and applied as much pressure as possible to his right thigh, trying to stop the bleeding, and with his other hand pulled out his phone, speed-dialing Bridgette.

A couple of kids raced over and cautiously watched him.

"Hey man, he ain't dead. He's chillin' on his phone," one kid said to the other.

"Hey dude, you're hurt real bad?"

They both backed off when they saw his gun.

"Thanks for the keen medical advice. Now get the fuck out of here before the po-po arrive and drag your asses to jail," he advised them, watching them back up toward the club house.

"Bill, where are you?" a frantic Bridgette answered.

"I'm at the golf course. Go figure. No, wait," he said right before he blacked out.

Chapter 40

Before we entered the house, Max steeped aside to make a phone call.

"When he returned, I asked, "Who'd you call?"

"Final arrangements. Let's ring the bell, see who's in attendance."

The door opened and we walked in. An older woman in a powder blue evening gown with matching heels, a diamond necklace draped around her neck, welcomed us.

"Gentlemen, welcome. You too, Kenny. Max, I see you brought Steve, as promised."

"I did. Steve, I'd like you to meet Mrs. Adams."

I thought she was one of the ugliest women I'd ever seen. Her makeup must have been held together with Gorilla glue, you could have gone spear fishing with her chin, her nose looked like a Belgian waffle and her eyes reminded me of a smoked salmon lying on ice in a buffet line. She should have had a hazmat label stamped on her forehead.

"Mrs. Adams, how nice to finally meet you," I politely said.

The simple explanation, she had to be the breadwinner or inherited some sick amount of money, and some poor, now rich, clever shmuck married her. You'd have thought with all this money floating around that someone would have coughed up the dinero's for a little plastic surgery. Somewhere in Hollywood, a "Walking Dead" set was missing a zombie.

"Mrs. Adams, nice of you to arrange this meeting tonight," Max replied.

I kept my facial expressions intact, better than the coaches in, "Porky's" who were flailing uncontrollably on the floor listening to Ms. Balbricker's idea of a penis lineup at the school. Max excused himself again and took another call.

I tried admiring the ambiance and beauty of the Adams' house: the floors, the walls, the paintings, anything to lure my eyes away from hers. However, my eyes failed me and continued to drift her way. I felt like an ancient Greek warrior fending off Medusa's snake-like spiked hair and fatal alluring stare which turned men into stone. I came up with a hideously obnoxious cough instead, courteously turning my face away which I performed twice rather than look into her eyes. She gave me this nefarious glance as Kenny and I followed her into a private room, off to the side of a spiral staircase which led to a second floor. I slipped to the right and began admiring her amazing assortment of books lined up throughout the room.

Max finished his call and joined Kenny and Mrs. Adams inside her magnificently decorated room. The books were sitting in alphabetical order on white and grey custom marble shelving. Sliding ladders were built into the ten-foot-high bookcases, making their access effortless. Three white leather sofas surrounded a large custom brick table with a glass top, covered with wine glasses and fresh flowers. Several portable wine carafes each held a bottle. Two large French doors draped in sheer white curtains led to a terrace somewhere in the back of her estate. I made a brilliant assumption; this must be her library.

"Well, if it isn't Steve."

I turned to my right and recognized the face that went along with the voice.

"Mrs. Black, uh, how nice to see you again. The night's getting more interesting by the second," I answered.

"It is."

She was surrounded by two large men who I assumed were her body guards. I hadn't seen this side of her before. Kenny stood by the door as did one of Mrs. Adams's men who pulled a gun on Kenny.

"Kenny."

Kenny gingerly pulled out his Glock 17 by the butt, holding it between his thumb and index finger. He handed it to Mrs. Adams's man.

Another man approached Max and asked us to calmly remove any weapons in our possession.

"Max, you didn't think I would just let you stroll in here without disarming you. I trust you, but…"

Max raised his arms and let her man disarm him. I pulled out both guns and turned them over to one of Mrs. Black's men.

"The kid had two of them," her man informed her.

"You can keep your third gun, Steve," Mrs. Black snarkily replied.

"One out of three."

"Why don't all of you take seats so we can get on with our business," Mrs. Adams said as she sat down on one of her sofas and crossed her legs. "Max you delivered Steve as promised, a man of your word."

"Delivered me. What are they talking about Max?" I said with a confused expression forming on my face.

Mrs. Black grabbed my shoulder and together we sat down on one of the white couches, her bodyguard moved in behind us.

"Safe and in one piece," Max answered. "You have something for me in return?"

"Max, what's going on?" I asked again only this time with more urgency.

She snapped her fingers, and a man dropped two duffle bags at Max's feet.

"Kenny, check these out. Make sure all the money is there. No offense, Mrs. Adams."

"None taken."

"Seriously?" I asked. "What's going on?"

"Why, Steve," Mrs. Black began as she put her hand in my lap and turned to face me. "Your friend sold you out," a cheerful Mrs. Black answered, pointing Max's way. "You see, Max is a businessman first. We made him an offer he couldn't refuse. A movie cliché, but pretty much explains why you're here."

I stood, but her man grabbed my shoulders and pushed me back down on the couch. He placed a gun against the back of my head.

"I apologize for the betrayal, but business, struggling of late, the offer they made, delivering you to them… well, I couldn't say no."

"You lied to me?!"

Max was expressionless and turned towards Kenny who was counting the money.

"You still haven't learned your lesson, Steve. Fucking you over pays more than aligning with you," Mrs. Adams said.

"All here, Max," Kenny commented.

I couldn't keep my mouth shut any longer. "Mrs. Adams, you are the ugliest human being I've ever laid eyes on. How in the hell do you walk past a mirror without it shattering?"

"You cocky little bastard," she said her face turning red even under all the makeup. "I'm going to enjoy watching them torture the shit out of you. Boys, escort Steve to the basement."

"Torture me?"

"Come on, Steve, you know why," Mrs. Black happily added..

"I have no idea what you're talking about."

"I'll give you a hint… Albert."

It all became crystal clear in that moment. They were the ones dogging me.

I turned to Max. "You can't let them do this to me. Max."

"My business dealings are more important than you are. You came out of nowhere, surprised us all. But it turns out, you're worth a small fortune… and our Chinese friends really want to meet you and are willing to pay handsomely for that pleasure," Max added.

"Steve, you just blindly walked into this." Mrs. Black grasped my hand in hers. "What were you thinking when you came to Vegas, we were a bunch of ignorant hicks waiting for someone like you to come in here and save the day? Rescue us from what, each other? The only thing any of us really want to know is what drugs you took to become this naïve? And how do we score them?"

The room broke out in laughter.

"Clever, but you forgot one thing."

"What's that?"

"I've slept with many women and to be totally honest with you… we are being honest?"

"Sure, I'll play along," Mrs. Black answered.

"How are you running girls when you're one of the worst lays I've ever experienced? And after being with you, I thought someone would be arresting me for being a necrophiliac."

She laughed. "I'm going to do things to your manhood you never even dreamed of, especially when I run a nice, thick, long glass tube up your big dick and shatter it with a rubber mallet. The things you're going to say to me, right before I do it."

Max interjected: "Well then, before we finalize our transaction, I'd like to take a moment and congratulate you, and like your late husband Harold, may he rest in peace, and remind you again, in a more tasteful and fitting way than Steve's elocution."

"Max."

"To once again remind you that you are still a lying, conniving bitch who will do anything for a dollar, including betraying your own country," Max concluded.

Mrs. Adams stood up in protest as Kenny dropped both bags by the door, overpowered her man, took back his Glock, and put one bullet in his head. Without hesitation, he surgically took out two more bodyguards including the one holding a gun at my head. The bodyguard standing behind Mrs. Adams managed to pull his weapon out, but Max took his legs out while subduing his weapon and killed him with it.

Max moved toward both women and motioned Mrs. Black, using his gun, to get up and move off to the side of the room while shoving Mrs. Adams in the same direction. I followed Max's lead, hopped over the couch, and repossessed both my Glocks.

"What the hell, Max?"

"Cutting-edge planning."

"Not from my end it wasn't."

"How many more are coming through the doors, Belinda Adams?" Max asked while firmly pressing his gun under her chin, driving it upward and causing her neck to overly flex backwards. "Steve, put your gun on Mrs. Black. She is a plethora of information, especially when it comes to you. I'm sure you'll find what she knows equally fascinating and irritating."

I did what Max ordered. She gave me this inappropriate you're turning me on look.

"You've got to be kidding me. Now?"

"Why Steve, I clothe you, fuck you, and now you're going to shoot me? Not very appreciative, is it?"

"I'm an asshole. What can I say?"

"Three, Max. I mean four. I have four more men on property."

"You're such a lying bitch." Max took the butt of his gun handle and cracked Mrs. Adams on the top of her head. Her knees buckled and she collapsed. Max gripped her hair with his left hand, protecting her from dropping to the floor. He had her undivided attention as she wearily glanced up.

A deafening shotgun blast came through the terrace doors along with a dose of bright night security beams. The buckshot made the curtains dance wildly, destroying a lamp, table, part of the door, and striking Kenny. He careened off the wall, dropping straight down. I caught Mrs. Black reaching between her legs; I assumed she wasn't trying to get herself off. I instinctively hit her with a straight right to the jaw. She went down instantly, unintentionally spreading her legs wide open. Her short dress rode all the way up her thighs stopping at her waist revealing a holstered gun and her habitual lack of undergarments. I bent down, yanked the gun out, and slipped it into my inside sports coat pocket.

Max turned toward the gunfire, pulling Mrs. Adams up by her hair, wheeling her in front of him, using her as a shield. He placed his gun next to her right ear and fired off several rounds at the French door curtains which were now rhythmically flowing outward through the newly shattered glass into the hot desert night along with the cool air from the library. Mrs. Adams clutched her ear, screaming in pain.

"They shoot at me and they'll hit you."

He shook her head violently, placing the hot gun flush up against her neck.

There were additional shots coming from inside the house just outside the library doors. I witnessed the man who shot Kenny flex wildly after being hit multiple times while trying to crash in via the terrace doors, his shotgun flying above his body. I took several steps toward Kenny and froze as the door exploded. I fired my Glock nonstop, aiming at the midsection and head of the person who came charging through the door; he lurched violently backwards. I continued to fire with reckless abandon, my remaining bullets springing out of the clip into the barrel and lodging in the door, staircase, and hallway wall. Entering the library would cost you your life.

Another hail of gunfire sounded to my right, near the house entryway. The shots sent several men, who appeared to be hiding outside the library doorway, to the ground. I released the empty clip into my hand and shoved it into my pocket. I reached into my holster and retrieved a thirty-

434

round clip. I put one in the chamber, fired two shots at the men lying on the floor and two more into the staircase just to remind anyone else who wanted to risk coming through the door that I was armed and ready. I ran up to Kenny, kneeled next to him while keeping my gun and eyes trained on the door. He looked up at me while I assessed his injuries and concluded they weren't fatal.

"You're going to make it Kenny."

"Steve, get back here!" Max shouted.

I yanked Kenny toward Max while scanning the door and staying low.

"Are those your men out there?" I asked.

"They better be. Now get back here!" Max ordered.

Mrs. Adams might have been old, but she was tougher than a one-dollar steak and knew how to protect herself. She jammed her spiked heel into Max's foot causing him to wince in pain, accidently releasing her. In cat-like precision, she pulled out a small knife from under her dress and stabbed Max once in the lower back. As she reached back for an encore performance, a bullet screamed through the French doors, hitting her directly in the face. The impact partially lifted her off the floor; she landed spread-eagle on her tiled floor, face up. As I knelt next to Max, I checked out Mrs. Adams. A bloody hole replaced her eye as blood pooled around her.

Mrs. Black came around, transforming into a psychotic demon, viciously trying to grab me between my legs with her long black razor-sharp nails; I blocked her hand.

"You really need to chill out."

"Fuck you!" she screamed.

"Steve, keep her alive. She's coming back with us."

"What little secrets are you hiding from me, Mrs. Black?"

She wheeled on her side and threw a side kick at the back of my knee, buckling it, forcing me to the ground. Like

435

a lion pouncing on an antelope, she jumped on my back, locking her left arm around my neck. While trying to choke me, she also attempted to wrangle the gun out of my hand. She was extremely athletic and physically violent. Max struck her with the bottom of his gun, landing a blow on the back of her head. She unwittingly released me and crumpled to the floor, landing on all fours. She was breathing erratically and heavily. She clutched her head and unceremoniously fell over onto her back.

Max pointed his gun at her stomach. "The drugs, the intel, the lavish parties, the two of you sponsored, over. We know every room and hallway in this place is wired with well-hidden Chinese high-tech cameras and sound equipment. The two of you illegally extracted intel at your little soirees, selling it to the Chinese for cash."

"What about the Russians, Max? They involved in this?" I asked.

"They can't afford to pay what the Chinese do; they've been circumvented at their own game."

The shooting stopped as three men cautiously entered the room pointing their guns at the ceiling.

"Don't shoot, Max."

One man ran over to Kenny, one guarded the door, and the other approached Max.

"We need to get out of here, Steve," Max insisted.

Three more men entered the room and I instantly recognized one of them.

"Claude?"

"Steve, nice to see you again."

"I'm sure it is. You here with that one?" I said pointing at Mrs. Black.

Mrs. Black went wild and started kicking and screaming when she saw Claude. Several of Max's men held her down and placed her in handcuffs.

"You fucking fagot traitor!"

436

"Virginia, it's been a real joie de vivre working for you. I can only hope they extract intel in a proper way, fitting for a woman of your exquisite caliber."

I looked over at Max. His injuries apparently weren't life threatening because he maneuvered around as though nothing phased him. A tough man's tough guy.

"Do tell, Max. Claude works for you?"

"Been working for us and the US government for the last twenty years. I saved his life twenty-five years ago. The Iranians were going to execute him because, let's just say, he wasn't being Muslim enough."

"They were going to execute him for being gay?"

"That would be the politically incorrect truth."

"You saved me because I helped you and several of your undercover operatives; you thought I could be useful."

"And here we are, you proving me right again."

"He's been spying on Mrs. Black, and that's how you knew. Damn. You're good, Max."

"Thank you, but right now, we need to evacuate."

"Claude, you sneaky gay bastard."

I gave him a big hug.

"Thanks for being here."

"Well Steve, look around, you had a lot of help tonight. Sonny was a great man and Virginia is a money-hungry sociopath."

Two men grabbed Mrs. Black under her arms as three men took Kenny out of the room and down the hallway. I noticed at least a half dozen bodies distributed about the stairs and hallway as we made our way out of the house and onto the circular drive.

There were four or five dead men scattered on the grounds lying under the bright Adams house security beams. Max's men, armed with AK-47's, were scanning the property as we climbed into the back seat of his car. One of Max's operatives took the wheel as Claude jumped into the passenger seat of Max's Bentley.

437

Four men took Mrs. Black in their vehicle and four more into a third car carrying Kenny. In total, three cars drove out of the Adams estate while one stayed briefly behind. Those men must have been on an evidence-destroying mission, because as we drove off, they were tossing objects through the windows and inside the front door. They sped off and were quickly behind us when the Adams house rocked from explosions. On the way out we slowed down as the lead car picked up one of the two security guards we passed on our way in. He jumped into the front seat of the car while it still moved. The feet of the other guard were lying in the rubble of destroyed security equipment as we drove off.

"Max, you had your men everywhere. That's how they walked in undetected. But I still don't understand why Mrs. Black, she was so nice to me. She could have just stayed in the shadows."

"Your identity as Sonny's son—they somehow figured out he wasn't your real father. They were going to exploit you, find out exactly what it is you can or cannot do, then sadly, they would have gotten rid of you. She completed her first assignment, gained your trust. As you figured out by now, you were not supposed to leave with me tonight."

"I was the bait."

"Yes, but there's still some players out there, and we need to find out who they are."

"So, we're not done."

"I wish I had better news for you. But on a positive note, tonight we made progress. Maybe Mrs. Black will reveal, after some very unethical and painful procedures are administered, the intel we need to wrap this up. You're entitled to live a normal life."

"Hard to imagine a government where human life has such little value."

There was reflection and silence as we drove out of the estates. We passed the first security check point—two more dead security men.

"How are you holding up? You killed a man tonight," Max asked me like a concerned father.

"I'm processing it."

"He might have had orders to take you alive too. We'll never know until we extract the truth out of Mrs. Black."

"I'd like to be there for that one."

"I wish I could make it happen."

"I understand."

An awkward silence loomed in Max's car as we turned on the 215 ramp north.

"I can remember the first man I killed," Max continued. "I see his face often in my dreams but in the end, I made peace with it. Hopefully, you'll evolve past this too."

"Your dreams say something else Max. I think you did it for love of country and of course, self-preservation. The details of what happened are trivial."

"You have the wonderful gift of rational thought for such a young man."

"Maybe I inherited it from Are. A stupid reason to throw someone down a hole and torture the shit out of them, don't you think?"

"Well put," Max said has he grabbed his back.

He couldn't hide his pain any longer.

"You're in a world of pain."

"In your opinion. I'll only admit to being a little sore."

I smiled at Max as I glanced back at where the Adams house used to be and saw the flames rising against the dark desert sky. The flames glow, a stark reminder of why I now personally wanted to torture Mrs. Black.

"I didn't see Bill, Bridgette, or Boris at the Black house."

"They were doing some reconnaissance."

"Reconnaissance? For what?"

"Like I like to say, it's above your pay grade."

Chapter 41

*****

Vicki stood at a safe distance watching as North Las Vegas and Las Vegas fire departments battled the fire, surrounded by dozens of police and rescue vehicles, the entire area sealed off. She knew there were casualties, and as promised, the morgue would be seeded with more victims. Hopefully, no one she knew would be tallied in the latest count.

Vicki's captain came up to her. "This had to be a drug deal gone wrong. I've never seen anything like this. Looks more like a war zone."

"The hundreds of fifty caliber rounds in the street tipped you off?"

He gave her an annoyed look and walked away.

"Hey, Captain."

He turned around, "Yes."

"I'm calling it a night. Won't be anything to do here until late tomorrow morning. You okay with it?"

"Yeah, sure." He continued to walk toward the Las Vegas fire battalion chief.

Vicki arranged a meet with Knuckles at Tight Racks in an hour. A strange place for a meet but he was already there and besides he wouldn't show up at Metro without a warrant. With The Graveyaad temporarily shut down, it was as good a place as any.

*****

We arrived at the east side door of Tight Racks. Moshe and Claude assisted Max getting out of the car and

441

into his back office. The back of his suit jacket stained with blood.

"Which hospital are they taking Kenny too?" I asked as we all walked up the back club stairs.

"We use a special emergency clinic," Moshe replied.

"Max, why aren't you going to that clinic and getting stitched up?" I asked.

"No need to. I have a doctor waiting inside. The late charming Mrs. Adams didn't hit any organs."

"You're a doctor too?"

"No. But I've unfortunately acquired enough medical knowledge to know the difference between needing a doctor and a hospital emergency room."

"Like the difference between being injured or being in pain?" I asked.

"Exactly," Claude replied.

"Where's everyone else? Bill, Bridgette... what's going on?"

"They went after Woody," Max replied.

"You went after him without me?"

"Too much violence, didn't want to risk getting you shot."

"What do you call what went on at the Adams house, a church social?"

"You're still alive."

"I needed to be a part of taking Woody down."

"What, you thought we were forming some sort of wild west posse and you were invited? You're roll tonight was a part of the bigger picture."

"And Woody, is he dead?"

"No. The door to taking him out is still open."

"Where is he? I—"

"I've assigned one of my men to escort you home," Max cut in. "Now's not the time. I'm a little busy."

"So, it's going to be like that?"

"Yes."

"I think I can make it home without an escort."

"Humor me. It's not safe out there. Bensman, do me a favor and tag along with Steve, see he arrives home safely."

"Sure thing, Max. Come on, Steve. Let's go."

"No stopping anywhere. And when you arrive home Steve, clean up yourself and your firearms. Wait for my call."

I backed off. Max had gone through a lot tonight.

"I understand."

I got behind the wheel of my Tundra with Bensman in the passenger seat as my personal escort. We left Tight Racks driving south on Las Vegas Boulevard.

"Bensman, Bridgette okay?" I asked fishing for answers.

"She's fine."

"Bill and Boris? I didn't see them at the club either."

"I'm going to personally kill Woody the next time our paths cross," an agitated Bensman stated.

"No, I get first shot at that son-of-a-bitch."

"You're going to find out anyway… things didn't go as planned, there were complications."

"Complications?"

"There was a shootout that took place at Woody's private warehouse. We lost some men, all friends, including Boris. Bill's been shot up, but he's going to make it. Woody, Letterman and Eddie escaped. "I'm probably going to get my ass chewed for telling you. I thought you should know."

"What the hell happened?"

"I've said too much already."

"Okay, then, where's Bill?"

"At the emergency clinic we use. He lost a lot of blood but I was told he'll make it."

"That's a relief. But I'm sorry to hear about Boris. I really liked him."

"He was a unique individual."

443

We veered off to the left on Paradise and were several blocks from Sahara when I noticed some unusual driving activity in my rear view mirror.

"Bensman, you see what I'm seeing?"

"I do." He reached into his jacket and retrieved his weapon.

He looked back several times making sure the car behind us wasn't about to rear end us or run us off Paradise. What neither of us saw was a car turning directly in front of us; it slammed my Tundra into a parked car. Luckily, my seat belt and the steering wheel kept me from sailing through the front windshield. Bensman was not as lucky. The broadside impact caught him as he was looking in the passenger side mirror. The abrupt snap to the left broke his neck.

I barely had time to see the driver run out of his car, smash the window, open my door, and drag me out. A car stopped alongside us. The driver ran around the front of his car and joined the first man. The two of them tossed me into a back seat. The driver of the stopped vehicle pulled a gun and joined me.

As I shook off the cob webs I recognized both men.

"Steve, you've been a busy boy. One of your old friends wants to see you."

"Letterman, you—"

"Woody's not pleased. He has a specially prepared room waiting for you."

He smiled, reached into my pockets while holding his gun close to my temple, and began emptying them.

"Steve, a lot of hardware for someone so young," he said as he continued to empty out the three guns and two clips and put them in his pockets. He gave my Glock with the thirty round clip hanging out an extra glance and then tossed my cell phone out the window.

"If only we were on a boat cruising Lake Mead, I could have just tossed you overboard. The excess weight you're packing would have sent you speedily into a four-hundred-foot grave."

I stared at him knowing I was in deep trouble.

"Nice to see you again, Steve."

I looked in the front seat. "You, you were the one at the Graveyaad screaming at Kurt."

"Nice memory. Too bad you don't have much time left for recall opportunities."

"Jerry something or other, right? Nelson, Jerry Nelson."

"The kid does have a good memory, Letterman."

"Good for him. Woody's going to let me ask him a couple of questions. We'll see how good that memory is," he said winking at me.

I tried to say something clever, but Letterman plunged a needle deep into my right shoulder.

"You talk too much."

"The public health commission is going to be notified about your unsanitary medical—"

Chapter 42

I woke up in a folding chair in a small room, a green nineteen-thirties light bulb fixture swinging several feet above my head, which by the way was pounding. When most of the drug-induced fog cleared out, I made out two shadows in the background talking quietly to each other. I tried to move, but felt and saw duct tape binding me to the chair. They noticed my conscious state as I inconspicuously tried to squirm my way out of their tape job. One of them came up to me and my opportunity to pretend to be unconscious evaporated; I should have remained still, kept my eyes closed.

"Nice of you to join us again," one of the men said, slapping me across the face.

"Hey, Woody! Your boy's awake."

"You look different with your eyes open," I said, recognizing him from the Rio. "Too bad Tony's not here to kick your ass again, finish the job he started."

He smirked and slapped me a second time, this time with more passion. "Woody, you've got to let me have the first crack at that this smartass."

Woody came out of the shadows and into the light. He grabbed the top of the light, shining it directly in my face.

"Sorry, Mike. I'm afraid I've offered Letterman first dibs."

Letterman put on some black leather gloves with open-ended fingers. They looked more like driving gloves. Unfortunately for me, they were going to be just as effective.

"Steve, so glad you could join us again," Letterman said as he wound up with his right fist and unloaded a forceful uppercut into my stomach.

I braced for it, but the pain radiated down my legs and through my toes. I became concerned at the prospect of endless body and face punches continuing throughout the morning and into the afternoon.

"Is there a point to this?" I asked with less pep in my voice.

"Does it matter if there's a point? Right now, let's just say, you're the entertainment," Woody happily announced, rubbing his hands together in excitement.

"You're in an overly good mood considering you and your band of criminal merry men just got their asses handed to them."

"Letterman, you see that. That's what I'm talking about. He's all wrapped up in duct tape, sitting in a flimsy chair under a hot light, took a gut punch, and yet he has this unwavering intestinal fortitude to continue to act cocky. Letterman, I can't imagine either of us acting so imprudent under these vexing conditions. Give him a dose of your adjustment counteractant."

"With pleasure, boss."

Letterman took his right fist and jacked my left jaw, knocking me and the chair to the hard concrete floor. I took the punch well considering my awkward situation, and managed to keep my head from cracking on the floor too. Mike picked me and the chair up like a cotton ball and repositioned me in the exact same spot.

"This is fun, boss. Thanks," Mike said.

Letterman repeated his first effort only this time using his left fist and using my right jaw. I went down a second time and Mike dutifully dragged me up again and cheerfully placed me back in the same position.

Woody intervened. "I need to ask him a couple of questions before he enters dreamland."

"Sure thing," Letterman said taking a couple of steps back while throwing some air punches.

I never appreciated an intermission as much as I did this one. The ominous taste of blood began to form in every corner of my mouth. I turned my head and spit it out and

447

onto the floor. I thought about expectorating it in Woody's face, but I'm sure that would have earned me another punch or six to my face. And right now, I considered every second not being hit to be a major victory.

"Steve, you seem to have extensive knowledge of this evening's events, which is one of the reasons I had you followed out of Max's place and brought to this little niche. Perhaps you were privy to the information and could shed some light on the person or persons who provided you and your friends with this data."

"You and Letterman killed Sam and her mother. Go fuck yourselves."

"That's definitely going to cost you smart ass. Letterman, tenderize him again and don't be affable."

Woody stepped aside as Letterman began choking me out. I tried to kick and twist, but the duct tape performed as advertised and kept me from any kind of movement. Letterman performed his assignment like a true professional. He knew exactly what to do. What a horrific last thought, Letterman's face. I could feel the room closing in around me. He released me and I began to cough while gasping for air.

"Nice coaxing," an excited Woody said as he began to ritually rub his hands together only this time faster, like a boy scout trying to create a fire.

"Now, let's try this again while you can still talk. How did you know about the drug deal at the warehouse?"

I stared at the floor. Woody grabbed my cheeks in his right hand, squeezed hard, and lifted up my head.

He leaned in inches from my face. "Deaf one, I said, how did you find out about the drug deal going down at the warehouse tonight?"

I believed in my heart that Letterman would kill me as soon as I revealed any information and it would be methodical, gradual, and excruciatingly painful. I knew my time was short. Letterman was strong, and being tied up made it easy for him. I did the only thing I could do; I reevaluated my previous position and spit as hard as I could into Woody's face, my bloody spit running down his chin and onto his western-styled suit coat.

He backed off, stepped into a punch, and unloaded it into my mouth, knocking me over backwards. He jumped on top of my chest and hit me in the face several more times before Mike pulled him off.

"Boss, he still needs to talk," he said while forcefully holding him off me.

Woody angrily shook him off. "Letterman, Mike, place him under the light again. I need to see what I'm doing."

They followed his orders and lined me up. I feared the entire process would be a rinse and repeat, many times over. Jerry Nelson entered the room, a glass of water in his hand. Letterman took it and held it next to my mouth. "You getting thirsty, Steve?"

"Ice would be nice," I said trying to force a smile.

"Here," Letterman said, throwing the water in my face.

The water actually felt good for a moment until I realized he tossed it in my face to keep me from passing out. I dragged my tongue across my upper lip and took in several drops of the mixture of blood, water and sweat while glancing up at Letterman.

"Thanks, asshole," I said while trying to lift my head up.

Letterman cocked his fist and was about to continue the process of unloading on me again when Woody held his arm back. He looked down at me.

"Steve, this isn't going as planned. I tried to be nice, even friendly. You just aren't cooperating the way I know you can. Mike, please bring in my tool box."

With an obnoxious smile, Mike answered, "I'll be right back."

449

He exited the same door Nelson came through.

"You're left-handed, right Steve?"

"I'm ambidextrous."

"Nelson, what are you still doing here? Go back out front and keep an eye out for any unusual activity," Woody ordered.

"My bad," he replied as he swiftly left the room.

Mike returned and set down Woody's tool box and repositioned himself at my right side. He grabbed my shoulders.

"Have you ever played Operation, Steve?" Woody asked.

I looked up at him and for some insane reason I began to think of all the good times I could have had with Vicki.

"What are you grinning about?" Woody asked with a stern look on his face as he opened the latches of the tool box up and flipped open the top.

I thought I heard some loud noises in the direction where Nelson exited. Apparently Woody, Letterman, and Mike heard the same commotion. I guess I wasn't hallucinating after all. Loud gunfire from the front of the building perked me up. The three of them pulled out their guns and backpedaled behind me.

"Mike, check the front. See what's happening."

Mike took two steps toward the door, then ran to the back of the room shouting, "Fuck this shit!"

He fired two shots at the front door before he went down in a hail of gunfire.

Letterman grabbed Woody. "We need to get out of here."

They both fired at the opened door.

Flashlight beams shined through the door along with continuous gunfire.

"Police. Drop your weapons!"

Letterman ran toward the back firing nonstop. I closed my eyes and waited for that Sopranos ending, never hearing my life ending fatal shot. Woody froze and dropped his gun. A door slammed behind me as the gunfire in the room ceased. I reopened my eyes as a flashlight beamed off my beaten-up face, forcing me to look away.

"Woody, how nice to see you. Boys, cut Steve loose. The two of you, see if you can find Letterman."

They rushed to a door behind me and left. I didn't recognize the voice, but I was grateful to whomever put in the effort. The tape binding me stuck to the chair as I wiggled my way to freedom. I stood and fell back down again. I shook my head several times, stretched out my legs while placing my head in my hands, accessing the damage. Letterman and Woody had done a number on me, but my senses were returning.

"Woody, at last we meet."

"You aren't Metro."

"Surprise."

"Fazio. What are you doing here? And why in the hell are you in my building shooting at me?" a bewildered Woody asked.

"I'm here on business."

"Well, as you can see, I have a package, still breathing, you're probably interested in. You can take him out and finally reacquire your father's old limo company," he said pointing his finger at me.

Five of Fazio's men surrounded Woody and me.

"I guess you *are* here for me," I said looking directly at Fazio.

"I knew you'd be here, Steve, but I'm here to settle some other business with Woody. You're just an added bonus."

"You and I don't have anything to discuss, Fazio," Woody insisted.

451

"I disagree. I do have something to discuss with you."

"And what could you possibly have to discuss with me?"

"Hans."

"What about him? I think he's dead. And you can thank this one."

He pointed directly at me a second time.

I slapped his hand away, much to the chagrin of Woody.

"Hans reached out to me a couple of days ago; he and I came to a mutual understanding."

"On what?"

"I would leave him alone, give him a get-out-of-jail card and in return he would turn his drug operations over to me and take a measly ten percent cut."

"Those are my connections… and they aren't for sale."

"Woody, I think you missed the entire point of this conversation."

"And that is?"

"Hans put a contract out on you, seventy-five-thousand dollars. I've been paid in full, and even though he's dead, I am still obligated to fulfill the terms of our agreement."

"I'll give you one-hundred-thousand dollars to void your deal with him, and you can keep his money. It's a big payday for you and a win-win for both of us."

"You're offering me Hans's money, which by-the-way, I already have. Besides, that would be unethical."

"Okay, two-hundred-thousand dollars."

"That'll be chump change compared to what I'll be making off your drug routes, arms deals, and of course all of those poor women you've been sodomizing and killing."

"That fucking cockroach. I knew I couldn't trust him."

452

"That's rich; he said the same thing about you."

One of Fazio's men put a gun to Woody's head.

"Hold on a second," I said, finally standing on my feet again.

Fazio looked my way.

"You can stand too. Bravo."

"You gonna kill me too? Is that where this is headed?"

"Actually, I need you around. When I came back to Vegas, I thought you were my biggest obstacle in order to reacquire my father's old limo company. However, along the way and with some persuasion from a loyal soldier, I decided to keep you around and in charge of YLL."

"One of your soldiers?" I asked.

"Tony, he spoke highly of you and explained to me the advantages of keeping you dutifully employed."

"Tony worked for you this entire time?"

"Don't get me wrong. His loyalties belonged to Sonny, but he served us too. When Sonny died, all bets were off. He fed us the intel we needed for our return to Las Vegas."

It was reassuring to me that Fazio had no clue who my real father was or else I would be rewrapped in duct tape and escorted to some third world gulag.

Woody cautiously slid toward the back door when one of Fazio's men grabbed him by his sports coat and threw him on the ground.

"Where do you think you're going?"

Woody looked up at Fazio, brushed himself off, and got to his feet.

I walked over to Fazio. "I have a deal for you."

"You have a deal for me?"

"Yeah. I want you to let me do Woody."

"You want to shoot him? Sure, be my guest."

"No. I want to fight him. If he wins, he owes you two-hundred grand and you let him live. If I win, well… there won't be much left of him."

Fazio's men smiled and laughed. They were excited at the thought of a blood-sport killing. Fazio's two men returned from searching for Letterman.

"He's gone. No sign of him."

"That's too bad. He needed killing," a disappointed Fazio answered.

"Do we have a deal?"

Fazio walked a couple of steps away and contemplated my offer. He quickly returned. "Yes, but not here. We have to leave."

With that statement, everyone moved to the front of the building and sat down in three running cars, all equipped with drivers. I was surprised at the amount of soldiers Fazio already recruited in Vegas.

"Steve, these belong to you?" Fazio asked, handing me my Glocks.

"Yes, thanks. I thought Letterman had them."

"We took them off Woody's dead driver. I heard about your thirty round clips and figured those guns must be yours.

"They are and they feel light. I see why—no magazines."

"I have the magazines. Once you take out Woody, you can have all four of them back," he said flashing the magazines.

Woody, Fazio, and I sat in the back seat of one of his cars. I sat behind the driver, Woody in the middle, and Fazio behind the passenger seat. The front seat was occupied by one of Fazio's men who pointed a gun directly at Woody. He immediately became irate.

"Eddie, you piece of shit!"

I couldn't believe it; Eddie, the wheelman, working for Fazio.

"Hey Woody, how does it feel to have someone stick it to you?" I said trying to smile, my jaw still aching and sore.

I made a circle with my right thumb and index finger and held my hand up for Woody to see. I slid the middle finger of my left hand inside and out of the circle. Woody didn't move a muscle.

*****

Letterman reached a car parked several blocks away under a carport at a small pest control company. The worn-out-looking 2004 blue Toyota Corolla's body was purposefully made to look neglected, but under the hood it was all power. Woody stored it there in case of an emergency. But for now, it was every man for himself, and he was taking it. He held his left shoulder tight with his gun hand while the blood leisurely ran between his fingers.

He dropped to his knees, reached under the driver's door frame, and retrieved a key hidden inside a magnetic box. Letterman got back on his feet and opened the car door. Once inside the car, he turned the key and the car started right up. He glanced down at the gas gauge, the needle pointed to full. He put it in gear and carefully drove away, keeping the lights off.

There were police, fire, and emergency vehicles traveling up and down the street he just vacated. When it was clear, he turned the lights on and drove twenty minutes to an all-night outdoor storage unit on east Boulder Highway. He parked, entered a gate code, and walked back to his unit.

The place looked like an old dump, perfect for what he needed. He turned the tumblers of two pad locks protecting his unit and opened the door. He switched on a battery-operated camping light which enabled him to see the room's contents. The only other light was provided by a couple of security lights attached to some older wooden poles towering twenty above the faded gray storage sheds.

The unit buildings were surrounded by an eight-foot chain-link fence, barbed wire intertwined at the top. The place was so cheap and run-down, electricity wasn't even an option anymore, but that suited his requirements perfectly. He reached into several boxes, took out cash, guns, a knife, and two passports.

A first aid kit sat on a higher shelf which he pulled down, opened, and began working on his arm. He freely poured the antiseptic on the wound, relieved to see the bullet only tore a small piece of his arm. With some needle and thread he had stashed in his medical kit he began to sew his arm back up, pulling the stitches tight. He found some crazy glue in the kit and applied it to the tightened stitches.

Letterman threw his bloody sports coat and shirt on the floor and picked out new ones he had hanging on a three-foot-long clothes rack. He would change as soon as he could get the bleeding to stop. Lying in a corner of the eight-by-ten-foot unit sat a packed suitcase with everything he needed to escape Nevada and or leave the country.

Chapter 43

*****

Vicki entered Tight Racks and was greeted by an overly cheerful bouncer until she flashed the man her badge. He motioned her in as she cut in front of the small line of men anxiously awaiting their turn to join the strip club melee. Once inside, her ears were treated to the gyrating music permeating throughout the club purposely geared to create sexual excitement. She scanned the hazy smoke-filled club, her eyes slightly burning, looking for Knuckles. She briefly stopped to admire an exotic dancer mastering a pole with several rows of dollar bills strategically draped in her G-string.

She finally located him in a semi-private corner table along with a couple other men enjoying the company of three scantily-dressed women performing a variety of lap dances. The table was loaded down with cocktails and cigars, each one trying to hang on to their positions in the ash tray. She received several intriguing glances from some of the male patrons who wantonly eyeballed her as she glided and maneuvered past them.

Vicki observed several females located at a table next to Knuckles, reveling in the company of some topless women performing a variety of sensual acts across their laps. The seated women locked their eyes on her as she approached Knuckles. A dancer doing a lap dance at a nearby table playfully grabbed her own breasts while lasciviously running her tongue across her upper lip when her eyes locked in on Vicki's. The entire atmosphere felt toxically seductive as she approached his table.

Knuckles playfully removed the dancer off his lap when he saw Vicki standing at his table. He jammed a twenty in her hand and patted her on the ass.

457

"Later, baby."

The pounding music made it almost impossible to hold an intelligible conversation. Vicki motioned with her thumb across her shoulder that the interview needed to be held outside of the club.

"I'll be right back!" Knuckles shouted, addressing the two men sitting at his table.

They both nodded, unphased by his sudden departure. A large arm suddenly draped Vicki's shoulder, gently pulling her to the right. She nervously turned her head and looked up to see who was violating her space. She eased up when she recognized Max.

"Are you here on business or pleasure?" he asked loudly whispering in her ear.

"Business," she said twisting her head sideways giving Max a strange look.

Knuckles moved towards them and nodded at Max.

"I see." Max leaned down toward her ear again. "You can use one of my private rooms for your meeting if you'd like."

Vicki thought about it for several seconds and shook her head yes.

"This way." He pointed in the direction of the room, tenderly moving her forward as he guided her shoulders.

Max was still in pain from the knife he took earlier as he cautiously steered her safely through the crowd while Knuckles trailed closely behind. Within a couple of minutes, Max stopped at a door guarded by a large bouncer who stepped aside and opened it.

"Thanks, Max, I appreciate this."

He nodded and left them as they entered the dimly lit room, the bouncer promptly closing the door once they entered.

"This looks like as good a spot as any." Vicki pointed to an empty table with several steps rising above the room floor protected only by a sheer red curtain clinging to a golden rod.

There were four booths in the room and they were all empty. She slid the curtain open and the two of them entered the first booth positioning themselves on opposite sides. There were four flush mounted Bose speakers allowing the club music to flow in.

"Quite the setup," Knuckles said. "I've never been in here before."

"Too much money to spend on a lap dance?" Vicki answered.

"Something like that. So, what's got your panties in a bunch? What's so important that you had to see tonight? I don't like be dragged away from my friends."

"First of all, I didn't drag you, and second of all, it didn't look like your friends gave a rat's ass whether or not you were there. They seemed to be doing fine on their own."

"Get on with it, detective?"

"The night Sonny disappeared, you were there, the last place he was seen alive."

"Yes. But there were other people there too. I didn't kill him. He and I were friends. What's your point?"

"You saw who killed him, kept it to yourself until that information became worth something, and then you sold it to the highest bidder."

"That's a mouthful, detective."

"I know you did it, so let's not play games. Tell me what you saw and who benefited from it."

Knuckles gave Vicki the finger and stood up. She pulled out her gun and aimed it at the middle of his forehead.

"What, you going to shoot me in a strip club?"

"You're a bookie. What are the odds I aerate your head and claim you attacked me? Give me one of your infamous odds."

Knuckles sat down and angrily stared at her.

"What, shy all of a sudden?"

"I was there, so what, I didn't have a thing to do with his death. It was an accident, okay? He and Sherry, who he was banging regularly, got into it because of something Hans said, which by the way turned out to be total bullshit."

"What are you talking about?"

"Hans told Sherry he heard from a reliable source that Bridgette and Sonny were hooking up, you know, bumping uglies on a regular basis.

"Great phraseology, Knuckles. And what happened when Sherry heard this?"

"What do you think? They got into a nasty fight in Sherry's office. She was loud, and from where I was sitting, I overheard a lot of it even though the music was on. The bar crowd was sparse that night and I'm sure only a couple of us overheard the fight. Sonny walked out of her office and toward the back door. He was not a happy man, Sherry followed him. That's the last thing I saw."

"And Woody bought that information from you, right?"

There was a long silence as the two eyeballed each other. Then Knuckles confirmed Vicki's hypothesis. "Yeah."

"How did that go down?"

"Woody's been after the Graveyaad for a couple of years now."

"And how did you know that?"

"Sherry and I were tight; I ran my book out of her bar, and in return I brought in a lot of customers—some were big slot players. We both made out."

"I don't understand. What did she ever do to you that would make you turn on her so viciously?"

"Nothing. Look, my book got hit hard during a three-week stretch of the baseball season. I got greedy, covered more action than I should have. I didn't lay enough of the money off; I ate too much. I lost over a hundred grand and panicked. My reserve funds were almost tapped out; that's how I came up with this idea to raise some needed cash. I called Woody, told him I had information that would make it easier for him to get Sherry to sell. Woody jumped all over the idea."

"Some friend you turned out to be. You got her and Sam killed."

"That was never supposed to happen. It was an inside tip, that's all. I regretted it the day after I did it. I got on a hot streak or my customers went on a cold streak over the next two weeks, however you want to phrase it. I more than doubled what I was down. I hated what I had done to her."

"But you still took the cash. How much did Woody pay you?"

"Fifty-thousand, plus, he agreed to let me run my book out of the bar, zero vig."

"Did Sherry kill Sonny?"

"She was tough enough to skin a live rattlesnake, but murder? Never."

"Then why is Sonny dead?"

"I promised to never say a word about this to anyone, but she's gone now. It doesn't matter much anymore."

"And you've kept your word until now?"

"Yeah, who the fuck was I going to tell?"

"Alright, tell me what she said."

"Sonny stormed out, she grabbed him and threw a punch at him, he ducked, slipped and fell down the stairs. Sherry began to laugh at him, until she realized he was really hurt. She ran down the steps and tried to help him, but he didn't respond. She tried to revive him, but he was gone. Buster came down the stairs and joined her. She was freaking out."

"What happened next?"

"Buster settled Sherry down and came up with this plan. First, he pulled Sonny under the steps, grabbed an old

461

painter's tarp, and tossed it over him. He found a couple of old orange construction cones they used to block off the parking lot during special events. He used them to seal off the back parking lot. Buster came up with the plan to dump Sonny in the desert and torch his car. He was afraid she would lose her license, or worse, get convicted of first or second-degree murder."

"All of this over an accident. You realize how many people have died because of this?"

"But she didn't kill him. When they came out twenty minutes later, he was gone."

"Yet, you told Woody she killed him."

"Yeah, shit happens, and Woody bought into it. That's the way it went down, We're done here. I'm leaving."

"You don't get to walk away from this."

"Watch me. You know who I know and you can't prove jack shit."

He got up and headed to the exit.

"One last thing before you go."

He turned around and looked back at her. "What?"

"I'd be very careful. Change is in the wind, and when Woody finds out you scammed him, he's going to skin you alive."

He walked out of the room. Vicki sat there a moment collecting her thoughts, figuring out a game plan.

Max walked into the room. "I saw Knuckles leaving. Are you okay?"

"Yeah."

"We have a more pressing issue to deal with."

"What issue?"

She slid out of the booth.

"Steve never made it home from here."

"Where is he?"

"He was supposed to go straight home after we came back to the club. I had one of my men take him, but he never made it back."

"How long ago?"

"It's been over an hour."

"Shit. I'll get on it."

"One more thing."

"What's that?"

"When he didn't answer his phone I sent one of my men to his house and along the route he found Steve's Tundra. It was on Paradise just before Sahara. The road was blocked off. My man parked and checked out the scene and saw his truck. It was involved in a three-car collision. Someone hit his truck head on. My man was found lying dead in the passenger's seat dead.

"No sign of anyone else?"

"No."

"They must have kidnapped him. Jesus, he's in serious danger, Max. I'd better go."

Vicki left the club and went back into her car and made a call to Charlette.

"Vicki, I was just about to call you," Charlette answered.

"It wasn't Lisa."

"Who was it?"

"I can't say."

"Right. I understand. Thanks for calling me and letting me know it wasn't Lisa."

*****

Charlette hung up and wiped some blood off her right hand onto her turquoise tee shirt.

463

"Lisa, thanks for the informative chat. I actually believe you."

Lisa sat on her apartment floor, barefoot, blood on her face, tee shirt, and the floor.

"Get out of here!" she shouted, tears running down her cheeks, mixing with the blood already on her face.

"Great news, Lisa. I'm not going to kill you tonight."

Lisa started to get up.

"Oh, and before I go, you're fired, bitch."

*****

Vicki called the two detectives assigned to Steve's case and informed them of the situation. She knew they would immediately begin to compile footage of the crime scene, trace the getaway vehicle and or vehicles escape routes. She called her partner Dustin to discuss their next move.

"You have him?"

"Hopefully."

*****

Chapter 44

The car parked behind an older building on West Charleston. One of Fazio's men dashed to the door and unlocked it.

"Why we stopping here?" Woody asked.

"What better way to settle a score than in the arena, especially this one. Get out."

"So, this is where Woody and I get to square off?" I asked.

"This is the place."

Several men trained their handguns on us and escorted us through the back door. The place inside smelled like two-week-old unwashed armpits. When the lights came on, I saw why.

"This is a gym?" I said, checking out the ambiance.

"Now I know why everyone thinks you're so intelligent," Fazio answered.

"Who thinks I'm intelligent?"

"Do I have to spell it out for you?"

"You know, don't you?"

"Yes."

"So, you have other irons in the fire besides acquiring YLL."

"Yes."

"What are you two talking about?" an annoyed Woody asked."

"Keep walking Woody," Fazio ordered.

Woody kept walking towards the ring. Fazio and I stopped.

"He doesn't know, does he?"

"No."

"You going to tell him?"

"No. This is between you and I," Fazio said pointing to the ring.

"Any more odiferous and I'd swear we were in a manure factory," Woody complained.

"Ah, the smell of competition. I love this smell!" Fazio yelled. "You two, get in the ring. And take your shoes off or anything else you don't want bloodied."

"Are you kidding? All my crap already has blood on it, mine" I replied.

"Then you're good to go. Peter, make sure the windows are covered."

"Got it, boss."

"Pick a corner, then come out fighting on my cue. I'll give you the signal."

I'm sure Woody was happy to be alive and being given an opportunity to walk out of the gym. We did as we were told, picking opposite corners. I did a couple of stretches hanging down off the ropes and rotated my neck around my shoulders several times. The beatings issued by Letterman and the asshole standing across from me already had me sore and aching. The beat down I was going to administer to Woody would be painful and prolonged. However, the objective of this fight was to eliminate Woody, not beat him down.

I sensed by his body language that he was nervous and I could smell his fear from across the ring. This fight couldn't bring Sam back, but I would be going vigilante on his sorry ass.

"The rounds will be two to five-minutes, depending on how many times my glass needs to be refilled. Any questions?"

One of his men brought him a wine glass and filled it.

"No. Ding," Fazio chirped.

I moved quickly to the center of the ring, Woody slid left along the ropes, slightly leaning backwards, calculating a move that would take me down.

"A fair fight. Something you're not accustomed to, is it Woody?" I said taunting him with my fists. "Man up, bitch. Let's get this on," I said doing a quick Ali shuffle for heightened effects.

Woody didn't answer instead he lunged at me, using the ropes as a mild catapult, launching a right roundhouse punch and himself directly at me. I was cocky and careless as Woody's punch caught a piece of my forehead causing me to slightly stagger backwards. I shook it off and got my head back into the reality of my situation.

Woody dipped back into the same trough and tried it again. This time I easily sidestepped him and threw a right cross to the back of his head. He went down and bounced off the canvas floor. To my surprise he rolled onto his feet and quickly stood up, ready to go again.

Even on the mend from having been punched out almost to unconsciousness still wouldn't make this much of a contest, as long as I didn't get to full of myself. I knew it, and Woody did too. In the back of my mind I wondered why Fazio would piss two-hundred-thousand down the toilet and let me annihilate him.

I walked towards Woody blocking his every attempt to avoid me. I backed him up against the ropes and unloaded a right frontal kick to his chest. A shocked Woody bounced off the ropes and sprung forward directly in front of me, where I crushed him with a left hook. Blood flew out of his mouth as he bounced off the canvas twice and rolled over on his back. It felt exhilarating to land a punch that flush. But he didn't go lights out, not like he did at The Rio.

He started to get up, but I pounced on his chest and landed a straight right to his nose. More blood splattered across his face, my hand, and the ring. I felt his nose flatten when I made contact; I'd broken it for sure. I pulled the semi-conscious Woody up, wrapping my right hand around his throat, squeezing it while I sat comfortably on his waist.

Fazio shouted, "Ding, ding, ding!"

467

"That's not fair!" I argued as I lifted up his head and then pushed it down to the blood-stained canvas. "It's been less than a minute!"

"My gym, my rules. Boys, help Woody over to his corner."

Eddie entered the ring along with another one of Fazio's men and dragged Woody back to his corner. Some black guy slid between the ropes bringing a stool with him. He then applied a wet rag to Woody's face from a bucket that magically appeared in the ring. He began restructuring Woody's blood-soaked nose and put in some cotton plugs.

"Steve, go back to your corner," Fazio ordered.

"Where's my corner man and chair? How about a quick massage while they work on him?" I asked as I leaned back against the Everlast turn buckle and took deep cleansing breaths.

"Sorry, your guy took the day off," Fazio said smiling at me.

I trained my eyes on a wall clock, trying to gauge the amount of time Fazio would allow Woody to recuperate between these makeshift rounds. When Fazio gave us the next, "Ding" I would charge Woody and beat him as hard and as often as I could.

Suddenly, I noticed Fazio had a small mic in his hands.

"Testing, testing. Great, it works. Steve, can you hear me?"

"Yes... I can hear you."

"Listen up, I have a couple of announcements to make. First, I'd like to thank that lying, cheating, scumbag Woody for so graciously attending and participating in tonight's preliminary bout, which by the way is officially over."

"What!" I stuck my head through the ropes, getting ready to jump in front of Fazio.

Two men with guns trained on me instantly changed my mind.

"Preliminary bout. What the hell are you talking about? Who else is fighting here tonight?"

Like locusts descending on a corn field, in came Letterman through the back door, pounding his fists together while making his way to the ring. He climbed in, never taking his cold laser eyes off me. Eddie and another one of Fazio's men frisked him and removed a gun and knife. He tossed them out of the ring into the waiting hands of another one of Fazio's men. Eddie assisted Letterman and helped him remove his shirt, revealing a black wife-beater tee. He also had a makeshift white bandage on his shoulder with fresh blood stains leaking through and a couple of small, coagulated blood trails that left dark red tracks down his shoulder.

"Fazio, what's he doing here? You were just shooting at him."

"Let's just say we've agreed to a brief cease fire."

"It looks like one of your men's rounds caught a piece of your boy," I said grabbing my shoulder and pretending to clear my eyes of tears.

"What?" Fazio said.

"And Fazio, don't forget to make arrangements with your life insurance company; take out a substantial policy on your boy before you ding him in," I added.

"How cocky and self-assured you are. Letterman couldn't wait to get here and be on this morning's card."

"Letterman, I can't wait to bust you up," I said, feeling my veins bulging on the side of my head.

"Hey boy, just thinking the same thing about you, except you won't be leaving here. Take a good look at my face… it'll be the last thing you see on this earth.

"Wait, wait, wait. Letterman, Steve's right. You have been shot."

469

"That bullet I took didn't even hurt my feelings. I'm ready to do him," Letterman angrily fired back.

"This is an unfortunate set of circumstances. Letterman's injured, he's damaged goods. The Nevada Athletic Commission would never approve of this. Therefore, he's being scratched. Letterman, get out of my ring."

"I'm not leaving until Steve is dead!"

"C'mon, leave him in, Fazio. He and I have unfinished business to settle."

"Letterman, get out! Last warning."

He leaned over the edge of the top rope and gave Fazio an icy stare.

"You heard me. Get out, or do you need some assistance?"

Several of Fazio's men standing next to the ring turned towards Letterman.

Letterman yanked his shirt out of Eddie's hand and obliged, gingerly sliding between the ropes.

"I'm sorry, Steve. You'll have to reschedule your death match with him down the road. I'll even book it for you, that is, if you make it out of here in one piece."

My spirits took a turn for the worst. Fazio had something else in store for me and looked confident in the outcome.

"Eddie, you're already in the ring. Why don't you fill in for Letterman. You and Woody can be partners in a tag-team event. And sadly Steve... no one volunteered to be your partner. My apologies."

"So, that's how it's going to go down?"

"Looks that way."

"What about your integrity? Didn't you make a promise to Tony?"

"I cut you loose and let you live. You chose to be here with Woody. I fulfilled my obligation of integrity and

470

my word to Tony," he said while slowly making the sign of the cross.

"With pleasure," Eddie said as he tossed off his shirt and threw it on a chair just outside the ring. He looked much tougher with his shirt off.

Eddie turned towards Woody and quietly said, "You left me hanging out to dry earlier."

"It was Letterman's idea. Don't worry, I'll make it up to you. Let's just get out of here in one piece."

"This is going to cost you Woody."

"Letterman, sit down over there." Fazio pointed to a third-row seat on the aisle. "Johnny, sit behind him and keep your Berretta pointed at his head. If he does something egregious, put a hole in him. Make that several holes."

"With pleasure," Johnny answered while nudging the barrel of his gun against the back of Letterman's head.

"Hey," I said to Letterman as he sat down. He looked directly at me. "I'll be seeing you around."

"You can count on it, boy. And one more thing."

"I'm all ears."

"You lucked out; they ain't tough like me."

This night was full of surprises, he actually appeared to want me to take out his boss and Eddie so he could personally do me. How sweet. Never figured him to have a warm spot inside that venomous exterior.

Apparently, Fazio was going to give Woody every possible chance to win; make him cough up the two-hundred-thousand dollars he agreed to.

"And Eddie, toss Sal your gun. No cheating," Fazio ordered.

Eddie sourly complied. He reached behind his back and pitched his gun out of the ring to a waiting Sal.

"Woody, looks like you're with us again, Fazio comically ascertained," his voice coming out garbled and cracked through the speaker.

471

Fazio pounded the mic several times, hoping to clear up the distorted sound.

"Testing, testing. Cheap Chinese garbage. Someone make a note to fix this damn thing."

Woody joined Eddie who tossed out the chair to the corner man sitting in a front row seat.

"We're ready," a heavy breathing Woody replied.

"You better not run away and leave me hanging," Eddie said looking directly at Woody.

"There's a nice five-thousand dollar cash bonus waiting for you when we get Steve. That work for you?"

"I can live with ten," he said peering down at Woody.

"Done. Ten thousand it is."

"Hey Woody, if you were Pinocchio, you'd have a new snout by now," I said gently stroking my nose.

"You're going to die smart ass."

Two of the three people I hated most in the world were in the ring. Barbra would have been a runaway fourth choice, but she would be facing enough charges to keep her occupied for the next several decades.

"Ding," Fazio chirped again.

They both slid along the sides of the ring moving in opposite directions. Their strategy, get me in the middle. My plan, somewhat different. I charged Woody who dove through the ropes and landed on the floor. Eddie lunged at me from behind hoping to wrap my neck in his grip and take me down like a cowboy tackling a calf. His plan went south when I pivoted and landed a straight left into his mouth. He staggered but regained his balance.

"You're going to need to do a lot more than that, Stevie boy," he confidently replied shaking off the blow to his head

"There's a lot more of that in your future."

While bantering with Eddie I made the mistake of losing track of Woody outside the ring. He dove back in

472

behind me and grabbed my left leg with both arms, and held on tight. Eddie seized the opportunity and crashed into me with his left shoulder, the impact driving us both back against the ropes, then propelling us forward.

Eddie landed on his side and rolled up to his feet. Woody's grip caused me to fall flat on my chest. I twisted on my back and kicked Woody in the forehead, driving him backwards into a couple of chairs. That move gave Eddie enough time to drop a knee into my chest using all his weight. The impact forced most of the air out of my lungs. Eddie took his right fist and landed a punch on the side of my head. Fortunately, I moved my head slightly away from his blow and only a minor portion of his punch did any damage. I drove the knuckles of my left hand deep into his exposed solar-plexus as he began to accelerate downward directly at my head for the second time. He made a weird grunting sound and fell over onto his left side, clutching his chest with both hands.

I rose up to one knee when Woody flew over the ropes and onto my back, driving my face hard into the canvas. He rolled up and over me and, in an instant, regained his balance. Survival, adrenaline and some sort of amphetamines must have been fueling him.

Woody and Eddie were facing me again as I jumped to my feet and went into another defensive stance. Blood began to trickle from my left eyebrow and into my eye. As I wiped it off, Eddie bent over and pulled a knife from a sheath hidden under his pant leg.

"Let's see how tough you are now," Eddie said as he tossed the knife back and forth between hands.

Another knife entered the ring near Woody. He scooped it up immediately. He put it in his right hand as the two newly armed men cautiously approached me with renewed vigor.

"Place your bets!" Fazio yelled out. "New odds coming in as we speak."

The laughter in the background was all at my expense. Letterman didn't think it was funny, he just stared at me.

They both took a couple of baby steps away from each other while cunningly closing the distance between us. Eddie had those wild, crazy eyes, and in my mind, would strike next. Woody being a pure psychopath and unpredictable would probably wait for Eddie to make the first move before he engaged.

I did a feint move on Eddie and they both jumped backwards.

"You've got the knives. Come and get some!" I screamed.

Fazio's jovial expression mounted with every second of this spectacle.

"Fazio, where's my knife?" I asked while breathing hard.

"Did you check your house lately?"

"You're a real comedian."

"I'm happy you think so."

"It's a shame you don't have the cjones to be in here with us!" I yelled making sure all his men heard me.

"Just be thankful I'm not!" He bobbed his head and grabbed one of the ring ropes trying to save face amongst his crew.

His men pathetically nodded and mumbled positive encouragement.

"Now!" Woody shouted.

They took two steps toward me, a kind of all-out charge, but Woody stopped short and left Eddie one-on-one with me. With the knife in his right hand, he lunged. Unfortunately, at that moment, I realized he knew how to handle a blade. He stopped at the exact moment I tried blocking his hand with my left arm. In my mind's eye, those two years of fencing were finally going to reap some reward. However, he ducked, pirouetted, and caught a piece of my right forearm and right side, just above my hip. I instinctively grabbed my side with my left hand and peeked at it to assess the damage. The cut wasn't deep but it was bleeding.

Eddie jumped back, laughing. In that moment while I was staring into his lifeless charcoal eyes, a hideous grin began to form across his face and his eyebrows rose. His confidence level hit a new crescendo.

"What's wrong, Steve? You don't look so good."

He came at me again, taking countless swipes as I jumped back each time, trying to avoid being slashed. I recognized his strategy, drive me towards Woody who kept circling me, waiting for the perfect moment to drive his blade into my back.

I had to make a move now or end up getting carved like a Thanksgiving Day turkey.

"Come on, Eddie, less talk. Bring it. Show me what a real mental-midget like you can do with a knife."

He took the insult personally and lunged at me, swinging his blade several more times. I pretended to jump backwards but instead made a move for his knife hand as he lunged forward. I caught his right wrist with my left hand and slid my right hip under him. I flipped him on the top rope and watched as his back completely arched. The ropes elasticity propelled him through the air where several metal chairs broke most of his fall. However, his head landed awkwardly on the cold hard concrete floor. He tried to stand and act unphased by the rocky landing and prove to me he wasn't hurt, but his plan dissipated like a fart in a hurricane. He crumpled to one knee and then to the other, clutching the back of his head. Concrete floor one, Eddie zero.

Woody took advantage of the moment and caught a piece of me. I avoided being gutted by his blade, but he still managed to create a small cut on my left side between my hip and ribs, which began to bleed instantly.

Flowing with confidence Woody tried the same move again. His expression went from satisfaction to horror when I caught his right hand, reverse spun him and shoved the blade deep into his stomach, then jerked it out. He doubled over, clutched the hole in his belly with both hands and dropped to his knees. I had them both on their knees, Eddie on the floor and Woody in the ring. I rotated to my right and draped my right leg over Woody's back, looking like a cowboy on a bull.

"Foul!" Fazio yelled. He was jumping around in protest, agonizing over the money I was about to deprive him of. My mind flashed back to my earlier conversation with Max, the complex internal processing of killing a man. Using my pent-up anger as a guide, I decided killing him would comfortably find a place within my conscience.

"Yeah, foul this!" I hollered using my right hand to dig up a swatch of his hair and pull him backwards. I'd seen this maneuver dozens of times on televised wrestling bouts, without a knife, but this time it was for real, and Woody was the fading star of the script. I continued to pull his head back almost to the point of breaking, using my right knee as a wedge to drive it deep into his thoracic vertebrae. He tried to grab me with his blood-soaked hands, but I had him at an awkward disadvantage. I held him there for several seconds while I caught my breath.

"This is for Sam."

I leaned forward, focusing my eyes directly on his. I thought I saw the evil in this man dissipate and drain into vapor just before I drove the knife up and under his chin, holding it there while I relished in his suffering. He went into convulsions as his bloody hands clutched my arm. I twisted the blade several times, watching him squirm uncontrollably like a worm trapped on hook. I was savoring the sight of his warm blood running down my knife-clenched fist. Woody gave me this dismayed and bewildered look right before I yanked the blade down and out of his neck and slid it across his throat, holding his head while his arms helplessly collapsed.

He died in my grasp, the weight of his body feeling like a three-hundred-pound sack of wet potatoes. I continued to hold his head backwards, watching as his blood rhythmically pumped out across the canvas.

"Fuck you, Woody," I unremorsefully whispered in his ear before finally letting his lifeless body drop.

The gym went silent; nobody saw this one coming. I stood over his corpse like a Roman Gladiator in the arena, celebrating a triumphant kill in front of a screaming, blood-lusting crowd.

Fazio's men appreciated the effort and began to cheer and applaud. Fazio stood next to the ring with his jaw open in disbelief.

"Letterman, what a great ending to a fight. Am I right?" Johnny asked.

"If you say so."

Letterman cautiously stood up and walked toward the ring.

"Go slowly, I've got Mr. Barretta trained on your back," a cautious Johnny said while standing up and standing in the aisle.

I raised my arms, looked over at Letterman, who was approaching the ring. I then turned to Eddie. I didn't have to say a word to him; he knew what I wanted.

"Don't go in there!" A woman's voice reverberated throughout the gym. Everyone turned in her direction, including me. I had trouble seeing her until she walked past Fazio and stood next to Eddie, grasping his arm.

"You," I said.

"That's right."

"Hey honey, just in time to watch me kill Steve," Eddie said flipping his knife grip to grip.

"Julie?"

"We meet again, Steve.

"What happened to your college education in La Crosse?"

"Let's just say subject material at UWL wasn't pertinent in regards to my chosen profession."

"Which is?"

"International finance, spying, terrorism, assassinations… the usual classes not found on any college itineraries.

"You're a plethora of perplexities."

"The parties just getting started Steve, buckle up."

"Well, I think I'm ready to go home," I said sarcastically and started reaching for the ropes."

"You can stay where you are. Fazio… Eddie and I will be taking Steve off your hands."

"If that's what you want, Julie," a still stunned Fazio answered.

"What the hell? You're taking orders from a wet nose freshman?" I asked.

"Money talks, and she has extremely deep pockets."

"Julie has deep pockets?"

"Yes, and we have an understanding, a partnership of sorts we formed to accomplish mutual strategic objectives. Her partners have unlimited funds for a wide variety of ventures.

"How convenient for you."

"It is, and I hate to interrupt this college reunion," Fazio began. "But first, Letterman, you need to take that dead lump of shit out of my ring."

An unfazed and stoic Letterman walked back to the ring and climbed in; Johnny's gun, still zeroed in on his back.

"There's some large trash bags in the janitor's closet," the black cornerman announced.

"If you could retrieve several of those bags for Woody's sake, it would be deeply appreciated," Fazio answered.

"Yes sir."

He moved swiftly to the closet.

"Johnny, take Paul and Mario and help Letterman remove Woody,' he said using his hands wildly to direct his men.

"You better move quickly Fazio or you might end up in the Metro holding tank. Rumor has it they've been alerted to a situation at a certain gym," Julie suggested.

"How thoughtful of you to be so… thoughtful."

"Again, the guest of honor will need to be staying here with us," Julie calmly added. "The fuss about Steve made for a mostly wasted trip to Vegas. Turns out, he isn't worth as much as previously advertised."

"I don't understand," Fazio said.

"What do you mean, I'm not worth as much?" I curiously asked.

"When it was discovered you were Are's son, it drew a lot of attention, the kind of attention that attracts big money players. Are inherited many talents from his encounter. The powers that be, especially the Chinese, thought he might have bestowed some of those powers on to you. They had some interesting plans for this young man and shelled out a lot of money too. Turns out, you're not very special after all, just slightly above average, except of course in that one unique area between your legs where I do believe you accelerate."

Julie walked over to Eddie, who gave her this WTF look and planted a long, hard kiss on his mouth. Eddy picked her up and they both hugged.

"You and Eddie."

"Kind of a, holy shit moment," Julie said, laughing at me.

"You make me want to puke."

"And Poor Mary, never saw that one coming, Julie and me," Eddie added. "She paid us nicely for that phony underage scam we ran on her. And Julie, Mary and me… so unbelievably hot.

"How did you know Mary was here?"

"Julie bugged Sonny's place as soon as we learned you were coming to Vegas."

"And you found everything out through Goldhabber."

"We did," Julie answered, surprised to hear I figured it out.

"And Mary's role?"

"Did what we told her to do, prison was never an option for her. We worked her like a crack whore. Fortunately for us, we heard the whole conversation at the pool. She was falling in love with you, how charming. The bitch talked too much and we couldn't allow her to expose us, now could we?" Eddie concluded.

"That's why you killed her?"

"Did I?"

Julie had this evil look on her face as she listened to Eddie's explanation. Letterman, Fazio and his men listened to the conversation like a captive audience watching a soap opera plot unfold.

"That means you won't be able to make a dollar off me, unlike your blackmailing scheme with Mary."

"That sums it up nicely. But you're still going to have to die Steve, just like those two whistleblowers in the back of Ramone's limo," Julie continued.

"It was you?"

"Was it?"

Fazio climbed into the ring, "You took quite a beating tonight kid, and yet here you are. You have some serious skill sets. When this is all done and, the kicker of course, if you make it out of here in one piece, you should consider joining my organization. You're smart, tough and have a razor-sharp tongue. I like that, except for the part where you tried to embarrass me in front of my crew. Don't ever talk to me like that again."

"Thanks, but for now I'm just going to concentrate on these two."

"Just remember, I wasn't here today," he said gently squeezing my cheeks within his right thumb and index fingers then releasing my cheeks and patting my left one. "Good."

He climbed out and stood next to Julie.

"Fazio?"

"What?" he asked, turning around to look up at me.

"Thanks for delivering Woody."

"My pleasure."

Letterman and Fazio's men drug Woody through the ropes, creating a horizontal blood trail, then wrapped him in the large plastic garbage bags.

He'd only been dead ten minutes but I could already smell his rotting corpse polluting the gymnasium air.

"Dump him in the desert," Fazio ordered.

"He's not your problem anymore," Letterman interjected. "I'll take care of him."

"You're about to be one lonely man, Letterman. Nevada, officially off limits to you."

"I understand."

"I'm almost going to miss you," he said with a smirk.

As Woody was being taken out of the gym, Fazio got close up in Julie's face. "And just to be clear, our business is completed."

Julie reached into her jacket and handed Fazio two envelopes. "For now."

He grabbed the envelopes, smiled at her and shoved them in his suit coat inside pockets. All of his men except for one walked towards the back door.

Fazio made a final turn and directed another comment Julie's way, "Oh and by the way, I hope Steve kills you and Eddie… I don't like Chinese."

"Before you leave, you have something that belongs to Eddie," Julie said with her hand open.

Fazio nodded and one of his men pretended to toss Eddie his gun. Another one came up behind Julie and frisked

481

her, taking his time when he checked out her bra and between her legs.

"What's this about Fazio."

"Keeping the fight fair."

"I took her Glock, a magazine, a serrated blade, and this little dandy," Fazio's man Peter said displaying all her weapons. "She's clean now."

I immediately recognized the strange weapon in Julie's possession.

"You killed her!"

"She should have stayed in La Crosse or moved back to Texas. Either way, she shouldn't have come to Vegas. It was a bad judgement call."

"There's a special little corner in hell with your name on it."

Eddie took exception to my comment, as did Julie.

"I'm going to enjoy killing you," Eddie said.

"Killing you is going to be extra special," Julie added.

"You're going to both pay for this," I said pointing my knife at their faces.

"This is way more entertaining than any soap opera. Who knew you were such a conniving bitch Julie?" Fazio proclaimed.

"You better watch your tongue, Fazio."

"Or what, Eddie? You gonna pay some thug to hurt me?" Fazio said.

"Julie and I have a way of disposing of undesirables," a cocky Eddie boasted.

"Like sneaking up behind helpless women and strangling them? You guys are real tough."

"I'm warning you, Fazio."

Peter took one step towards Eddie and kicked him in the back of his left knee. Eddie went straight down.

"Not so tough," Peter said mockingly.

"You want to threaten me again, Eddie?"

The room went silent for a few seconds as tempers cooled. Eddie stood up flexing his knee several times.

"Fazio, we may still need each other down the road," Julie reminded him. "So let's drop all the macho bullshit. Give Eddie and me our weapons back and walk out the door."

"You're right, Julie. We might need each other in the future. Peter, toss Julie back her monomolecular sci-fi weapon or whatever you call it."

"Fazio, it's a custom-made garrote, pistol grip handles, an effective weapon for—"

"Strangling," Fazio interjected.

"Yes."

"Julie, you do have a flare for the macabre," Fazio declared.

"It's a killing tool I've mastered."

"Peter, toss it to her." He did and she caught it with one hand. Fazio clapped. "Athletic too. Show me how it works."

Julie put the weapon in her hand and pointed the handles at Fazio. "You see this button?" She pointed to the end of one of the pistol grips.

"Yes, I see it."

"Watch." Julie pushed the button and pulled apart the garrote exposing sixteen inches of steel wire. "You loop it around the neck and pull."

"Jesus Christ, that weapon is out-of-control!" Fazio shouted.

She pushed the button again and guided the two ends together.

"Eddie, you're sleeping with a lunatic," I interjected.

"Keep it. And here are the rest your weapons." Fazio nodded at Peter who handed her weapons back.

Johnny tossed Eddie his gun back too.

"Why, thank you Fazio," Julie said politely.

"Don't thank me just yet. If there's one bullet hole found on Steve's corpse I'll put a contract out on the both of you. Is that clear?"

"No shooting him," Julie said with an ear-to-ear grin.

"Steve, good luck." Boys, time to leave," Fazio ordered. "Julie, my apologies. The Chinese were wise to bankroll you."

As Fazio and his men were leaving for the second time, he directed a parting comment my way. "Oh, and Steve, no hard feelings kid, but business before pleasure. And remember, be careful who you align with."

The comment was a crock-of-shit but making sure I saw him place my Glock and clips on a chair next to the back door while Julie and Eddie focused their eyes on me, priceless.

I nodded.

Chapter 45

The door closed and it was down to Eddie, Julie, and me. Eddie, who was fully recovered from the blow he received to his head and the kick to the back of his knee came up to the ring and stopped. He didn't say a word and just stared at me.

I looked at him and noticed that the cuts on my sides were beginning to somewhat coagulate and the cut above my left eye stopped bleeding. Finally, something working in my favor.

"Julie, Metro's not really on their way, are they?" I asked not taking my eyes off Eddie.

"No. Maybe, the Chinese are wrong about you."

"I keep hearing that."

I leaned over the top rope and flashed Eddie the knife in my blood-stained hand. "You stepping back in?"

"I am," Eddie replied as Julie put the garrote in her back jean pocket, grabbed the top rope across from me and jumped into the ring, knife and gun in hand.

She stuffed the gun behind her back, took off and threw her jacket on a chair, exposing her braless beige wife beater. She was well toned, even more muscular than I remember from our one night stand in La Crosse.

"You guys are the quintessential psychotic couple," I snarkily threw in.

"Flattering, but you're still going to die," she said garnishing a smile and shaking her long black hair out right before retying it back up and twisting it into a bun.

I knew I couldn't take them both. Julie had to be ex-military, probably Russian, and I'm sure possessed skills I hadn't seen before. Eddie and I were closely matched, but fighting them as a team; I'd be dead meat.

Julie did a couple of feint moves towards me, swashbuckling her knife which captured my attention and allowed Eddie to sneak back into the ring. He shoved his gun behind his back too. Apparently, Fazio's warning made an impact on them. I was not going to get shot.

They parlayed together in the opposite corner, discussing their strategy. I leaned against the turn-buckle running dozens of defensive scenarios in my head; each one ended up with me being stabbed or strangled. They broke apart and quickly closed in, approaching me from opposite sides.

Eddie would engage me before Julie, definitely a guy thing. I guessed wrong. Julie came in hard and fast swinging her knife accompanied with ballet footwork precision. But I had already figured out my best strategy. I thrust my knife at her mid-section, forcing her to retreat for an instant. Eddie tried attacking me from behind.

"Screw this," I said right before I jumped through the ropes and onto the concrete floor.

I needed every inch of space I could find to defend myself; fighting the two of them in the ring was suicide. They followed me out of the ring. I shoved my knife in my back pocket, picked up a folding chair and closed it. I'd use it as a shield. Not the greatest plan ever designed but better than standing around exposed in the ring.

Once again, they decided to come at me from opposite sides. My heart began to pound, my breathing became erratic and my mouth tasted like I ate a bucket of sand. This is what a rabbit must experience when surrounded by a pack of coyotes; it's impeding sense of doom.

Everyone's strategies blew up when the main lights unexpectedly went out, revealing a barely visible dull red exit signs above each door. Instinctively we all froze as our eyes adjusted to the poorly illuminated gym. I reacted the quickest and flung a chair into Eddie's path, hitting him flush and knocking him backwards. I stumbled and made a move for the back door, kicking and tossing chairs out of the way.

Julie came up with a better plan, jumping back into the ring, crawling to the opposite side, and sliding back onto the gym floor, cutting off my retreat. I heard Eddie banging chairs behind me; he would be all over me in a few seconds. I found another chair, folded it, and swung wildly from left to right at Julie. My first swing missed, but as I stepped into my return backswing, I managed to land one on her shoulder and forced her to backpedal several steps.

I heard Eddie on my tail, wheeled, and swung the chair sideways, hitting him on the side of his head with the top part of the chair. It felt like hitting a ninety-mile-an-hour fastball in the meat of the bat. He went down hard and fast. Julie immediately came up behind me her garrote already opened and tried to pull it around my neck. It forced me to drop the chair. Fortunately, I managed to slip my right arm in between the wire and my neck, my forearm taking the brunt of her executioner's grip. I swung her around toward the ring and jammed her into it, trying to reach behind her head with my left arm and lock it. Blood freely began to run down my right arm as the garrote's wire began burrowing deep into my skin and muscle.

Failing to reach her head, I dropped to one knee and pulled her on top of my back, causing her to momentarily loosen her grip. I jumped back to my feet and used my right leg to push off with all my strength. The two of us fell backwards, and as we hit the floor, I tossed my head violently backwards into her nose forcing her to release her grip. I spun out and pulled the garrote and wire out of my right forearm. I crawled a couple of feet away and grabbed my right arm, holding the garrote in my left while applying pressure to my arm.

My eyes had already adjusted to the dim red hue lighting in the gym and I was able to make out her image as she tried to get up. I rolled on my right side, dropped the garrote and pushed off putting a claw grip into both of her eyes. She screamed and began an onslaught of kicking and

487

punching at my arm and hand. I didn't have enough strength left to hold on and released her. I picked up the garrote again as she got on all fours and was about to crawl away when a fully recovered Eddie jumped on my back. The two of us crashed on top of Julie. The impact forced the air out of her lungs. She made this hideous demonic sound while gasping for air. I landed face down on the gym floor and was momentarily stunned. Eddie promptly jumped to his feet, picked up a chair and slammed it into my back.

The lights unexpectedly came back on, momentarily blinding all of us. The back door swung open and bounced off the wall.

"Put your hands up. You're all under arrest!" I heard a female scream.

Eddie paused for a second and then reached behind his back and pulled out his gun.

Two ear-piercing shots rang out, both hitting Eddie, driving him backwards and to his right. Julie tried to get up on her knees and opened her mouth, trying to speak. I pounced on her back with her garrote in my hands and tightly cloaked it around her unprotected neck, crisscrossing my bloody arms and pulling back as hard as I could. She was flat on her stomach and tried to grasp my arms. I rose up and used the weight of my right knee against her back. Within seconds her blood streamed across the wire, her fingers wildly clutching at it. I stared down at the back of her head, pulling the garrote tighter until she finally went limp, her blood rhythmically pumping out of her severed carotid artery and pooling on the gym floor.

When I was sure she was dead I released the weapon and collapsed on top of her.

The front door swung open and a man wheeling a gun charged through.

"We're secure, Dustin!" Vicki shouted, her fingers resting on Eddie's pulse.

He lowered his gun and walked toward us. I tried standing but collapsed onto my left side.

"Steve, you're bleeding," a concerned Vicki said as she leaned over and took me in her lap, placing her hands over my wounds. "Dustin, call 9-1-1 and get an ambulance here, now."

"How did you—"

"I put trackers in your precious thirty-round magazines, figured the two of you were inseparable. However, they didn't work as efficiently as we would have liked. I'm sorry we were late."

"A lot of work, getting you to see me again."

Dustin pulled his phone out from under his sports coat and made the call.

"We need to leave!" The cornerman shouted. "The building's on fire!"

"What?!" Vicki said as smoke began swirling inside the gym.

"You," she said pointing at the black cornerman, "help me get him outside."

"It's Hank, officer."

"Hank, help me get him outside. Dustin, come here, give us a hand."

The three of them dragged me out the back door and into the small parking lot. Flames began to rise along the sides of the building and over the roof.

"Someone torched the gym!" Hank frantically yelled.

The three of them set me down.

"Julie's garrote, you have it?" I said running out of breath. "She killed Mary with it."

"No. I'll be right back."

"What are you doing?!" Dustin shouted.

"I got this, take care of Steve."

*****

489

Vicki raced through the back door and into the smoke-filled gym. She turned her flashlight on and shined it on Julie's body. The emergency exit lights came on as the electrical power to the gym shut off.

She placed her arm around her mouth, fighting to keep the smoke from entering her lungs. She knelt down, lifted up her almost severed head and unwound Julie's weapon. It was still imbedded deep around her bloody neck. She did the best she could to pull the weapon together and shoved the garrote in her inside jacket pocket. There wasn't time for police etiquette, procedures or time to drag both bodies out. She made a split-second decision, sidestepped Julie and grabbed Eddie under the arms.

*****

Hank saw Vicki dragging Eddie through the burning gym door and ran up to help her. Dustin was busy rolling up his sports coat under my head for support.

Vicki and Hank were almost next to me when an ear-deafening explosion rocked the inside, sending glass and debris in all directions, creating a fireball that rose high in the Neon lit sky. Vicki dove onto the asphalt, dropping Eddie while covering her head. Dustin rolled on top of me, trying to keep the fiery debris from landing on my body. Hank took the brunt of the blast and flew face first hitting his forehead on the asphalt parking lot.

The first LVFD truck arrived, followed by several Metro patrol vehicles and a variety of ambulances companies.

490

*****

Bridgette stood in the alleyway, watching the building burn. As soon as the building exploded, she left.

*****

Vicki brushed several embers off her blazer and came over to Dustin and me who sat up and did the same. Vicki ran over to Hank, who appeared to be knocked out by the blast. Several paramedics rushed to our aid and began working on Hank and me.

"Do you know what happened here?"

"Not a clue," Dustin answered.

"Let's move him over here," the paramedic said, pointing to the wall of a neighboring building. "Too dangerous to work this close to the fire."

Several more paramedics came to my aid and began working on me as the fire department set up to extinguish the blazing fire.

"He has multiple stab wounds, contusions. He's lost a lot of blood. Sir, can you hear me?"

Vicki showed her badge to the paramedic. "His name is Steve."

"Steve, stay with us."

The last thing I remember that night was Vicki dropping to a knee and taking my hand.

"You're in good hands, you're going to be…"

Chapter 46

I awoke to the sound of a heart monitor beeping. As I opened my eyes and focused in on my surroundings I noticed that the monitor was hooked up to me. I closed and reopened my eyes several times, nothing changed, I was in a hospital room. I began to panic when bloody images of knives, wires and guns started dancing around the room. I tried to move my hands but they were handcuffed to the bed railings. I tried kicking my blanket off but my legs were chained.

I sat up as far as my as restraints allowed.

"Where is everyone? Hey, someone! Get me out of here!"

"Mr. Mueller, it's okay. Relax," a nurse reassured me as she walked up to me.

I opened my eyes again and came to the conclusion I had died and punched a first-class ticket to hell.

"Oh no, not me. Screw you, I'm getting out of this place!"

"Steve, please calm down. Doctor Tucker, he's coming out of his coma."

"He'll be fine", said the man dressed in a white lab coat with a custom embroidered name strewn across the left pocket.

The doctor shined a small light into my eyes, the brightness having the same effect as an acetylene torch.

"Don't look directly into the light, son."

"Jesus," I said, taking a poke at the light with my left hand, which apparently wasn't cuffed to the bed.

"Your eyes do look much better. How are you feeling young man?" He pulled back the light.

"Probably better than I look."

"Probably not. You took one hell of a beatdown, son."

"You should have been on this side of it."

492

"No thank you. I'm a doctor, I get paid to clean up messes like the one you were in. But it's promising to see you haven't lost your sense of humor."

I dragged my tongue across my teeth searching for cracked ones. I opened and closed my jaw several times, pleased to find it wasn't wired shut.

"Doing a little self-inventory?" the Doctor asked.

"I can see why you chose the medical profession."

"Yeah, you'll be fine. Just take it easy, and you should be out of here sometime tomorrow. We need to make sure the swelling from your concussion has subsided enough so we can release you."

"How bad was I?"

"You ended up here, didn't you?"

"Where's here?"

"UMC. Any of it coming back to you?"

"Unfortunately, yes."

He patted my shoulder. "Again, take it easy son. You'll be fine."

I reached around my neck and felt a gauze bandage.

"By all rights you should be dead. The wire someone used to try to kill you almost did you in."

I watched him and the nurse walk out and closed my eyes as the repugnance of what I had done, and witnessed, dominated my thoughts. Eventually though, these thoughts would subside and get buried deep inside my psyche.

"Hey you."

I reopened my eyes to see Vicki standing over me. She placed her hand on my shoulder.

"How's the patient doing?"

"What are you doing here?"

"The hospital had orders to inform me when they were going to bring you out of your induced coma. I sat outside your unit along with the Metro officer assigned to protect you."

"Protection?"

493

"Woody and Letterman are still in the wind and I don't believe they've left Vegas. Do you remember anything about the men who attacked you?"

"I don't remember much of anything."

"Forget that, baby, it doesn't matter. I've really missed you."

She leaned in and kissed me; it was the perfect remedy until I began to have trouble breathing. I gently tried to push her back but she leaned in and kissed me deeper, her lips devouring mine. I tried to say something, but I was paralyzed. I finally managed to shove her away and gasped for air.

"You're just too cute."

I looked up and freaked out when I saw Mary's face as she opened her mouth and tried to kiss me again.

"Mary?!"

*

"Steve, you're okay. Nurse, get in here. He's coming around!"

"What's happening?"

"You were in a coma. You're coming around. Nice to see you again."

"Vicki, what are you wearing?"

"Vicki? Dude, remember me?"

I refocused my eyes, shaking off the fogginess. "Russ... nice to see you too."

"For a second I thought you were suffering from some sort of brain damage."

"How long have I been in here?"

"Three days."

"How are you feeling, Mr. Mueller?"

"Like I came out of a very real nightmare."

"How do you know you're not still in one?" She placed her hands around my neck and began choking me.

Shit, shit, I'm trapped in my head. No, it can't be. I'm paralyzed... I can't move my legs, my arms. Do something. Move. Why can't I hear anyone? I can't see... there's no way out. I'm stuck in my mind. Oh help. Please, somebody help me! I don't want to be stuck in here for all eternity. Please, somebody help me..."

*

"Doctor, do something!"

"Steve, come on. Time to join us. Wakie, wakie."

I opened my eyes, ecstatic when I saw my nurse and that my hands weren't handcuffed. I wrapped my arms around her arm and kissed it.

"Is he always like this?"

"I'm not the person to ask."

"Vicki?"

"Hey you." Vicki turned to the nurse. "Uh, how's the patient doing?"

"Shit, it's happening again. I can't do this forever."

"What are you talking about?"

I focused intently on Vicki. "Are you actually here or is this going to turn into another nightmare?"

"That isn't a very pleasant thing to say to someone who's been keeping an eye out for you the last several days," the nurse interjected.

"Vicki, please do me one favor."

"What do you need?"

"Kiss me. You never have to talk to me or say another word to me. Just please, kiss me."

The nurse stepped back and Vicki grabbed my head softly and kissed me. I closed my eyes and prayed when I opened them, I would be back in some sort of reality again.

"That suffice, Steve?"

I stared at her. "I'm sorry, but I've been having these insane visions and I needed to believe I've returned to some sort of reality. So please, don't fly away and leave me here."

She took my hand. "You're back, Steve. I'm sorry you had to go through all of those heinous circumstances, but. . ."

"But what?"

"But there's probably more to come yet."

"You mean because Letterman's still out there, right?"

"Of course not. You killed him. You killed Woody and strangled Mary, remember? You also have the right to remain silent…"

"NO! Not again, not again. This can't be happening again. NO!" I screamed as I tried to fight my way out of the bed.

I saw one of the nurses put a dose of something into my drip system.

"Hey, what are you giving me?! Get away from me!"

The room faded to black.

*****

"What did you give him?" Vicki asked the nurse.

"We gave him diazepam; that should knock him out for a while. The propofol we used earlier to awaken him out of his coma, as you witnessed, had an undesirable result. Most people don't have that kind of reaction to the drug."

"That was incredibly painful to watch."

"But you looked like you enjoyed the kiss," the nurse said as she started to leave the room.

"He'll be alright, won't he?"

"Yes, don't worry," she answered as her words trailed her out of the room.

Vicki sat down in a chair next to the door.

"Sergeant, you okay?" the Metro officer on duty assigned to protect me asked as he peeked into the room.

"Not really."

*****

Chapter 47

I awoke to the sound of a heart monitor machine's rhythmic beep. I looked around the room. Russ looked awkward as he slept in a chair surrounded by a plethora of hospital personnel racing around. I scratched an itch on my nose.

"Hey, my hands work," I said smiling at my hand scratching my nose.

I remained still, not wanting to create a disturbance in this calmness. I closed my eyes and reopened them. Kurt was reading his iPhone on the same chair I just observed Russ in. Nightmares. I remember nightmares. Where'd Russ go? How'd Kurt get in here?

"Hey," he said.

He put his phone in his sports coat pocket and walked over to the edge of the bed. "Welcome back, kid."

"Where am I?"

"You're in the back of a limo getting a blow job. Where the hell do you think you are?"

"Thanks for the warm greeting... and fuck you too."

"Hang on," he said turning toward the unit desk. "Hey nurse, he's awake!"

An older nurse walked through the door and came up to me as Kurt stepped back.

"How are you feeling, young man?"

"Like someone dragged a bucket of shit through my mouth."

She picked up a plastic cup with a straw sticking out, bent it, and placed it against my lips. "Here, take a sip."

I followed orders and wasn't pleased to feel the burn in my throat.

"My throat."

"A minor reaction to a surgical scope and the repair work the doctor did around your neck. You were one beat-up young man, you're lucky to be alive. Those knife wounds almost opened up holes in your stomach and that wire cut across your arm and neck."

A Metro officer walked a few steps into the room and spoke into his shoulder radio. I couldn't make out what he was saying, but he didn't appear to be kicking up his heels in joy.

"Kurt, what's he doing here?"

"Just making sure you don't have any unwanted visitors."

"Where am I?"

"UMC, ICU unit."

"You used the word unit twice," I said with a broken smile.

"Now I know you're back. I'll start calling everyone, let them know you've joined the living."

A doctor walked into the room. "Steve, how are you feeling? You know you were close to bleeding out; your knife wounds almost killed you. However, our amazing medical staff and this wonderful surgeon standing next to you did a great job. Son, you're one lucky young man."

"Quite a mouthful, doctor. My thanks to you and your wonderful staff. And by the way, luck had nothing to do with it."

"Yeah, you're better. Nurse, I'll be back in a couple of hours. If he keeps improving, we can move him out and into a private room," he said right before he exited the room.

"How to make friends and influence people," Kurt added.

"Kurt, where's Russ? How's Bill? How's business?"

The nurse shook her head and left the room.

"Good, they're gone. Kurt, come here, I have some things to tell you."

Chapter 48

It was Friday, and after a week of hospitalization and several Psycho Therapy sessions, I arrived safely home. I was tucked away in my recliner, in front of my seventy-five-inch HD TV when Bill limped into the room and joined me. Even after being shot twice, he looked like he was recovering faster than me.

Dino and Russ were running the company in my absence and business was brisk. The new limousines finally arrived and with the added publicity or morbidity highlighted by the number of attempts on my life made chartering a limo from YLL a novelty. They released George from the psychiatric unit and he was back to his old self. His sister Barbara was in deep crap. They rang her up for perjury, conspiracy, drug possession, possession with intent to distribute, and attempted murder. She would be in CCDC lockup for months. To my delight, her bail was denied because she was a major flight risk. She'd be on the first Tijuana taxi headed south to Mexico.

George was asleep in his room, performing some of his famous eyelid research. Metro had several cars patrolling the area who apparently were on the up and up. Of course, we had our own version of security tucked inside several drawers throughout the house, the pool, and within arm's reach. I wouldn't say my life had returned to normal, but the prevailing winds were definitely in my favor.

Unfortunately, my mind continually drifted back to that night, the blood, the rage, the death and my self-preservation instincts taking me back to primal. Daily, I fought the good fight, trying to recover and overcome everything that happened. I'd either win or end up spending the rest of my life sitting in a dayroom, somewhere in an isolated psych ward, with a cheery name no one could pronounce.

The doorbell rang and both Bill and I instinctively reached for our weapons. I looked at him and laughed. "Letterman's at the door. Care to get that?"

The latest security technology had been installed in the house. I glanced down at my phone, pushed the button on my high-tech app, and the door unlocked.

"Don't the two of you look comfy," She said as she walked in.

"Thanks for dropping by, Vicki," I replied.

"You need me for anything?" Bill asked.

"I think I've got this."

"Good, I have some computer work to do, so if the two of you will excuse me… "

He pulled up his crutch and slowly hobbled away.

"Have a seat," I said, turning off the TV, pointing to my couch.

"You're looking better, Steve."

"Feeling better too. How are you holding up?"

"I'm holding up. Working with the DEA and the FBI has been an experience in and of itself."

"The big boys in crime investigations. You're moving up in the world."

"I'm a useful bystander, pinned with a courtesy tag from the Washington elite."

"You here to tell me something new or are you here on a phishing expedition?"

"Unfortunately, the latter."

"Well, fire away, detective."

That comment got me into some hot water.

"Listen, I've had your back through all of this. I don't deserve to be snarked at."

"I'm sorry but it seems like you stonewall me whenever I ask you a question about these investigations. I didn't ask for any of this crap. How about a couple of answers for a change?"

I realized I jumped down her throat again and wished I hadn't gone down that road. "I'm sorry," I said, trying to deescalate the tension.

I pushed the foot rest switch down and tried to abruptly stand. I grabbed my side and using my right arm leaned backwards and fell into the chairs waiting arms. Vicki rushed to my aide and kneeled beside me, putting her hand on my shoulder.

"You're supposed to be taking it easy. I'm sorry if I flipped your switch."

"My bad. You have a job to do."

She assisted me into a more comfortable position. I took in a full dose of her perfume; it should have been labeled charmingly intoxicating. Our eyes locked and I couldn't take mine off hers.

"In the hospital, your hallucinations were hard to watch," she said taking my hand.

"You were there?"

"You don't remember?"

"I only remember that crazy nurse plunging whatever into my system and the room collapsing. I awoke several hours later; Metro officers were peeking in on me for the next two days."

"Well, I did, but you weren't in the best of conditions. I received daily updates. I'm here now."

"To ask me questions, right?"

"Yes."

"Well, fire away. My vocal chords are sore but functional."

She moved back to my living room couch. "What really happened that night?"

"You wearing a wire?"

"No."

"I don't think I could handle jail time."

"You're not going to jail, alright? I've pieced most of it together, and that garrote helped to solve Mary's murder. Will you tell me what happened?"

"Several people attacked me, kidnapped me, I escaped… with these wounds. You came into the gym and shot Eddie."

"That's your story? I'm calling bullshit. You were stabbed, twice, almost strangled and beat to a pulp. It's amazing you're still alive."

"When I have something more to add to my story, as my mind goes through the healing stages, I'll make sure you're the first one I call."

She came back over to me. "I can't help you if you don't tell me everything that went on."

"You mean like bearing my soul to you and you walking out? That kind of help?"

"That's unfair. I—"

"Walked out, left me standing at my front door modeling my birthday suit. I've never felt more naive than in that moment, thank you."

"I apologize. I had a lapse in judgment."

"At my expense."

She walked to the door and opened it.

"Before you leave."

"Yes."

"Tony, Sam, Sherry, any leads?"

She quietly closed the door.

Chapter 49

Two weeks passed. Several detectives dropped by routinely to throw questions at me, which, by design, I didn't have answers to. My body healed quickly, and I began to work out, lifting weights, punching and kicking my heavy duty MMA training bag and swimming. I stopped in at YLL several times and pushed some papers around my desk. I had a cavalcade of employees come and go from my office with the congratulatory welcome backs and hope you're feeling better routines.

It was a typical hot, late evening, September, a Wednesday night. I sat by the pool, in the process of killing a second beer when my iPhone lit up.

"Metro and the FBI got you working some long hours," I answered.

"I need a favor," Vicki answered.

"A favor. You know what time it is?"

"Yes, and since when do you chase sheep this early?" she said, her voice sounding playful.

I could almost smell the alcohol permeating through the phone.

"What do you need at eleven-thirty?"

"I need a ride from the Tuscany Hotel. I think I've had too much to drink. I thought you might be able to give me a lift."

"Lyft, a very unpleasant word to use around a limo driver."

"Ahem. Ride. I could use a ride."

That brought a hesitant smile to my face but since I was only on my second beer, I thought this would be a great opportunity to make amends for being such a dickhead the last time we saw each other.

"Sure. Give me thirty minutes. I'll call you when I'm in the valet area."

"Thank you."

The line went dead.

"I wonder why she called me and not one of her friends," I mumbled.

As I left, I noticed Bill passed out in front of the TV. I put on some nice clothes, my Glock and walked out the door. I took the newer Tundra, turned my Waze app on, and started driving. I took Maryland down to Flamingo constantly checking my rear-view mirror for any signs of a follower. An endless stream of taillights on West Flamingo lit up the Vegas night as far as the eye could see.

I made the left into the parking lot and followed the road until it u-turned back into the valet. I told one of the valets I had a charter, showed him my limo card. He pointed me to an area twenty feet away. I put a ten in his hand, parked, and called Vicki.

The combination of music and chatter was so loud, I could barely hear her.

"I'm out front in valet."

"On my way."

I stood by the tail gate anxiously waiting to see her. When she finally came out, she had company. I took the short walk to the door. She and her female companion wore low cut backless evening dresses, matching shoes, and purses. Vicki in black and the blonde who held on to her in sequined scarlet red.

"I see you're not alone," I brilliantly surmised.

"This is my friend, Jill."

"Hi, Jill. Looks like you ladies had a really good time tonight."

"Tonight? We started at four o'clock," a loaded Vicki corrected me.

"Yes, we've been tossing them back for a while," Jill added.

I immediately assessed they were both tanked, but the tall blonde apparently could handle her liquor somewhat better or else maybe drank less.

505

"I'm glad you called me instead of trying to make it back on your own."

Jill and I helped Vicki in first. She turned, clumsily stepped up on the running board, her dress riding up her legs just below her waist. It became impossible not to stare. Jill maneuvered her into the middle of the backseat, then seductively worked her way in. I closed the door and dutifully ran around to the front and climbed in.

"Where to ladies?" I said, adjusting the rear-view mirror so I could see them both.

Jill rattled off an address and I punched it into my Waze app and began driving.

"Since four, huh?"

"Since four," Jill answered.

Balancing the visuals of the road and the back seat became a challenge. I observed Vicki's head resting on Jill's left shoulder, her hand on her thigh. Jill had a mischievous expression on her face. Vicki's eyes began scouting mine. Those eyes, I missed those eyes.

"Jill is my lesbian friend; she says I have nice tits and a hot body."

"I can't argue with that," I answered not knowing where this was going.

Jill took her hand and smiled at me. Vicki looked down and closed her eyes.

"I also have nice tits," Jill slyly remarked.

"I'll have to take your word on that but you do fill out a dress nicely," I answered.

Jill leaned forward between the bucket seats. Vicki's head slightly jerked sideways causing her to momentarily reopen her eyes. Jill pulled her dress top down and made sure I saw her chest. Vicki gazed up at me trying to anticipate my reaction.

"Just so you know I'm telling the truth."

"I never doubted you."

She tucked her breasts back inside her dress and slid back to her original place in the back. She readjusted Vicki's head back onto her shoulder and tenderly kissed the top of her head. Vicki smiled at me.

"You two a couple?" I asked, as a monster knot began forming in my stomach.

"We're really good friends, neighbors too," Jill remarked.

"You really like her, don't you?" Jill asked, cutting through our cat-and-mouse conversation.

"I like Ferraris too, but as you see… "

"You've had some rough waters to navigate."

"I have, and to answer your question, unfortunately we're only tied together because of some bad—"

"I saw it on the news," she cut in. "Answer my question."

"Let's see. I'm a victim, slash suspect, in numerous murders, I'm younger than her, and I think, well, and I think she thinks that's a problem."

"You've got some problems, Steve."

"I do."

"How old are you?"

"Twenty-four."

"You're only nine years apart."

"Maybe Vicki should be involved in this conversation, Jill."

Vicki slumped over, softly landing in Jill's lap. Jill lightly ran her fingers through Vicki's hair.

The knot in my stomach began to grow larger.

"She got really loaded today. I think the pressure of her job is taking an awful toll on her," Jill answered.

"Her job is a tough one and getting worse no thanks to yours truly. She's seen so much violence since I've been in Vegas. I don't know how she does it."

"You were almost killed several times."

"You seem to know a lot about me."

507

"You really do care for her, don't you?"

"I do. And I understand why she needs to distance herself."

Our conversation ended. Within several minutes I came to the end of our trip. A sleeping Vicki missed out on an interesting conversation.

"We're here." I parked the truck out front and opened the passenger side back door. "Let me help the two of you out."

"This isn't her house; I'm stopping by and meeting some friends. Here's *our* address." She handed me a note.

"I thought you were both going home together."

"This hot blonde is still in play for the evening." She glanced at Vicki. "As you can see, she's not."

Before Jill exited, she gently raised Vicki's head and kissed her.

It felt like a pallet of bricks came down on me.

She closed the door, leaned in to me and kissed me on the cheek. "She really cares for you, make sure she gets home safely."

Vicki was lying across my back seat.

"I have this."

"I'm sure you do," she answered as she walked into the three-story apartment building.

I locked her in the back and finished the remaining fifteen-minute drive to her place. Jill's note included a security pass code for the gate, the door, and a condo number. I found a parking spot and helped her out of the truck.

"Thank you for helping me to my place," a tired Vicki commented.

Nice to know Vicki wasn't a mean drunk. She was trashed and could have acted any number of ways. Many hidden personalities have been revealed under alcohol-induced evenings. Happy and stupid drunks are among my favorites. I had to prop her up; she had an extreme case of wobbly legs.

Once inside I pushed the elevator up button. While we waited I held on to her tightly, placing my right arm around her waist. Her head delicately rested on my shoulder allowing her long flowing black hair to cloak my jacket. Her perfume's alluring fragrance began to overwhelm me again.

The elevator came and I carefully maneuvered her inside and pushed the third-floor button. A moment later we exited the elevator and walked to her door. She handed me the keys and leaned against the wall. I fumbled around and finally found the right one and let us both in.

Her place, a lot more revealing than her office. An abundance of art, family pictures and knick-knacks were strategically placed throughout. She threw her purse on the couch and stumbled toward what appeared to be her bedroom. I stood there not knowing what to say or do.

"Do you need anything?" I blurted out.

"I'm okay. Wait a second. I want to pay you for our ride."

"You don't have to; glad to help."

I patiently waited for her to reemerge from the bedroom while continuing to look around her place. Within several minutes Vicki walked out of her bedroom wearing only a soft blue tee and black lace panties. She walked directly toward me in a seductive gait. My heart started racing.

"You've been seducing me with your eyes all night, playtime is over."

"Whoa, we've been down this road before and I'm the one that ends up being thrown off the cliff."

She pushed me on the couch, mounted me, put her hands behind my head and pulled me in, laying a wet juicy kiss on my lips. Unfortunately, it tasted like a vodka martini.

I pushed her slightly back, "Vicki, stop. What about your girlfriend?"

"Girlfriend. You mean Jill? We're just friends. Why, did she say something?"

"No, the way she acted, like the two of you were a couple."

"We're not. Remember the girls? They've missed you." She pulled her tee shirt off.

"Vicki, you're loaded."

She pleasantly pulled me off the couch and towards her bedroom, kissing me several times along the way. Once inside, she started to undress me. She was so beautiful, but in her current condition, less attractive.

"Vicki, stop, you're trashed, you don't know what you're doing."

"I know exactly what I'm doing. You want me... here I am," she said slurring some of the words.

I pulled her in tight and held her.

"Please, not like this. I know this sounds like a cliché but I wanted our next time to be special."

"What are you, a schoolboy?" She pushed me away.

"Go on, get out. You're not ready for someone like me."

She crawled partway toward her pillows and passed out face down.

Having been with way too many party animals, I knew I couldn't leave her lying that way. I pulled down her comforter and rolled her over on her side, her head near the nightstand. She rolled on her back and tried to pull me into her, playfully wrapping her legs around my waist.

"Steve... "

She went out again and for a few seconds I stared at her body lying there. I couldn't believe this was happening. I rolled her back on her left side and covered her up, kissing her on the cheek.

"Sleep tight."

I went into her bathroom and took the waste basket and placed it next to her head on the floor. I turned out the lights and partially closed the door. I heard her wretch and ran back into the bedroom and helped her to the bathroom.

"Apologies. Thank you."

She pushed me away and slammed the door. It sounded like she unloaded all her alcohol in two heaves. She flushed, came out of the bathroom, and hugged me.

"I'm having a bad night. Would you mind sleeping on the couch? Just for a few hours. I'm not used to being this drunk."

"Of course I will."

She asked the perfect question. I would have been afraid to leave her alone in her present condition. I made myself at home, turned on the TV, and shut the volume off. My curiosity began to get the better of me and I started to nose around her condo, looking at pictures, knickknacks, and rummaging around her cabinets. Her place was small, and before long I sat back down on the couch and drifted off.

It must have been around three in the morning when I was startled out of my sleep by the front door creaking opening. I came out of my sleepy state, sat up, and was surprised by the person standing over me.

"What are you doing here? And how did you get in?"

"I'm here for you, and none of your business."

Letterman pointed his gun at me. "You and I are going to take a little ride. Resist or make any noise, and I'm going to kill your heart throb in the other room. You and I have some unfinished business."

He pulled out my Glock and tossed it in the direction of the kitchen.

"How did you know I was here?"

"It's what I do; wait for perfect moments."

I put my shoes and sports coat on and with Letterman pointing the way we walked toward the door.

511

"I don't think you're really his type," Vicki said, standing next to her bedroom door wearing shorts, a tee shirt, pointing her Glock at his chest.

Letterman wheeled toward her voice, changing his line of fire from me to her. I dove to the ground. Vicki fired several shots directly at his chest, hitting him. He fell backwards against the wall, knocking down a painting.

I looked at his chest and didn't see any blood.

"He's got a vest!" I shouted.

Letterman winced in pain but managed to maneuver for a shot at Vicki. I dove on top of him, grabbed his gun hand with my right, and threw an elbow into his mouth, the force bouncing his head off the floor. He dropped a bone-crushing left elbow on the top of my head. I was momentarily stunned but stayed focused and held onto his gun hand knowing Letterman was more than ready to use it on both of us. He still managed to squeeze off another round. The shot sailed high and to the right of Vicki. She ducked and took cover behind a leather chair.

I gathered all my strength, took hold of his gun hand in both of mine, slid forward, and delivered a bone crushing right knee to his lower jaw, sending his blood splattering across the wall and to the floor. Letterman fought with his mouth open, exposing a portion of his tongue which I mangled from the explosive impact of my knee. I had turned his teeth into ivory saw blades, severing a portion of his tongue. He screamed in agony, blood running down his chin. Vicki stood up and aimed but couldn't find a clean opening.

Letterman had plenty of fight left. He reached his left arm around my neck and maneuvered himself into a perfect position, twisting himself on top of me. As we rolled to the right, we crashed into a reading lamp, the impact causing the glass table which held it to shatter on her tiled floor, sending glass in all directions. He sported a deranged look while trying to maneuver the gun near my face.

"I'm going to blow your face off, motha-fucka," he said unable to pronounce the words with clarity.

While Letterman focused all his energy trying to jam his right gun hand into my face, I took advantage of the situation and used my training, thrusting my right index and middle finger into his eye. Any other human being would have reared back in pain and submitted. Letterman fought back like a man overdosing on PCP, acting unphased by my actions. He managed to pin my right arm back to the floor.

Vicki squeezed off two more shots, hitting Letterman in the back of his vest driving him down and forward. He fell across my face, his belt scraping against my nose. The impact of those shots should have knocked him out, but he slid back and continued almost unphased, grinding it out with me on the floor.

He was better trained and stronger than me. He rolled me over, this time onto my right side, and using me as a shield scattered five shots toward Vicki. Fortunately, I wrestled his gun hand, making it impossible to accurately line up any of his shots. The rounds scattered in different directions, taking out stucco, wall art, and family pictures.

I heard Vicki's footsteps slapping against the tile and knew she was charging us. I did the only thing left that I could do. Exhausted and out-matched, I drove my head into his right wrist, buried my teeth deep into his arm, and clamped my mouth tight. He started slapping the gun against the side of my head, opening a cut and drawing blood. If Vicki didn't react quickly enough, I would be knocked out and he would finish pulverizing my skull. On the verge of blacking out, I heard a deafening gunshot. Letterman's arm went limp, his blood splattering across the side of my head.

Vicki stood close enough to take the final shot. I raised my throbbing head, my body wobbly, and looked down at Letterman. A small piece of his head was missing, which brought a brief smile to my face. I rolled over on my right side and with my left leg managed to kick Letterman's dead body away from me.

Vicki dropped to her knees and pulled me in tight.

"You're hurt," she said.

"You know if Letterman has aides, I'm screwed, right?"

She smiled and wiped his blood off my face.

"Don't you mean, we're screwed?"

An ear-to-ear smile appeared on my face, as she hugged me tighter.

"You break my heart... and you're going to end up like Letterman."

"Not if it takes you that many shots I won't."

"You can be such an adorable asshole." She kissed my cheek. "Let's get you cleaned up. I refuse to sleep with anyone this messy."

Chapter 50

Vicki radioed the Metro squad units parked several blocks away, awaiting her call. But they were already on their way. Letterman was smart and cunning, parking anything resembling a police unit anywhere near Vicki's condo would have tipped him off. We walked to her front door where she opened it partway and then moved on to the bathroom. We immediately heard sirens closing in on her condo.

She wet down two towels and used the first one to wipe the blood off the side of my head. She opened her medicine cabinet and pulled out an antibiotic spray. She aimed it at my wound and sprayed a couple of times.

"That's not so bad," she said, smiling.

"That depends on what side of the towel you're on."

"Hold this against your head," she said as she went into her bedroom and threw on some clothes.

I followed her instructions. She came back into the bathroom and used a second towel to wipe the blood off the rest of my face. She kissed my cheek, hugged me, and led me back into the shot-up living room.

Several metro officers with their weapons drawn entered the condo.

"Letterman is over there," she said pointing to his body.

"You okay?"

"We're fine."

She took my hand and led me to the kitchen. This is where I popped the question.

"Letterman?"

"We knew he'd never stop hunting you; it became personal. We used you as bait, flushed him out. He was still hiding in Vegas, waiting for the right moment to make his move. Everyone, including Letterman, knew I was the lead investigator. He bugged my condo, a move we anticipated. We caught it early, waited for the right moment, and made our move. We hoped he'd take the bait tonight… and as you can see."

"Nice of you to dangle me out in front of him. And Jill?"

"I asked for a favor and she was eager to oblige. "He would have never left us, I mean, you alone."

"A Freudian slip?"

"No… I meant us."

A conglomerate of abbreviated agencies joined the Metro officers. It became overly crowded; you could walk on heads from one end of her condo to the other, never touching the floor.

"But you were so trashed."

"Not quite as drunk as I played."

"What would have happened had I taken you up on your offer?"

"I knew you wouldn't."

"You have more faith in me than I do."

"I have great instincts."

"I only have one thing to say about that."

"What's that?"

"Jill's right. You have an amazing body."

Vicki smiled, took my hand, and kissed it.

Chapter 51

The desert sun came up over Black Mountain, displaying an array of red, orange and yellow colors through some scattered clouds. For the most part, our presence at the crime scene was no longer needed. Vicki and I were beyond exhausted after the countless replays of this morning's events. Her stack of paperwork would have to wait until late this afternoon.

"I can't keep my eyes open anymore," I said, partially yawning.

"I know. I'm exhausted too."

"Why don't we go back to my place? My bedroom's a tomb during the day, and without a light, it's impossible to know the time of day. You can have my bedroom, get some rest."

"Dustin, Steve and I are going back to his place. I need some sleep."

"Sure thing partner. The CSIs will be here for a long time. Go for it."

"Good, tell the Captain I'll be in later this afternoon and take care of the paperwork. And Dustin… "

"Yes."

"I'm shutting off my phone. You know where to find me."

He gave us both that phony I didn't see that coming look. "I got this."

Vicki put together a quick overnight bag and within a few minutes we were down the elevator and in my truck. Officers were still out front checking I.D.'s before they permitted anyone from entering or leaving the building.

The morning sun was proudly pounding out another September one-hundred-degree day. The inside of the truck was already a casualty. I started the Tundra, jacked up the AC, and we were on our way.

I never envisioned this ride, Vicki with me on our way to my house, but I had thought about it, countless times.

At the red light at Green Valley Parkway and the 215, I turned to her. Her head was resting on the side of the high back bucket seat as she stared at me, her eyes wide as a pair of harvest moons, her hands folded on her lap, looking vulnerable.

I reached my hand across the console and gave her a reassuring smile. She took my hand as our eyes locked. She unsnapped her seat belt, leaned across the console, and kissed me. Her thoughts intertwined with mine—joyous, euphoric, rapturous. I felt an energy unlike anything I experienced before.

The blaring sound of a horn jolted me out of my exhilarated state, demanding I pay attention to my driving. I grabbed my hand back, gave the man behind me a courtesy wave, and started down the highway. I did a double-take at Vicki, still content, looking at me.

"Buckle up. You okay?" I asked as I picked up speed down the on ramp.

"I'm tired, Steve. I just want to shower last night off and get some rest."

"Not to brag," I said glancing at my driver's side mirror, surpassing the speed limit and pulling into some moderately heavy traffic. "My shower is legendary in its healing powers. It magically erases a variety of ailments."

"Really? You don't say? My cure happens to be among those."

"Your cure is already programmed in and waiting."

"That sounds so nice," she said rolling her head on her shoulder, closing her eyes.

Vicki was asleep by the time I entered the security gate. The guard recognized me as we rolled through and I pulled into my circular drive.

I walked around to her side of the truck and opened the door. Vicki was awake, her gun pointed at my chest.

"Did you think I was just going to collapse into your arms?"

"Uh, yeah?"

She slid out of the truck and holstered her gun.

"Right answer," she said as she put her arms around me and backpedaling me to the front door, kissing my neck, cheeks, and lips.

I fumbled for my keys unlocked the door and pushed it open. I grabbed her waist as we pirouetted into the foyer. I kicked the door closed, reached over, and locked it.

George stood expressionless in the living room, dressed in his pajamas and holding a steamy cup of coffee.

"Good morning Steve, Sergeant."

Like ice bucketed, we froze and acknowledged George.

"Hey, George. You picked a nice day to be home at ten."

"You know me and bad timing."

"Like the Titanic and icebergs."

"Mister Sharpe," Vicki girlishly acknowledged him.

"Sergeant Spicuzza."

"Vicki stopped by to perform some unauthorized cavity searches."

"Steve," she said, punching me in the arm.

"You two make a perfect couple," George calmly declared, walking back to his bedroom.

We both enjoyed the awkwardness of the moment. I took her hand and pulled her into the bedroom.

"Take me to the healing waters," she demanded as she took off her tee shirt and threw it on the floor.

I was too excited to speak and just pointed. She put her gun on my nightstand and tossed off the rest of her clothes.

"You coming?"

I quickly undressed and guided her to the shower.

"Wait."

519

She went into the water closet while I switched the shower heads on, getting the temperatures right.

She emerged looking as sexy as a woman could look. There were still minute drops of Letterman's blood on my arms, face, and hair that needed to be expunged.

She waded in, making sure the water wasn't too hot. When she felt comfortable, she pulled me in and started to rub out the blood stains. The drain turned a momentary pinkish red but soon returned to clear.

She guided me closer to her, and together we embraced under the warm healing Vegas water, letting the events of earlier this morning take their turn swirling down the drain.

After drying off, we both crawled into bed and under the covers. The thermostat was set at seventy degrees, perfect for sleeping when it's one hundred degrees outside. I grabbed the remote and turned off the light. She spooned next to me, kissed me, rolled over facing away and pulled my arm across her body holding my hand firmly on her breasts.

While yawning she said, "I'm really glad you invited me to stay here."

I caught myself yawning back and answered, "There's no one I'd rather be with."

"Me too."

Chapter 52

I woke up and while muffling the light of my iPhone, I glanced at the time: two in the afternoon. Vicki, was still out cold, rhythmically breathing, deep and slow. Creating as little movement as possible, I moved to the edge of the bed, my battered body still aching from Letterman's punches. Still using the iPhone light, I gingerly pulled open the nightstand drawer. I stared down at the key Charlette gave me hiding next to a Glock, two thirty-round clips and the security envelope.

In my gut I knew whatever was attached to the end of this key would create another shit-storm, and for the moment I preferred the peace. Everything I could have ever wanted I had. My friends were safe, my enemies at bay, and the woman of my dreams sleeping contently several feet away.

The key, like a tornado siren at midnight, screamed for me to act. I couldn't just let it sit there knowing there was a piece of my life buried in a box, sealed in concrete, in a vault several miles down the road. All I had to do was go there, open it, uncover the mystery. Every second I hesitated, time would reach out and drag me into its curiosity abyss.

I closed the drawer and partially shined some light on Vicki, who was still lying on her right side. The sheet rested just several inches above her waist, her right arm under the pillow, her long black hair flowing across her neck and shoulders.

Did I want to take the risk of losing everything I had over something in a vault box? Or maybe I was paranoid. But my brief history in Vegas screamed, Pandora's Box. Was I ready to go down this road again? My answer was an easy one as I looked at Vicki.

I closed the drawer, delicately glided next to her and began to playfully kiss her shoulders. I heard her moan softly as she rolled over onto her back, her eyes struggling to open. As soon as she managed to lock her eyes on mine, she abruptly flipped me on my back, climbed on top of me and smiled.

"Never wake a sleeping tiger."

*****

A mini bus pulled into the Washoe County Parole Office. Seven men exited the bus. Six went into the office while one hung back. A limo approached the man and stopped. The front door opened as a chauffeur approached him.

"Mister Huntsman, welcome back. Your father's waiting in the car." He opened the back door. "Get in."

He entered the car and the chauffer closed the door, standing next to it like a Marine drill instructor.

"Dillon, welcome back."

"Thanks, Pops."

"Get your parole papers in order and call me when you're done. Woody was murdered and I know by whom… we have work to do in Vegas."

"You're back in?"

"Just until I clean up the mess your brother made."

Thanks for reading Short Rides In Long Cars.

Chapter One of book two, Long Rides In Short Cars is on the next page. The book should be out sometime in the summer of 2022.

Chapter 1

I jumped onto the ledge of a snow covered, six story, flat rooftop ledge on Manhattan's west side. Two of the three wiseguys assigned to keep me healthy, freaked out and started to run to my aide until I pirouetted towards them.

"What, you thought I was going to end it all?"

"That wasn't funny, you could have slipped, got my ass in a whole world of trouble," the taller of the two wiseguys angrily said.

"I'll keep that in mind if I decide to take a nose dive."

This was not how I imagined spending my Groundhog Day. It was just past midnight as a gentle wind swirled light snowflakes across the cold Manhattan skyline.

I glanced over my shoulder down at the alley below, littered with snow covered garbage and an out of place black town car parked along the side of the building. There was zero traffic and it was eerily quiet, except for the distant sounds of sirens, none of which were coming my may.

Once again, I was being threatened. This time however, not in Las Vegas but in New York City. I jumped off the ledge and landed a couple of feet in front of the two wiseguys who were intently watching my every move.

A third one entered through the rooftop door. A dimly lit bulb at the doorway and the city lights, provided more than enough light to see what he was dragging behind him, folding chairs.

The little wiseguy, short, ornery looking, dressed in black slacks, a dark gray overcoat and a black English racing hat which covered half his head. He reminded me of Joe Pesci in "Goodfellas". He could have passed for his doppelganger.

Without taking his eyes off me he yelled out, in an almost comical New York mob lingo, "Hurry up Bosco; I'm getting tired of standin here!"

"What do I look like, a pack mule?" Bosco shouted back in the same lingo only running out of breath with each step.

The tall wiseguy, about six-four, wearing a long black wool button down coat, matching pants and Fedora, which shaded most of his face. I gathered from his tone and mannerisms that he was the boss of this three man crew.

He chimed in with his exquisite New York mob lingo, "No, you look like someone chased a cockroach up your face with an ice pick. Hurry up, set them down here and open them."

Bosco hurried and opened the three folding chairs, slamming each one hard against the rooftop.

"Here!"

"That wasn't so hard pencil dick," blurted out the little wise guy.

Bosco had to be the wiseguy in training, the gofer of the crew. He took a step back between the two wiseguys and awaited his next order.

Bosco was dressed in a camel colored overcoat, dark jeans, black work shoes and a Yankee baseball cap trying to hide his pocked face. He could have been the All-American poster boy for failed acne medications.

"Aw, it looks like were a chair short Stevie," the little wiseguy said mockingly with a forced smile.

I looked down at the ground and slowly raised my head and stopped when my eyes locked into his.

"No, it looks like you brought two too many."

The little wiseguys expression changed instantaneously and with a look spawned in hell he took an aggressive step towards me.

I used my left hand and pulled out my 9mm Glock from under my coat, loaded with hollow points, aimed at the little wiseguys head and pulled the trigger. The loud crack of the Glock momentarily stunned Bosco and the tall wiseguy as the little wiseguys face exploded and he staggered backwards, crashing into his chair, landing lifelessly on his back.

Bosco, standing in the middle of the group had trouble reaching behind his back for his gun. His long overcoat made it impossible for him to react quickly enough to respond to my shot. With one hand reaching behind his back and the other fumbling to lift up his coat I fired the second and third shots into Bosco's exposed chest. Bosco collapsed awkwardly, landing on his back too, his head careening hard off the snowy rooftop surface.

After taking out Bosco with those two shots, I took evasive action and dove onto the rooftop surface knowing full well the tall wiseguy would have his weapon drawn, in hand and about to fire.

As the tall wiseguy pulled the trigger, I landed on my stomach facing him. But there was only silence, the gun didn't discharge.

"Shit!" The tall wiseguy yelled.

He forgot to push the safety off.

I reeled off four consecutive chest shots from my belly position. The tall wiseguy already having flicked the safety off with his right thumb was about to fire as the first of four shots hit his chest. He managed to pull the trigger but the impact from the Glock rounds sent his arms flailing in different directions as his shot sailed wildly off the rooftop surface. The second third and fourth shots sent him backwards heel over heel until he dropped and crashed against the rooftop ledge.

I stood up and walked towards the tall wiseguy. As I closed in my jaw almost unhinged when I saw his eyes open wide followed by a sadistic grin. He was stunned, not dead and raised his gun hand towards my chest. Without breaking stride and still focusing on his face, I fired one more shot, the kill shot, to the middle of his forehead. The impact sent his head bouncing off the ledge as his body rolled over onto his left side.

I walked up to him, my gun still pointed at his head and said, "You got something to say now?"

I ripped open his coat.

"Bullet proof vest, you son-of-a-bitch. Do all of you assholes wear them? I said loudly across the rooftop."

I got up and walked over to Bosco, keeping my gun trained on his head, just in case he had one too. I stopped and looked at his bloody body.

"I guess you were too cheap to buy one," I said watching his blood pool on the rooftop.

I kicked him once and added, "I guess your wiseguy aspirations had a few holes in it."

I thought I was funny.

I moved on to the little wiseguy, took a long hard look at him and kicked him twice.

"With that sink hole in your forehead I guess all the body armor in the world wouldn't have saved your sorry little ass."

I turned around and slowly walked back to the tall wiseguy. When I got back to his body I noticed that the cold night air had already caused the blood on his head, mouth and on the roof to coagulate.

I kneeled and put my gun in his mouth. "Got anything else to say... I'm waiting?"

*****

"Hey, get off the ledge, we wouldn't want anything to happen to you limo boy," the tall wiseguy shouted.

I quickly snapped out of my daydream. "If I only had a gun," I quietly said to myself.

I turned and faced the three wiseguys and jumped off the ledge. All three wiseguys took a precautionary step back.

"Whoa, a little jumpy aren't we? You already searched me, remember? And it looks like we're a chair short."

"Find another chair Bosco," the tall wiseguy ordered.

"Are you fuckin kiddin me?"

"Do I look like I'm fuckin kiddin you? We need to make our distinguished guest as comfortable as possible. Now get the fuckin chair."

Bosco immediately walked towards the rooftop door, his gait hastened by the tall wiseguys command. The tall wiseguy sat down followed by the little wiseguy.

He stretched his long legs and crossed them, interlocking his fingers behind his head and asked, "So, how does a kid from Vegas end up spendin Groundhog Day on the rooftop of a warehouse in New York? You know, with such delightful company like ourselves?"

I backed up to the ledge using my right hand as a feeler and when I touched the ledge sat down.

"You mind?"

I reached into my coat pocket and pulled out a Cuban cigar.

"Yeah go ahead kid, why not?"

The little wiseguy stood up and walked up to me, reached over, grabbed the cigar out of my hand and opened it. He crudely bit off the end and spit it out.

"Got a light?"

I reached back into my coat pocket and pulled out a lighter. I leaned in, flipped the lid open, thumbed the wheel several times until a flame shot out and consumed the wick, eye-balling him the entire time. I placed the lighter in front of the cigar. The little wiseguy puffed several times until smoke came billowing out of his mouth. I snapped the lighter shut directly in front of his nose and placed the lighter back inside my coat pocket. He slowly backpaddled to his chair with this cantankerous grin plastered across his face and sat down.

"Thanks," I sarcastically said.

"You're welcome."

"So, do you gentlemen have names? I mean I know who Bosco is but-"

"We do," the tall wiseguy cut in. "Come on, you're a smart kid. You own Yo Leven Limousines, so why don't you tell me and my associates here why *you* think you're our guest this fine, chilly, snowy evening?"

Bosco walked up to me and slammed a chair open at my feet. He walked back to his chair and angrily sat down.

"Yeah, we have some time to kill and an interesting selection of toys to do it with, so why don't you fill us in, Stevie," the little wiseguy interjected, feeling full of himself.

I slid off the ledge and sat down on my newly placed chair.

"Great, you want to hear my life story. Why, that's really kind, thoughtful and caring of you."

"No, dumb-shit, just how you screwed up and ended up here. And don't give us some phony bailout excuse about not knowing exactly why you're here either!" The little wiseguy shouted out in a way that should have scared the snowflakes off the roof."

I turned to the tall wiseguy, "Why don't you put a leash on that monkey. And this Bosco character, he looks like the quintessential organ grinder. Maybe those guys can drum up a few extra bucks performing on the streets."

The little Wiseguy jumped up knocking over his chair, reached inside his coat pocket and took a quick step towards me.

"JOHNNY!"

The little wiseguy stopped dead in his tracks.

"That's two names," I said.

"Shit. We've got instructions to follow; you can settle this later, Johnny," the tall wiseguy said, never taking his eyes off me.

Johnny picked up his chair, reopened it and sat down.

"Instructions?"

I hunched over letting my arms dangle and scratched my arm pits while making ape faces.

The tall wiseguy took control of the situation. "Seriously, we do have some time and I'd really like to hear your story; or do you want to sit here all night and swap insults?' He asked in a calm voice.

"It's an incredible story, but without pictures and pop-ups the little monkey might not be able to follow the story."

Johnny stood up, picked up the folding chair and slammed it on the roof.

"That a boy, Psycho!" I said standing up and kicking my folding chair towards Johnny. "Here, see what you can do with this one."

Johnny grabbed the chair, raised it over his head and then gently placed it on the rooftop and sat down.

"I can't wait till I get the green light to rearrange your body parts you cocky fuck."

I leaned back and sat on the ledge, "Be careful what you wish for."

"Steve, are you gonna to tell us or what?" the tall wiseguy interjected.

"Sure. It all started to fall apart for me about five months ago. But in case you didn't know before I became the owner of YLL I used to work as a psychiatric attendant in La Crosse, Wisconsin." I stated while looking directly at Johnny. "You know the place where that pissant monkey should reside."

There was no reaction this time, just a blank stare.

Bosco tried to open Johnnies smashed chair. "That's toast," he said as he tossed it back down.

He flipped the broken chair off to the side and sat down again.

"Before you go on, there are several things we already know, like Lakeside," the tall wiseguy began. "And we also know about how you and that hot sergeant you were shacked up with took out Letterman. But what we don't know is how you managed to shit everything down the toilet."

Johnny started laughing, "I can't wait to hear it… I'm all ears."

"That you are my short, undeveloped, simian, fledging. But I think there's a little more to this story than what you seemed to have heard."

Johnny pulled up his left sleeve coat and looked down at his watch. "The clocks tickin Stevie boy."

"Alright. When I came to Vegas I was this wide-eyed kid who thought he had it all. I inherited a house, bank accounts, cars, jewelry and a limo company. What I didn't know… it was all bullshit. Everything had already fallen apart and I was suddenly the captain of the fatally iceberg hit Titanic.

"Stop." The tall wiseguy quickly cut in. "You got everything back, except for Sonny's missing money."

"Hey, this is my story and I'm telling it my way."

"Sure, go on."

"It was the next afternoon, right after Letterman tried to kill me. I was home, happy to be alive. But I couldn't let Sonny's death turn into a cold case.

"Letterman was some badass, you got lucky," Johnny said.

"He *was* a dangerous individual, but as you can see, I'm here and he's not," I said looking directly at Johnny.

"Go on,"

"I had a key to a private vault. I was hoping Sonny had left me a clue to his missing money. I knew going there would probably create another shit-storm but…"

Special Thanks:

Kelley Raberge for modeling my cover.

Krista Wagner.

My wonderful wife Connie.

My daughters Sara and Angela.

People of Las Vegas, Nevada and La Crosse, Wisconsin for making my life exciting.

And to all the brave and loving mothers who gave their children up for adoption.

Made in the USA
Middletown, DE
26 February 2022

61819798R00295